THE WINDS OF DESTINY

THE WINDS OF DESTINY

Charlotte E. Craig

THE WINDS OF DESTINY

iUniverse books may be ordered through booksellers or by contacting:

iUniverse
1663 Liberty Drive
Bloomington, IN 47403
www.iuniverse.com
1-800-Authors (1-800-288-4677)

ISBN: 978-1-4917-7626-1 (sc)
ISBN: 978-1-4917-7627-8 (e)

Library of Congress Control Number: 2015914148

Print information available on the last page.

iUniverse rev. date: 09/21/2015

THE REALM OF
ELSSADOR

EPIGRAPH

"There are winds of destiny that blow when we least expect them. Sometimes they gust with the fury of a hurricane, sometimes they barely fan one's cheek. But the winds cannot be denied, bringing as they often do, a future that is impossible to ignore."

- Nicholas Sparks (Message in a Bottle)

PROLOGUE

The hooded figure bent under the branches that hung low over her path, the horse galloping beneath her body, flicking mud up onto her damp cloak. The night was dark around her, distorting the trees in the forest this woman rode through, making them look like the dark creatures locked deep inside her memory, the creatures she had known to be dead. But this news that she had received made her question that knowledge. This news that an ancient darkness was reawakening was what brought her so far from her home, forcing her to charge out of her city and ride towards this forest to meet with the one who gave her this information.

The woman soon approached a clearing and quickly tugged on the reins of her steed, pulling up slowly and scanning the area before sliding off her saddle. She gripped her reins tightly, carefully moving further into the clearing, not caring that her skirts were soaking in the muddy puddles beneath her. All she seemed to be able to focus on was what was placed in the middle of the clearing. A well, built up of plain grey stones was what sat at the heart of this deep forest. In the darkness, she could see the moss that had grown over the ancient structure, sticking between the cracks in the bricks. It looked like any other ordinary well, but this woman knew it was much more than that. Powerful magic was built into its very stones, just like the other Windows of the Portal *that had been destroyed long ago. But not this one. This one was kept for the very reason this woman had come here. This well played a great part in what would save every last creature in the realm of Elssador.*

"Have you brought the Key?" a cool, female voice asked from across the clearing, startling the woman. She instantly looked up from the well, spotting the speaker just stepping out from the shadow of trees across the clearing, her golden eyes glowing brighter than usual.

"Yes. You know I keep it with me always," the woman replied. She dropped the reins of her horse and approached the well, pulling her hood back and allowing the rain to spit down on her blonde waves of hair as she slipped an object from her sleeve. The moonlight reflected off the silver object as the woman held it in the palm of her thin hands, reaching it out over the well towards the other woman.

The other woman stared at it for only a moment before taking it and closing her slender fingers around the object, holding it tightly in her fist. She stood still for a moment, allowing the magic of the object to send tingles through her hand, down her arm, along her fingers. The object seemed to pulse, a sign that the magic of the well was calling out to the object, a sign that this woman didn't call her friend all the way here for nothing.

Reveling in the breathtaking feeling of the magic surrounding her, the woman closed her eyes, feeling the wind gust through her long brown hair. Then, she opened the palm of her hand, placing her other one over the bracelet, whispering words that would have sounded like gibberish to most people, but the woman across from her knew them well. She recognized them as the Ancient Tongue, *a language that only few in this age knew how to speak, one that was only used to cast spells.*

When the other woman was finished with her incantation, she passed the object back to her friend. At first, it felt hot on her skin, then it began to cool until it felt just like it had been before the other woman held it. The only thing on the object that marked her spell was an engraving, written in the Common Language *and not in the old runes she expected.*

A name was carved into the fine silver, the name of the one who would soon come, and a reminder of the danger that followed them.

"Have you seen them?" the blonde woman asked, still staring at the bracelet. "Has the Wanderer's Sight served you well?"

"*The Wanderer's Sight has always served me well, my dear friend,*" *the other woman replied, a sudden tightness in her voice, "He reveals to me what must be revealed, nothing more. All he gave me was that name.*"

"*So how are we to decide if this person is the one to save us or to destroy us?*" *the woman answered, finally looking up from the bracelet. She looked to her friend whom she found was reaching out to her, covering her hand that held the bracelet.*

"*The Wanderer knows what he is doing, he has always known. Please trust him, Arianna. If not him, then please place your trust in me,*" *the other woman said to the blonde-haired one. She let her hand fall away once she could see the words settling in her friend's light blue eyes.*

The blonde-haired woman – Arianna – let out a long breath and a nod before closing her fingers tightly around the object. She then stretched her fist out over the mouth of the well where she released the silver object, expecting there to be some loud crack *or* pop *to sound as the object entered the next realm, but she heard nothing.*

"*It is done,*" *the other woman said. Arianna looked to her just as she was turning away, back into the shadowed forest where she had come from. On a normal day, Arianna would have felt offended by her friend not saying farewell, but she knew why there were no goodbyes. They were going to see each other again, hopefully, very soon.*

Arianna looked down into the darkness of the well and – despite the fact that she knew her words probably would never be heard – she whispered down into the abyss, "Save us, Carter Olsen."

CHAPTER 1

CARTER OLSEN

The brisk winter wind blew against my face, biting my cheeks as I walked through the dark streets of South River. The small Canadian town was quiet – as it usually was – but the starless sky above seemed to emphasize that silence as I crossed the main road towards the sidewalk in front of a dark windowed café. Three pairs of eyes followed me as I passed the house-like building and I pulled my grocery bags closer to me, taking a glance at the group of boys to my left. They were huddled together in the cold, smoke pouring from their mouths and up into the air around them, forcing one of them to let out a cough. Their eyes continued to follow me as I passed them, pressing forward towards the field at the end of the sidewalk, and they only turned away once I had disappeared from their line of vision.

I made my way through the field, shivering as the winter winds grew stronger, threating to blow me back the way I came. But I managed to keep going, with thoughts of a warm house and a hot shower filling my mind. I hurried my pace as I passed the small local police station and library building with about three or four cars parked in front of it. I could see the lights of phones reflecting off the mirrors and windows of the vehicles as I continued on, knowing that these people were probably using the library's free internet to scroll through their *Facebook* or *Instagram* pages.

Eventually, I crossed another road and rushed on to Alfred Street, keeping the image of a steaming, hot shower in my thoughts as another gust of wind blew snow and small pellets of ice against my face. I walked along Alfred for only about a minute before turning onto Tebby Boulevard, following the curve of the road towards my home... well... my new home, I suppose. I had been there for seven years and it was still hard for me to call it that, to think of it as a place of comfort, of belonging, when I seemed to feel none of that within its walls.

It had been seven years since I moved into this house with my aunt and uncle and their four children. It was a rough transition, but a whole lot better than the alternative that most orphans had to face. It was my Uncle Gabe who insisted I come to live with them when my dad died, when he had been taken from me by the dark hand of cancer. It was only a short while before Uncle Gabe and his wife signed the school papers and other legal documents, stating that they were my official guardians.

Aunt Mary was reluctant to have me join her family, as she had also seemed reluctant to befriend my father – her husband's brother – when he was still alive. She never seemed to like my dad and me. Thankfully, her dislike for him seemed to fade after his death, but it soon came rushing back at the idea of having me move in with them. Of course, I wasn't too thrilled about the transition either, not just because I disliked Aunt Mary as much as she despised me, but because I knew it would never replace the home I had with my father, the home that I would never return to.

I hurried towards the front door of the house, nearly tripping over the tire-swing that hung from the massive willow tree in the front yard as I did so. I placed the grocery bags on the porch and quickly dug out my keys, catching them as they slipped out of my numb hands. I quickly unlocked the door and shoved it open, letting out a sigh of relief as the warm air began to cover my skin, almost instantly removing the chill I brought in with me from outside. I immediately hauled the grocery bags in, closing the door before the cool air found its way to Aunt Mary, who I knew would snap at me for letting all the warm air out.

The house was quiet, making me wonder if everyone had gone to bed already. When I checked the clock on the other side of the hall, I felt my heart sink. It was past eleven, past curfew. If Aunt Mary discovered me walking in at this hour I would be grounded for weeks! She was usually a strict woman with her own children, but her punishments seemed to be more severe towards me. With her kids she was a bit more lenient, more open to letting punishments pass, but she always made sure mine remained.

Silently, I began to take off my snow-covered boots, placing them on the mat beside the closet where I then hung up my coat, wincing as one of the hangers dropped to the floor. Afterwards, I picked up the grocery bags and made my way into the kitchen, flicking on the oven light and beginning to unload the items from the ridiculously noisy bags into the fridge. Suddenly, the overhead light came on, making me gasp and instinctively reach for one of the kitchen knives from the sink. I whirled around, gripping the knife tightly to find someone far worse than the expected intruder.

There she was, Aunt Mary, standing with her bony hands on her small hips, her cheeks only a shade of red darker than the fluffy, pink robe she wore. I swallowed hard, lowering my knife as she continued to stare me down with her dark brown eyes, sending more chills through my body than the air outside did.

"You better have an explanation for this," Aunt Mary said, sounding surprisingly calm, despite the fact that her eyes were boring holes into my skin.

"I was picking up the groceries you wanted me to get," I replied, my voice coming out flat in attempt to hold back the anger rising in my chest.

"You mean the groceries I asked for four hours ago?" she scolded, breaking her calm and collective state. "For goodness sake, put that knife down!"

I blinked, looking down at my hand to find that I was still holding the knife, gripping it so hard that my knuckles had just begun to go white. I wasn't even aware of myself raising it before Aunt Mary's demand for me to put it away. I swallowed hard as I slowly lowered the blade, but before I could even move to place the thing on the counter, Aunt Mary had snatched it out of my hand, putting it back in the sink. Her silence as she reached for the grocery bags continued to make me shiver. I stood still, awaiting for more of her wrath, but she didn't say a word...until of course she pulled the eggs out of the bag. Yellow goo dripped from the carton, landing with a splat on the hardwood floor.

"Go upstairs," Aunt Mary said through a tight jaw, still staring at the eggs.

"But I'm not done putting the..."

"I said, go upstairs!" she snapped. I stared at her for a moment, surprised by this response. Normally she would have made me put every single item into the fridge and clean up every last drop of the eggs off the floor, then she would force me to do extra work by washing the remaining dishes. Never was she this lenient with me. Unless...

"Is Marlee up again?" I asked.

Aunt Mary just nodded her head stiffly, but no matter how stern she made her features look, she still wasn't able to hide the worry in her eyes, "She had another nightmare and is asking for you. Now do as I say."

I turned away from her, rolling my eyes as I made my way out of the kitchen and towards the stairs, taking the steps two at a time. It wasn't unusual for Marlee – the youngest of Aunt Mary and Uncle Gabe's children – to wake up from her dreams. It had been happening for the past two years, exactly half of her life. The first few times she had had these dreams, Aunt Mary tried to comfort her, but Marlee would just shove her away or cry harder. Everyone tried to calm her down after these dreams, but my arms were the only ones she seemed to accept. Once I had settled her down, she would tell me about her dreams, explain them to me as if she was sitting in front of a television, watching it happen through the screen. Sometimes they were so bad that she would wake up in a cold sweat, but sometimes the dreams were good and they woke her for reasons I didn't understand.

"They woke me because I wished they were real," was what she usually told me when I asked her why the good dreams woke her up, but I had sensed something off about her words that made me wonder if I had been lied to.

At first, no one was worried about Marlee's dreams, knowing that everyone had nightmares, but once they started happening more often, our anxiety kicked in. Aunt Mary wanted her to see a doctor so he could order tests for her, but Uncle Gabe insisted she leave it be, that Marlee would one day grow out of it.

About a year had passed since Uncle Gabe had assured us the dreams would go away, and yet the nightmares continued to plague her, waking her up about three times a week. That week it had been the fourth time they woke her, as well as the fourth time I had to deal with it. I didn't mind, of course. Marlee was the only one in the whole house that I truly enjoy being around, who I *wanted* to be around. She had always felt like a younger sister to me rather than a cousin, and I believed that she felt the same towards me.

Ever since I arrived, Marlee had been attached to me, ever since she could walk she had been following my every move, wanting to be where I was every minute of the day. For most people it became annoying, I knew for sure it would set off her older sister Sophie, who was only four months younger than I, but for someone as lonely as I, it was comforting to know that there was someone left in the world who loved me.

I walked past the two rooms on the landing, one of which was the twins' rooms – Justice and Jeremy – and the other Aunt Mary and Uncle Gabe's. I could still hear his snores as I turned into the hallway on my left, making me wonder how anyone got any sleep in this house. As I made my way down the hall, I tried my best to avoid looking too long at the family photos that lined it, knowing that some of them contained images of my father and me. Seven years later, the pain of only being able to scc his facc in a photograph continued to press at my heart.

Once I was at the end of the hall, standing before Marlee's bedroom door, I reached out for the handle, but immediately jumped back as someone pulled open the door from the other side, slipping out into the hallway. I tried to breathe quiet breaths, in hopes that Sophie hadn't noticed that she had startled me, but I could tell by the amused curl of her lips that she already had.

"So, did she ground you again?" Sophie asked, her grin turning into a wicked smirk as she crossed her arms, leaning on her hip. Sophie was considered to be a pretty girl, some would even say beautiful, but not to me. All I saw when I looked at my younger cousin was a pest, a huge pain in my neck.

"No," I fired back, scowling. Sophie's smile faded instantly and she raised her dark eyebrows, her blue eyes widening in shock. "Don't act so surprised or disappointed. If anything you'll be the one getting grounded tonight."

"Pfft," Sophie said, letting out a laugh. "Why do you say that?"

"Because I'm not the only one who got in past curfew. You just entered the house yourself," I said, taking note of the red lipstick that coved her full lips, her tight jeans and frilly top that she seemed to be trying so hard to cover up with a sweater. Even her dark hair, which she usually let fall down her back in long waves, was pulled back into a braid.

Sophie stiffened instantly at my words, pulling the sweater tighter around her, "You're not gonna tell, are you?"

"If you don't get out of my way I will," I threatened, staring her down until she gave into my commands, slowly moving away from the door and down to the end of the hall where I heard the door of the bathroom click shut.

With a frustrated sigh, I slowly opened the door before me, quietly moving into the bedroom that was lit up by the small lamp beside Marlee's bed, placed in the middle of the room. The other two beds – mine and Sophie's – were pushed up against opposite walls on either side of Marlee's. She was sitting up when I entered the room, the covers pulled up over her small legs and a picture book in her hands. I bit my lip, trying hard not to laugh. The book she was trying to read was upside down. The cuteness of the situation overwhelmed my heart, making it swell with joy, eliminating all the anger and frustration I had been feeling earlier.

"You're late," Marlee said, probably sensing my presence, because she didn't even look up from the book she was attempting to read.

"Sorry," I answered, approaching her bed with a sudden guilt swirling in my stomach. Normally, I was there for her when she woke up from her dreams, in the bed only a few steps away from hers. Sometimes she even curled up next to me, not even seeking my words of comfort, only my embrace. How horrifying it must have been for her to wake up and find me not there. The thought sent a sudden ache through my chest, reminding me of how shocking it was for me to be with my father one moment, and then the next find him lying in a hospital bed, the heart monitors beeping…

"Was it a bad dream tonight?" I asked Marlee in an attempt to erase these horrible memories from my mind.

"No, not really," Marlee answered with a shrug of her small shoulders. I pondered that for a moment, silently tallying how many good dreams she had had in the past six days. I was glad to find that the good ones were the majority.

"Do you want to tell me about it?"

Normally, Marlee would nod enthusiastically at this question and begin to explain immediately, but this time she seemed hesitant as she dragged her big blue eyes away from her book and toward me, "Nah. I don't think you're ready yet."

"Ready yet?" I chuckled. "What do you mean?"

"I mean you *will* be ready, just not right now," Marlee answered. Sometimes I was taken aback by how witty this child was, how wise she could sometimes be, but most days I smiled in the face of this side of her. She was truly an incredible child, one who knew how to make me smile, despite the anger or sadness I had been feeling.

"Do you think you'll be able to fall back to sleep without me tonight?" I asked.

She shook her head, closing the book and beaming up at me, "I want you to tell me the story!"

"Again?" I groaned, staring at her with pleading eyes. It had been the fourth day in a row that she had asked me to tell her the same story. It was a tale that my father told me as a child about two brothers who live in a grand kingdom they have promised to protect. Then, a dragon comes and begins to threaten the kingdom, but the two brothers manage to go on an adventure to try and stop the dragon and rescue their people. The first night, I was hesitant about telling her this story, for fear that it would provoke her dreams, but she had fallen into a sound sleep almost immediately after I had told it.

Marlee didn't have dreams like most four-year-olds. Sometimes I was happy only my best friend – whom I told everything to – and I knew about what really went on inside her mind. Her dreams were filled with creatures, dark creatures that always seemed to attack her in her sleep, tear at her limbs, and bite into her flesh. Then there were the good dreams she had, dreams of kings, queens, magical kingdoms filled with creatures that I couldn't even begin to understand.

When most children dream about magical kingdoms, they dream about living there, basking in the magic, in the luxury, but Marlee seemed to only dream about their politics. I remember one night when she woke up, not even needing me to ask her if she wanted to explain what she had dreamt. She just grabbed my sleeve tightly, practically tearing the fabric with her little nails. Her eyes were wide as she began to tell me about the magical world she kept dreaming about, how two races had been fighting with each other since the beginning of their time. Marlee explained to me that this conflict made them blind, blind to the fact that a greater war was arising. That a darkness was coming.

I had never seen her so shaken before, even when she dreamt about strange creatures clawing at her flesh. It always made me shiver whenever she explained these strange dreams to me, making me worry even more about her well-being. Even during the day, after she had these dreams, she would go on speaking to me as if they were real, as if they were visions she was receiving, not nightmares. Marlee always seemed glad to share the wonders of her imaginary world that seemed a little too dark and dangerous for a child to conjure up. She always spoke about it with a smile on her face, with a hope glittering in her eyes. It was only then, as I began to tell her the story about the two brothers and the dragon, that I realized how much it bothered me that Marlee didn't explain this particular dream to me. More than anything, it made me even more worried about her.

Soon – not even three minutes into the story – Marlee had dozed off, her little head falling onto her pillow, her light brown hair spreading over the blue sheets. I smiled down at her weakly, stroking her hair as Sophie slipped in through the bedroom door, quietly sliding under her own covers and rolling over to get some sleep. I yawned as I continued to stroke back Marlee's hair, suddenly feeling the weight of my exhaustion, which forced me to rise from Marlee's bed, and pull the covers up over her small shoulders. I bent down to kiss her on the forehead and turned off her lamp before exiting the room, heading for the shower.

I allowed the hot water to sear my skin, to wash off all the dirt and left over chill from my walk across town. As I rinsed the soap out of my hair, I began to think again of Marlee and her wild imagination, began to wonder if I should be encouraging Aunt Mary to get her some help or to let the stage pass on its own. My weariness was what forced me to save these wonderings for the next day, what drew me out of that hot shower and eventually into my soft bed.

I curled up under my covers, not caring that my wet hair was dampening my pillow. Before I dozed off, I stared at a picture of my father and me – a habit that I had developed over the past seven years – that rested on my windowsill. We were at the lake, our hair soaked from swimming for hours. He stood with his arms around my shoulders, giving the camera his usual wide grin. I smiled a bit as I stared at the photo, knowing that the two of us were probably laughing at something when it was taken.

My eyes began to grow heavier and heavier, preventing my thoughts from drifting too far. Before my exhaustion completely enveloped me, I glanced out my window, finding a single, bright blue star gleaming against the black sky. The sight reminded me of something that my father had told me once as a child. I closed my eyes as his words repeated in my head, listening as if he were right there at my side speaking them…

"Darkness can't last forever," he had said. "One day you might come to a point when you feel as though it does. When that time comes you have to believe, Carter Leanne Olsen. You have to believe that the light can overcome it…"

* * *

I pushed open the front door and braced myself for the cold winter I was about to step out into. I moved out onto the landing and immediately the cool air began to bite my cheeks, just as it had been doing to the rest of the family that was beginning to pile into the mini-van parked in the long driveway.

Aunt Mary was leaning over the back seat, probably buckling Marlee up so they could be on their way to North Bay to get some shopping done. Sophie stood next to her, leaning against the side of the mini-van with a bit of a pout on her face. The sight made me roll my eyes in disgust, even though I was quite used to seeing that expression, which was usually followed by her familiar whine when she wasn't getting her way with her mother. Aunt Mary seemed to be doing a good job at putting up with her oldest daughter, replying with a calm and patient tone she never used with me.

The sound of the front door closing behind me made me turn, even though I knew it was Uncle Gabe who had closed it. He was a tall man, a big man, with hands the size of my face, yet he was far from frightening. I could always count on him to crack a joke and sometimes even lessen the punishments his wife placed upon me. He flashed me his familiar wide grin, sending a tiny sharp pain through my chest at the resemblance between him and my father.

"So, you've decided to come with us this time?" Uncle Gabe asked, running a hand through his red curls. "I thought you hated coming with us on shopping day."

"Oh, you know I do," I replied with a weak laugh as a memory of previous shopping days I was forced to come along on shot through my mind. It wasn't just shopping that bothered me. But having to sit in a car with the twins shouting in the back seat, Sophie screaming at them to shut up, and Aunt Mary trying to scold them from the front for an hour – which was approximately how long it took to get to the nearest shopping mall – made me want to throw myself into a snow bank. I shuddered even at the thought. "I was just coming out to ask Aunt Mary if she would let me go to Tom Thompson. You know, since my week of being on house arrest is over?"

Uncle Gabe chuckled his usual low, comforting laugh, and placed a warm hand on my shoulder, "Well, I suppose that's one way to define being grounded. Personally, I don't see why you can't go, but…"

I groaned immediately, knowing exactly what his response was going to be. He seemed to always have some excuse for me not to go to Tom Thompson Park. Of course, Uncle Gabe was a lot kinder with his words, whereas Aunt Mary usually just objected plainly. I wasn't even sure why I was even bothering to ask for permission, knowing that the answer was always *no*. But I needed to try, not just because I wanted to get out of shopping day, not just because I wanted to hang out with my best friend, Tyler, it was because I needed to escape. Tom Thompson was always that for both Tyler and me, an escape from reality, an escape from our regular lives, from our pain...

"Gabe, we need to get going," Aunt Mary hollered over to the two of us. She looked drained already, her eyes wrinkled with weariness. She heard a cry and turned towards the willow tree in the front yard, clearly noticing the red-headed troublemakers climbing up the tree. Uncle Gabe let out a sigh and moved past me, approaching the twins, asking them nicely to come down and get in the van.

Before long, we were all seated in the van and were rolling out the driveway, turning off Tebby Boulevard and onto Alfred Street. I was seated between Sophie and Marlee, trying my best to ignore the twins in the back seat who were already beginning to get restless, as well as the sound of Sophie chewing her gum loudly in my ear, music blaring from her headphones.

"Do you have to chew so loudly?" I said to her once we had driven past the school on Ottawa Avenue.

"Sorry, wanna speak a bit louder? I can't hear you," Sophie practically shouted in response, sarcasm ringing in her voice. I gritted my teeth, gripping my knees to keep myself from reaching up and smacking her as she began to purposely chew her gum even louder.

I was so glad when we finally arrived at the *Kwick Way* – a popular stop for those who lived in town and those just passing through – that I actually let out a breath of relief. Sophie was the first to jump out of the backseat, hurrying away from the rest of her family and entering the small convenience store. I got out next, chuckling under my breath as I helped Marlee out of her car seat. Sophie was very good at making it seem as though

11

she didn't want to be seen with her family, when I knew full well that the reason for her rushing in without us was so she could flirt with Tyler Goodwin before I stole his attention.

I understood why Sophie – or any girl for that matter – would want to do just that. Tyler was the town prince; tall, blonde, and handsome. Every girl seemed to grow shy in his presence or hit on him in some way, all of them secretly wishing that they could spend the day with him, or that he would ask them out on a date. I nearly burst out laughing at that thought. If those girls knew Tyler as well as I, then they wouldn't keep wasting their time on him. Tyler was a naturally charming person, but he was a complete fool when no one was watching. It wasn't that he tried to hide the real him behind a veneer of charm that could win the hearts of many women, it was just that people were so blinded by his beauty that they seemed to be able to look past his goofiness.

When we were younger, I used to sometimes wish that people looked at me that way. That my classmates would be able to see past my shyness, my snort when I laughed at things that most people didn't find funny... It only ever seemed that Tyler was able to accomplish that, until we became friends, of course. Since then, those weightless wishes seemed to fade away, vanish from my mind. We met in grade two when we were placed in the same reading group. I remembered how shy I had been around him, how silent I was, but he didn't seem to mind. I just sat there, slowly warming up to him, listening to him read to me and laughing when he did. It was then that we struck a friendship, realizing our similar interests, despite the fact that to others we were unlikely friends.

I always cherished my friendship with Tyler, knowing that we had become more like siblings rather than just best friends. He had been through everything with me, through my father's death, through my first fight at school when a kid was daring enough to point out the worthless orphan girl as she walked by. To everyone I was always known as the girl whose mother burned to death in a fire, the girl who lost her dad to cancer, the orphan... To Tyler I was none of those things, I was Carter Olsen. I was his best friend, his sister...

The bell above the door rang as I walked into the store behind the rest of the family. I could hear Tyler already greeting everyone as they walked in, reminding them that if they needed any help, he was there for just that.

"Morning, Tyler," Uncle Gabe greeted in return with a smile as he passed the front counter that his daughter was leaning over, seductively twirling a strand of her dark hair as she continued to speak with Tyler. It only took me two steps towards the counter before Sophie shot me a deadly look and rushed off to some other part of the store.

I smiled at Tyler as I reached the counter, wagging my eyebrows, knowing that my teasing annoyed him.

"Stop it," he said immediately, rubbing a hand over his face. "Just don't."

"I didn't say anything," I grinned, putting my hands up in surrender.

"Yes, but you were going to," Tyler replied, "And the answer is yes, she tried to get me to come with her to David's party next weekend."

"And what did you say?"

"I didn't get the chance to answer. You chased her off," Tyler noted, gesturing to the spot where Sophie once stood. I continued to smile, knowing very well that Tyler would refuse to go with her. To him, Sophie was just another girl trying to claim him as her own, another pest... I was happy that we had that in common too. "I feel like we should give her some credit though. She's been the only one brave enough to actually ask me out."

"You mean *desperate* enough," I corrected, allowing him to give me a shove away from the counter, especially as a customer came up behind me. He greeted her with his usual friendly smile as he scanned her items, asking her about her grandchildren, how her husband was doing. It was normal for people in town to know everything about everyone, or even to say hello to new people in the streets who were only staying with family for a couple of weeks. It was one of the many things I loved about South River, the only world I had ever known. Tyler and I had plans to leave one day, to venture out to the city, explore the land outside of our small town. It was my father that placed that idea in our minds and it was because of him that I didn't think it could ever be done. Whenever I thought of leaving South River, which held the memories I had made with my dad, it felt as if I would be leaving him, despite the fact that he was gone to me.

"So," Tyler began once the lady he was helping gathered her bags and headed towards the door, giving me a small smile as she exited. He leaned across the counter, his hands folded in front of him and his blonde hair – that looked so much like mine – falling over his emerald-green eyes, eyebrows raised. The position made him look even more handsome and I could have sworn that I had heard Sophie swooning from the back of the shop. "Are we still on for Tom Thompson?"

"I don't know," I said, taking a look over my shoulder at Aunt Mary who was urging the boys to choose only one candy, not seven or eight. I lowered my voice as I turned back around, whispering so that only Tyler could hear, "You know how Cruella Deville feels about me going there, how she reacts whenever I ask…"

"Yeah, I know," Tyler replied with a nod, but even his bright tone couldn't hide the disappointment in his eyes.

"Besides, I think they might need me to watch over Marlee when they do their shopping," I said with a sigh. Tyler's eyes shifted past me and a small smile drew itself across his lips. I turned as well, knowing already that it was probably Marlee standing behind us, waiting with a box of *Smarties* in her small hands. Uncle Gabe stood at her side, giving Tyler and me a suspicious stare.

"I hope you two aren't plotting against my wife now," he teased.

"No, sir," Tyler grinned, letting out a nervous laugh, making it seem as if Uncle Gabe intimidated him when I knew full well it was Aunt Mary's wrath that he feared, "Is there anything I can help you with?"

Marlee nodded slightly and approached the counter, sliding her box of *Smarties* onto its surface, then scurried back towards Uncle Gabe, hugging one of his long legs. She too seemed to melt in the presence of Tyler. It was almost as if his charm worked on everyone, no matter what age they were. Tyler quickly scanned her item and then accepted the cash Uncle Gabe offered him, returning the change as another employee walked out of the back room, wearing the same blue uniform Tyler wore, rolling up her sleeves as she approached his cash.

"My shift, Goodwin," she said to Tyler, who willingly stepped back, giving Uncle Gabe, Marlee, and me a wave goodbye before disappearing into the back room. I watched as the door closed behind him, my mind drifting to the secluded woods of Tom Thompson, the calm and quiet that seemed to drift between the branches over the frozen lake, and even along its very ground.

"Go," Uncle Gabe whispered in my ear as Marlee rushed off towards her mother. I looked at Uncle Gabe, knowing that I was probably giving him a bewildered expression, for he laughed, repeating his previous words. "Well, go on."

"You're letting me go?" I asked, then glanced over at Aunt Mary whom I felt eying the two of us, probably wondering what we were whispering about.

Uncle Gabe gave me a nod, then winked as he patted my back, "Yes. You can go. I'll cover for you."

I beamed, squeezing his arm in thanks as Tyler exited the back room, dressed in a jacket with a red hoodie underneath. His face lit up as my eyes met with his, clearly recognizing that my plans had changed. He approached Uncle Gabe and me, pressing his lips together as if to hold back the excited smile that was threatening to spread across his face.

"Just be back before dinner," Uncle Gabe added, his tone filled with warning, but his blue eyes stirring with humour.

"Aye Aye, Captain," I replied with a salute. Out of the corner of my eye I could see Aunt Mary's face growing red and noticed her quick approach. I instantly grabbed Tyler's hand, pulling him with me out of the store just as Aunt Mary reached her husband. I could hear her already calling after me just as we exited the building, her shouts muffled by the closed door.

Tyler and I jogged towards his truck parked at the end of the small parking lot, the two of us climbing in. He started the engine as I buckled up and before long we were cruising down the street, making our way towards Tom Thompson.

CHAPTER 2

A NAME

Snow covered the usual path Tyler and I took through the small woods of Tom Thompson Park, piling up on the trees surrounding us. It weighed down their branches so that they curved over, aiding us in navigating our regular route. We absentmindedly moved in silence, the two of us taking in the peace and quiet the woods brought us. I felt like I could breathe clearer here, as if the quiet park broke me free of the heavy chains that came with living with Uncle Gabe and Aunt Mary's family. It was almost as if I was being set free, free to do as I please, free from obligation, and free from worrying over Marlee.

I felt excitement ignite inside me as a fallen pine tree began to come into view, marking our destination. It was one of the reasons people rarely ventured into the woods, why they all decided to enjoy the lake and the Frisbee golf. No one knew how the tree had fallen, but some people had theories, believing that it had fallen over in a storm, or that a grizzly bear had knocked it over. All the theories seemed to be on the right track, but Tyler and I had been past the tree often enough to recognize the cut marks on the end of the trunk.

Tyler was the first to climb over the tree, then reached a hand down to help me over it as well. Together, we jumped down, the snow nearly reaching our knees. Despite the biting cold it sent though my skin, I wanted to slump down into the snow, lay there and watch the light clouds move over the blue sky, and fully take in the peace of this little clearing, this spot that was marked as mine and Tyler's.

I wanted so badly to do as my heart desired, but I seemed to be stuck, already basking in the peace that this little clearing brought me. It had been a while since I had been here, almost two weeks. Now that I was back, gazing at the trees surrounding us, at the familiar, dried up well that sat in the centre of the clearing, it felt like coming home after a long, long journey.

Soon, I began to take control of my body again, stomping towards the centre of the clearing, about to take a seat against the snow-covered well when Tyler suddenly reached out to me, yanking me back before I got too close.

"Wait! Be careful!" he shouted, nearly making me have a heart attack. That was until I began realize what he was about to tell me. I rolled my eyes and gave him a frown, not wanting him to continue. As if recognizing the look in my eye, he smirked smugly, doing just what I wished he wouldn't, "What? It's magical, remember?"

"Ty, it's not funny," I snapped, giving his arm a punch. He winced, rubbing the spot where I had pounded him. Even amidst his pain and the frustration in my tone, he continued to grin.

I rolled my eyes once more, turning away from him and beginning to brush the snow off the stone well. I knew Tyler meant for his words to be a joke, but what this jest referred to was not a subject I was willing to poke fun at anymore.

There was one time, about a year back, when I decided to bring Marlee to Tom Thompson with us, despite the fact I knew Aunt Mary and Uncle Gabe would have opposed the idea. Ever since she stepped into the clearing, since she laid eyes on this old, beat-up well, she had begun to ramble on and on about it, her imagination gobbling it up. She came up with the idea that it was no ordinary well, but a portal into another world to that still didn't have a name.

As I finished brushing the snow off, taking a seat on the edge of the well, I began to realize that Marlee had begun to have those dark dreams not long after that visit. It was almost as if she had become so obsessed with her imagination that it even slipped itself into her dreams. If Aunt Mary knew about that she would have certainly blamed me, even though I did nothing to place such ideas in her mind. All I did was bring her to a park, invite her to be part of our little escape.

"She's been having the dreams again, hasn't she?" Tyler asked, his smile fading.

I gave him a nod, not needing to express the anxiety stirring within me. He knew how much I loved Marlee and had been noticing how her dreams had been weighing me down.

"You know it's normal for little kids to come up with imaginary worlds, to dream of a different reality. In fact, it's normal for everyone," Tyler said, attempting to encourage me. I smiled weakly, remembering when I had gone through all those possibilities as well.

"But normal people don't dream about them just about every night. They don't feel their imaginings harming them," I replied, shaking my head. "I just don't get it."

"Maybe your uncle's right, maybe it's just a phase," Tyler answered.

"I hope it is," I sighed. "Marlee's too young to come up with some of the things she has, too young to even understand them. Half the time I have trouble following along."

"Like what?"

"Have you ever heard of a *dryad*? Or an *egurra*?" I said, not surprised by the shake of Tyler's head. "Neither did I until I asked Marlee to explain it to me. She says they come across as looking human, but their souls are not like ours. She says their spirits are attached to the trees somehow, that they can feel what the forest feels, communicate through the trees..."

"That doesn't sound too complicated."

"Then there are the Eggura, who – according to Marlee – are a special kind of dryad. That they only appear once every hundred years, that they're immortal. She also happened to explain to me that they are even *more* closely tied to the trees. So close, in fact, that their lives depend on the tree's survival."

Tyler was silent, understanding filling his green eyes, "You said she made that up?"

I gave him a nod and our conversation died, the two of us losing ourselves to our own thoughts. I was only drawn out of my own when Tyler began to smile again, snickering.

"Is something funny?" I asked, using a hint of the same sort of sass I used with Aunt Mary and Sophie.

"Well, I'm just remembering a little blonde girl trying to convince me that unicorns existed," he grinned.

A felt a smile spread across my own face and my cheeks grow red with embarrassment, "I find no humour in that."

"Really? Then why are you smiling?" Tyler teased. I shook my head, still trying to hold back my grin. Tired of my pretense that I didn't find his remark humorous, he reached out to my face, pulling my cheeks back until I smiled widely. I laughed despite the fact I was begging him to let go of me. Only when I had almost fallen back into the well did he cease his foolishness, pulling me forward so I wouldn't fall.

I slid off the well after that, taking a seat in the cold snow, not caring that it had begun to soak into my jeans. Tyler did the same as I, lying back in the snow with his arms and legs stretched out, still laughing at what he had said before. I smiled as well, recognizing just how much I had missed being with him in this place, how much I needed it to cope with the rest of my hectic days.

"Did you see that?" Tyler said abruptly, sitting up.

"See what?" I asked, propping myself up on my elbows and scanning the sky above us, just as Tyler was doing.

He was silent for a moment, still, only his green eyes moving around. Then he suddenly grabbed onto my arms, shaking me and pointing to the sky, "There! Do you see it?"

I squinted, trying to make out what he was pointing at. Soon enough, I began to see it. Two butterflies, flapping their little orange wings as they flew towards the well. As they neared, I noticed something between them, an object that their little black legs were clinging to. I sat up straighter once they landed on the well, releasing the silver object that glittered in the sunlight. Tyler and I both stared at the two butterflies, shocked and confused about what they were doing here in the middle of winter.

After a few moments, they began to flutter their wings again and flew up into the sky. I expected them to fly south, where they should have been during this cold season, but instead they wheeled and flitted downwards into the mouth of the well. Tyler and I got up immediately, rushing towards the well and staring down into its dark hole.

"Do you see them?" Tyler asked, squinting his eyes as if it would allow him to see through the darkness within the well.

I ignored his words, my focus no longer on those two butterflies that had seemed to vanish before my eyes. I expected the sight to shock me even more than it did, make me wonder if I had actually seen what I had, but my attention had turned to something even more surprising. The object the butterflies had dropped remained upon the stone well, right in the spot where I had been sitting before. Slowly, I picked up the object, recognizing it as a bracelet. It had a thick chain, the silver rings attached to a flat plate in the middle. I sucked in a breath, feeling my mouth go completely dry as I stared at the plate, rubbing my thumb across the single word engraved into it.

It was a name.

My name.

Carter.

* * *

Marlee's excitement grew more and more as Tyler continued to drive the three of us towards Tom Thompson Park two days after the incident with the butterflies. Aunt Mary had left me to babysit Marlee that day, letting me know that *after* I had made plans to go with Tyler to Tom Thompson. Any other day, I would have canceled on Tyler, knowing that bringing Marlee to the very source of her nightmares was a bad idea, but that day I was desperate to go. I had been up for almost two whole nights, racking my brain for answers on where this bracelet had come from, why my name was carved into it. I knew the bracelet meant something the moment I touched it, knew that the answers weren't going to come to me easily. Eventually, I had reached the conclusion that the well was the only place I would find those answers, the only place where I could get even a clue as to what this bracelet was, what it meant.

"The dryads and the aprimorads hate each other, you know," Marlee said suddenly as we continued on our drive, the Tom Thompson sign just visible in the distance.

"Whoa, that's a big word," Tyler chuckled, glancing at her from one of the mirrors. "Is that even English?"

As if Tyler hadn't even asked her a question, Marlee continued with her previous words, forcing Tyler and me to share a worried stare, "The bad man likes that they hate each other. I don't know why, but maybe it's just because he's mean. Mean and tricksy."

"Hold on, but if this world is made up of aprimorads and dryads, then how does the kingdom survive if they keep fighting? You know, always trying to kill each other?" Tyler asked, clearly not being able to help himself. I shot him a deathly stare, which he only looked to for a split second before returning his eyes to the road ahead. I let out a sigh and leaned against the window, shaking my head as Marlee answered his question.

"There are other creatures too, they just don't fight with each other. A long time ago, four magwas became kings and queens. They came from our world and made everyone get along, well, everyone except the morbiens."

"*Morbiens?*" Tyler and I said in unison as he pulled up into one of the parking spots, turning off the ignition and unbuckling his seatbelt. I did the same, but instead of getting out the car like he had, I turned to look at Marlee, noticing the slight paling of her cheeks at the mention of that word.

"I don't like them," Marlee answered in a small voice, "They're tall, bald, and don't have noses. They smell like blood and they kill people. They scare me."

"Are those the things that try to eat you in your dreams?" I questioned, staring into her blue eyes that were suddenly filled with fear, the same fear I had always seen when she awoke from her nightmares. She gave me a small nod of her head, confirming my words to be true.

I got out of the car after that, stepping out into the dull day and coming around to the other side of the truck where Tyler stood, already beginning to pull Marlee out of her car seat. Once he had unbuckled her, he passed her off to me and she immediately wrapped her arms around my neck, clinging to me tightly as Tyler closed the door. As she held onto me, her cheek just brushing up against mine, I noticed how cold she was, although there was sweat beading down her brow.

"You okay, little girl?" I said to her, brushing back a strand of her hair. She gave me a little nod, her eyes looking so distant, as if she was beginning to get caught in one of her dreams.

"Want me to take her?" Tyler suggested, putting his arms out. He had that look on his face, the one where his brows creased together and his jaw tightened. It was the look he always gave me when he was concerned about my wellbeing. I knew it was then that he was beginning to notice the dark rings around my eyes that I had discovered that morning, a result of not getting enough sleep.

"No, I'm okay," I answered immediately, forcing strength into my voice. I didn't like it when Tyler worried over me, when he stared at me as if I were a grenade, or as if I would drop dead before him at any second. I knew where that drastic thought came from, for it happened to me whenever Marlee woke up, her skin as cool as ice, reminding me of my father the day he died. His hands had been so cold, his skin so pale, eyes dark... I had looked at him the way Tyler was staring at me then, wondering when death would take him, knowing that it could have happened at any moment.

"You sure?" Tyler pressed, taking a step closer to me.

"I'm fine, I promise," I assured him, adding a sigh after my words, letting him know that there was nothing to worry over.

Soon, we were making our way through the woods again, reaching the fallen pine tree and climbing over it to the other side. The moment I let Marlee down into the snow, she was smiling, giggling, as she rushed towards the well. Tyler and I both stood still for a moment. Only when he saw that I wasn't going to move to go after her did he take a step forward, jogging towards Marlee who was standing beside the well, the only thing in the clearing that I seemed to be able to pay full attention to.

Slowly, I began to approach the well, unclipping the bracelet, which I had attached to my left wrist that morning, and rubbing my thumb over my name once again. I had done that over and over again within those past two days, seeing if the name would eventually rub off, but it hadn't. It was carved into the silver, permanently engraved into the bracelet. What was even stranger were the markings I had found on the back of it. There were four of them, evenly spaced out along the back of the plate where my name was. At first I had thought it might have been an Asian language, but after hours of searching the internet the night before, I found no matches. None of the letters of my name looked the same as the one's marked on the back of the bracelet. What fascinated me even more about them was how they seemed to vanish depending on what angle you turned the bracelet. If you tilted it forward you could see the markings as if they were etched into the silver like my name was, but if you tilted it back, it was almost as if they weren't there at all.

I could hear Marlee continuing to blabber on and on about her imaginary world in the well as I took a seat beside the old structure, still examining the silver bracelet. The questions I had those nights before came flooding back to me; *Why is my name on the bracelet? Did someone send it? If they did, then who was it?*

"The bad man's coming back, Carter. Did you know that?" Marlee said, shoving her face really close to mine, implying that that wasn't the first time she had asked me the question.

"Yeah, yeah," I answered with a nod. She gave me a weak smile then and returned to Tyler. I could see the two of them out of the corner of my eye. My thoughts once again began to drown out their conversation, making it seem as though I was in a different place than they were. It was only when Tyler approached me, a playful grin lighting up his face, did I return to them.

"Well, well, you brought the bracelet after all," Tyler taunted. I glared up at him, knowing that his words were meant to cheer me up, but he of all people had to know that I was seriously not in the mood. "Last I checked you weren't the jewelry type."

"You know I'm not," I said flatly, rising from the ground. I turned then, looking at the bracelet and then down into the well. "Where do you think they went? The butterflies we saw last time we were here?"

Tyler's smile faded and he stood next to me, his senses clearly kicking in. He always knew when something was troubling me and when it was a good time to try and relieve me of my sour mood. Now was not that time and I was glad that he soon discovered it.

"I have no idea," Tyler answered with a sigh. "It's like they just vanished, dissolved into thin air."

"That's impossible. They had to have gone somewhere," I said under my breath just as an idea popped into my mind. Without words, I clipped the silver bracelet back around my wrist and gripped the well tightly, having a silent debate with myself. I could hear Uncle Gabe's words of warning in my mind as I continued to lean over the well, knowing that he would try to talk me out of the plan I was slowly building. He was always the one who held me back from my own curiosity, reminding me to think of the consequences and the safety of my plan, which always seemed to fly right over my head whenever I became over-curious, over-adventurous. *It's reckless behaviour, Carter Leanne,* he would say. Somehow, whenever he spoke it, I got the feeling he was thinking of my father. The look of *deja vu* always seemed to gleam in his eyes as he held me back from my dangerous curiosity, making me even more frustrated.

I'm not his little brother or his daughter, I thought. *I'm no one's daughter.*

It was those words that finally allowed me to pull myself up onto the top of the stone well and swing my legs over the side, letting them dangle over the dark mouth of the well. Just as I was about to slide down, Tyler grabbed hold of my arm, holding me back and staring at me with a strange intensity in his eyes.

"What do you think you're doing?" he whispered, glancing at Marlee whose cheeks had returned to their usual pinkish colour. She was pressing her small lips together, her eyes wide as if she was holding in her excitement.

"I'm going to find some answers," I answered, attempting to pull my arm out of his grasp, but his hold tightened.

"Then let me go," he volunteered, that concerned expression taking hold of his face once more. I opened my mouth to respond, but was quickly interrupted by Marlee who seemed to not be able to contain her excitement any longer.

"Can I go too? Please! Please, can I come?" she pleaded, skipping over towards the well.

I found myself growing angry, feeling the rage against her request well up inside my chest. The only reason she wanted to venture down into the well was to get to the world she believed lived beyond it, the world that was beginning to drive me insane, "Marlee, stop it! There is no world in here, okay? It's all in your head."

The moment the words spilled out of my mouth I wished them back, especially at the sight of Marlee's heartbroken expression, and the way Tyler looked at me, with his mouth opened slightly in shock. He knew I never got upset with Marlee, no one ever did. I was the last on the list of people who would ever snap at her the way I had then and it broke my heart to think that, making me feel nauseous. Tears began to rise in Marlee's blue eyes and I knew I couldn't stay there any longer, I couldn't stand to watch her cry on my account.

"Watch her. I'll be back in a minute," I muttered to Tyler as I turned my back to them, beginning to slide myself down towards the uneven stone of the well, shoving my feet between the cracks in the bricks. I twisted my body around, beginning to climb down into the well, and catching a final glimpse of Marlee and Tyler, the two of them watching as I climbed down into the dark abyss.

The first minute of climbing down made me panicky, the darkness around me making it difficult for me to place my feet in the right places as I continued to climb down into the well. I moved at a slow pace, my feet fitting into the stones almost perfectly until I nearly reached the bottom. In the darkness, I had accidently placed my foot on a loose stone, forcing me to lose my footing in my hold on the wall. I scrambled, trying to regain my position, but I was already falling fast, letting out a scream as my body collided with the hard ground, my head bouncing off of it.

I was still for a few moments, the area around me looking fuzzy, blurry, and distorted as my vision began to adjust. Once it had, I began to notice a strange sort of light in the well. It was no longer dark, but glowing with a beautiful golden light, as if the sun had poked out of the clouds above, shining down into the well. I propped myself up on my elbows, my vision still adjusting, and scanned the area, noticing that the well had not been completely empty after all.

My mouth fell open in shock as I used the wall to help myself stand, the golden light continuing to fill the space around me.

"Gold," I mumbled, staring at all the golden objects that were scattered around the ground I stood upon. There were golden cups, plates, necklaces, even vases. *I guess maybe this is the reason why someone cut down that pine tree,* I thought, smiling to myself at the idea. But my grin soon faded as I began to take in the strange silence around me, only able to hear my own breathing echoing around the well around me.

I stared up at the opening, expecting to see Tyler staring down at me from above, asking me if I was okay after my fall. But there was nothing there, only the grey sky and the thin white clouds moving across it. A strange feeling began to take its place in my stomach as I continued to stare up at the opening of the well.

"Marlee? Ty?" I called up to the opening.

I waited for a response, but the only voice that replied was my own echo.

Strange, I thought as I fiddled with the bracelet. *Did they go back to the car to wait for me?* I buried that thought immediately. Tyler wouldn't have left me behind, he would have wanted to wait until I had found what I needed to find. I was suddenly reminded of why I had come down into the well in the first place and immediately began to scout out the area for those butterflies, checking cracks in the stone, inside some of the golden bowls and cups. As I searched, I found that I couldn't shake that unsettling feeling swirling in my stomach, couldn't bury it no matter how hard I tried.

Once again, I found myself staring up at the opening of the well, repeating my call to Tyler and Marlee, once more blessed with the sound of my own voice. My head spun, aching from my fall, worry, and disappointment. From what I could see, there were no butterflies down here, just the gold and the plain stone walls. After only after a second more of staring at the gold in hesitation, wondering whether I should take some back with me or not, did I begin to climb back up the well. This time I was careful with my footing, moving slowly, despite the fact I was desperate to see Tyler and Marlee again, to shake off that bad feeling that still made my stomach churn.

Eventually, I made it back to the top, holding onto the well tightly as I lifted my head out of the opening, my grip tightening at the shock of what I was seeing. The area surrounding me was a clearing, one that looked so similar to Tom Thompson, but instead of a perfect blanket of snow, there was fresh, green grass. The clearing was filled with the smells, colours, and sounds of spring. Above me, I could hear the birds chirping, singing away as the wind blew against their branches, sending a few leaves off their stems.

At that point, all I wanted to do was climb back down into the well, but my body couldn't take it. I could already feel my feet slipping again, my arms shaking as I continued to hold myself up. I grunted as I began the process of pulling myself out of the well, sliding onto the warm stone, and adjusting myself into a sitting position before pushing myself off onto the grass. I looked around in awe at the forest, completely captivated by how green the leaves were, how much the colour of the bark resembled the rich colour of chocolate. The forest was healthier than any wood you would find in South River.

The thought of that small town reminded me of Marlee and Tyler, forcing me to scan the wood with my eyes. There was no sign of them, no tall boy with blonde hair, no little girl with those big blue eyes, no anyone! The forest looked completely empty, but it did not feel that way. I could sense life all around me, just not the ones I was looking for. There was nothing in that wood that gave me comfort, no sign of anything familiar.

"Tyler?" I shouted in a panicky tone into the empty forest. "Marlee?"

There was no answer. The only reply I got were the birds that continued to sing to one another. Slowly, I started further away from the well, continuing to call out for my best friend, my tone becoming more desperate, more afraid. My shouting only calmed when I felt my foot catch on something, when I tripped and landed face down on the ground. I yelped, using my hands to catch myself just before my nose collided with the earth. I twisted my body, turning quickly to see what I had stumbled upon.

It was a dead man, laying on the ground with an arrow stuck in his dark, bare chest and another through his neck. Fresh blood covered the areas around his wounds, creating streams that ran all the way down his chest to his strong stomach. The sight and the smell forced me to my feet immediately and made me back away as best as I could with my legs suddenly turning into jelly. I reached out for the tree beside me, using it to catch my balance as I willed myself not to throw up and to move my gaze away from the dead man's ghostly eyes.

Suddenly, there was a whizzing sound that forced me to look up. I let out a cry, finding an object soaring towards my face, embedding itself in the tree I was leaning against, and missing my head by only a centimetre. I instantly moved my hand away from the tree as I stared at the object more closely.

"It's an... *arrow*?" I said to myself, grabbing the shaft and yanking the object out of the tree. I stared at it blankly, taking in the sharp point and beautiful purple fletches.

My mind was so struck by the arrow that it took me a couple of minutes to recognize the noise that was resonating through the forest. It sounded like hooves galloping across a plain and it was growing louder. I spun around, catching sight of five men astride their horses charging across the path ahead, racing towards me with shining metal objects at their sides that I recognized as swords. I pressed my back against the tree, watching fearfully as the horses and their riders encircled me, aiming their bows and swords right at my head.

All five of them seemed to wear the same things; metal helmets, shining armour, and a deep purple tunic underneath their chainmail that identified them as knights. I stood there in front of them, paralyzed with my mouth half open in amazement as one of the men moved his horse forward, forcing me back against the tree even more tightly. Unlike the others, this man didn't wear a helmet, leaving me in even more of a shock than the sword he held at my throat. It was his eyes that struck me first, for they were unlike any eyes I had ever seen. They were beautiful, filled with the green-blue colour of the sea, but it wasn't their beauty that caught me off guard, it was the fact that they glowed. *Literally* glowed. Perhaps it was his dark hair and golden skin colour that made it seem as if his eyes were luminescent, but as he continued to look me over – clearly not pleased with my leather jacket and jeans – that glow seemed to fade until his eyes became the same light as my own.

"Who are you?" he said in an accent that sounded almost British. I stared back at him in awe of his costume, of the weapons that he and his men held. His horse whinnied, breaking through my state of shock as he repeated the question, "Who are you, girl?"

I continued not to answer his question, feeling afraid of the weapons they brandished, especially since I didn't have one of my own. My eyes found their way to the dead man before me, to his belt where the hilt of a dagger peeped out its scabbard. Before I – and the men before me – could even register what I was doing, I had already leapt towards the dead man, drawing his dagger and threatening the group of knights.

They began to chuckle as I stood with my knife at the ready, my hands shaking with fear.

"Please," the same man with the sea-green eyes said. "We will not harm you if you cooperate."

I don't trust them, I thought. *I don't trust* him! *He shot an arrow at my head!*

The knights remained still on their horses with smug looks upon their faces, clearly convinced that I wasn't capable of saying no, of defying their orders. They were certain that I was going to give up my dagger and surrender. The thought made me grip the knife tighter, making my knuckles turn white.

I don't think so, I thought before hurling my knife at one of the men and making a run for it, not needing to look back at the knight to know that my dagger had met its mark. His cries of pain called after me as I ran. As did the sound of their horses, of their hooves stomping against the ground.

I knew I didn't have a chance at outrunning them. Heck, I couldn't even run more than five laps in gym class let alone outrun five horses! I blocked these thoughts out of my mind, trying to focus on the road ahead and not on the sound of the riders approaching. I raced towards a tree, quickly grabbing onto a low branch. I pulled myself up onto it and began to climb, knowing full well that the knights had caught up to me. I could see them circled around the base of the tree as I glanced down to adjust my footing.

"No use in hiding up there, sweetheart!" I heard one of the knights shout, forcing me to look down at him in disgust. Part of me wanted to reply with a rude remark, but I suddenly found myself unable to speak and wishing I hadn't looked down in the first place. I grew dizzy as my fear of heights kicked in, forcing me to climb up the tree at an even slower pace.

"Don't look down, Carter, keep going," I mumbled to myself as I continued up the tree.

I had just grabbed the third branch when I felt a tug on my leg. I stifled a scream, looking down. One of the knights had clamped his hand tightly around my ankle. I attempted to shake off his hold, but his grip was too tight, seeming to grow stronger the more I struggled. He pulled on my leg with such force that I lost my grip on the branch and tumbled out of the tree onto my back, my head – yet again – bouncing off the ground beneath me. My head throbbed and my chest ached from having the wind knocked out of me. I coughed, my chest heaving, as the men lifted me to my feet, grabbed ropes and tied them around my wrists. Then they attached the other end to the saddle of the sea-green eyed man's horse.

"We move on towards camp," he ordered, glaring at me before turning around on his horse, leading his group towards the path they had entered the clearing from.

I stumbled behind his horse in silence, my head still throbbing and spinning from my fall. The ropes around my wrist tightened as I fell behind, making my bracelet dig into my skin, and driving me to keep up.

This is a dream. This has to be a dream, I thought frantically as we continued on our trek.

As we moved further along the path, the smell of smoke and meat filled the air as well as the low rumble of laughter and the sound of metal clanging against metal. Curiously, I looked past the horse's flank to find a camp creeping into view. Purple tents were set up among the many trees and campfires blazed at their doorsteps. There were soldiers, knights – like the ones who captured me – laughing and eating around the fires or practicing their skill with a blade in the small areas between the tents.

As we entered the camp, their swordplay came to a slowly halted, their attention seemed to fall on me, their prisoner. Gradually, everyone stopped what they were doing, each of them either looking me over with a look of distaste or delight. Some even looked confused, puzzled, making me wonder if this was their first time seeing a girl walk through their campsite. I refused to meet their stares and instead found myself looking at the ground, watching as I continued to drag my feet along the dirt path.

The horse I was attached to slowed to a stop, forcing me to pull up behind it. I was very aware of the silence that had fallen over the camp and the fact that just about every soldier was standing around us, watching as the boy in front of me slid off his saddle and began to untie the rope I was attached to. I waited for him to untie the bonds around my wrists, but instead he grabbed my arm gruffly, pulling me along with him towards a large tent with a purple flag waving at the top. Two mermaids were on the flag their tails intertwined, wrapping around the trident that stood between them.

"Wait here," the boy said, drawing my gaze away from the flag. Two guards came to my side as the boy released me, both of them holding onto my arms with a grip only a little less strong than his. The boy continued to stare me down, suspicion gleaming within his eyes as he turned his back to me, entering the tent.

That was when I noticed how badly I was shaking. My fingers trembled as I stood between the two guards and sweat was beginning to pour down the side of my face. I was scared in a way I hadn't been afraid before. My head continued to spin as my anxiety grew, but I knew it wasn't just because I was afraid of what these men might do to me. It was also the aftermath of all my trips and falls. I could feel myself beginning to sway, my body growing weary as the boy emerged from the tent.

He approached me, waving off the guards at my side. They released me, but my arms still felt like someone was gripping them with full force. I stared back at the sea-green eyed boy, shivering as he crossed his arms, flexing his biceps. What was worse was his scowl. It was so intimidating, so angry. The look aged him, made him seem older than I first thought he was. I had been so sure that he was my age – maybe even a year or two older – but with his jaw set and his brow drawn in a firm line, he could've easily been in his early twenties.

"King Jordan Wallace of Lorien demands that you tell us your name and what your purpose in this forest is," he said, his deep voice ringing with authority. I remained silent, feeling my mouth go dry as he moved closer to me, looking less friendly with each step. "If you deny the king's wishes and refuse to tell us who you are, then I will have to give you to one of the men."

"To do what?" I barely whispered.

"Well, to do as they please," his frown cracked and a smirk replaced it. The men behind me chuckled and hooted, allowing me to understand what they would do to me if they had me. I suspected that the threat was intended to make me feel even more afraid, but instead it did quite the opposite. I grew angry, which made me aware of the blood rushing through my veins, urging me to do what my Olsen blood told me to do; *fight*.

I curled my hands into fists and whacked him across the face with my bound hands, sending him toppling backwards. The laughter from the men behind me stopped almost instantly at the sight and sound of my fist colliding with their leader's face. All of them seemed to suck in a breath, watching as the boy touched his upper lip, removing his hand to find blood smeared across his fingertips. He looked at the blood running along his finger and then stared me down with a deadly gaze.

"*You –*" He growled, raising his fist high in the air to strike me. I braced myself for the blow, but someone had suddenly reached out from behind him, grabbing his arm before his fist could meet my jaw.

"Julian," the voice boomed. The boy before me turned immediately, his angry expression softening as he stepped to the side, allowing the taller man behind him to come forth.

"We are not barbarians. This is not how we treat the women of these lands."

The boy – Julian – bowed his head to the man, "Yes, father."

Father? I looked from Julian to the man who still held a firm grip on his arm, noticing the resemblance right away. They had the same chestnut-coloured hair, but the older man's was longer, reaching his shoulders. He wasn't dressed in armour like the others, but instead wore a tunic with the same symbol I had seen on that flag sewn onto the front. In addition to the tunic, he wore something upon his head, a type of headpiece that anyone would recognize. A crown.

I suddenly felt uncomfortable in his presence. *Should I be standing? Bowing? Kissing his feet or some royal rings?*

The king turned his attention away from his son and instead looked to me with a much sweeter expression than the one his son gave me, "Do not fret, my dear. I apologize for my son's behaviour. He should not have treated you so wrongly," the king said, shooting his son a scolding stare over his shoulder, making Julian blush. "But as a precaution, I must ask you to state your name and where your allegiance lies."

I stood very still, finding myself unable to move, let alone talk. *Have I fallen through time?* I shook my head at my own thought. That was impossible and impossible things only happened in stories or dreams. *Man, how hard did I hit my head?*

"We may not have any luck in prying any information out of this one, father," Julian spoke up. "She has only spoken once and injured two men from your army since we found her." He gave me a glare, still trying to wipe away the blood on his lip.

"What land do you dwell in? Or is the forest your home?" the king asked, ignoring his son.

"Please," Julian groaned. "She is not a dryad. If she was I would have killed her by now."

Some of the men began to chuckle and even Julian let a small grin cross his face whereas my stomach churned at their words. *Dryads?* I thought. *As in Marlee's Dryads?*

"He is right, your skin is much too light to be of dryad blood," the king said. "But then again, you are something we have not seen before."

"I reckon she is from the east," said one of the knights standing close behind me. "From Lilamule."

Some of the knights grunted and nodded in agreement, but I continued to remain still, trying to process their words.

"Is that true?" the king questioned kindly. "It would not surprise me if a woman as fair as you were from the land of beauty. In fact, I am quite close with Queen Arianna. She is a dear friend and –"

"Father, you are much too reckless with your kindness," Julian snapped. "She is not from Lilamule, nor is she from any other kingdom in Elssador."

"And how did you come to that conclusion?" the king asked, raising a brow.

"Because," Julian continued in a tone less sharp than before, "I, your knights, we are aprimorads..."

Dryads? Aprimorads? I knew these creatures too well, knew them better than I wanted to. Marlee spoke about aprimorads more than any of the other creatures she made up. She said that they were human, but their senses were enhanced until they were almost perfect, blessing them with the eyesight of a hawk and the hearing of an owl. But if Julian and all the other men surrounding me called themselves aprimorads, that meant... *oh no.*

"We can smell the scent of her blood and it is not like any other creature we have smelled before," Julian continued. "She is different, therefore she is dangerous."

I suddenly felt my knees turn to jelly and I began to stumble. One of the knights reached out to me, holding me up so I wouldn't fall.

"Where –" I started to say, my words slurred. "Where am I?"

"Well you are in the country of Lorien, of course," the king replied, his eyebrows knitted together in concern.

"No," I shook my head slowly. The world around me grew foggy, the king and his son looking more and more like massive blurs as my vision started to cloud over, "Where?"

"You are in Elssador," the king responded. He said something afterwards, but I couldn't hear it. I had already faded into darkness.

CHAPTER 3

THE FIRST HUMAN

I heard Aunt Mary and Uncle Gabe's muffled voices beside me, their conversation soothing the ache in my head, comforting me from that bizarre dream I had just had. I felt the soft covers beneath me, the pillow under my heavy head, and began to feel the stretch of a smile forming on my face.

I was home.

I attempted to open my eyes, but found that I couldn't. They were so heavy with exhaustion, feeling as though they were glued shut. Quick conclusions instantly began to dissolve the sudden panic rising within me. *I guess I have a concussion*, I thought as the pounding returned to my head. *A pretty bad concussion.*

My body felt paralyzed as I began to focus on Uncle Gabe and Aunt Mary's conversation, not quite picking up the words they were saying. Eventually, I was able to move my fingers and soon my arm, moving my right one over to my left to see if I still had that bracelet. A let out a sigh as I felt the cool silver beneath my fingers, unable to tell if I was relieved that I still possessed it or frustrated because it meant there were several unanswered questions.

I forced myself to focus on the familiar voices around me and not on the bracelet, which only seemed to make my head pound even more.

"Uncle Gabe," I managed to say, my dry throat making my voice sound raspy. "Aunt Mary..."

The ability to open my eyes had slowly come back to me and they began to flutter open, allowing me to see only a single blurry figure hovering over me.

"Shh, m'lady. You must rest," the person I thought to be Aunt Mary said.

"Aunt Mary, I don't understand. Why –"

"M'lady," the woman replied. Her voice suddenly became clearer to me and I began to realize that it wasn't Aunt Mary's voice I was hearing after all, let alone Uncle Gabe's. "I am not this Aunt Mary that you speak of. My name is Hana. I am a maid sent by his lordship to see you back to health."

I rubbed my tired eyes and eventually found the strength to open them fully. My vision began to clear and the blurry figure started to take form, immediately forcing a blush to creep up the back of my neck. It really wasn't Aunt Mary at my side, and certainly not Uncle Gabe. This woman was far too small and delicate to be him. I pulled the wool covers that I was tucked into further up my chest, feeling embarrassed and exposed in the presence of this unfamiliar face. Under the warmth of the covers, I became aware that my clothing had changed, exchanged for a large cotton shirt, substituting as a nightgown.

"I need you to sit up slowly now, m'lady," the maid said. I reluctantly followed her order, slowly easing myself up into a sitting position and instantly feeling as though I was going to be sick. "That's it. Now if you drink this you will feel much better."

She brought a cup up to my mouth, resting it on my lips, and encouraged me to sip. The taste was awful, bitter, and earthy, forcing me to cough some of it up. She removed the cup from my mouth and placed it on the small table beside my bed, seeming to have expected my reaction to whatever it was she made me drink.

Once my coughing fit had subsided, I let my eyes wander around the room, taking in all of its strange and unusual features, like the grey stone walls, the small, shuttered window carved into one, the ancient-looking wardrobe beside it, and the tiny silver pot that sat alone in the far corner.

The sound of my heartbeat began to thunder in my ears.

"Where am I?" I asked the maid – Hana – as I continued to stare at all these foreign objects, my chest, once again, tightening with panic.

"You have been brought to the city of Titus, m'lady, the capitol city of Lorien," Hana replied, her voice soothing my distress, but not completely extinguishing my worry. *Am I still dreaming?* I thought as my heart began to thump even louder against my ribs, allowing another wave of nausea to wash over me.

"Now, m'lady, I must inform you that the court physician has instructed me to give you a dose of that medicine every morning and every evening, just before you go to sleep. He said that it should heal your concussion," she said, striding towards the window and opening the wooden shutters. I squinted against the bright light that streamed through it, bringing a hand to my brow to shield my eyes. Once they adjusted to the light, I began to see what lay beyond my room, letting out a short gasp at the sight.

"Those are turrets!" I exclaimed, gazing out at the large stone towers that were built into the walls. I gaped at them, very aware that the maid was giving me a strange look, one that probably questioned my sanity. My joyful feeling started to fade the longer I looked out over the medieval city. The smile it had brought me turned into a frown as I realized what all of this meant. I was still dreaming. My nightmares weren't over.

"You should probably dress, m'lady," Hana said.

I turned to her, my heart sinking even more at the sight of what she had pulled out of the wardrobe. It was a beautiful gown, made of deep green fabric. Sewn onto the low neckline was a complex pattern, adding a bit of life to the dress.

"In that?" I said, arching a brow, my eyes darting between the gown she held in one hand and the deadly corset she held in the other.

"Of course," Hana chuckled until she realized the seriousness in my tone. She cleared her throat, composing herself. "I beg your pardon, m'lady. Is there something else you wish to wear?"

Yeah, sweats and a t-shirt, I thought instantly, but knew by the city beyond my window and her reaction that she wouldn't have a clue as to what those were.

"Is there anything a bit more... casual?" I said.

"I can wash up your old clothing if you'd like?" Hana responded, still eyeing me curiously. I opened my mouth to reply with an enthusiastic 'yes', but she continued on with her words, "Although – if it is right for me to say, m'lady – I would not walk into the king's court in such attire."

"The king's court?" I exclaimed.

"His lordship asked to see you the moment you woke," Hana said. "I shall find a servant to fetch you a tub so that you may wash."

"Thank you," I answered, completely dazed.

She placed the gown and corset at the foot of my bed and gave me a little bow before exiting the room. Once she was gone, I began to move myself, sliding my feet out of my covers, and scooting towards the edge of my bed at a pace my grandfather would have used. I still felt a bit woozy as I moved, but not nearly as bad as I did minutes before. I assumed that was the medicine doing its work.

My hands gripped the edge of my bed as I looked back out that window, watching as the wind blew against the flags hanging from the towers. I needed to wake up from this dream... or whatever it was. As far as I knew, dreams only lasted this long if you were in a coma. *Could I be? Am I back at home in a hospital, unconscious?* All I seemed to understand from the new world around me was that I didn't belong in it. I belonged in my reality, on Earth, back at home with Tyler and Marlee.

I suddenly remembered something Uncle Gabe had told me once, about a world you travelled to after death. *Earth is only the beginning,* he had said, *but it's more than that. It's a test. The dead don't stay dead forever, some rise. They rise and live in a world without sickness, pain, or grief. But others are blind and the only way they can see this world is if they choose to see.*

This place felt like Earth, but filled with kingdoms, names of places and races that I didn't recognize. Could it have been the world that Uncle Gabe talked about? I pushed that thought out of my mind quickly. I was silly to think that. This place was just the same as the world I came from. It was full of pain, sadness, sickness... and death. An image of that man I found by the well flashed through my mind, making me feel nauseous.

No. This was a nightmare. A nightmare that I really, really wanted to end.

But how?

Suddenly, my door flew open and Hana entered, followed by two servant boys who carried a large wooden tub. Hana carried a bucket of steaming water in her hands and began to pour it into the tub as the two servant boys left the room. She placed the bucket against the wall and then reached into her apron, pulling out a bar of soap which she placed in the tub.

"I will return to help you dress when you have finished your wash," Hana said.

I felt the urge to tell her that I was capable of dressing myself and that I would prefer it, but then I thought of that corset and the laces I would have to do up myself. It was quite an impossible task for one person. I gave her a slight nod, allowing her to leave the room to let me undress.

I pulled the large shirt over my head and threw it on my bed before stepping into the tub. The water felt good against my body, it moistened the dryness, making my skin feel smooth. Depending on how long I had been unconscious, I probably hadn't had a bath in days. I washed myself like I would in a normal bathtub, but when I went to reach for shampoo all I could see was the single bar of soap. I reached up to touch my oily, tangled hair and shrugged, taking the bar of soap and beginning to lather my hair with it, dunking my head under the water to rinse it off.

Once I had rinsed off all the soap, I got out of the tub, reaching towards my bed for the towel that was left for me. I wrapped myself in it, quickly drying my body and hair before putting the large shirt back on. Moments later, Hana gave a knock on the door. I called her in and she told me to take my shirt off again. I hesitantly did as she demanded, allowing her to pull a thin underdress over my head and then begin the long process of lacing up my corset. I let out a gasp as she got to my mid-section, reaching for my stomach that was being squished by the laces. Once she had finished doing it up, I put on the green gown, turning my back to Hana so that she could do up the many buttons.

"There," Hana said, patting my shoulder. I could see her grinning behind me in our reflection in the mirror I stood in front of. I watched as she began to give my damp hair a quick brush before handing me a pair of slippers, and rushing me towards the door, barely giving me time to take a look at the stranger I saw in the mirror. From what I could see, the corset made me look thinner, almost two sizes smaller. My figure seemed less square and more hour-glass, like Sophie's.

A knight stood outside of my room in the dimly lit hall where Hana led me. He was wearing the same costume as the knights I had seen before, a purple tunic and silver armour, topped with a sword at the waist. He gave me a slight bow and then turned, guiding me down the hallway towards the staircase at the end. I took note of the skeptical look he gave me over his shoulder as we went on our way. Clearly I was right about not being welcome. I suddenly remembered that knight, Julian, and the scowl he gave me the moment he spotted me in that forest. The thought made me wonder how many of his fellow knights he had convinced of my danger. *What danger can a human bring to them?* I laughed to myself, making the knight's suspicious stare harden.

Eventually, the knight and I made it to the bottom of the spiral staircase and out into the sunlight. My mouth fell open as I stood in the courtyard, gazing up at the thick walls surrounding me, at the knights that stood guard upon the tall towers. Never in my life had I been to a castle or ever dreamt I would step foot into one, yet in this dream I somehow knew every detail. It all looked so real – *felt* so real.

I forced myself to bury that ridiculous thought by paying attention to the knight who had already begun to make his way towards an inner gate up ahead, leaving me in front of the entrance of the stairwell we had just exited. I picked up my skirts and caught up to him just as he reached the gate.

"What part of the castle are we in?" I asked him.

The knight looked over his shoulder at me like I was delusional and responded in a tone that implied that that was something I should know. "We are about to enter the main bailey, the courtyard surrounding the keep," he answered, pointing to the large building at the back of the courtyard. It was built up onto a small hill where stone steps led up to its grand doors.

I continued to gape at the city as we passed under the gate, watching as the knights moved along the curtain wall, staring out into the great span of land I could just see through the opening of the front gate. My eyes locked on a large flag that hung just above the entrance. It was that purple flag I had seen before, the one with the mermaids hugging the trident. The flag seemed to wave over just about every tower and peak in the citadel.

The knight guided me through a row of shops and past a well in the centre of the courtyard where people were filling up their buckets and jugs with water. They watched me as we passed by, their eyes glowing like Julian's had. I wasn't sure why, but the sight sent an eerie feeling through my mind, making me worry even more for Marlee. When she spoke of aprimorads, she never mentioned that their eyes glowed, but that didn't mean she didn't know they did.

We climbed the steps towards the keep and approached the guards that stood by the door, just beneath a stained glass window. It was a picture of four people, three boys and a girl. Each of them stood with their hands out, revealing the various objects they held. The girl had a butterfly, the boy to her right had a sword, the one to her left held a flame, and the final one held what looked like a bolt of lightning. I wondered who they were and almost asked the knight guiding me, but the guards at the door had already pulled them open, allowing the knight and me to walk into the grand throne room.

There were whispers from the end of the room where a wooden throne sat upon a dais. It was occupied by the king I had seen before I had passed out. He was speaking with a man with slick black hair, dressed in a long robe that matched his reptile green eyes. As I approached them, their words grew quieter, their conversation dying down. The two of them turned to me, the king with a kind gleam in his eye, and the man beside him with a suspicious one.

"My lord, the girl as you requested," announced the knight in front of me with a low bow.

"Thank you, Drinian," the King replied with a nod. Although his eyes showed me kindness, his tone was hard, holding that authoritative sound that his son had. "Did my squire treat you well?" the king asked after a short silence. I stood in the middle of his court, just a few feet away from his throne, fiddling with the bracelet still clipped around my wrist. I spotted Julian over by one of the columns beside the dais his father sat on. He leaned against it, his expression still set in a scowl. The look hardened even more as I continued to stare at him, forcing me to turn away and blush.

I looked back up at the king who was awaiting my reply. I did not feel any kindness in the room, only a tension between the three royals before me. I was more than unwelcome, I was unwanted. But then why did the king place me in a room in his castle? Why not throw me in a dungeon?

I opened my mouth to respond to the king's question, but one of my own slipped out, landing me in even more trouble, "Why am I here?"

"I beg your pardon," the man with the black hair exclaimed. "You will address the king as Your Highness or Your Majesty!"

"Mortimer," the king groaned, rubbing his temples, "it is alright. She is not accustomed to our ways. Besides, I believe the question she asked is much deeper than the inquiry you took it as."

The corners of the king's lips twisted upwards into a small smile, making me regret the true meaning of my question.

"I just want to know why you haven't killed me yet," I said in a smaller voice than before.

"King Wallace does not execute under suspicion," Julian piped up. "He must be certain of your allegiance before that stage comes."

I swallowed down the lump that had formed in my throat and tried my best not to wipe my sweaty hands on the skirts of my dress.

"Please, I ask that you do not fear me," the king said softly, leaning forward in his throne. "I do not think you are a spy as my son and steward do –" He gave the man beside him, Mortimer, a quick gesture, "– but I still would like to know who you are."

I bit down on my bottom lip nervously, glancing between the steward and Julian's dirty stares and the king's caring one. The king seemed to carry a fatherly presence with him, reminding me of the dad I had lost. The reminder forced me to look down at the purple carpet beneath my white slippers, blinking back tears that threatened to fall from my eyes.

"My name is Carter Olsen," I answered quietly.

"May I ask where you are from, Carter Olsen?" the King said.

I stayed silent, hesitant about telling him where I came from. Even though he had saved my life and made sure that someone watched over me until I was back to full health, I still didn't trust him. I didn't trust any of them.

But it's a dream, Carter, I reminded myself. *You have nothing to lose.*

"I'm from Canada," I said eventually, knowing that they probably had no idea what I was talking about.

"Canada?" the Steward repeated slowly, his brows raised in question. "Is that a village from Boron?"

"No. It's in North America," I said. "You know, snow, maple syrup, a pretty bad summer Olympic team." I began to laugh at my own joke, but my laughter faltered when I stared back at the three confused faces before me.

"Canada," the King began to rub his bearded chin. His eyebrows were knitted together into a firm line as if he was trying to remember if he had heard the name before. "That is an earthly country. But you cannot possibly be a magwa?"

I tried my best to hide my surprise at the accusation. I was really going to have to get Marlee to forget about that well just to break myself free of this dream.

"No," I responded stiffly. "I'm human."

All three of them suddenly starred at me like I was a rare piece of silver or gold, like I was valuable, unique. I started to fiddle with the bracelet again, shifting uncomfortably on the spot. No one had ever stared at me like that before, especially not three men.

"That is impossible," Julian mumbled. "No one can travel in and out of Elssador. No one is supposed to. That is why the Portal –"

"Silence," the king hushed his son who reluctantly pressed his lips together, still looking outraged by my presence.

What are they talking about? What portal? I thought rapidly, my eyes darting between the three men. Dreams like this always woke me up. The ones where it got so confusing and frustrating that your brain couldn't take it anymore. *But shouldn't I know what this portal is? Don't you dream about things you know?* I suddenly began to think of Tyler and Marlee and all the other faces I knew so well. If you did dream about things you knew, then why weren't they in my dream? I seemed to know nothing here, not one person and not one rock.

I started to question myself again, wondering once more if this really was a dream, but once again I had pushed away the thought. It was a dream. None of what I was seeing was real, no matter how much it continued to feel like it was.

"Thank you, Lady Olsen, for your cooperation. I dismiss you from my court to do as you wish, just as any member of this castle is allowed to do," the king smiled. Mortimer and Julian shared a disagreeable look, proving that their suspicion towards me had not subsided no matter what their king said. "I shall send my squire with you to the kitchens immediately. Seeing as you were unconscious for two days I think it would be wise for you to have a nice meal, would you agree?"

My stomach growled loudly. I blushed, knowing that they had probably all heard it, "That would be great. Thank you, *My Lord*."

He shook his head, still smiling, "As part of this castle you are allowed to call me what you wish. King Wallace is one I hear often."

I returned his smile and curtsied – like I had seen Hana do – before his squire led me out of the keep. I peeked over my shoulder as we left to see that Mortimer and King Wallace had both risen from their seats, exiting the throne room through a door on the left wall, leaving Julian alone to stand with his arms crossed over his broad chest, watching as I exited the hall.

* * *

The squire, Drinian, had led me to the kitchen's where I eventually found something to eat. He stood by the door, watching me closely as I walked around the room, the smell of stew and fresh bread filling my nostrils. My stomach growled as I watched the kitchen ladies walk around the room, carrying pots of soup and plates of meat.

"Can I get you something to eat, m'lady?" one of the cooks asked. She held a tray that carried a bowl of stew and a few slices of bread on the side. The aroma made my stomach growl even more and I realized just how starving I really was.

"Here," the cook smiled, handing me the plate.

"Thank you," I said, taking the tray from her and sitting down by one of the counters, practically devouring the delicious stew. I received a few puzzled looks as I dipped the soft bread into my soup. I supposed it was something unheard of in my dream world.

I also became very aware of the king's squire hovering over my shoulder, munching on a green apple as he observed me eating. I felt the hairs on the back of my neck stick up as I finished my meal. Once I was done, a kitchen maid approached me and took my dishes. The squire tossed his apple into an empty barrel and waited for me by the door.

I decided that I was going to take King Wallace's advice and explore the castle. Drinian gave me a short tour around the keep, taking me through the throne room again and then around towards the library where I gaped at all the shelves of books that seemed to cover every wall and corner. Then Drinian took me back down to the main bailey where Julian and his knights were gathered. They were laughing as they took turns shooting arrows at targets that were set up in the courtyard. A small crowd of townsfolk had gathered to watch. They cheered every time a knight's arrow met its mark on the board, clapping even more as the knights bowed to them, relishing their applause.

Drinian brought me towards the crowd, over to the stables to get a better view of the entertainment.

"Stay here," he ordered, before turning on his heel towards Julian and his knights.

Julian looked up as Drinian approached, clasping his shoulder, and – to my surprise – grinning as their little game continued. I was struck by Julian's smile, startled even. I didn't think it was possible for a man who scowled as often as he did to produce such a charming grin.

Julian's smile continued to grow as Drinian took a bow from one of his fellow knights and stood beside Julian across from his target. Arrows were nocked as one of the other knights shouted "Load!" then at the word "Aim!" they all drew back, and then... "Fire!"

Loud thumps reverberated across the courtyard as the arrowheads met their wooden targets. The only person who managed to shoot his arrow dead centre was Julian. A few of the knights groaned when they realized he had won, but the others cheered loudly along with the crowd, making me feel as if I were at a hockey game or some football match. I clapped along with them, but soon became distracted by the stable around me. I looked up at the thick wooden rafters and down the walls towards a basket of arrows resting against the side of the barn. I glanced at Drinian who was busy groaning at his loss against Julian and then moved towards the basket. I picked up a long thin bow, immediately noticing the beautiful markings it had all up its limbs.

I knew quite a bit about archery. My father used to shoot. It was his weapon of choice when he and Uncle Gabe went hunting. He spoke about it often, explaining all the different parts of a bow to me, like the limbs, the grip, and the nocking point. He even let me try it, allowing me to fire at one of the targets he had painted into one of the many trees in our back yard. I remembered him demonstrating how to do it, then stepping back to let me take the reins. My hands had shaken as I stepped towards the target, still not fully understanding how it was done. My father remained silent as I lifted the bow, aimed at the red dot, and fired, my arrow landing on the first white ring around the centre. My mouth fell open in shock as I stared at my shot, but my dad applauded, patting me on the back as if it was something expected. As if he knew that I would be able to do it.

As I stood by the stables with this bow in my hand, I felt all those memories come flooding back. All those times I spent with my father in the back yard, practicing. I remembered the feeling of holding a bow and arrow, how strangely familiar it felt. I had never held one until the day my father taught me, yet as I fired, it felt as though the strength to do it was in my blood. I suppose it was. My father never missed a target and neither did I.

My fingers seemed to be itching to reach for one of the quivers beside the basket of bows, to grab an arrow and join in with Julian's game. I looked up at him, watching as he continued to fire more arrows at the targets, making the crowd shout with joy. There was no doubt that he still suspected me of being a spy. He didn't trust me as much as I didn't trust him. If I were still a dangerous threat to him then demonstrating my ability with a bow would only make matters worse.

But this was a dream. This was a world within my mind where no one could hurt me, where the rules were only my own. If I created them, then that meant I had the right to break them.

What do I have to lose?

"You shouldn't be doing that," someone said from behind me just as I pulled an arrow out of the quiver I had my eyes on.

I jumped, wheeling around with bow and arrow gripped tightly in my hands. A stable boy – about my age – stood before me dressed in brown rags that matched the colour of his short wavy hair. His voice seemed hard, but when I caught the look on his face I knew he found this situation amusing. His light brows were raised slightly, a grin tugging at the corners of his lips.

"Why not?" I asked the stable boy. "I'm just trying it."

"Yes, and you may miss and shoot one of the knights or worse, the prince," he said. I scowled after him as he moved a little further into the stables. He bent, using his pitchfork to rake strands of hay into a large pile. I never expected to see a strong – and not to mention attractive – stable boy. I always thought of them as anyone else would; ugly, smelly, and... well, wimpy. That's how they were mostly displayed in movies anyway. This guy was different than what I expected. He had some edge to him, a bit of sass that set my teeth on edge.

"Do you doubt my aim?" I questioned.

"Have you ever used a bow before? Have you ever shot an arrow?" he replied with a slight smile.

"My father taught me how to use one when I was seven. I've been shooting ever since," I said proudly. It was the truth, my seventh birthday was when my father decided to teach me, but the last part of that statement was a lie. Besides Aunt Mary not allowing me to touch my father's bow – which I knew to be stuffed away somewhere in our attic – I hadn't wanted to use one. This was the first time since he died that I wanted to wield it.

"Beg your pardon, m'lady," the stable boy said with a respectful bow. "I did not know you were so skilled with a bow."

I caught the grin on his face as he turned away to continue his work. There was no doubt that there was sarcasm in his voice. Anger bubbled inside of me and all of a sudden I had the urge to prove myself to him. I immediately nocked my arrow and drew back my string as the man who was shouting commands said *aim*, and then I fired, my arrow soaring through the air and landing dead centre on the target Julian stood across from.

A weight seemed to lift off my shoulders when I shot, a sense of comfort flooded through me, but it wasn't long until the weight returned. It rested heavily on my shoulders as I began to realize the silence that surrounded me. My relieved smile slowly faded as I looked around at the crowd, at all the eyes that were locked on me. Even the knights stood still, watching as I slowly lowered my bow, blushing as their stunned silence continued.

Julian was the first to move. His face blazed red as he stalked towards me, gripping his bow until his fingers paled, "You have an excellent skill with a bow, *m'lady*," he spat. "It may be different where you are from, but ladies of the castle do not use weapons."

"Yes, but I'm not a lady of the castle, am I?" I snapped back.

"This is a knight's game. A game of men. It is not safe for a women to engage themselves in dangerous activities such as this."

"Then let's change that. Let me play."

"I do not trust you, Carter Olsen," he responded, his blue-green eyes narrowing. "How do I know that your intentions for playing are merely an attempt to try and beat me, not to kill me?"

"If I wanted to kill you I would have," I said confidently. "I never miss."

"I highly doubt that," Julian snickered.

"Challenge me then. Prove me wrong."

Julian stood stiff for a long moment, the muscles in his body tensing. He swallowed hard, not even trying to conceal his irritation with me. He glanced down at his bow and then headed back towards the targets.

"The first person to shoot all the targets with a perfect score wins," Julian instructed as he walked up to the red line. There was no applause from the crowd this time, nor any words from the knights that stood there with their jaws dropped in shock.

Julian ordered them to move out of the way and they silently did as he bid. I started to move after him, towards the targets, but I felt someone grab my arm, pulling me back a step. I turned, looking into the stormy grey eyes of the stable boy.

"You are making a big mistake, m'lady," he whispered. "Prince Julian has been training with a bow since he was a small boy. He has had practice on the battlefield and not once has he missed target, no matter how fast it was moving."

I smirked. I could tell that Julian was good with a bow, but he wasn't the only one who had excellent aim. I pulled my arm from the stable boy's grasp and continued on after Julian. He was standing at the line with an arrow already loaded. I stood at a short distance behind him, watching as he aimed at the first target and then fired. He waited for the arrow to land in the centre, then he nocked another, shooting arrows as he walked down the red line, passing all the targets. Even on the last one he hit the red dot, but the arrow wasn't completely centred just as his other ones weren't. I held back my smile as Julian turned to me, bowing with a smug look on his face as the crowd applauded.

He moved out of the way for me as I stepped up to the first target, pulling an arrow out of the quiver that one of the knights held, and nocking it. I breathed as I pulled my bowstring back towards my cheek, squinting as I aimed. Once I knew I was in position I shot at the target, watching as my arrow landed dead centre, only an inch or two away from Julian's. I could see his smug expression slowly fading as I continued down the line of targets just as he had, each one of my arrows landing at the centre.

The silence that had fallen over the crowd when I first shot my arrow returned. They all stared at me in awe. Even Julian, with his hands at his sides, his full lips parted slightly. I stared back at him, trying my best to hold back the smile that was tugging at the corner of my lips. As if taking note of my struggle, he clamped his mouth shut, his cheeks burning bright red. I wasn't sure if it was out of embarrassment or rage. Soon the silence in the crowd broke as the stable boy began to clap. Then everyone else joined in – except for Julian and his knights of course – with a cheer as loud as they gave their prince.

I walked away from the knight's who continued to stare at me as if I had beaten all of them and not just their leader. I made my may back towards the stables – feeling the prince's careful eyes watching me as I went – to put my bow back in the basket. I stepped into the stables, poking my head out the door to see the knights as they started packing up their targets and weapons while Julian jogged past the barn and hurried into the keep.

I found a bench to sit on and let out a loud sigh, closing my eyes and allowing myself to smile as I let the good feeling of using a bow again sink in. More memories of the many hours practicing with my dad in the fields of the family farm began to pop up, putting my puzzled mind at peace.

There was one time in the fall, just after we went apple picking, where we decided to have a little practice. My dad would toss the apples into the air – completely ignoring Aunt Mary's protests – and I would shoot them, watching as they stuck to the trees in the distance. I remembered us laughing at Uncle Gabe jumping out of his skin as one of my arrows shot past his ear. My father had hunched over in laughter, chuckling to the point of tears. Uncle Gabe had marched towards him, beaming as he tackled him to the ground and I hopped in to join them.

That was my favourite memory of my father, but it was also the worst. About an hour after that, when the sun was setting, we were walking inside for dinner. My father volunteered to clean up outside, insisting that he would catch up. He seemed pale in the orange sunset and his eyes looked as though they were full of pain. I had noticed his dramatic weight loss over the past few months. Every time I went to ask him about it he would brush it off and change the subject. He never told me he was sick. He didn't tell anyone. My father was very secretive, sometimes too secretive for his own good. I always had to pry information out of him and then he would point out how much I acted like my mother, forcing us both to shut up. It was a subject that brought us great joy, but also unbearable pain.

Uncle Gabe and I walked inside the house, but we waited for almost an hour and still my father hadn't returned. Uncle Gabe went outside to check on him. Minutes later I heard the door swing open and both Aunt Mary and I rose from our seats. She made it to the doorway first, immediately turning back and shoving me out of the way. I tried to move past her, trying so hard to break down her barrier. But when I had, I wished I hadn't fought so hard. Uncle Gabe was standing there with my father's motionless body in his arms. The sight made my own body go completely numb. Every inch of me was paralyzed except for my eyes, which travelled from his pale face and towards the blood stain on the front of his shirt. I remember feeling empty, abandoned, thinking he was dead. Thinking that he had left me. Uncle Gabe must have known these thoughts were playing through my mind. He looked at me with his soft blue eyes, assuring us all that he was still alive.

We got him to the hospital immediately and they told us that these were his last hours. There was no hope for recovery. The cancer had spread everywhere, invading every organ in his body. That was the last day I saw my father, the last day we spoke. I remember him lying in his hospital bed, requesting to speak to me, only me. Uncle Gabe brought me in, standing silently behind me at the foot of the bed.

"Carter, my brave, beautiful girl," my dad whispered. "I love you. Remember that, alright? Everything I did and everything I didn't let you do is all because of that. Because I love you. The time is coming for you to take heart, Carter. The time for you to be brave is coming soon."

"I can't be brave," I said. "Not without you."

My father smiled, lifting his cold hand to my cheek, wiping away my tears with his thumb. "You have heart, Carter. A heart of courage. When the time comes you'll see it and you'll learn how to use it."

Not long after those words the steady *beep* of the heart monitor stopped.

My father was gone.

"My apologies, m'lady, but I need to get through," a voice said. I snapped out of my thoughts instantly and looked up to find the stable boy standing before me, his pitchfork in his hand. He smiled weakly, gesturing to the cabinet behind me.

"Oh, yes. My bad," I quickly stood up from the bench and hurried behind him, instantly wiping away my tears. I hoped he hadn't seen them. I hated it when people saw me cry. Even Tyler hadn't seen me do it. Not Tyler and certainly not Marlee. I hadn't even cried at my father's funeral. I waited until I was home, locked in my room and sobbing myself to sleep more nights than I could count.

"I must say, m'lady," the stable boy said over his shoulder as he pulled a bucket out of the cabinet. "I seemed to have underestimated your abilities."

"Thank you..." I paused. "Uh, I don't think we've really been introduced."

The boy stood up straighter, staring at me with sudden curiosity, "Most people just call me *stable boy*. They do not have time to learn my name."

"I have time," I answered with a shrug.

"My name is Abias. Abias Wood," he responded with a kind smile.

"Carter Olsen," I replied, shaking his rough, calloused hand. "Are you sure you're actually a stable boy?"

"I am fairly certain," he chuckled, lifting the bucket in his hand and gesturing to the area around us. He was witty, funny, a quality that lots of people were attracted to. I laughed with him as I walked at his side towards the well at the centre of the courtyard.

"Did you ever consider being a knight?" I asked curiously, eyeing his muscular build as I helped him fill the heavy buckets with water. "You know, fighting battles? Defending your people? Being a hero?"

"Do you always ask this many questions?" Abias said over his shoulder with an amused raise of his brow. I gave him a slow nod. "Well," he replied, "you can do all of those things without being part of an army. I believe that it is not knighthood that defines one as a hero. Besides, there hasn't really been a war worth fighting in these lands for years. The last true war fought was the one King Wallace and the magwas were part of."

"King Wallace is a magwa?" I exclaimed as I took a bucket from Abias and started to carry it back to the stables alongside him. I tried my best to keep up with his long legs. Even with two heavy buckets in his hands he seemed to be going twice my speed.

"Indeed," Abias replied over his shoulder. "He is the man with the lightning bolt in his hands on the window above the keep."

"Who are the others?" I continued to question. I always was curious when Marlee spoke of magwas. Out of all the creatures she invented they seemed the most normal and – in my dream – certainly the most kind. They were creatures that also looked like humans, but they were blessed with special abilities, powers that marked them as different. I found myself becoming more and more interested in her imagination. I had always wanted to understand how she saw things, figure out why this imaginary world was so important to her, why it became part of her dreams at night. Maybe that was why I was having this dream in the first place, to see the world the way she saw it.

"The man with the flames is King Caleb Monahan," Abias answered. "He rules over the land of Boron. The woman, that is Queen Arianna Ross, she rules Lilamule, the Land of Beauty. When you arrived here we all assumed that is where you were from," he smiled kindly as he unlatched the gate to one of the stalls where a brown horse waited thirstily. It took me awhile to realize that he had complimented me, but when I did, I felt my face grow hot.

"It seems that news here spreads fast," I said. Abias seemed to know that I was a stranger to more than just the city of Titus. I looked around at others that passed us by in the courtyard. Every one of them seemed to be trying their best not to look at me as they continued with their daily routines. Could they all sense that I was different just like Julian had? Could they smell my foreign scent?

Abias smiled at me and shook his head as if I had voiced my questions rather than thinking them. "Not necessarily," he replied, placing the bucket by a wall and closing the gate behind him. The brown horse started to lap the water as we walked further down the aisles of stalls, "Aprimorads have a very good sense of smell. We smell more than just fragrances, we can smell blood as well. That is how we identify different creatures whose appearances resemble ours. But you, you're blood smells different. It is stronger than what we are used to smelling. When you arrived in these walls everyone was suspicious."

"Then how come the king and his son were so surprised when I told them I was human?"

"Because King Wallace – as I have said – isn't an aprimorad. Therefore he does not have our sense of smell. As for Prince Julian, he – like the rest of Elssador – has not smelled human blood before."

"Then how do you know that's what I am?"

Abias raised his eyebrows, flashing another grin in my direction before turning on his heel towards another pile of hay, giving me no answer. "The last magwa on that window," he started, continuing with our original topic, "that would be King Austin Ross, the ruler of Oscor, the Land of Might. He claims to be the rightful ruler of Elssador."

"Claims? You mean he's not?" I asked. Abias was about to respond, but was stopped by the sound of a loud bell ringing and a few shouts from the front gates.

I looked to Abias and his eyes were wide and watchful, glowing more than they were before. "That is the visitor bell," he mumbled, dropping his things onto the ground and starting out into the courtyard. I ran out after him, out of the stables and into the square where groups of people were gathered to greet the visitors as they filed in on their horses. Julian and King Wallace had emerged from the keep and rushed down the small hill to see who was entering their city. One of the men spotted the two of them coming his way and immediately got off his mare, heading straight for King Wallace.

"My Lord," he bowed lowly.

"What is it Lord Sebastian?" King Wallace clasped his hand and looked into the other man's eyes worriedly.

"My scouts have seen morbiens on the shores of Mitus. They ride on ships with black sails. It seems as though they are heading here, to Titus," Lord Sebastian said lowly, looking around at the villagers who stood by, trying to get a good look at their guest. I left Abias – despite his protests – and snuck up close behind Julian, listening to the leaders speak.

"Then we must evacuate the city," King Wallace concluded, speaking to Julian, his squire, and Mortimer. "We will get our armies on every wall surrounding the castle. The women, children, everyone in this city must leave and go to Mitus."

"But, My Lord, if they are to take Titus, won't they plan to invade my city as well?" Lord Sebastian noted.

"It is just temporary. They will not take this city if we stand and fight. Mortimer," King Wallace said to the steward, "announce this to everyone and make sure they are out of this city in less than an hour."

"Yes, Your Majesty," Mortimer bowed his head and started toward the crowd with a few knights following after him.

"Sebastian, how many men do you have with you?" King Wallace asked as they started up the hill. Abias hurried towards the Lord's horse, taking the reins and guiding it into the stable. He gave me a look of warning as he went, but I continued to ignore him, moving behind King Wallace and his cabinet as quietly as I could.

"Two hundred, Your Highness," Lord Sebastian replied. "I brought almost all of my men. There are still about eighty guarding Mitus."

"Good," King Wallace said, pulling up and allowing Lord Sebastian to continue up to the keep. He turned, his eyes resting on me. By the gleam in his eye I could tell he knew I was there the whole time. Julian came walking up the stairs, about to pass us and continue up to the keep, but his father put out a hand, preventing him from moving any further. Julian blinked, clearly just as confused as I was.

"Julian, I want you to guard Carter. To see that she makes her way out of the city alright," King Wallace said.

Julian's jaw dropped and he instantly began to protest, "But, father, I am to remain here. I am to guard Titus alongside you!"

"This is a new order, Julian," King Wallace snapped, narrowing his eyes on his son. "You are to lead our people to Mitus safely and Carter as well." King Wallace took a step towards Julian, placing a hand on his cheek and whispered, "Guard her with your life."

His last words puzzled me, but they sent a completely bewildered expression across Julian's face. King Wallace walked away and continued toward the keep, leaving Julian and me to stand at the stairs in shock.

After a moment of us standing still on the steps, watching as King Wallace disappeared behind the doors of the keep, Julian shook his head and turned back around towards the town, refusing to look at me. "This way," he gritted through his teeth, pushing past me and striding towards the stables. I rolled my eyes and hurried on after him. Clearly he didn't want to be seen with me, but why? Was it because I was human? Abnormal? *I am far from abnormal, Hawkeye.*

I followed him down into the centre of the courtyard and through an alley that brought us towards the stables. I could hear him grumbling to himself as we continued on, but didn't quite catch any of the words. I could only assume he was cursing his father's decision, maybe even me.

"Julian –" I started, about to tell him that I didn't need his help out of the city, but he whipped around and glared down at me before I could make another peep.

"Listen here, *human*," he growled. "I am going to make something very clear. You may have noticed that I do not want much to do with you."

"Then we agree on something," I shot back. He clenched his jaw and walked away.

"I suggest you keep your pretty little mouth shut if you want to be alive by dawn," he said over his shoulder as we turned into the stables.

"Is that a threat?" I stopped walking, crossing my arms, and raising a brow the way I had seen Aunt Mary do countless times.

"Not from me. From the enemy," he said, turning. He moved closer to me as he spoke, taking several steps until my back was pressed up against the cold castle wall. I could feel his hot breath against my skin as he searched my eyes with his cold ones, sending a chill through my body, "The morbiens, they will show you no mercy, no compassion, and no honour if you fall into their hands. They will rip your body to shreds while you are still breathing and eat you for their supper. They were born and bred in the darkness, therefore they are empty. No soul to cry out with and no love to share. It is not me you should be afraid of, Olsen."

As he said those last words I swore I saw a bit of sympathy in his eyes, a bit of fear even. I assumed it was just my imagination because the look was gone before I could even comment on it. His scowl returned, along with his icy stare.

"I suppose you and morbiens aren't so different then," I muttered. I expected him to lash out at me, to lift his arm to strike me just as he had almost done when I first attacked him, but instead he smirked.

"You don't know me, Olsen," he said. He took another step towards me, his smirk transforming into a slight sneer. "And I think we shall get along much better if you stop pretending like you do."

CHAPTER 4

CLARISSA'S LULLABY

It had been several hours since we left the city. It was already getting dark by the time Julian decided to get everyone to stop in a valley to rest for the night. Several of the villagers immediately began to unload their belongings and settle down by a warm fire. About a dozen of them were already lit and I was still trying to figure out how to start one without matches or a lighter. Having no clue what they used here, I picked up two sticks and began to rub them together, very aware of someone chuckling beside me.

When I looked up, I saw that it was Abias, seated before a large fire that sizzled and popped not far from where I was. He was watching me, obviously trying to hold back a grin. I turned away, continuing to try and make at least a spark with my sticks.

"It will take you days to start a fire like that," he said.

"Well, how else am I supposed to do it?" I sighed, tossing my sticks down and putting my hands on my hips.

"There is always the option to share," Abias gestured towards the flames that danced before him, luring me forward. I gave in, rising from the ground with my saddle bag in hand. I took a seat beside him on the ground, immediately feeling comforted by the warmth of the fire.

"Has Prince Julian left you?" Abias questioned, scanning the perimeter as if expecting him to be near.

"He went to meet up with the other knights. Something about night guards, night watches... You know, prince stuff," I replied, settling down beside his fire. His muffled laughter made me look up from my saddle bag that I had begun to rummage through with my brows raised. "Is something funny?"

"Well, I think you may have been just a bit misinformed," Abias replied, turning his head towards two people walking in the distance. One of them was a girl with honey-coloured hair that blew back in the light wind, tendrils of it flying past her flawless face as she walked alongside a boy, her hand linked with his. I noticed that it was Julian right away, recognizing those blue-green eyes even before he looked up, dragging them towards the pretty girl at his side. She was speaking to him as they walked, her eyes trained on the road ahead, but Julian's were fixed on her, a sweet smile spreading upon his lips. He looked at her as if she was the most beautiful being he had ever seen, as if he could look upon her for the rest of his life and the image would still hold its magnificence.

I remembered my father looking at photos of my mother like that, even the way he spoke her name made it seem as though the thought of her was something he could think about forever. He rarely spoke of her to me, but when he did, a light smile would form on his lips. He would get caught in a daze, staring off into nothing as if she was in the room standing there before him. I didn't need my father to tell me stories about the woman who gave birth to me to know that he loved her. I saw it in the way he stared at her picture, at the way he avoided speaking about her, and even the way I caught him looking at me. It wasn't that he was ashamed of loving her, it was that her name brought him pain. He loved her so much, maybe too much.

"Her name is Talia Bennet," Abias started to explain. I kept my eyes locked on Julian as the two of them stopped moving along the path and turned, standing chest to chest, gazing back at one another. "She is a village girl, a nice girl. She and Julian are to be wed at the beginning of next month."

"*She* is going to marry *Julian*?" I said, my tone coloured with exclamation.

Abias chuckled, "It would seem surprising, but they are a smart match. She brings out a light inside him that I and everyone else had thought burnt out years ago."

I finally drew my gaze away from Talia and Julian, not just because they both leaned in for a tender kiss, but because Abias' words sparked confusion inside of me. He spoke as if he knew Julian as more than just his prince, as if he knew him as well as his father did.

"Bread?" Abias offered, lifting up a loaf of it with a tight grin, making me wonder if he could see my many questions being written across my face. Hesitantly, I accepted his request, ripping off half of the loaf and taking a large bite out of it before returning my attention to my saddle bag.

I began to dig through it, pulling out a loaf of my own bread, along with some fruits and cheese. I looked under an extra gown that Julian had gotten Hana to pack for me, hoping to find at least a dagger at the bottom, but there was nothing, only the bottom of the leather bag. I silently cursed Julian. I was defenceless without a weapon. Sure, I was surrounded by armed knights, but if those morbiens were as bad as he made them out to be, then it would be every man for himself if they decided to attack.

I shuddered at my own thoughts. *Since when did I start thinking like a soldier?* Yes, I knew how to shoot an arrow, but that was just a hobby. I could tell by the sharp blades attached to every knight's belt that archery wasn't just something they practiced to pass time. It was a chance at survival. I may have had the skill to kill someone, but not one part of me wanted to do it, no matter how heartless my enemies may be.

Watching my father die made me want to make sure that everyone lived, but it wasn't just his passing that revealed to me how much I hated death. His wasn't the first one I had witnessed. He and Uncle Gabe would take my grandfather hunting every Father's Day. There was one time when I begged to come along. I looked up to my father the way Marlee looked up to me. I wanted to spend every moment by his side, doing what he did. He was hesitant about letting me come along, in fact all three of them were. I wasn't entirely sure what made them agree that I could join the hunt, but the next thing I knew we were packing up the van, heading out into the back woods on the outskirts of South River.

We had moved deep into the forest, wandering around for what felt like hours until we saw a deer. The four of us stopped, holding our breaths as the innocent animal approached a tree, chewing on its green leaves. Uncle Gabe lifted his gun to shoot, but my father held him back.

Too loud. I could see the words in his eyes as he shook his head at his older brother. Uncle Gabe nodded, a smile appearing on his lips as my father opened up the large bag he had brought with him. He pulled out his bow and an arrow along with it. He rested the arrow on his bow string, pulled back, and released. The arrow didn't even make a sound as it flew off of his bow, shooting through the forest and embedding itself in his target.

We approached the deer, laying motionless by the tree it had once been eating from. My father knelt down beside it, taking a hunting knife from his belt and driving it into the deer's flesh near where his arrow stuck. I remember gasping at the sight of the blood that streamed out of the wound. I had felt like I was going to faint, but instead I made a run for it, charging through the forest with my father's calls chasing after me.

I hid behind a pine tree, curled up in a ball and sobbing into my arms. If I didn't understand death before, I did then. The sight of the deer's pale eyes had startled me, but seeing my father harming it after it was already mortally wounded made me go into complete shock. I was horrified and suddenly scared at how calm my dad had been as he pulled out the arrow.

Footsteps approached me and I knew just by their sound that it was my father. Dirt and pine needles crunched beneath him as he lowered himself next to me. I didn't want to look at him. I was afraid to. But he wasn't afraid. Why wasn't he afraid?

His arms folded around me and immediately I melted into their embrace even though it was the last thing I wanted to do. After seeing what he did to the deer, I didn't think I could bear to even look at him. But the comfort of home was what I needed in a time of pain and he was my home. He had always been my home.

Suddenly, he began to sing, stroking my hair as a familiar song escaped his lips. It was a lullaby, one that he had sung to me often. The haunting tune put my mind at rest and the comforting words dried my eyes as he continued to sing;

My love, my love
why must you cry?
This fear will soon pass by
My love, my love
why must you feel so alone
when you are so close to home?

My love, my love
I'm right here by your side
with my arms stretched wide
My love, my love
Please don't frown
I'm right here, smiling down

My love, my love
I'll always be right here
even when I disappear

"That's pretty," Abias said, his words breaking through my thoughts. I flushed, only realizing then that I had been singing it out loud instead of in my head. The weight of Abias' gaze weighed heavy on me as he continued to comment on the song, "A beautiful song."

"Oh," I said, feeling my face grow even hotter, "It's a just lullaby. Something my mom made up. My dad used to sing it to me when I had nightmares and stuff," I swallowed, feeling a lump form in my throat. *Don't cry*, I snapped at myself. *Don't you dare.*

"If your mother is the writer of this song, why did she not sing it to you?" It was an honest question, but to me it felt like more of a clarification, as if he already had a feeling that she was something missing in my life.

"She died when I was really young. I never knew her," I replied carefully. I didn't know why I was telling Abias all of this. The only one that had heard me talk about my mother was Tyler. When I was younger it was a hot topic. I often wondered who she was and why she was never around like other kid's moms were. Questions like that had haunted me through my early years, but close to the time my father died I seemed to ignore those thoughts. Yet, now that I was in Elssador they seemed to be popping back up, forcing tears to well up in my eyes. I blinked them back, turning my head in attempt to hide my tears from Abias, but he had already seen them.

He instantly reached out to me, resting a gentle hand on my arm, "I'm sorry. If I had known, I wouldn't have –"

"No. It's fine." I wanted my response to be kind, but I seemed to force the words out sharply as I pulled my arm out from under his hand. A hurt look crossed his face, forcing guilt to swirl around in my stomach, "Sorry. I didn't mean to talk to you like that. You were just being kind."

"No," he shook his head, beginning to poke at the fire with his pitchfork. "I'm used to it."

I looked him over, feeling a sadness settling in my heart. I pitied Abias. The way he spoke to me made it seem as though people had been treating him like dirt his whole life. Besides my humanity, he thought I was different than everyone else, that I spoke to him like a person rather than a worthless stable boy.

"You think Julian would let me travel with you instead?" I said.

Abias looked up, his eyebrows knitted together in confusion. I gave him a small smile which spread one on his own lips, "If he really is as irritated by your presence as he seems, then I am sure he would put you into my care freely."

He spoke in a light tone, but the look in his eyes betrayed it. Was it doubt swirling between the dark grey flecks in his irises? Or was it a bit of fear? I decided to ignore it and instead let out a light laugh, "Good. At least now I can travel with a friend."

A funny look appeared on Abias' face. I suddenly found him staring at me as if that was the highest compliment I could give him, "You consider me a friend?" His voice was coloured with surprise, making me wonder if he had ever had a friend, someone to protect, someone to act like a fool with, someone who knew the deepest parts of your soul...

"Yeah," I said, with a nod. "I do."

*   *   *

"Carter, we've got to get moving."

I could feel Abias' hands on my arms, shaking me awake. He continued to tell me to get up until I slowly opened my eyes. The sunlight burned them and I groaned, immediately rolling onto my stomach and burying my face in my arms.

"What time is it?" I grumbled.

"The sun is just rising," Abias replied. "We have slept in far too long. Others have already begun to pack up their things."

I slowly lifted my head, adjusting to the light, and watching as Abias moved towards our fire, stomping out the last bit of flame with his foot. He took our saddle bags next and began to load them onto our horses as I prepared myself to get up off the ground.

"Sleeping in," I muttered as I rose. "I don't even wanna know what their definition of early is."

It didn't take long for the two of us to get ready to go. Abias was already holding both of our horses' reins in his hands by the time I walked over to him. I attempted to pull myself onto my horse just as I had seen everyone else do, but I soon discovered that was an impossible task with this stupid dress on. *I wish someone would just give me a pair of pants already! Or better, I could wake up and find myself back home in a pair of comfy sweats.*

"Would you like help up?" Abias offered from beside me with a huge grin on his face. *Morning people,* I silently groaned.

"No. I got it," I assured him, trying my best to use a tone as pleasant as his.

"Here," Abias chuckled, quickly tying his horse up again, and then coming over to me. I felt his strong hands grip my waist and then –

"What do you think you're doing?" a familiar, unpleasant voice grumbled before us. I looked up, not at all surprised to see Julian seated high up on his horse, his eyes narrowing at Abias

64

and me. Abias immediately removed his hands from my waist, taking a step away from me, and gave Julian a bow.

"My Lord," he said. "I was just assisting Lady Olsen onto her mare."

"Thank you for your help, Stable Boy, but I think you should stick to caring for horses. It seems to be the only thing you succeed at," Julian answered bitterly. I glared up at him. It was only hours ago he was walking alongside Talia, smiling brightly and letting his hard exterior fall away. I supposed she was the only one that could break down his strong walls.

I glanced over at Abias who hung his head, refusing to meet his master's eyes. He wasn't sad, he was boiling with anger. Abias said he was used to having people talk down to him. So why did he let Julian's voice bother him? Was there some deeper meaning to Julian's words? The more questions popped into my head, the more I began to feel out of the loop. There was something these two weren't telling me. I was missing a massive piece to their collective puzzles.

"Olsen, get on your horse. We are about to depart," Julian ordered. He pulled on his reins, about to turn away.

"Wait," I called after him. He rolled his eyes and stared at me with an impatient expression. "I'm done travelling with you."

"That is not for you or me to decide. I am following my father's command," Julian replied.

"King Wallace ordered you to get me out of the city safely. You've done your job," I said.

Julian's horse took a few steps closer to me, making him look even more superior, "Elssador is not a good place for a woman to be wandering off on her own."

"I won't be alone. I'll be with Abias. He'll make sure that I'm safe."

"Olsen," Julian hissed, "it is not my duty to advise you otherwise. It is my pleasure. It may just be the only kindness you receive from me that I give willingly."

"I trust him," I answered, looking over at Abias whose gaze was still locked on the ground beneath him. "My life is in his hands now."

Julian stood very still for a moment, gripping his leather reins so tightly that I thought his fingers might begin to bleed, "Fine. Do as you wish."

He turned slowly, hesitantly, and then rode off towards his knights at the front of the line of villagers. Abias turned to me silently, once again placing his hands on my waist. He bent and lifted me up onto my saddle.

"Are you comfortable?" he asked as he slipped my feet into the stirrups.

"I would be even more so if I had a pair of breeches like yours," I said, making a small smile appear on Abias' face.

"Women in these lands don't wear trousers," he answered as he pulled himself onto his own horse, kicking its flank and moving forward in a trot. I rode alongside him, joining the long line of townsfolk that moved along the dirt path. "I didn't think it was something women found pleasure in wearing."

"Trust me. We find great pleasure," I insisted.

"Careful. Talk like that might start a revolution, one that you will be named the head of." His tone was teasing, but I wondered if maybe he was being serious at the same time.

"What do you mean?" I questioned.

"Elssador's people are preparing themselves for change. All they need to begin that change is a leader who is not afraid to stand up to His Royal Highness," Abias said, raising his eyebrows at me. "The people have been speaking of your challenge to Sir Julian. It might be different where you have come from, but no man would ever dare to stand up to the next in line for the throne. It's a dangerous move, Carter, but you did it anyways. It seems as though you have some courage buried in your heart."

I paused, taking in what he had said. *Me? Brave?*

You have heart, my love. A heart of courage, my father's words repeated in my mind. *The time for you to be brave is coming soon.* A strange feeling washed over me, forcing the hairs on the back of my neck to stick up.

It's just a dream, Carter. Not a coincidence. Just a dream. Only a dream.

"You do not believe me," Abias observed. "You don't believe me just as you don't believe in this world around you."

"I don't think I understand. What –"

"You know what I speak of. You think this is all a dream, do you not?" Abias said.

I paused. There was no use in hiding it. The fact that this was a dream was the reason I didn't care that I went head to head with Julian. It wasn't because I was brave. It was because I had nothing to lose.

"It has to be," I sighed. "I fell down a well and hit my head. It's the logical explanation."

"*Logical* to your world maybe."

"Well it seems that me being here isn't very *logical* for your world either."

"There is a reason why you are here," Abias said firmly. "Whatever it may be, good or not, there is a reason. We just don't yet know it."

I let his words sink in as he started to ride past me and further up the line of people. He rode towards a child who had slid off her saddle. I watched Abias as he hopped off his horse and helped the child back onto hers with the sound of my heart thumping in my ears. When I said I trusted Abias earlier, I meant it, but I didn't know why I did. Watching as he refused a reward of money from the child's mother made me realize why. He was Tyler. Every bit of his charismatic smile, the compassionate look gleaming in his eyes... it was all him. Abias was covered in every inch on my best friend that I loved to the ends of the earth. As he got back on his horse, riding towards me, his light brown curls began to get lighter until they were the golden colour of Tyler's hair. His strappy build began to morph into a tall, lean one. His stormy eyes became green like the grass his horse galloped on.

I felt a pain in my chest as Abias returned to my side. He made me see how much I longed for my best friend, how much I wanted a piece of home. Worry suddenly began to take control of my mind, filling it with questions that made me feel sick. *What if I never get out of this dream? What if I'm dead? What if this is like a second world or something that you pass through before you go to that place Uncle Gabe always talked about? What if this was just another test?* That meant that I was stuck in this world until my time here was complete. That also meant that I would never see Tyler again... or Marlee.

"You seem troubled," Abias observed.

"What? No, no, I'm okay," I assured him, putting on my best fake smile. "I was just –"

Suddenly, there was a shout from the front of the line, cutting off my words. Everyone stopped moving forward as two Lorien scouts rode down the line. As they drew closer, I could see that their mouths were sealed shut and their legs were tied down tightly to their saddles. Their eyes were wide as they passed us, filled with warning. Suddenly, there was a noise off in the distance. A growling and howling from up ahead. Wait, no... *from behind.*

I whipped my head back towards the forest we just left and a spear shot down from one of the high branches. It hit an old man who was walking at the back of our line. He stumbled, falling to the ground with a cry. I turned away quickly at the sight of blood splattering out of his body and onto the green grass.

"Carter, we must ride quickly," Abias urged. I nodded in agreement and we surged forward. Everyone was wailing in panic, moving as fast as they could, but seemed to get nowhere with all their belongings dragging them down.

I stayed close to Abias as we rode, but I noticed someone falling behind. It was a little girl, struggling to move her small legs as fast as the woman running ahead of her did. She looked as though she was only four years old, Marlee's age. She was crying, screaming as crowds of people ran past her, accidentally pushing her to the ground in their terror. I instantly pulled up on my reins and steered my horse around.

"Carter, where are you going?" Abias shouted after me. His arm reached out towards my reins as if to pull me back, but I was already galloping towards the girl.

As I approached her, a tall, dark creature came up from behind. He was dressed in black, making his pale skin stand out even more. His eyes were dark, but as he stared down at the little girl, screeching in horror beneath him, they began to blaze with red. He licked his fat lips, snickering as he raised his blade to strike her. Before the blade could get anywhere near her throat I was on top of her attacker. I had leapt off my horse, throwing my body onto to him, tackling him to the ground with me on top.

I didn't have time to check and see if the little girl had gotten away. The creature had already flipped me onto my back, pinning me down, putting his heavy arm over my throat. I stared back at the creature who sneered at me, the sight of him allowing a sliver of fear to settle within me. He didn't have a nose, only a pair of gills on the side of his face that flared as he chuckled, finding pleasure in the fact that he was suffocating me.

I reached my hand out, feeling only the soft grass beneath my fingers, finding nothing useful to hit him with. Hope was restored as my hand passed over a sharp rock. I gripped it tightly, quickly bringing my hand up to his temple. He fell back at my blow, releasing me, and clasping his bleeding forehead. I got up, immediately hunching over to cough and gasp for air. As I did, I began to smell a strange aroma that had suddenly filled the air. It smelt like blood. I stared around at the villagers, still trying to escape. Only a few of them had been struck down, each one covered in scarlet liquid, but not nearly enough to cause the whole area to stink of blood.

I froze. Blood. Blood *and* sweat. That was the best way to describe the stench and the only way that I was able to define what these creatures were. *Morbiens.*

Suddenly, the morbien was on me again, shoving me down onto the ground and rolling me onto my back once more. He climbed on top of me, pinning me down the way he had before, with his legs crushing my arms. He placed an arm across my chest, holding me down as he drew a dagger from his belt, pointing the sharp tip at my throat. I struggled beneath him, racking my brain to figure out a way to slip out from under him, but it was no use. He was too strong, too heavy.

"Pretty, pretty girl," he said. I shuddered at how inhuman he sounded. His grin was even more sickening. It spread wide, reaching his gills, and revealing his sharp, crooked, yellow teeth. A disturbing joy seemed to fill his red eyes as he slowly – with a strange, uncharacteristic gentleness – moved his dagger down the side of my face. Julian's words suddenly leapt into my mind as I felt the sharp edge of his blade against my cheek: *The morbiens, they will show you no mercy, no compassion, and no honour if you fall into their hands. They will rip your body to shreds while you are still breathing and eat you for their supper.* It wasn't just death they wanted, it was mutilation, torture.

I felt my throat go dry as his sharp teeth were revealed once more. He leaned down towards me, licking his lips as if to take a huge bite out of my face. I didn't give him the chance to even place his lips against my cheek. Instead, I was the one to take the first bite, digging my own teeth into his skin. I could taste his bitter blood in my mouth and immediately wanted to roll over and retch into the grass. The morbien shouted at the pain I had caused him, but he didn't release me. It was almost as if the bite I took was as small as an insect's, even with the blood oozing out of the bite marks I had created in his skin.

"You have fight, girl, but not enough," he chuckled, leering at me. "You were the reason we are here. You made it so easy too, *human.*" He sneered and once again pointed his dagger at my throat. This time there was no delay, no hesitation. He began to cut my skin open, forcing me to scream at the pain and the feeling of thick, hot liquid pouring down my neck. I opened my watery eyes, noticing the joy that each drop of my blood gave him. *They were born and bred in the darkness. No soul to cry out with and no love to share.*

Was this how I was going to die? Or was this how I was going to wake up from this dream? You couldn't feel pain in dreams, nothing could harm you, nothing could kill you. You can't die in dreams because you don't know what it feels like to die. But then why could I feel every painful tear of my skin? Why was my head throbbing, my vision failing? *Why* did I feel I was dying?

Suddenly, the feeling of my throat being cut open was gone and the weight crushing my ribs was released. I began to gasp for air, sobbing at the agony it caused me. The morbien may have stopped cutting my throat open, but the sharp pain remained. I forced myself onto my side, trying to see where the morbien had run off to, why he suddenly abandoned his kill. The answer was

Abias. I could make out his broad figure standing before the tall morbien, his pitchfork meeting the morbien's blade. The sound of their weapons scratching against each other echoed over the sound of the villager's screams.

I felt my body slowly getting weaker as I watched Abias protect me. My eyes grew heavy and my vision clouded even more. My body felt light, as if I was ascending up into the sky upon a cloud. I heard someone whispering into my ear, begging me to answer them. I wanted to respond to their panicked cries, but my throat wouldn't allow me, nor would my tired mind. Something slid underneath my body, something strong and warm. It lifted me higher and higher into the sky, the sound of many horses, of swords being thrashed at bodies, and the continuous cries of terror slowly fading away into silence.

CHAPTER 5

ANOMALY

I woke up to the smell of burning wood and a warm fire blazing before me. I expected to find Abias at my side, but instead I found that it was Julian seated on the other side of the flames, the light of the fire reflecting off the weapon he held on his lap. He was staring down at his sword intently, wiping its sharp tip with a cloth that was stained red. A memory of the taste of that morbien's blood in my mouth made me want to retch.

"I see you're still alive," I mumbled, sitting up slowly against the trunk of the tree I was resting beside, groaning as I did so.

"It is a pleasure to see you too," Julian responded, looking up from his weapon and flashing me a fake smile.

I scowled as I continued to prop myself up against the tree. My body felt as weak as it did before I passed out, just after that morbien had cut me open. I reached up to my throat, expecting to feel my open wound, but I found it to be sealed shut. I ran my finger along the warm straight line. The wound seemed to only be an indent in my skin.

"Here," Julian said. I looked up, finding him moving towards me in a crouch with a canvas of water in his hand. I glanced at the water and then back up at Julian, questioning his sudden kindness. He rolled his eyes, stretching the canvas out to me more, "It's yours. Take it. You've been out for quite a long time so you'll need it."

"How long?" I asked, noticing the sudden rasp in my voice as I took my canvas from him, immediately bringing the bottle

to my lips and gulping down the cool
dry throat, making me sigh with pleas

"Four, maybe five hours. Easy there
me as I continued to chug my water,
and we still have one more day to go

I reluctantly put the canvas back
him to put the cork back in it and retu
watched him closely as he took a swig
wondering what in the world he was
me? Didn't he have Talia to attend to
questions swirled around in my mind
"What happened?"

"Your throat got sliced open," Julia

"I got that, thanks," I scowled. "I

"My father arrived at the scene wi
They murdered every morbien in their
I expected to find joy in his expressic
came in to save us, but there was only d
across Julian's face.

"There's more, isn't there?" I queri
Titus? Wasn't King Wallace supposed t

"He did, but he failed. He lost the
was too strong," Julian replied gravely.
drop of anger in his tone, the rest was
I noticed a shine in his eyes, the glisten
head to stare at the fire. I suddenly felt
my own heart breaking for his, for King
the people living in that city. Those m
home, probably destroying it in the proc
one's belonging, was just as horrible as lc
For me it had equal value. My father was
my safety, and illness destroyed him. I k
consuming Julian and all of Titus' inhat

I looked around at the trees surroun
fires blazing, the villagers sticking clos
down to sleep for the night. It didn't see
of them were missing, but I remembered
being struck down, all the screams and

faded a
wasn't
I suc
"W
not –"
"He
There is
Julian
spoke, t
betweer
At t
Abias
locked
to save
seeing a
his pitc
heart b
would
would'
giving
back. I
as serio
be ther
was do
withou
I sn
line, pr
pulling
"W
"I
obviou
polishe
smell c
"N
sheath
with y
Jul
stand.

ay into unconsci ousness. People had died. Even if it
any, lives were st **i** ll lost.

lenly thought of **A** bias and panic flooded through me.
ere's Abias?" I sa **i** d over to Julian. "Is he alright? He's

s with his family **,** recovering from very minor injuries.
10 need to worry. He is alive and well... unfortunately,"
uttered. I could **s** ense the tightness in his voice as he
e hatred, once ag **a** in making me wonder what happened
them.

at moment I di **d** n't dwell on Julian's hatred towards
or did I let his ru **d** e comment get to me. My mind was
n one thought al **o** ne: *He saved me. Abias risked his life
tine, to save som* **e** *human that he just met.* I remembered
blurry image of h **i** m fighting off that morbien, slashing
fork out at the **d** isgusting creature in my defence. My
gan to warm wit **h** comfort. That was something Tyler
ave done for me **_** No matter how difficult the fight he
e tried to protect me. He promised that he would once,
ae a smirk as he **a** ssured me that he'd always have my
made his words seem humorous, but really they were
is and unbreakab **l** e as wedding vows. Tyler promised to
for me when I w **a** s at my worst, just as I did him. Abias
1g just the same, **m** aking the powerful vow of friendship
even having to s **p** eak a word.

iled, reaching u **p** to my throat again and feeling that
ssing on it until **a** sharp pain shot up my neck. I winced,
my hand away in stantly.

at did you do to my neck?" I said, looking up at Julian.
aled it," Julian **s** aid as if it was something completely
. I gently touche **d** my scar again, staring down at his
l blade. I was be **g** inning to wonder if it really was the
' burning wood I woke to.

w come on," Jul **i** an sighed, rising from the ground and
1g his blade. "M **y** father has requested another audience
u."

in stepped towa **r** ds me, putting his hand out to help me
grabbed it and i **m** mediately felt dizzy once I was up. He

74

held onto me as I staggered, allowing me to lean on his arm as he guided me away from our campsite and down a small path towards a purple tent set up between two tall trees.

"Why did you heal me?" I asked Julian as we neared our destination.

Julian's pace slowed, but he didn't come to a complete stop until we were three feet away from the opening of the tent. He turned to me then, letting out a loud irritated sigh, "You were losing a lot of blood when I found you during the attack. I pulled you out of there and healed you once we found shelter in this wood."

"*You* decided to save *me*?" I said, completely taken aback by this news.

"My father gave me orders to protect you with my life," Julian replied, giving me a hard look. "All I was doing was performing my duty. Do not mistake it for anything besides that."

"Trust me, I'm not," I shot back coldly. "But that duty was passed down to Abias, remember?"

"I do remember," Julian said through his teeth, his words coloured with loathing. "I also remember other things about that stable boy, things I will never forget. It was for that very reason that I raced back to find you. Now come on. My father is waiting."

Julian offered me his arm again, but I just walked passed him, continuing to wonder how Talia could love a man like him, a man who was so full of anger, hatred... and brokenness. I decided that I needed to stop judging Julian. Something had happened to him, something that cut deep into his heart, slicing it down the middle so that it was identical to my own. There was more to Julian than met the eye. The more I realized that, the more I wanted to know what made him who he was.

I entered the purple tent, finding King Wallace seated in a chair with Lord Sebastian, Mortimer, and his squire present. They were deep in conversation until I entered, forcing them to close their mouths and look my way.

"The human, as requested," Julian announced, coming into the tent seconds after me.

I shot a glare in his direction.

"Leave us," King Wallace said, looking to the three men at his side.

Mortimer looked from me and back down to the king, eyes wide, "But Your Majesty, we were just discussing –"

"I know and we can speak more about the matter later," King Wallace assured him, rising from his seat and placing a hand on Mortimer's shoulder. "The three of you should get some rest. Today has been a day of great sorrow, but our journey is not over yet. You will need your strength to complete it tomorrow."

"Yes, my lord," Mortimer said. He, Drinian, and Lord Sebastian bowed to their king before leaving me alone with him in the tent. Julian made his exit after his father released him from his duty only a few seconds later. He practically ran out of the tent once King Wallace gave the word for him to leave. My guess was that he was rushing off to see to Talia.

King Wallace gestured to a chair across from his and I willingly took a seat, still feeling incredibly weak. King Wallace sat down himself, looking me over with a concerned expression, "How are you feeling?"

"I'm fine. I just feel tired that's all," I replied.

"I am sorry that I called you here when what you need most is rest, but I needed to speak with you alone, in regards to what transpired earlier today."

"You mean the attack?" I assumed.

"Indeed," King Wallace said. "That creature that attacked you, do you know what it was?"

"Yes," I answered with a nod. Memories of Marlee talking about them in the back of Tyler's truck played at the back of my mind. "My cousin told me about them. She said they were there in her dreams, trying to attack her. She dreams about this world a lot, speaks of it often. In fact, she knows more about this place than I do."

"She is one of the Njohuri then," King Wallace smiled.

"The what?" I questioned, leaning forward in my seat.

"The Njohuri. Humans are not supposed to have any knowledge of our world, but there is a crack in the divide between Earth and Elssador. Magic seeps through that crack along with knowledge. A great force chooses certain humans to know about our world for reasons beyond our understanding and perhaps even theirs."

I thought about Marlee, about how all it took was one visit to that well for her to start dreaming about Elssador. Maybe this was the explanation for all of that madness. I buried those thoughts almost instantly, reminding myself how impossible that was. How impossible everything around me was.

This is a dream, I assured myself. *Nothing but a dream.*

"You understand what I speak of, but you are refusing to believe it," King Wallace observed. "You are under the impression that this is all happening inside your mind. Is that correct?"

"It has to be," I said with a sigh. "Everything that is happening to me, around me, it's all impossible and those kinds of things only happen in dreams."

"I am old, Carter, much older than I seem," King Wallace said. "Many years ago, I used to have nightmares from things that had happened in my past. Things I had seen, things I had heard, and things that I had done that came back to haunt me when the sun went down. Each time I was near death in my dream or each time a blade was pointed at my throat, I would wake. If this is a dream, Carter, then you would have already awakened."

This information brought me down to Scenario B: the Second Test. If this wasn't a dream, then I was dead and passing through a second earth. But wasn't that conclusion just as unrealistic as actually climbing out of a well into a new world? My head started to pound with frustration. King Wallace reached out to me as if sensing my distress and took my hands in his, mirroring my concerned expression.

"Carter Olsen, I do not believe you are dreaming, just as I do not believe that you were brought here by mere chance," King Wallace said.

"So you think that maybe I was meant to be here?" I said, remembering Abias saying something similar: *There is a reason why you are here. Whatever it may be, good or not, there is a reason.*

"I do," King Wallace nodded. "This is no dream you are in, Carter. It is reality."

I paused, looking away from King Wallace's pleading eyes and down at the silver bracelet that was still clipped around my left wrist. Everything that was happening started when I found it, when those butterfly things flew up out of the well and gave it to me. Maybe it was all leading me towards this second test, towards a world more dark and dangerous than Earth. Perhaps even to my death.

King Wallace was right. I didn't want to believe anything he was saying. If I believed it then that meant I couldn't ever go home. I couldn't see Marlee or Tyler again. If this world around me was truly real, that meant I was stuck here. I was cut off from Earth, dead to it. My head started to throb with confusion and exhaustion as I continued to question and rewrite my theory of where I was.

"I don't understand," I said. I noticed the quiver in my own voice and immediately wished it would go away. I didn't want King Wallace to see the panic brewing within me, the fear that was knocking away at my heart, asking to come in. I didn't want anyone to see how lost and alone I really felt. "I don't understand any of this."

"Neither do I," King Wallace said. I looked up, surprised by his response. A small smile tugged at the corners of his lips. "But what I do know is that you are a mystery, Carter Olsen, an anomaly."

"So then you agree with me? That my being here is impossible?"

"Yes... and no," King Wallace answered. I studied him closely as he released my hands and rested his on the arms of his chair. "There was a Portal that existed long ago. It was created to be kept hidden and safe so that one day, when the time came, creatures from Elssador could enter your world."

"To destroy it?"

"No, no," King Wallace chuckled. "To protect it. The Portal was a powerful device, made from the hands of the High Diviner himself. Legend even states that he placed part of his soul within this Portal, a spirit, so that he could live amongst his people.

This spirit – this being – is known as the Wanderer. He was the one who controls the Portal, who allows people to travel between realms. He was the Portal itself, a device of sorts that only the deep, old magic of this world could unlock."

"What happened to it?" I questioned, sitting up straighter in my seat.

"It was destroyed," King Wallace said, "Power is something that every mortal being desires. Deep within our hearts we all want it. The Portal tempted many, especially those who sought to take Elssador for their own. There was a wizard, Zeth, who was the enemy in my days. Magwas were the chosen creatures to protect Earth and we did for many, many years, but soon war broke out within the race. The war was over a prophecy, one predicting the coming of four magwas that would take up the four thrones of Elssador. Zeth desired to defy the prophecy that chose me and the other three current rulers. He started to recruit magwas of his own who shared his desire for power. My kin and I, we knew that once Zeth controlled Elssador that he would soon want more. Earth was going to be his next target and all he needed to take it was the Portal.

'Eventually Zeth got hold of it, but my kin and I arrived to meet him with most of Elssador at our side. We took the Portal and immediately knew what must be done. Earth would not need magwas to protect them if the window between the two worlds were closed. So we took the Portal up to the highest tower in the city of Damon. On that tower, we destroyed the Portal, crushing it with the sword of a great wizard and friend, Ensindior. He was the Caretaker of Liliamule at the time, dying from a curse that was cast upon him by Zeth. My kin and I set the Wanderer free, just as Ensindior sent us out to do. But destroying the Portal did not stop its power. Just because we had destroyed the Wanderer's body did not mean that he was gone. The magic of the Portal still lingers, the Wanderer still lives and he will continue to do so until the Portal is remade."

"What happens to him when it's remade?"

"The one who remakes it will become the Wanderer, will become the one to determine who and what enters and exits this realm," King Wallace said. "The Portal has not been remade,

Carter. There is no one alive powerful enough to do so, therefore it was not some wicked force that allowed you into our world. It was the Wanderer."

"But why? What could your world possibly need from me?"

King Wallace paused for a moment, his dark eyebrows falling into a straight line. It was only then that I could see the resemblance between the king and his son. They had the same anxious expression, the same frown, and it had the same effect on me, making me feel smaller, like a child being stared down at.

"King Wallace?" I said, realizing how far off he had suddenly began to look. I followed his gaze to where it locked onto my bracelet.

"May I see that?" King Wallace asked kindly, but I could see the intensity in his eyes as he continued to stare at the object as if he had seen it before. I nodded slowly, unclipping the bracelet and slipping it off of my wrist, placing it in his hand. He stared at it intently, flipping it over in his hands, letting his finger trace the engraving of my name on the front.

"Where did you find this?" King Wallace questioned, with an urgency in his voice that I didn't think was there before.

"It came out of the well when I was near there with my friend," I replied with a raise of my brow. King Wallace's frown deepened as he continued to examine the bracelet.

"How did it come to you?"

"I – I'm not really sure. Some butterfly things carried it up to me," I said, wanting to laugh at how strange that explanation sounded. But King Wallace remained serious, nodding at my words as if it was the answer he was expecting to escape my lips.

"The Nuntii, messengers from the Kingdom of Lilamule," King Wallace mumbled. "But why would she – this doesn't make sense."

Yeah, tell me about it, I thought, leaning back in my chair. I wanted to know more about what King Wallace was saying, but this was one of those few moments where my exhaustion beat out my curiosity. All I felt like doing was nestling down in the soft grass and getting some sleep, drifting off into my subconscious. Another image of that morbien popped into my head, his crooked smile, his blood-red eyes, and the words he had hissed into my ear: *You were the reason we are here. You made it so easy too...*

Maybe giving myself up to my dreams wasn't such a good idea after all.

"It is a very lovely bracelet," King Wallace's voice broke through my thoughts, drawing me back into our conversation. He placed the cool silver object back in my hand, folding my fingers over it and giving my fist an assuring squeeze. "It is something of great value. You should be very careful not to lose it."

＊　　＊　　＊

It was nearly dark when we reached the city of Mitus. The city was a bit smaller than Titus, built up with the same grey stone, but instead of its walls circling the keep, it was a perfect rectangle, a tower standing at each vertex. Beyond the city walls, I spotted massive ships floating in the vast ocean with the same purple flags waving from them. I felt a twinge of excitement at the sight of them as I imagined what Tyler's reaction would be if he were here with me, gazing out at the grand vessels that sat upon the glittering waters. I immediately stopped my thoughts from traveling too far on the topic. I couldn't think about Tyler anymore. Not Tyler, not Marlee, and not even the rest of my family. If I was right about my being in a second earth, then that made them my past and I knew that it wouldn't do me any good to dwell on that.

"The country of Lorien is known as the land of the ocean men," a voice said behind me. I jumped slightly – making my horse lurch – and turned to find Abias trotting up beside me. It was the first time I had seen him since the attack, since he had protected me from that morbien. He didn't seem to have too many wounds, only a bruise or two on his arms and a scratch across his cheek. "Those ships – in the older ages of Elssador – used to be used for war, but today they sail out all across Elssador. Some to collect goods from the other kingdoms and some in search of unknown lands."

"It's not really as fun as it sounds," I half-teased with a smile which he returned weakly. I watched him closely as we continued to follow the line of people – led by King Wallace and his knights – towards the front gates that opened as our group approached.

"How are you doing?" Abias asked, gesturing to my throat.

"Oh. It's fine," I reached up to my wound, running my finger over it again. The skin surrounding it was still tender, sending a shooting pain up my neck as I pressed harder on the scar. Julian had given me a couple swigs of medicine, but it seemed to be healing very slowly. "It's a good thing you were there to get that morbien off of me. If you weren't I think it would've been much worse."

"It was Prince Julian who rescued you from that battle," Abias said, his smile growing weaker with each word.

"Yeah, but he was following orders. You weren't," I replied. "So I'm thanking *you*."

"Well," Abias said, his handsome smile returning, "if you are ever in need of rescuing, m'lady, then I will be there to do so."

I laughed at his chivalrous tone, but my joy only lasted for a short while as images of Tyler began to return. Once again Abias was turning into my best friend. Once again he was becoming more and more of a reminder of the person I seemed to be missing the most.

Soon Abias and I filed into the courtyard amongst the rest of the knights and villagers. Those with horses walked to the stables to remove their saddles and others moved out of their way, gathering with family members. I slid off my horse – with only a little help from Abias – and followed the knights in. I removed my saddle bag and slung it over my shoulder, allowing one of the knights nearby to tend to my horse. I was practically shoved out of the stables by the many people rushing in and out, so I decided to stand out of their way as I waited for Abias to place his horse in a stall, watching all the villagers as they continued to find their friends and family.

I spotted Julian helping Talia down from her horse, gently holding her waist as they moved on towards King Wallace and Lord Sebastian. They were all staring down at a map – probably one of the city – pointing at the different buildings and roads within the walls of Mitus. My guess was that they were trying to work out sleeping arrangements, places to lodge the hundreds of people rushing about.

As I scanned the crowd, I noticed a somewhat large family huddling together in the centre of the square. A grey-haired woman stood beside an older man who leaned on a crutch, smiling as four, tall boys gathered around them. The boys were all wearing the same argent silver armour with the purple and white crest of Lorien upon their cloaks.

"Carter," Abias said as he emerged from the stables. I wheeled around, looking at him over my shoulder. "I shall be back soon. I just have to see to something."

"Okay," I responded blankly as I watched him run off towards the family I had been observing. He hurried over to the older woman first, leaning down to give her a big hug. She kissed him on the cheek gently and Abias moved out of the way so that one of her other sons could lean down and wrap the old woman in his massive arms.

This was Abias' family; four older brothers, a father, and a mother. I couldn't help but continue to watch their family reunion. To most people it seemed normal, but to me it felt like watching something new, something foreign. It was beautiful, yet it tore at my heart, making me realize how much I longed for something like that. To have a father and a mother waiting for me to run into their arms, to have them worry over my well-being, to have them cry tears of joy at the knowledge that I was alright... It was all I had ever dreamed of having, yet it was so incredibly impossible.

But maybe there was a chance it wasn't. If this really was a second earth I was in, maybe my parents had passed through it as well. Maybe that meant they were still alive, roaming this world, waiting for me to find them. I felt a flame of hope ignite inside of me and found myself beaming as I visualized what it would be like to be with my dad again, to meet my mother, to actually see them together. The thought seemed so realistic, fulfilling every crook and corner of my dreams. But perhaps it was still very false, still too far and impossible for me to reach.

What if I'm wrong, I thought. *What if this is really just a dream? Or a magical world inside a well?*

I felt the corners of my mouth twitch downward and tears sting the back of my eyes. My breathing became quick and heavy with all this unknowingness, suddenly making me feel as if I was about to break down in the middle of the courtyard. The heavy weight of grief pressed hard on my chest, forcing me to turn away from Abias' family as tears began to cloud my eyes.

I ran. I ran as far away from that family as I possibly could. I turned into an alley between two buildings and pressed my back up against the cold wall, letting the tears fall, stream down my face as I slid onto the ground. I bit down on my lip, trying so hard not to make any noise as I cried with my face buried in my knees. If someone found me like this I would never be able to live with myself, to live with the shame that I believed came with my tears. To me they were a sign of defeat, of brokenness, and I couldn't bring myself to admit that that was what I was. I was broken and the one person that could make me whole was gone. He was dead.

"Carter," a voice said from the end of the alley. I could tell by the kindness in his tone that it was King Wallace, but I still refused to look up even as his footsteps neared me. "Carter, please look at me."

I caved, slowly lifting my head up to find him kneeling down in front of me. I quickly began to wipe the tears away from my puffy eyes, but he took hold of my wrist gently and folded my hand in his. I glanced from our hands and into his kind, electric eyes that were filled with sincerity and what I thought to be love. The same love that had filled my father's eyes whenever he looked at me.

"There is nothing wrong with shedding tears," King Wallace said.

I stared back at him, about to protest, but I had been exposed. King Wallace was seeing me, my brokenness. I always thought that if someone saw it they would turn their backs on me, cast me out, and let me drown in my own sorrow. But King Wallace didn't. He just stared back at me compassionately, smiling a weak, yet encouraging smile that made me cry even more.

I closed my eyes as my tears continued to fall, allowing King Wallace to put a loving arm around my shoulders and pull me into his chest. As I cried into him, all I could think about was my dad. It didn't feel like King Wallace was holding me, it felt like my father's warm embrace. It was his heart I heard beating as my ear pressed up against King Wallace's chest, his hand gently rubbing my back as I continued to sob. The lullaby that he used to sing to me slipped into my mind and I could hear my father's voice as he sang that beautiful, haunting tune…

My love, my love
why must you cry?
My love, my love
I'm right here by your side…

CHAPTER 6

IT HAS COME

King Wallace escorted me to a room inside the keep once he and Lord Sebastian had worked out all of the sleeping arrangements. There were several empty bedrooms in the castle, but they were reserved for the knights and royals, which apparently seemed to include me. Most of the people in Mitus offered their homes to the villagers from their neighbouring city, but most of the peasants stayed in inns. Titus seemed to be double the population of Mitus, making the city feel crammed. There was a person each way you turned. I think that was why I spent the rest of that evening in my room. It was the only place I could be alone.

I stayed in there for a few hours until Julian knocked on my door – which just so happened to be across from his – to tell me that dinner was about to be served. I followed him down to the great hall where King Wallace and his royal court sat. Everyone began eating as soon as Julian and I took our seats, chomping down on their juicy meat and sweet tomatoes. I ate very little, not feeling as hungry as I was before I watched Abias get the happy ending I longed for. I sat silently as the king, Lord Sebastian, Mortimer, and Julian spoke of plans to possibly move some of the people into a neighbouring village to decrease the population. Talia and I were completely left out of the conversation. At first we sat silently, shooting each other several awkward looks, but neither of us knowing how to begin a conversation. I let out a small, relieved sigh when she decided to speak up first...

"I hope you are enjoying your time here so far," she piped up as the men continued to discuss urgent matters. Despite the fact that she was clearly feeling awkward about how she began our conversation, her tone was light and a small smile tugged at the corner of her pink lips.

I let out a light laugh, "Well, that attack sure added some excitement."

"Indeed," she said with a giggle. It was a sweet laugh, one that matched the gentle look in her pretty eyes. It again made me wonder how on earth she could have fallen for Julian. The two of them did look good sitting side-by-side, both of them with the same fair, golden skin and fine hair. But Talia was like the sweetness that filled your mouth when you bit into an apple, whereas Julian was the rough, hard skin surrounding it. I wanted to ask how the two of them met as I continued to try and understand how she fell in love with a man like him, but she continued on with the topic of the attack, her words forcing all girlish thoughts out of my system.

"I must say, it is not something we are used to. It has been a long while since morbiens have attacked our people, especially a major city," Talia said. "There have been no sightings of morbiens in these lands for years."

"None at all?"

"My fiancé tells me that they have been seen near the borders of this kingdom, that there have been reports from the others that they have seen them too, but they have never made an attack, not until yesterday," Talia explained. I stared down at my plate, trying to piece this information together. I arrived in this second world and soon after creatures that were said to be either dead or in hiding appeared, forcing an attack on Lorien's people.

That morbien's words once again came back to haunt me: *It was because of you... because of you... you...*

"Why have they decided to attack now then?" I asked, knowing that she herself probably didn't have an answer to that. "Who sent them?"

"Their leader has known to be dead for centuries," Julian interjected, answering for Talia. It was then that I noticed everyone's attention on Talia and me, on the words spoken between us.

"We do not know why the morbiens have decided to attack," Mortimer said, joining in on our discussion just as Julian had, "All we do know is that it began when you arrived here."

I looked to King Wallace who sat at the head of the table, his hands folded out before his empty plate. I expected him to stare back at me, assure me that what Mortimer was saying wasn't entirely true, but instead I found him to be studying my bracelet again. He looked at it as if it were some puzzle he couldn't quite understand. It was the same look he had given me when he discovered that I was human, the same look, I realized, he had given me ever since.

Soon the four men returned to their previous conversation and Talia and I finished our meal in silence. Once everyone was finished, we were released from the great hall to do as we wished. I headed straight for my room, wanting nothing more but to lay on my bed and tell myself that this was all a dream, that none of it was real no matter how much I was starting to believe it was.

It had been a couple hours since dinner and I was still curled up in a ball under my warm covers, staring out the window at the moon that hung in the sky, suddenly finding myself unable to close my eyes. My brain was too wired as images of the attack and previous events of the day kept playing through my mind, along with more and more questions about the unknown land around me. I shuddered at my own thoughts, at the vivid images of that morbien pinning me down to the ground, of the screams of others that were being attacked...

I closed my eyes tightly, willing myself to think of something else. But when I did, all I could think about was all the things I didn't know. *Is this a second earth? If so, are my parents here? Are they alive? If not, am I stuck in a dream? A coma? WHAT?*

My eyes popped open and I let out a frustrated growl, tearing the covers off my bed and running a hand through my hair as I paced back and forth in the moonlight that shone through my window. Soon, I found myself moving towards the door to my room, opening it gently, careful not to wake Julian who was sleeping in the room across from me. I continued to be silent as I closed the door, moving through the dark hallway towards the double doors at the end of the hall. I swung them open and was immediately pushed back by a gust of wind. I wrapped my arms around myself, stepping out onto the tower before me, into the cool night air, towards the stone railing. I leaned against it, looking up at the sky, taking in the beauty of the stars blinking against the darkness. They may have been pretty, but they were unknown. I had hoped to see the Big Dipper or the Milky Way, something to remind me of home, but I couldn't find them. The constellations were so different, reminding me how far away from home I truly was.

I began to think of Marlee as I watched a shooting star fly across the sky. I began to wonder where she was, what she was doing, if she was upstairs in our bedroom, waiting for me to come and sit on the edge of her bed and read to her. I wondered if she was trying to fall asleep without me, but couldn't because she knew something was wrong. If I was dead, Aunt Mary and Uncle Gabe wouldn't have told her. If they had, it would've broken her, ripped her heart out the way my father's death had done to me.

My longing for the place I called home suddenly grew stronger, making me wish that I was there with Marlee, holding her, assuring her that I was alive, that I hadn't left her. Tears began to sting my eyes as I reminded myself that that too was something utterly impossible. I was dead to her, to everyone back home. The thought that I would never see her again began to sink in, making my heart ache. But it wasn't just her I was leaving behind, it was Tyler, Uncle Gabe, my grandfather, even Aunt Mary and the twins, Sophie...

What was the point in living in a world where you felt so alone?

This question continued to play over and over again inside my mind as I stepped even closer to the edge of that tower, leaning over the railing and starring down at the long drop beneath me. I expected that sick feeling to rise in my stomach as it always did when I stood upon high places, but instead I began to feel alive with fear. It woke me up, made my head buzz even more.

I want out of here, I thought as I continued to stare down at the city below.

Going home was something I wanted more than anything, but if I was right about being in a second world, then there was a possibility that my mother and father were alive, that they too were walking upon this second world. I closed my eyes tightly, trying my best not to let out a howl of rage into the night sky. Instead, I felt hot tears sting my eyes, run down my cheeks, and my body began to shake with terror. The truth was, I didn't know what to do. This thought fuelled my anger, my frustration, my fear.

Carter Olsen didn't know what to do.

Carter Olsen just didn't know.

This feeling gave me a sense of *deja vu,* sending goose bumps and shivers through my limbs as I was once again reminded of my father laying in that hospital bed, his skin as white as the pale sheets beneath him. As I stood up on that tower, lifting myself on top of that stone railing until I was standing even higher above Mitus, I began to feel so helpless, so worthless. A hollow feeling settled in my chest, forcing more tears to fall from my eyes, blurring my vision as I stared down at the ground beneath me. All of this reminded me of when my dad died, how I felt when it truly settled with me that he was gone. My world had seemed to have fallen through my fingers, crumbling into ash. Falling though that well, climbing out and finding unknown territory around me... it brought back all those helpless feelings, perhaps made me feel even worse.

I was alone.

So utterly alone.

King Wallace and Abias may have been there for me, given me a small sense of comfort, but I knew it would never fill the warmth my father gave me, that Tyler and Marlee also provided. I was alone and there was nothing I could do to change that. Except maybe one thing, one way that would make my father's head turn away in shame, one that made me shake even more.

After long minutes of hesitation, of stepping down from that tower and then back up, I closed my eyes tightly, trying to force out my pervious thoughts. If I was going to do what I was about to, I wanted to do it knowing that there was a time when I was happy. I wanted to do it with my mind set on the faces of the people I loved most and of the times that I shared with them. But most of all I wanted to think about my dream, of my parents standing before me, holding hands as they watched me race towards them with tears of joy falling from my eyes. To think about what it would've been like to actually hug my mother, to feel the warmth of her embrace, to actually meet her and see her real face, one that wasn't just a picture on my father's dresser. I wanted to see my dad again, to hear his warm laughter, to see him poking fun at Uncle Gabe. I wanted him to hold me again, to feel his warm embrace and listen to his heart thumping against his chest, assuring me that he was still alive, that he hadn't abandoned me.

I kept my mind on these thoughts, my eyes still closed as I took a step closer to the edge of the tower and another until I was falling, and falling, and falling…

*   *   *

I could sense that there was someone watching me. Someone sitting at my side, leaning over my face, and creating a shadow over my eyes. Normally the thought of being watched would make me shudder, send a shiver through my limbs, forcing me to wake up and smack whoever the creeper was. But my heart felt no fear, no will to attack this person despite the fact I didn't know who they were.

I slowly began to open my eyes, taking in the blurry figure hovering over me. His image began to get clearer, allowing me to see a head of dark red curls and a pair of green eyes staring down at me. My heart pounded with excitement at the sight of the figure and the relief of not lashing out at this person washed over me as I looked at the man at my side.

It was my father, dressed in a white shirt and pants that matched the colours of the floor, my bed sheets, and the walls surrounding us. I blinked several times, making sure that my eyes weren't deceiving me, that it truly was him that I was seeing and not just a projection of a memory.

"You," I breathed. "You're... are you really here?"

My dad threw his head back in laughter, making me break out into my own fit of giggles.

"Yes, Carter, I am," he answered. The sound of his voice sent warmth through my bones, filling my heart with comfort. I remembered spending countless nights, trying to remember the sound of his voice, wondering if it had been deep and rich like Uncle Gabe's or raspy like my grandfathers. But it was neither. It was smooth, soft, clear... it was the sound of home.

"But you can't be. You died... didn't you?" Everything in my brain seemed to be jumbled up and messy. It was like the place I awoke to wiped me clean of all my memories, perhaps even all I was before I arrived. My heart felt so light, like it was drained of all anger and sorrow.

"To your world I'm dead, but to this one," my father smirked, "I am very much alive."

"Where am I exactly?" I questioned. Part of me wanted to get up from the bed I was confined to, but I felt as though something was pulling me back, holding me down. I ignored the feeling, assuring myself that my body was just tired. But that feeling lingered at the back of my mind, letting me know that something wasn't entirely right.

"Back in Elssador, probably laying in a bed just like this," my dad answered, gesturing to the sheets that were fit snugly against my chest. "There is no way anyone could have jumped off a tower that high and walked off without an injury. Even someone as strong as you."

He smiled, bringing a hand to my face and stroking my hair back just as he had always done to assure me that everything was going to be okay. But the gesture did nothing for me. It didn't mask the feeling of uncertainty and confusion that his words brought me.

"I jumped off a tower?" I asked, closing my eyes as I tried to force memories back into my mind.

"Yes, you did. You jumped because you wanted to find me and your mother, because you were tired of being alone," he said. A light bulb seemed to go on in my mind, making all the jumbled memories and images piece back together. Me standing upon that high tower, the feeling of the wind pressing against my face as I pushed off, the sensation of falling... I remembered it all, even the deep sadness I had felt before I had jumped. But I never remembered the sudden stop, the bone-shattering feeling of my body colliding with the ground.

"Did – did I die?" I stuttered, suddenly feeling the fear that I had been missing before. It wasn't death I was afraid of, it was the fact that it had been something I wanted. Death had been my intent. Yet lying in that bed, under that white ceiling, I didn't feel dead at all. In fact, I felt quite the opposite. My body was burning with life, with an energy that I hadn't experienced before.

"No. You're not dead. You're just asleep," my father explained, continuing to stroke my hair back. "But you *could* have died."

"How do you know all of this?" I said.

"I never left you, Carter," he spoke as if this was something I had forgotten, something that should have been seared into my memory. "I promised you that I wouldn't leave you no matter what."

"But you did." Even the calming silence and the faint, soothing sound of water crashing up against a shore couldn't wash away the bitterness in my tone. It couldn't even completely wash away my anger that seemed to be slowly returning as I remembered all those nights of crying myself to sleep, days of sobbing in the shower, going for long walks just so I could scream into the sky, all those times I felt so alone, so abandoned...

"Did I ever tell you about the day my mom died?" my father said. Curiosity sparked inside me and I shook my head. "I was young. Maybe seventeen, eighteen. She was sick, like me, but to a greater extent. She had been ill since the day I was born. As time passed, the illness spread, eventually slowing her heart. When I heard she was gone, it felt like my heart had been cut in two. Unlike your uncle – who keeps his hurt bottled up inside." My father raised a brow, giving me a look that implied that this was a characteristic obviously passed down to me. "I let out my anger, my grief. Your Uncle Gabe found me in my room the night she died, sitting on top of a pile of broken glass from my window, blood smeared all over my hands. After that I became consumed by my grief, always trying to busy myself with other things so I didn't have to think about the pain that was eating away at me. It took me awhile to fight it, to remember something my mother had told me, a promise that I passed down to you..."

My father paused, waiting for me to finish what he had to say, but I found that I couldn't speak. My throat felt tight, making me feel as if I was about to cry. I knew the words. Only then, after hearing his story did I remember them. He had said it to me one of the nights I woke up from nightmares, begging him to stay with me until I could fall back to sleep. *I won't leave you, Carter*, he had said. *No matter what may come.*

"Those words," my father said with a slight smile, reading my mind like he had always done. I swallowed, trying to hold back the tears that stung my eyes. I supposed that I had been so caught up in my own grief that I had let his words fly right over my head. I was so consumed by my loneliness that I hadn't really thought about what his promise truly meant.

"When you said that, you were talking about the place we're in now, weren't you?" I said. "We're in that world Uncle Gabe told me about."

"Perhaps," my father smirked. "Or maybe I'm just an image in your mind, a memory." I raised a brow, about to ask a hundred more questions, but instead he laughed, giving me a gentle pat on my shoulder as he shook his head. "Now isn't the time to worry over this. I am real and I am here with you. That's all that matters right now."

"But *why* am I here? Why are *you* here?"

My father's smile faded slightly, his green eyes suddenly stripped of all humour, "I'm here because of you. I'm here to get you to believe."

"Believe? In what, the tooth fairy?" I jested, trying to lighten up his mood. Normally he would've chuckled a bit at my jokes, then shot back with an even cleverer one. But the corners of his lips didn't even budge. They remained in their straight, serious line.

"No. To believe in something you are refusing to," he replied.

I froze, suddenly losing the ability to smile as well. "Elssador. Is that it? Is that what I'm refusing to believe in?"

"Yes," my father nodded. I gave a roll of my eyes which sharpened his tone. "Elssador is real, Carter. It is impossible, yes, but there are some impossible things that we need to be possible, that are made possible for our sake."

"You think there's a reason I'm here too, don't you?" I asked, thinking of King Wallace and Abias and the similar words that came from both their mouths regarding this topic.

"Everything happens for a reason, Carter. The good things, the sad things, the strange things, they all shape us, mold us into the people we were intended to be, the people we are *meant* to be."

"And Elssador is doing that for me?"

"Yes," my father finally smiled, beginning to stroke my hair again. "It's changing you. I can see it already."

There were thousands of things I wanted to ask him. I tried to sit up to do so, but I felt that force again, that strong vigour that seemed to be holding me down. I tried to move my arms, lift them to hold my father's hand, but all I seemed to be able to do is clench and unclench my fists.

"You can't fight it, Carter, the force that's holding you down," my father said in a soothing voice.

"You mean I can't stay?" I was always good at reading between the lines, especially his.

"No, you can't," he shook his head, pushing back another stand of my hair until it curled around my ear. "You're going to wake up soon."

It didn't feel like I was going to get up. In fact, it felt as though I was going to fall right back to sleep. My eyes grew heavy, making me struggle to keep them open. I could feel myself slowly slipping away into unconsciousness, away from him.

"I don't want to leave," I managed to say.

"I know. I don't want you to either. Neither does your mother," my father replied, glancing over his shoulder at the door at the back of the room. Through the small window carved into the white wood, I could see the back of a blonde head pressed up against the glass. I felt my body tingle with excitement, with joy, but it was soon defeated by my weariness. "But you have to go, Carter. You're story isn't over, not yet."

I was giving into my exhaustion, allowing my eyes to shut. But I could still hear him, feel his hand against my cheek and the softness of his lips on my forehead. "Believe, Carter. Believe and remember this," he whispered, "The time for you to be brave has come."

*   *   *

My heart leapt in my chest as if I had landed from my fall off that tower. My eyes shot open and I sat up straight, taking heavy breaths as I scanned the space around me. My father had been right, I was in Elssador, laying in a bed, the bed I was trying to fall asleep in before I had jumped off that tower. The bed, of course, was not nearly as soft or comforting at the one I was laying in when I was speaking to my dad. My chest began to ache with longing as I thought of him, as I began to miss him all over again. But the feeling soon passed as his last words continued to ring in my ears, as if he was still speaking them to me although he was no longer physically at my side: *The time for you to be brave has come.*

"– and now you're awake," I heard someone say. His voice broke through my father's words, forcing me to look to my right, towards a chair at the corner of the room that was occupied by Abias. I blushed, wondering how long he had been talking to me.

"What?" I said. Abias let out a light laugh, getting up from his chair and moving towards me. His eyes seemed weary, shadowed by the dark circles that people always have when they don't get enough sleep.

"I was just letting you know how long you have been unconscious," Abias answered. "After three days people began to give up. The court physician just about declared you dead. But both King Wallace and I knew it could not be true. It seems that all you really needed was a bit more time."

"I guess so," I half-laughed. I felt slightly boggled as I sat up a bit straighter. *How could it have been three days?* I thought. *I was only gone for a few minutes, not* – "Ouch!" I winced, placing a hand on my side, right where my skin and muscle covered my ribcage.

"Oh yes, you may want to lie back down," Abias suggested, helping me rest my head back on my pillow. "I have to go find the King. I shall be back," he said as he strode across the room towards the door. He swung it open and stepped out, but before closing it, he poked his head back in and with a wag of his finger said, "And don't you go wandering off."

I tried to laugh, but eventually it turned into a cry of pain.

"Don't worry," I groaned. "I couldn't even if I wanted to."

CHAPTER 7

NOT JUST A BRACELET

I was lying in my bed for a long while until Abias returned with King Wallace and what looked like the court physician. He immediately rushed over to my bedside with his bag of instruments in hand, leaning over me and beginning to check on my injuries. King Wallace stood at the end of my bed, crossing his arms with a faint smile pressing on his lips, and a knowing look in his silver eyes. Clearly Abias' words proved to be true, King Wallace was confident that I wasn't truly dead.

"This is remarkable," the court physician marvelled as he checked my pulse, my temperature, and my pupils, which he claimed were only slightly dilated. "You should be dead, m'lady. In fact, I was certain that you were. You were as cold as ice, you weren't breathing..."

"Yet here she is. Perhaps humans are stronger than we thought them," King Wallace said with a proud smile.

The court physician instructed me to lift my arms so that he could check my side. He pressed his cool fingers into my tender skin and I bit down hard on my lip, trying to muffle my cries of pain.

"You seem to have a few broken ribs, a bruised arm..." he said, moving to the end of the bed and rubbing his thumbs on my ankle. I cried out instantly at the sharp pain shooting up my leg, "Oh, and a sprained ankle."

Suddenly, someone came barging through my bedroom door, making the doctor swear and drop a couple of his instruments.

It was Julian who had come in, clearly in search of his father, but when he saw me his face was wiped of all expression.

"She's – how is this – I thought," Julian sputtered, clearly befuddled by my resurrection. His expression quickly changed from one of confusion to one of anger, "I thought you were dead!"

"You sound like you wish I were." I shot back.

"Of course I didn't – don't –" a blush was creeping up on Julian's cheeks as he continued to stutter on his words. "You know what I'm trying to say."

He was right, I did know and I smiled because of that knowledge. He was glad I wasn't dead, relieved that I was alive and well. I continued to find comfort in that thought, but also began to wonder why? We had, after all, disliked each other the moment we met.

"Thank you, Maurice," King Wallace nodded to the doctor.

"I shall be back soon with her medication," the court physician, Maurice, replied, gathering all his things and then exiting the room. The sound of the door closing behind him sounded much louder than it probably was. It echoed over the unsettling silence that had fallen upon the room, emphasizing the tension among the three men standing before me. I noticed Julian shoot Abias a deadly stare, then turn his head away to stare at the opposite wall, as if he was pretending that Abias wasn't even there.

"I am surprised that you have such minor injuries," King Wallace said, clearing his throat. It was quite obvious that he was trying to mask that tension between his son and Abias, but he did it in such a way that made me wonder if he knew what caused that hatred. He moved across the room and took a seat on the edge of my bed, folding his hands on his lap, "According to Mr. Wood you had quite the fall off that tower."

"You saw me fall?" I asked Abias. I could feel my cheeks heating up and I knew I was blushing.

"I found you lying in my cart of hay," Abias replied. "I walked away to go and get something and when I came back I saw you falling. If I hadn't accidentally left my cart there, you would have hit the ground and then you really would have been dead."

"How heroic," Julian sneered. Abias shot him a look. It wasn't a deadly one, but it wasn't a very kind stare either, "I suppose we should just leave all the saving to him then? We all know how good he is at that."

What occurred next happened so fast that it took me a few seconds to register what was going on. Abias grabbed Julian by the collar, spinning him around, and pinning him up against the wall with a strength that made me let out a gasp. Julian was the most shocked by this, blinking his eyes in surprise as Abias shouted into his face.

"It wasn't my fault!" I thought I heard him say.

"If you were doing your job she would still be here!" I heard Julian yell back. They continued to shout back and forth at each other until I couldn't understand a word either of them was saying.

King Wallace shot up from my bed and turned towards the two of them as if to grab them and pull them apart. But instead he just stood there, holding his hands out at his sides. I saw something spark on his finger tips as if a bolt of lightning was going to shoot right out of the palm of his hand.

"Enough!" King Wallace said loudly over their shouts. Their bickering stopped immediately at the change in King Wallace's tone. "You two are both aware of what I am capable of. I do not want to use my magwa powers, but if there is an outburst like that again, you may be the ones to set it off. Do you understand me?"

"Yes, My Lord," Abias said, dropping Julian's collar and stepping away from him. I expected Julian to argue with his father, to persuade him to lock Abias away in the dungeons. Wasn't attacking royalty against the laws here? But Julian did nothing. He didn't even look up at Abias, nor at his father, who was giving him a hard, scolding look. Instead he straightened out his shirt, smoothing out the creases where Abias held it.

"Now, away with you both. I would like to speak with Carter alone," King Wallace finished.

Julian gave his father a shy, apologetic nod before exiting the room. As he walked out the door, the light of one of the torches at my doorstep lit up the side of his face, allowing me to notice the shine of tears in his eyes. Julian didn't seem like the kind of guy to cry over someone giving him a smack over the head. He was fierce, strong, and much too proud to get upset over something as small as that. Something very large would've had to be thrown at him to break down his mighty walls, something that only King Wallace, Abias, and he seemed to know. My mind was burning with questions, but I didn't dare ask them. Now was clearly not the time.

"I'm very sorry, My Lord, truly," Abias said, bowing his head lowly.

"I know you are," King Wallace's voice was tight, but Abias seemed to relax a bit at his response, bowing once more and then, with sad eyes, slipped out of the room.

My mind was racing with even more thoughts now. Abias and King Wallace's short conversation seemed to hold a deeper meaning that went beyond my understanding. I bit down on my tongue, trying so hard not to interrogate King Wallace as he turned to me again, his hands no longer sparking. He removed his crown from his head, running a hand through his greying hair. He seemed drained from recent events – from worrying over my safety or that argument between his son and the stable boy?

"I apologize for that," King Wallace said, slowly turning to face me with his eyes fixed on the floor. "I would share with you the tale, but I do not believe I am the right person to tell it."

I gave him a slow nod, despite the fact he was still refusing to meet my eyes. Something in his voice made me feel sad, resembling the gloom that seemed to be overtaking him. I wanted to say something to cheer him up, but I was never good at comforting people. The only person I seemed to be able to cheer up was Marlee, but even then all I needed to do was sit at her side and hold her. I was thankful when King Wallace let out a sigh, taking a seat on the side of my bed and began to speak, "I suppose I should speak quickly so I can let you get some rest."

I nodded despite the fact I didn't agree. I had been out for some time, the last thing I needed was some sleep.

"Maurice's analysis of how you must have fallen off of that tower is a very good one," King Wallace stared, with a weak smile, "but I do not believe one word of it. Would you care to explain what really happened?"

I swallowed back tears that immediately began to fill my eyes. I didn't want to tell him what happened. I didn't want to live with that heavy burden of shame weighing me down, but most of all, it was his pity I was trying to avoid. He was a king. He had more important things to worry about than some human girl that decided she didn't want to live anymore.

The events that happened after I jumped off that tower began to creep back. *Believe and remember.* I could hear my father's voice as if he was sitting there next to me, whispering it into my ear. Maybe he really was.

I let out sigh and began to explain to King Wallace what happened, starting with the reason I jumped off the tower. I fiddled with my bracelet as he continued to listen to my story and noticed as I reached the end how his eyes flickered towards it, making me wonder if he had been doing that that whole time.

"Interesting," King Wallace cogitated, tapping his lips with his fingertips. It seemed to be the only word that could escape his lips. He said it at least three times before I interrupted him.

"My father said that I couldn't stay with him because my story wasn't over. What do you think he meant by that?"

"Everyone that lives has a story, a part to play in the course of the world. Most people would call it destiny," King Wallace replied.

"Destiny?" I repeated, trying hard not to laugh at the topic. "Do you really believe in that stuff?"

"I fulfilled a prophecy predicted hundreds of years before I was even born," King Wallace said. "If it wasn't the powerful pull of destiny that brought me to this throne, then I'm not sure what it could have been."

I paused, considering his words, but also sorting out the overload of questions, trying to pin-point the right ones to ask. Instead, I discovered a statement, one that I was afraid to admit, but I knew I couldn't hide its truth any longer. The more I considered it, the more I began to wonder why I had been scared of that truth, the truth that Elssador was a real place, a real world beyond Earth. If I had truly entered Elssador through that well, that meant that I could return the same way. It meant I could see Marlee again, Tyler, everyone I was so afraid of leaving behind.

"I believe now," I said abruptly just as King Wallace was about to say something else. He closed his mouth instantly and then smiled until the corners of his lips touched the lobes of his ears. "In Elssador, I mean."

King Wallace leaned forward and whispered, "I knew you would. That belief was always there. You were just refusing to face it."

"That's what my dad said." Those words resonated between us as if they meant something deeper than I intended them to be. Perhaps deep down I did. He reminded me of my dad the moment I met him and something told me that I reminded him of someone he once loved as well.

"I should let you rest," King Wallace said, rising from his seat. "Maurice should be back soon with your medicine."

He gave me a nod before turning away, still smiling, but I noticed how it began to falter as he turned towards the door. Something seemed to be irritating him, making the faint wrinkles around his eyes stand out, and the few grey hairs on his head shimmer, making him look older – or perhaps more his age. Was this because of the fight between Julian and Abias? The mystery of how I got here? Why it was possible I could be here?

My mind seemed to focus on that last thought as I remembered something else my father told me: *There are some impossible things that we need to be possible, that are made possible for our sake.*

"King Wallace," I said just as he reached the door.

"Yes," he answered, turning slowly on his heel to face me.

"My dad said something else to me, something both you and Abias have told me before," I started. "He said that there is a reason I am in Elssador. That I was *meant* to be here."

"Did he?" King Wallace said. I raised a brow, noticing the lie in his eyes almost instantly.

I had gotten quite good at noticing when people were lying to me. Ever since the day Uncle Gabe came in, carrying my father's limp body in his arms, I adopted that skill. Nurses telling me that he was going to fight it off, Aunt Mary telling me there was nothing to worry about, even Uncle Gabe, assuring me that everything was going smoothly. I thanked the heavens for that one doctor who told me the truth, who came out with a grim expression, looking at me as he explained the bad news. Since then, I had been able to tell when Aunt Mary was lying to me, but Uncle Gabe was the toughest to crack. He was a better liar than them, and certainly a better one than King Wallace.

"You wouldn't happen to know anything about that, would you?" I said. King Wallace pressed his lips together, standing with his back to the door, his eyes trailing the ground. When he finally decided to look up, I found him eyeing my wrist again, staring at that silver bracelet. I looked down at it as well, unclipping it and holding it out in the palm of my hand. "What is this?"

"A bracelet," King Wallace said. "Just a bracelet."

I paused, lowering my hand down onto my lap and gripping the bracelet tightly until I could feel it digging into my skin, "Please don't lie to me, King Wallace. I know it's not just a bracelet. If it were, you wouldn't keep staring at it."

"I apologize for my lies. You are right, Carter, it's not just an ordinary bracelet," King Wallace admitted after a long pause. "It's a message."

"A message?" I repeated, thinking of that four letter word on the back of the bracelet, the one that I couldn't seem to read. "From who?"

"It belongs to my friend Arianna Ross, the Queen of Lilamule. It is her most prized possession, which she keeps with her at all times," King Wallace explained. "She would only part with it if she fully knew and trusted the person she was sending it off to."

"I've never met her. She doesn't even know me." I said. "How can you trust someone you don't know?"

"I do not know why she sent you her bracelet, Carter, just as I do not know why she has put her trust in you. It has been hundreds – thousands of years since Elssador has had contact with the human world and never once have we needed their help, they have always needed ours," King Wallace replied. "Now is seems as though it is becoming the opposite."

"What do you mean?"

King Wallace pressed his lips together once more, continuing to stare at my fist where I hid this bracelet. "I mean that something evil is coming, something beyond my understanding, and it seems that you play a part in it."

"In bringing evil to Elssador?"

"Perhaps," King Wallace responded honestly. I stared back at him blankly, feeling the hairs on my arms standing tall and a shiver run through my body. "After all, the sky must be at its darkest before the dawn arrives. Maybe you are the one to call upon this evil, but perhaps you are also the one to break it."

I continued to give King Wallace a blank stare, not understanding one word of his riddles. I was not a cloud of darkness, nor was I a ray of sunshine that could break through it. I was a human, a girl, an orphan. If I were brought to Elssador for a reason – as everyone seemed to think – then it was because of me. It was because *I* needed to change. Maybe my father was the reason I had been brought to Elssador. Maybe it was supposed to show me that I didn't have to be alone anymore, that I could fully love those around me, open myself up to them…

Those thoughts only seemed half true. Something was clearly missing from them, something important, and something that King Wallace and I both couldn't seem to figure out.

"I need to see her," I said. King Wallace gave me a questioning look. "I need to meet with Queen Arianna. She's the one that sent the bracelet. She has to know why I am here."

"I have already sent word to Lilamule. She returned my letter with this." King Wallace reached into his robe, digging out a folded piece of paper, handing it over to me. I let my bracelet fall onto my lap and reached out to take the letter by one of its creased edges. I unfolded the yellow parchment, reading the two words that were inked on the page.

"'The Wanderer,'" I read aloud. I stared at the page for a few seconds more, expecting some magical explanation to appear beneath the name, but nothing happened. It was just those two words, "Is this it? Is this all she had to say?"

"It may not seem like much to go on, Carter, but I can guarantee you that those two words are very powerful," King

Wallace said. "It seems that neither Arianna nor I can give you the answers you seek, but the Wandering Spirit can, that is certain."

"But how do I find him? His name is The *Wanderer* after all. I don't expect he'd be in just one place. Is he even a person?"

King Wallace gave a laugh, taking the letter back from me and folding it back up, "He is a person and he does wander, but only when he must. I wrote back to Arianna asking if she knew where he could be found and she directed me towards the Dia Mountains."

"So when are we leaving?"

King Wallace laughed once more, but shook his head, "You will not be going anywhere until you are fully healed. Only then may you set out on your journey."

"You're making it sound like I'll be going alone." I gave a light laugh in hopes that he was making a mistake in his choice of words, but when he didn't respond with his own laugh, my heart sank.

"This is *your* task, Carter, *your* questions that need answering. No one else can seek them out for you," King Wallace replied. "But do not think I will be sending you out to wander this world on your own. A guide will accompany you on this quest, someone who knows these lands well, someone I would trust with my own life."

Oh, no, I thought. I rubbed my chapped lips together, trying to surpass a groan. I knew exactly who he was sending with me on this journey.

"Do not worry, Carter," King Wallace assured me as he pulled open my door. "My son will not lead you astray, nor will he fail to protect you if the need arises. I can promise you that."

The moment my door closed behind him and he was out of my bedroom I threw my head back against the pillow and let out a frustrated sigh.

CHAPTER 8

THE RED SUN RISES

The next morning, a maid came in early, shaking me awake and opening my shutters, allowing the morning light to sear my eyes. She began shuffling around the room, silently sweeping dust from the floor, filling up a bowl of water for me to wash my face with, and cleaning out my fireplace. Her silence seemed strange. When she was in my room the night before, cleaning me up and getting me ready for bed, she was buzzing with conversation. That morning she was as silent as the grave, working diligently and wiping at her eyes that seemed to cloud over with tears every so often.

"Is something wrong?" I asked, trying to get up, but was reminded by a sharp ache through my side how impossible that task was.

"No," the maid answered instantly, shaking her head. "Nothing is the matter, M'lady."

I took note of the fact that as she spoke she would not meet my stare. She gave me a small bow and moved towards my wardrobe, pulling out two gowns and asking me which one I would prefer. I could barely hear her because my attention had refocused on what I was seeing outside my window. It was the sky, the sunrise, which was all different shades of orange, yellow, and red. Most people would say it reminded them of fire – which it did – but for me it resembled blood. My dad told me once that when the sunrise is red, it means someone died and it was the way the earth paid its respects.

Suddenly all I could hear was the pounding of my own heart thumping painfully against my broken ribs.

"M'lady, the physician has finally found your medication," the maid said in a shy voice. I dragged my eyes away from the window and watched her come towards me, holding out a small vial in her hand. I took it from her hesitantly, studying the strange purple liquid that swished inside the vial.

"It is Umbedium, a medicine to cure all ills. It is made from the roots and leaves of the telmar trees, from the power of the dryads," the maid explained. "But the supply seems to be dwindling. In fact, people are saying that it's becoming quite a rare substance."

I took her words as a way of telling me not to waste it and popped the cork, chugging down its contents. I cringed the moment it touched my tongue and swallowed it down quickly, letting out a cough as I handed her back the empty vial.

"It tastes awful," I complained, grabbing my cup of water on my bedside table and washing out the taste of the medicine. After a few minutes more of lying back in my bed, I began to feel much better, as if the medicine was snapping my bones and ribs back in place. I tried twisting my foot around, anticipating a sharp pain that would cause tears to well up in my eyes, but the pain never came. It seemed to be fully healed.

I would have rejoiced in that news if my mind hadn't still been lost in the red sky beyond the walls of my room. Only then, as I continued to turn my ankle, stretch my bruised arm, did I realize that the maid wasn't the only person being strangely silent. All of Mitus seemed to be as well. The whole city seemed to be under a funeral-like quiet.

The maid returned to her work at the fireplace again, sniffling as she replaced the old, black wood with new chunks.

Something is wrong, I thought. *Something is very, very wrong.*

I forced myself into a sitting position on my bed, ignoring the ache in my ribs. It wasn't as agonizing as before, but the pain still made me feel dizzy. I slid my feet out over the side of my bed, placing them on the cool ground, and using my bedpost to help me stand.

"M'lady," the maid gasped. I heard a clatter as she dropped everything to the ground, rushing to my side. "You must stay in bed! You are not fit to –"

"I'm fine," I said, trying to use a pleasant tone, but it came out tight. The maid closed her mouth and quietly helped me stand. "I need a dress, preferably one that won't crush my ribs."

"M'lady, I must advise you to stay put. If His Lordship discovered I allowed you to leave when you are not yet well –"

"He won't. I promise," I assured her. "Just please, let me see what happened."

She stared at me before forcing herself to do as I asked. She was back at my side seconds later with a purple gown draped over her arm. She quickly unbuttoned my nightgown, letting it drop to the floor. She helped me step out of it and into an underdress and then she pulled the purple gown over it. She brought the long sleeves up over my shoulders and quickly did up the back. The moment I felt her delicate fingers fumble with the last button, I moved unsteadily towards the door. She pulled it open for me as I stepped out into the hall, then took my arm, assisting me down the stairwell, and out into the courtyard.

The area was empty, not a body was seen until the maid brought me towards the main baily. The sight I saw once we moved under the arch of the inner gate made me wonder why I had ever thought the city was silent. There were about a hundred or more people gathered in the courtyard, almost all of them hovering over bodies that lay limp and lifeless upon stretchers.

The maid at my side gasped in my ear, bringing a hand to cover her mouth in shock. I felt my own lips part, but no words escaped them. My throat had gone too dry for me to speak. All the people in the courtyard held grim expressions, many of them let out loud cries of anger or sobbed into a loved one's arms. Besides the horror of seeing all the villagers mourn over their losses, the dead bodies let off a stench, making me feel even more dizzy and unstable on my feet.

I began to walk further into the main baily, pausing a couple times to let a few knights rush past, carrying their injured comrades on wooden stretchers. I swallowed hard at the sight of one of them, of his leg that seemed to be twisted in an odd direction, the blood that stained his armour and covered his face. Once they were out of my way, I began moving again, only to be stopped by the sight of a family crowded over a familiar body.

The sight of the light brown curls upon the dead man's head made my stomach turn. My mind raced to an image of Abias and I felt my knees buckle, but the sight of the man's silver armour filled me with relief...and guilt. It may not have been Abias, but it was one of his older brothers. The other three boys stood over him, each of them looking very pale and grim. Their mother was on her knees, her body draped over her dead son's as she sobbed into his chest. Abias' dad knelt at her side, rubbing her back as if it would soothe her pain.

As I watched Abias' family grieve, I began to realize that he wasn't among them. I got up on my tiptoes, trying to see if he was hiding behind his tall brothers. But all I could see were the heads of another heartbroken family.

I started to move through the crowd again, this time heading towards the stables where I hoped Abias would be. As I limped around the main baily, snaking through the narrow paths that the villagers had made, I tried to avoid staring at the wagon that was being pulled out of the front gate, knowing that it was the dead they were bringing out to burn.

I made it to the stables, glad to find that I was right. Abias was standing before me, holding a broom and sweeping up the straws of hay scattered upon the floor. His grip on the broom was tight, making his knuckles resemble his pale cheeks.

"Hey," I said, limping into the stable. Abias gave a little jump, clearly startled by my greeting.

"You should be resting," he said, leaning on his broom.

"No, I shouldn't. I should be here, helping with all of this," I replied. My hand clenched into a fist and I dug my nails into my skin, trying so hard to keep my voice from shaking.

"It is not your duty to bury the dead, Carter," Abias said. His voice was uncharacteristically flat, holding none of its usual charisma.

"How did this happen?" I asked, glancing over my shoulder at the crowded courtyard.

"They came in the night, the morbiens," Abias explained. "Prince Julian rode out with his knights to meet them, but..." His voice cracked and he let the sentence drop. I didn't need him to explain anymore to know that they were vastly outnumbered.

"Does King Wallace know why?" I said. "I mean there has to be a reason for –"

"Morbiens do not reason," Abias snapped, his eyes burning with anger. "They are cold-hearted creatures, Carter. They enjoy the sight of our blood being spilt."

I swallowed, feeling my eyes begin to sting with tears. He was right, of course. I remembered that morbien sitting on top of me, grinning as blood trickled down my neck from where his knife pierced my skin. But this was the second time they had attacked the people of Lorien, the second time since I had arrived in Elssador. Something told me that this wasn't just a mindless hunt, this wasn't just about terrorizing people and feeding their bloodthirsty desires...

Does this all have something to do with me?

Abias was studying me as I stood, paralyzed by this horrible thought, and took a few steps closer, his eyes growing sad as if he understood exactly what I was thinking. He reached out to me, placing a gentle hand on my shoulder, speaking softly, "Blaming yourself will not bring my brother back from the dead."

I found that all I could do was stare at him. Returning his words with a nod would be a lie. Despite the fact that I knew every word he said was true, my heart didn't seem to accept it. I knew blaming myself wouldn't bring his brother back, it wouldn't bring any of the dead back. But that wasn't why I was placing all of their blood on my hands. I was blaming myself because this really did all happen because of me. All those people died because King Wallace was too kind and loving to murder me the moment his son brought me into his camp. It was becoming crystal clear that these morbiens were after my blood for reasons that I couldn't wrap my head around.

These thoughts began to weigh me down, forcing me to turn away from Abias. I felt the tips of his fingers trace down my arm as I shifted out of his hold and limped back towards my bedroom as fast as my ribs would allow me. I crossed through the courtyard, looking down in fear of meeting eyes with one of the mourning families. Seeing them grieve for their loved ones made my guilty feeling stronger, forcing me to feel unsteady on my feet, sick. I hauled myself up the staircase, finally allowing some of my tears to slide down my cheeks before reaching the top of the stairs, and stepping out into the hallway where my room was.

When I entered the corridor, I found that I was not alone. I pulled up, standing still as the other being in the room dragged his tired feet towards me. It was Julian, dressed in the same silver armour I met him in, but it wasn't nearly as polished and shiny as I remembered it. Blood and dust covered every inch of him; his clothing, hands, and even his face which held a blank, unreadable expression.

My eyes searched his as he took his final step towards me, leaving only a small gap between us. At first, he did nothing except stare. His eyes held nothing but the same sadness and grief I had seen in them when he told me Titus had been taken over by the same creatures that continued to try and harm his people.

After a few more seconds of standing deathly still, Julian reached down to my hand – still staring deeply into my eyes – and lifted it up to his lips. I sucked in a breath as they gently brushed against my knuckles, struck by this unexpected gesture. At first my brain was spinning with potential explanations for this kiss, but as he pulled away I felt something hard and mildly sharp press up against my palm.

Julian released my hand, allowing me to curl my fingers around the object as he slipped past me, heading towards the stairwell I'd come from moments before. I waited until I heard the door close behind him to look at the object I held in my fist, discovering it to be a folded piece of parchment. I quickly unfolded it, desperate to know why he needed to be so covert about getting a message to me.

The answer came the moment I laid eyes on the text:

We leave at sundown.

CHAPTER 9

BEHIND THE MASK

I tried to sleep as much as I could that afternoon, as well as drowning myself in the rest of the medicine the court physician had delivered to my door, preparing myself for the night ahead. The Umbedium may have tasted awful, but it sure did do the trick. Come evening, there was only a slight prick of pain in my side and the bruising down my arm had faded into a faint purple.

I lay down in my dark room, the only light coming from the setting sun outside my window. I watched as it slowly disappeared behind the shadow of mountains in the east, the sky becoming consumed by a dark blanket.

It was time.

Grabbing the candle on my bedside table, I approached my fireplace – which was still burning brightly – and allowed the flames to ignite the tip. I moved around the room, lighting the other candles on my mantelpiece. I approached my wardrobe next, swinging open the doors and pulling out the least restricting gown I could find. It still would have been better if I had a pair of breeches, something that I could actually run in if I needed to.

King Wallace spoke of my journey at dinner that evening, filling in Lord Sebastian and Mortimer on the matter, and speaking as if my trip were still a distant thing. Julian never spoke once about our early departure. I assumed the moment he had slipped that note in my hand that this was supposed to be a secret mission, and his avoidance of the topic at dinner confirmed that assumption.

Guilt took its place in my stomach as King Wallace promised to arrange a couple of bags for our journey, providing us with extra food and clothing. I desperately wanted him to know that Julian and I were planning on leaving that very night, but knew better not to say anything. Julian's flame of anger was already burning for me, the last thing I needed was to step even further onto his bad side. We needed to work together if we were ever going to find The Wanderer.

My mind drifted off to our conversation over supper as I continued to dig around in my wardrobe in search of a pair of pants...

"You must take horses as well," King Wallace had said. "They will be useful if you are attacked by anything unexpected."

"Like morbiens?" I asked. The look that King Wallace, Julian, and Mortimer had shared in that moment was seared into my memory. It was a look of worry and even fear.

"No, creatures far worse," King Wallace replied, "Morbiens are not the only creatures that roam the free lands of Elssador. They may just be the least of your worries."

"Would you suggest bringing a few knights with us, then?" Julian piped up. I watched him closely, wondering if he was just asking the question to hide his betrayal or taking notes for our trek that evening.

"It would be wise, yes," King Wallace had answered. "Not only will it assist in your protection against them, but it will also reduce the chances of your being hunted. Their aprimorad scent should mask Carter's human one."

"I suggest that you speak to no one else of this," Mortimer had whispered, his green eyes sending warning signals to all of us. "There is word that there are others that fight alongside the morbiens. You must trust no one you meet on the road, Prince Julian. Perhaps even those you think you may already know."

Mortimer's words had haunted me through the rest of that meal, even as I continued to dig around in my closet for something other than one of those stupid gowns. That was when I found it, folded neatly at the bottom of a basket, hidden underneath an extra bed sheet. Beaming, I pulled the breeches out and then the purple tunic, one almost identical to what all of the knights wore under their heavy armour. As I unfolded the clothing, a note fell out of one of the sleeves. I picked it up and read the neat script drawn onto the parchment;

> *The boots are under the bed.*
> *May the winds of destiny guide you, my child.*
> *- King J. Wallace*

I nearly dropped the note after reading it, my mind searching for an answer to how he could have known what Julian and I were up to. After a few seconds of standing still in disbelief, I began to grin. I supposed nothing went over that man's head. He was too wise, seeming to hold the answers to everything... well, besides one thing.

I fiddled with my bracelet as I moved towards my bed, shucking off my nightgown and changing into my new clothing. When I was finished buckling up a belt at my waist, I knelt down to retrieve the boots King Wallace left me, sitting on the edge of my bed and tying up the thick laces. A knock at my door interrupted me. I rose, rushing towards the door, knowing full well who it was. Sure enough, Julian had arrived, standing in my doorway dressed in an outfit similar to mine, but with silver armour strapped to his broad shoulders and biceps.

He stared at me, eyeing my clothing with a disapproving expression, "I preferred the gown," he grumbled, shoving me out of the way with his arm and welcoming himself into my room.

Did he just try to compliment me? I buried that thought and gently closed the door, assuming there were guards patrolling the end of the hall. When I turned to face Julian, about to tell him that his father knew of our plans to leave early, I was stunned to see what he held in his hands. It was a bow, the same one I had used when I challenged him in Titus.

"Is that for me?" I questioned hopefully, gesturing to the weapon.

"Listen," Julian sighed impatiently, staring me down, "I'm still not comfortable with the idea of you possessing a weapon.

Even more so now that many of my people are dead, slain by morbiens that seemed to be following you wherever you tread."

I clenched my jaw in an attempt to hold back the tears that began to sting my eyes. I looked away from him, unable to face the reality that he agreed with me. He too knew it was my fault all those lives were lost. *She is different, therefore she is dangerous*, I remembered him saying when we first met. It seemed Julian knew from the start that I was going to cause havoc, even if I didn't try to.

"You volunteered to come along, didn't you?" I said.

"Perhaps," Julian responded through gritted teeth.

"Why?" I hissed, glaring at him. "To spy on me? To make sure that I'm not one of those traitors Mortimer talked about?"

"Just as you would like to know why The Wanderer allowed you to enter Elssador, so do I," Julian snapped, taking a dangerous step towards me. "You are a mystery, Olsen, one that needs to be solved before anyone else dies."

The weight of his words pressed down hard on me and I closed my mouth, once again turning my eyes away from his.

"Here," Julian said, his voice as sharp as the edge of the blade sheathed at his hip. He shoved the bow and quiver into my arms, forcing me to stumble back a couple steps. "We are wasting time."

I moved further into the room with Julian, hanging my bow on my bedframe as I pulled the quiver over my shoulders, adjusting the strap until it fit snugly across my chest. The weight of the quiver on my back brought me a strange feeling of comfort, security. It was the same sort of relief that came upon soldiers or warriors in the stories Tyler and I used to read back home, but they were never afraid of that comfort. The feeling seemed to make them stronger. For me, it did the opposite. The comfort of holding an instrument of death in my hands terrified me.

"We will make our way to the kitchens from here," Julian said, snapping me out of my thoughts. "That way we can collect some food for our journey."

He was standing before my bedroom wall, the back one where the headboard of my bed was pushed against. Then, he placed the palms of his hands against the stone, pressing hard into it with a grunt as if a secret door would open at his touch.

"What are you doing?" I questioned. "Shouldn't we be sneaking through the courtyard?"

"Oh, yes, what an excellent idea!" Julian said, his voice dripping with sarcasm. "Let us run through an open courtyard where we will be seen by every guard along the walls."

"Okay," I snapped. "I get it."

"My family and I used to sail to Mitus for celebrations hosted by Lord Sebastian," Julian said, his voice suddenly free of all the sarcasm it held only seconds before. He stopped pressing against the wall, turning to face me as he continued to speak, "Spending so much time here, my sister and I discovered a passage which we used to steal sweets from the kitchens."

I nodded my head in understanding before the realization of his words struck me. *Sister? What sister?* I started to ask him this question, but my voice was muffled, cut off by the sound of spinning gears. Suddenly, the bed before me began to lift off the ground and fold up against the wall. At the same time, the floorboards began to lower, revealing a dark passage.

"My aprimorad vison allows me to see in the dark, but you will need some form of light," Julian moved away from my bedpost, which he had pulled down like a lever to open the doors of the passage. I could feel his eyes on me, hear his voice, but I found myself unable to respond. I was frozen in shock.

"I suggest you fetch a torch from the hall," he continued.

"You have a sister?" I finally asked after a long pause.

"I *had* one, yes. Now go and find a torch," Julian responded, spitting out each word. This was clearly a subject that you didn't speak with him about, one that most people would not dare pry into. But I wasn't like most people in Elssador.

"What happened to her?" I said. Julian's ocean eyes shifted away from mine and rested on the flickering candles placed on my mantelpiece. His jaw was clenched tight, his Adams apple bobbing as he swallowed back the tears shining in his eyes.

"She died," Julian answered, his demeanor unexpectedly calm. "Now, are there any more inquires I need to answer before you finally do as I say?"

There were many more questions. My brain was buzzing with them. But it wasn't my wonderings that justified my refusal to follow his orders, it was the fact that they were *his* orders. I hated doing as he said, bossing me around like I was one of his servants or knights. I was a human, not a creature of Elssador, nor a lady of the castle. Did he really have the right?

"We are wasting precious hours, Olsen," Julian warned, clearly recognizing my reluctance. "If you would like to reach The Wanderer within the next two days, then I suggest we waste no more time, understood?"

He was right and that irritated me even more. I gave him a dramatic roll of my eyes, turning my back to him and heading out into the hall. I left the door open as I stood on my tiptoes, reaching for the torch above me. I pulled it down and began to walk back inside to join Julian when my eyes met with another's at the end of the hall. I could see his armour shimmering in the torch light, confirming that he was one of the guards posted to patrol this area.

"M'lady," he started, "what is it you are –?"

I panicked, not even waiting for him to finish his sentence before disappearing back into my room, slamming the door shut and locking it.

"What happened?" Julian demanded as I pressed my back up against the door, breathing heavily.

"The guard, he saw me," I explained, heading towards the passage as the knight began to pound on my door. "We need to leave."

Julian nodded in agreement as I passed him, stepping into the entrance of the passage and sidestepping the slanted ramp with my feet to the side to prevent me from tumbling down the slope. I jumped down onto the flat ground, the torchlight flickering against the grey walls of the tunnel as I turned to find Julian rushing in after me. My room behind him was pitch black as if he had blown out all the candles before he entered the tunnel.

Julian gestured for me to continue on and before I knew it, we were moving in step with each other at a quick pace through the long tunnel. I squinted, hoping that the end of the passage would come into view soon. Even if Julian blew out the candles, it wouldn't stop the guard from breaking down my door and finding the mysterious passage opened before him.

It wasn't that I was afraid of the guard running to King Wallace with news that Julian and I had snuck out into the night together. This was his plan after all. What I feared was that more people would find out about our journey. Both Mortimer and King Wallace emphasized the secrecy of this mission throughout dinner. Once again I was haunted by Mortimer's words... *You must trust no one. Perhaps even those you think you may already know.*

I shuddered.

"Cold, are we?" Julian noted as we continued to move down the passage. I glanced at him, noticing a hint of a smile on his lips. I refused to reply to his words. Not because he was teasing me, but because I was angry, mad that he kept pushing away all the questions I had about his sister. *How did she die? How long has she been dead for? Why didn't he mention this sooner? How come King Wallace never said anything?* My questions were endless and they were also forbidden. A look of warning filled Julian's eyes, one that had the words 'don't you dare' written all over it.

"The end of the tunnel is not far from here," Julian said, avoiding my questions that he clearly assumed were being silently asked.

"How come you never told me you had a sister?" I said, ignoring his warning. Julian glowered, but I stood my ground, raising my brows in anticipation for an answer. *I am not a citizen of Lorien. I am not one of his people,* I silently reminded myself as Julian's gaze grew more deadly. *He didn't have the right to boss me around.*

"Because I did not think it was something you needed to know," Julian responded. "Do you really think I would expose my past to someone I do not trust?"

"Fine. What about your father? He trusts me. Why didn't he mention it?"

"Because my sister is *dead*, Olsen," Julian whirled, stepping in front of me so I could move no further. His cheeks were red with rage as he took a step closer to me, looking even more furious than before. "She died the same day my mother did. They died a horrible death, one that both my father *and* I witnessed. The mention of her name, any reminder of her brings my father a pain so great that all he can do is lie in bed for weeks on end. It is something that is difficult for both of us to bear."

Suddenly, Julian was becoming clearer to me. This was the explanation for his hard exterior, the thick walls he built around his heart, his consistent scowl... He wasn't just bearing the weight of his sister's death, but his mother's as well.

My guilt kicked in at that moment, making me want to take back all those questions I shoved in his face. If he had asked about my father I wouldn't have spoken a word. I would have done exactly what he did and avoid this painful topic. The desire to apologize filled my heart, but I found that I couldn't fulfill it. My body seemed to fall deeper into a state of shock as I realized that I had just seen Julian Wallace, the *real* Julian Wallace. Stripped of all his sarcasm, his arrogance, and his pride, which he used to cover up all the things I was seeing as we continued on our way.

He revealed his heart to me, whether he intended to or not, and I realized something that sent a strange feeling of warmth and comfort into my body. That hard look in his wet eyes, the grievous hunch of his shoulders he had as he turned away... it all led to the fact that Julian Wallace was broken.

CHAPTER 10

QUICKLY & QUIETLY

A loud crash echoed around the tunnel as Julian punched the large vent above us at the end of the passage. Julian stretched up high, reaching up to push the vent aside and pull himself through the opening.

"The area is clear," he whispered down to me.

I dropped my torch, quickly stomping out the flame – just as he instructed me to do only a moment earlier – before climbing up onto the same rock he had once been standing on, and grabbing hold of the hand he held down to me through the opening. I used my other hand to grab hold of the surface above, pulling half my body out of the opening, and welcoming his help to haul the rest of me up.

Julian released me once I was on my feet and moved over to a barrel by the start of a flight of stairs I assumed led out of the kitchens. I could barely see anything around me so I focused on Julian's glowing eyes, just as a reminder that I wasn't alone in the dark.

He returned about a minute later, holding two bags in his hands. He shoved one of them into my arms and gestured towards the pantry beside one of the wood stoves along the far wall, "Find some food to pack into this. I will stand guard until you are finished."

"What about the second?" I said, motioning towards the other bag he held.

"I already filled it earlier this afternoon with extra clothing and a few medical supplies," Julian replied, slinging the bag over his shoulder. "I also packed a vial of Umbedium. It would be wise for you to take some when we stop in the village of Maycock to rest."

I gave him a nod, heading towards the pantry he gestured to. I still couldn't see very well as I scanned the shelves, so I felt my way through the various items, recognizing the crest shape of a bundle of bananas, the smooth surface of an apple, and even bread and cheese in the pantry. I quickly stuffed as much as I could in the bag, closed the pantry and made my way back toward Julian. I hadn't even fully reached him before he came towards me, grabbing my arm and racing up the stairs.

"What? What's wrong?" I whispered, falling behind.

"Someone's coming. I can hear their voices down the hall. Now hurry, we must hide," he urged, grabbing my hand and pulling me up the rest of the steps with him, guiding me into a dark corner on the landing just as the door swung open.

"Are you positive it was this passage?" a voice asked. Julian tensed beside me, his eyes widening with fear and recognition. The voice sounded familiar to my ears as well. It was Mortimer, being led by the guard I had met eyes with in the hall.

"I am certain," the knight said as the two of them descended the steps, heading for the entrance to the passage Julian and I had climbed out of. "I saw her race towards her room. When I broke down the door I found the entrance to this tunnel."

They stood in silence after that, hovering over the opening in the ground as Julian and I continued to hide in our corner. We each held our breath in fear that they would be able to hear us. I wasn't too worried about Mortimer discovering our leave. What else could he do but tell King Wallace who already knew? It was the next words exchanged that sent my heart racing.

"She has betrayed King Wallace's trust, therefore she has committed treason, whether she understood it or not," Mortimer said, running a hand through his slick black hair.

"But, my lord, the punishment for such a crime is death," the knight slowly acknowledged, "I do not think King Wallace has the heart to send Lady Olsen to the gallows."

"That is right, Sir Landon. It would be as if he was watching Lady Liana die all over again. That is why I will see to the matter myself," Mortimer replied with a defeated sigh. My throat went dry at these words. Mortimer came across as reluctant to go through with this plan, but he also seemed to bow down to the law, even before his king.

"I fear his majesty will not approve of this," the knight – Sir Landon – said.

"I am the Steward, the King's advisor, and close friend. I know both him and the kingdom of Lorien well. If he shows leniency to a crime such as this, then he will surely lose control over his people."

As Mortimer continued to speak, I felt Julian's breath against my neck. I glanced over at him, trying my best not to turn my head in fear that the two men below us would sense my movement. That was when I felt his arm slide behind my back, his hand reaching for the handle on the kitchen door.

"Understood, My Lord," Sir Landon said with a slight bow, "What would you have me do?"

"Find her before she leaves the city," Mortimer replied, "When you do, bring her to my chambers to be questioned. If I believe her tale – whatever it may be – then she will be spared."

I felt Julian's lips gently brush against my ear as he whispered, "Go," and opened the door, placing a hand on my lower back to guide me out of the kitchens. He slipped out after me, closing the door behind him. Obviously we weren't fast enough, for I could hear the guard shouting from inside the kitchen and the sound of his and Mortimer's feet trampling up the steps.

"Come, Olsen. *Run!*" Julian hissed, grabbing my wrist and pulling me forward.

We raced down the hall, turning left into another one, and then slowing to a stop before a far narrower corridor. Julian put a hand out to stop me from moving any further and placed a finger on his lips, his eyes darting towards the guards that patrolled the hall.

Wait here, Julian's expression read.

I gave a nod, letting him know I understood his command.

Soon, I found myself waiting alone in the shadows, watching as Julian approached the guards standing on either side of a door at the end of the hall, but all I could hear were their whispers and hushed laughter. Before I knew it, the two guards were walking away from the door, towards where I was standing. I quickly sunk back into a dark corner, bracing myself as they passed by, moving straight down the opposite hallway.

Once they were gone, I slipped out of my hiding spot and raced towards Julian who was facing the mysterious door, using a set of keys to unlock it. At the click of the lock, he shoved the door open and hurried inside. I followed close behind him, entering into a long room filled with shelves and shelves of various kinds of armour and weapons.

I stared in awe at all the sharp objects, suddenly having the childish urge to touch all of them. A thought at the back of my mind forced me not to give into that desire. Suddenly, all I seemed to be able to think about were the words Mortimer spoke moments before. Only then, within the thick walls of a locked armory, was I able to register what he had said, forcing more questions to invade my thoughts.

"Julian, that girl Mortimer was talking about, Lady Liana, that was your sister, wasn't it?" I asked, looking over my shoulder at him.

"Yes, it was," Julian responded tightly as he moved further into the room after making sure he had locked the door, "and it seems Mortimer is under the impression that my father sees you as a reminder of her. The only reason I can think of for him taking your crime into his own hands would be because of that, because he would do everything in his power to protect my father's heart from being broken once more."

I ignored the part he said about this being *my* crime – since this was his plan after all – and allowed myself to be filled with understanding. That was the reason King Wallace had been so kind to me, the reason he showed so much care and fatherly affection. It was because when he looked at me, he saw the daughter he'd lost.

"Mortimer has long served our family and shown loyalty to my father," Julian said, continuing on with his previous words. He had walked even further into the armory, standing before a cupboard which he used the ring of keys to unlock, "There has not been a time in my life where Mortimer was not a part of it, nor a time when he would stop at nothing to protect us, especially my father. It seems that ever since Liana's death that desire to protect him has grown even stronger, as it has for me."

I studied Julian carefully as he continued to open the cupboard, swearing under his breath at how troublesome the lock was being. His words gave me access to even more knowledge of why he volunteered to come with me on this journey to find The Wanderer. It wasn't just because he was curious or suspicious, it was because he knew seeing his people die hurt his father, severed his already broken heart. My being in this city would only add to that heartbreak, not only because I reminded King Wallace of his dead daughter, but because as long as I remained in this city the morbiens would keep attacking. Julian wasn't coming along to protect me, he was accompanying me to protect his father.

"I do not see it," Julian said, his voice breaking through my thoughts. It was then that I noticed he had been standing still, probably for quite some time, watching me study him.

"You don't see what?" I asked.

"Liana. I do not see her in you the way my father does," Julian replied, "You are far more stubborn than my sister, too hard-hearted."

I ignored his words, not letting myself take offense at them. My mind ached to know more about his sister, especially now that I was being compared to her. I wanted to know the full story of how Liana died, no matter how long it took Julian to explain it. I came to his side with these thoughts burning in my mind and grabbed onto his arm just as he reached out towards the cupboard. He froze, staring furiously at my hand and then back to my face.

"How did she die?" I asked. My voice was level, suddenly matching the authority his held. Both Julian and I were surprised by the courage in my tone, "I'm not going anywhere until I get some answers and don't try and tell me it would be my loss because it won't be. It will be yours. How do you think your father will react when he finds out his son betrayed his orders?"

Julian's jaw tightened and I tried to hold back my smile. Blackmailing was surprisingly fun.

It was awhile before he finally gave into my commands, grabbing two cloaks out of the cupboard and then locking it, pressing his back up against its doors. He sighed, staring down at the ground like he was searching for where in this tale he should begin.

"We were traveling home from Mitus two winters ago, only a day and a bit more after Lord Sebastian's birthday celebration. On our journey home, we made camp in the woods, the same wood we stayed in on our way to Mitus only a few days ago. That night, our camp was attacked by a manticore."

"A manticore?" I said, my brow creasing in confusion.

"It is a lion-like creature, but three times the size, with wings almost as large and powerful as a dragon's. Its tail moves like a serpent, one ready to strike as a scorpion would it's prey," Julian described. Goosebumps began to form on my arms at his vivid description, "The creature's face is one I will never forget. It looked almost as if it could be an aprimorad until it roared, opening its cave-like mouth to reveal a full set of sharp fangs."

"It killed her," I mumbled, my body feeling numb.

"No," Julian's eyes grew dark with memory, "it devoured her. Her, my mother, and a few knights that came along with us for the journey."

I started to feel sick as I imagined what it must've been like to watch something as horrible as that, to see a beast eat away at the ones you love, crush the men who swore to protect you. The worst in all of this was how sudden their deaths were. Yes, they may not have suffered, but the ones the dead left behind did. Julian, King Wallace, they weren't just living with the guilt of not being able to save their family, but the guilt of not being able to say goodbye.

"Liana and I would have been sixteen that summer. We would have had a huge celebration together, commemorating our transition into adulthood," Julian said, a slight smile pressing at his lips despite the tears I noticed shimmering in his eyes, "This year we would have been eighteen. She would have been old enough to officially become head physician. It was what she had always wanted, to care for people, heal them..."
His voice trailed off, his small smile fading, and his eyes growing

hard, as if he just remembered something even darker than what he already told me.

"Now she cannot accomplish any of that," Julian added through clenched teeth, "And it is all because of that stupid stable boy –"

"*Stable boy*?" I exclaimed, suddenly feeling almost as angry as he was. "What does Abias have to do with any of this?"

After minutes of refusing to do so, Julian looked up at me, his pupils so large I could only see a thin line of the glowing sea-green colour that had filled his eyes before, "So I see he has decided not to tell you," Julian chuckled coldly, "I should have known he would be too cowardly to reveal such things, to give his new *friend* a glimpse of who he really is."

"What the heck are you talking about?" I hissed, taking a step towards Julian. He straightened up against the cupboard, staring me down in attempt to intimidate me.

"He was a knight at the time, being trained by one of his older brothers. That day he was instructed to stand guard outside Liana's tent, to make certain that she was safe through all hours of the night. When the Manticore attacked, I awoke to my sisters scream's. When I ran out to come to her aid, I saw Abias lying under a tree, staring as the beast dropped my mother's dead body to the ground and advanced towards Liana. Even when the beast had taken her, running away with her limp body in its mouth, he still remained where he was, doing *nothing* while the rest of us tried to do everything we could to save her!"

Suddenly, I was overwhelmed with even more understanding. The piece I had been missing to Abias and Julian's rivalry had placed itself together. Abias felt guilty for what he had done, for not being able to rescue Liana the same way no one else was. Julian was the one who created that tension between them, making sure Abias remained guilty for not saving his sister. I supposed it was a way for him to relieve himself of that same guilt, just a horrible way to cope with his grief. Although this puzzle seemed to be coming together, I still couldn't completely wrap my head around the idea that Abias would let someone die, that he would just sit there and watch as someone was being torn to shreds. He had risked his life for me several times since I met him. What made him unable to do the same for Liana?

"But I'm sure there was a good reason why Abias couldn't –"

"Enough, Olsen," Julian hissed, pushing himself off the cupboard and hovering even closer to me, still burning holes into my eyes with his deadly stare. "I know why he did not decide to save my sister that day. It's because Abias Wood is nothing but a coward. I suggest you put an end to your words of defense because nothing you say will change that."

"I refuse to believe it," I said, shaking my head.

"You can believe what you like. It does not matter to me if you wind up dead because of him," Julian replied with an arrogant smirk. I glared at him as he shoved a cloak into my arms and placed the handle of a twelve-inch dagger in the palm of my hand, "Tie your hair back and pull your hood up. These cloaks will conceal us as we sneak towards the stables."

I silently did as he instructed, braiding my hair back while continuing to glare at him as he tied his own black cloak around his neck. Then he moved towards another shelf, eyeing me as if taking in my measurements. He returned to my side only moments later, holding two leather wrist guards out to me.

"Why do I need those?"

"They will help protect you if we run into morbiens on route," Julian replied. "I would dress you in armour like mine, but you would just slow us down. Now come, we are already late. The others will be waiting."

"The others?" I questioned, sliding on the leather wrist guards, fumbling with the laces in attempt to tighten them. Julian reached out to assist, letting out an exasperated breath while he quickly adjusted the wrist guards.

"Yes, my knights," Julian replied, finishing up the last knot. "I took my father's advice and invited a few of them to come along on our journey. That way we will reduce the chances of being tracked," Julian lifted his hood up over his head until it was pulled up to the bridge of his nose, covering the faint light in his eyes. I did the same, letting my braid rest on my shoulder and tucking the extra strands behind my ears. Then we were off again, making our way to a door hidden at the back of the armory. We slipped outside of the warmth and into the cool night air. I shivered as a gust of wind blew across my face, threatening to push my hood backward.

"This way," Julian whispered, cocking his head towards the inner gate where a few guards stood watch, looking off into the east.

I followed Julian, sticking close to the walls, allowing myself to become one with their shadows. It was a dark night, one with thick clouds brewing in the distance. I bit down on my lip, swallowing a groan. Those clouds were going to be upon us shortly, pouring rain down on our backs, seeping into our clothes and chilling our skin. I really hoped Julian had packed a blanket in that other bag he had hanging off his shoulder as we continued to move beneath the tall walls.

We soon reached the inner gate where Julian put an arm out, forcing me to hide deeper in the darkness with my back pressed up against the stone wall. I glanced up to where his eyes rested on a guard who had turned, looking towards the door we had just come out of. After a few seconds of holding our breath – yet again – we were off once more.

My heart raced as we hurried past the inner gate and didn't slow until we had taken cover in an alleyway between two shops. I slid up against one wall just as Julian did the other. He poked his head out of the shadows, scanning the wide courtyard between us and the stables on the other side. The wooden shack was dark, pitch black, making it seem to me as if it were entirely empty, but I knew Julian could probably see his knights hiding in there. His eyes were glued to the wooden building that seemed all but cleared out to me.

"So, are you gonna apologize for being snippy with me about sneaking out through the courtyard?" I whispered with an amused smirk, "Because that sure looks like what we're about –"

"Shhh," Julian hissed. I could see the outline of his scowl, even with the hood covering so much of his face. He pulled it back ever so slightly, allowing me to see the seriousness in his eyes, "If we are to make it out of the city this night on horseback, we must move quickly and quietly. It seems that Mortimer has called for more guards to take up patrol while we were wasting time in the armory."

I didn't bother shooting a witty remark his way as I still felt somewhat guilty for prying so much information about his sister out of him. Instead I kept my lips pressed together, scanning the courtyard just as he was, probably working out a safe route towards the stables. I noticed several guards patrolling the front gate, their metal pikes shimmering in the faint moonlight. I glanced up at the sky just in time to see a dark cloud cover the moon, making it even more difficult for me to navigate.

"Alright," Julian sighed. All I could see were his eyes, which held the same adrenaline I felt boiling within my own body, "I have a plan and in order for it to work you must follow me and do exactly as I say. And I mean *every* word, do you understand me?"

"Yeah," I nodded.

"Good, then you must stay close to me," Julian said, "and follow my every move."

I nodded, doing just that as we slipped out of the alleyway and into the open courtyard, my shoulder brushing up against his arm. Julian moved more swiftly than I, his chest sticking out, and walking in a bit of a march. I tried my best to follow suit, just as he told me to do, walking in a way that made me feel like one of his knights. It suddenly clicked inside my mind that perhaps that was Julian's plan, to make me seem as just another one of his soldiers until we were safely outside of Mitus.

I could feel the eyes of all the guards on us as we moved towards the dark stables, but they said nothing, seeming to recognize the purple tunics poking out under our cloaks, taking us as just more knights being posted for patrol. I could only see the shadowed outlines of the men Julian invited to come along with us, spotting only about six of them as we entered the stables. The tallest one took a step forward towards Julian and stretched an arm out. The slap of hands being clasped filled the stables as Julian took hold of this knight's arm.

"You're late," the tall knight said, his glowing brown eyes flicking towards me, "Were there any complications?"

"Just one," Julian responded carefully, he too shifted his gaze towards me. "It seems we are not going to be able to sneak out of the city as secretly as we thought. More guards have been sent to patrol the walls."

"So how are we to leave?" the same knight questioned.

"We are to break out, fight through any guards that decide to stand in our way," Julian replied sternly. I watched as his outline faded into the shadows behind the knight he was speaking to. He returned moments later with the *clip-clop* sound of hooves trailing behind him.

"Prince Julian, these are your men. You would risk striking them down just to leave the city in secret? What if another band of morbiens attack while we are away?" asked the knight.

Julian didn't respond right away. Instead, he approached me, taking my hand and guiding me towards the horse he had brought forward in the dark. "There will be no more attacks on this city, Alexamian. I can promise you that."

Before he turned me around, we shared a long look, one that made me wonder if perhaps he hadn't told these knights *everything* about our journey. I held my tongue, forcing myself not to ask as I turned to face my horse. I felt Julian's strong hands grip my waist as he lifted me up with a quiet grunt. I slipped my foot into the stirrup, allowing Julian to release me as I swung my leg over the other side of the saddle. I held back a giggle of excitement at how mobile I had become with my new pants. I silently thanked King Wallace as Julian left my side and returned a moment mounted riding on a brown steed resembling mine.

"We must act as if we are scouts leaving the city to patrol the borders, nothing more," Julian instructed, twisting around on his saddle to look towards his knights who had hopped onto theirs. "Only charge at my signal."

"Yes, M'lord," his knights chorused.

Julian looked to me, raising his brows as if waiting for a similar answer to escape my lips.

"Yeah," I sighed, with a slow nod, "I understand."

Julian began at a slow trot out of the stables, followed by me, and then the six knights took up the rear, two of them flanking me. The hooves of our horses echoed across the courtyard, forcing the eyes of all the guards to fall on us, following our every move as we advanced towards the front gate.

"Halt!" someone shouted from above.

We all pulled up on our reigns before the gate, standing behind Julian who pulled his hood back, staring up at the guard with raised brows.

"Oh...uh... Prince Julian, Your Highness," the guard stammered, giving his prince a low bow, "My lord, I am sorry, but you are not permitted to leave. We are to make sure no one does. Lord Mortimer wants all to remain in the city."

"Your prince is ordering you to stand down and allow us to pass through this gate immediately," Julian said up to them, using that strong tone that always seemed to put these men in their place. "We must scout out the area to ensure there are no more attacks this night."

"His Lordship has already sent out scouts. They returned several hours ago," the knight continued to press on. I noticed a slight waver in his voice this time and suddenly felt sorry for him. He was clearly conflicted between these orders, not knowing which ones he should follow.

I sensed movement from the knights on either side of me. The tall one that Julian was speaking to in the stables – Alexamian – had moved his hand over to the sword at his hip, gripping the hilt tightly. The knight on my other side did the same, gripping his reigns as if preparing himself to charge out. My heart pounded in my chest, but I did the same as these two, unsheathing my dagger and holding it beneath my cloak.

"We come with my father's word," Julian continued to persuade. "He wishes for another patrol, just to ensure that all is well."

I took a quick look over my shoulder, noticing dark figures emerging from the shadows of the courtyard, moving slowly towards us, circling us in. I returned my attention to the front, staring up at the guard Julian was speaking to. He was standing very still, his eyes moving rapidly along the wall and then back to Julian.

"A-as you wish, My Lord," the guard stuttered after his long pause. He waved a hand at the guards who were beginning to encircle us, sending them back to their posts.

"Thank you," Julian responded with a slight bow of his head. The guard blushed, sticking out his chest and proudly

132

ordering someone to open the gate immediately. I held back my nervous laughter as best I could once we began to move towards the gate that was slowly opening before our eyes. *Julian sure does know what he's doing*, I thought as we galloped out of the city and into the valley that lay between us and the small village of Maycock, which I could just make out in the distance.

At least I hope he does…

*   *   *

We arrived in the village about two hours later, slowing our horses as we passed over the cobblestone road, lined with rows of houses and shops. A light rain began to fall on us, creating a slight sheen on the stone path as we moved through the empty streets. My eyes seemed to grow heavier with each hoof my horse put forward. The adrenaline that had surged through me a couple hours ago completely vanished, allowing my body to take in the feeling of exhaustion.

I forced myself to examine the unique details of the village in order for me to stay awake, noticing how quaint and quiet the small town was. It seemed to be only half the size of a football field, with the buildings all lined up along the road, breaking off into five rows. A small well was placed in the center of the village, just outside of an inn where the only source of sound seemed to come from. I could hear muffled laughter and chatter the closer we got to the brick building. It was the tallest of all – besides the mill a block down from it – and had a small stable attached to the east wing. Something about the village reminded me of a Western movie. All it seemed to be missing were a couple tumbleweeds and some cowboys riding around, spitting tobacco onto the street.

Julian got off his horse in front of the inn, his armour clanging as he did so. He passed the reins to Alexamian, who had walked up beside him while I was falling behind, marvelling at the small town. I watched as Julian moved towards the entrance of the inn, giving the door a loud knock. It took some time and a bit more knocking before someone finally opened the door. A man waddled out onto the front porch, his white shirt unbuttoned down to his mid-chest. I scrunched up my nose at the stench that accompanied him. Even standing a good five feet away I could smell the alcohol that seemed to be soaked into his clothing.

"Ah! My Lord Prince Julian, Son of the Lightning Man, heir to the throne of Lorien! It is always an honour to stand in your presence," the man said, slurring his words and giving Julian a dramatic bow.

"Hello, Mozko," Julian responded flatly, despite the small smile tugging at the corners of his lips.

"It has been quite some time since I've seen you walking through these doors," the man – Mozko – said, stumbling over his feet in an attempt to lean coolly against the beam beside him. Julian reached out to help stand him up but Mozko quickly caught his balance, placing a hand on the beam and giving Julian a smile.

"Yes, it has. About two years," Julian said. I quickly did the math in my head, recognizing that it had been about two years since Liana's death. Had Julian resorted to drinking away his sorrows that day?

Suddenly Mozko's grin faded, his eyes clouding over with memory. He gave Julian a slight nod, confirming my previous thoughts. It wasn't long before his smile returned, lighting up his face, "Have you returned to join in our celebration?"

"Celebration?" Julian asked.

Mozko let out a loud laugh, slapping Julian hard on the back as if thinking he was playing dumb with him. Julian just looked to Mozko with a frown and then to Alexamian who was snickering at Julian's drunk friend.

"For your wedding, of course!" Mozko beamed. "My sister tells me you two are to get married within the next month! I decided to honour that glorious day, seeing as she is in town and all."

"Talia's here?" I asked the knight at my side.

"Indeed," he nodded, "She arrived about a day ago, not long before the morbiens attacked. King Wallace sent many people over to reduce Mitus' current population. I suppose Sir Julian thought his fiancée would be safer here, with her brother."

The knight and I slowly turned our heads towards Mozko who had begun laughing again for no apparent reason. *Julian left his wife-to-be with that?* I thought, looking to Julian who seemed to be wondering the same thing as he began shaking his head and rubbing his temple while Mozko stumbled over once more.

"Mozko, could you get the innkeeper for us?" Julian asked once his friend had calmed his laughter. "My knights and I have great need to stay here this night."

"You *and* your knights? Or just you?" Mozko chuckled, wagging his eyebrows.

"Moz, please, just go along and fetch the innkeeper?" Julian sighed, growing even more impatient with his friend.

"Yes, yes, he will be with you in a moment," Mozko muttered as he turned to re-enter the inn, clearly disappointed in Julian's solemn mood.

Sure enough, the innkeeper emerged from the inn only a minute or two after Mozko left. The man was tall and lanky, dressed in a black tunic covered by a long tattered coat that reached the top folds of his boots. He placed a thin, bony hand across his chest and bowed lowly to Julian. The innkeeper turned to us next, staring at us with his glasslike eyes. I felt a shiver down my spine as he continued to look at us, seeming to always shift his gaze back towards me.

"Good evening," Julian greeted, forcing the creepy man to drag his eyes away from me.

"It is, My Lord. To what do I owe this great pleasure of your company?" the innkeeper asked, sounding so sophisticated. Probably too sophisticated for working at a shabby inn and wearing such tattered clothing.

"We wish to spend the night," Julian responded after a short moment of hesitation, obviously feeling uneasy about this man just as much as I was. He reached into his pocket as he continued to speak, taking out a small bag of coins and placing it in the innkeeper's hand, "It would be most appreciated if our stay was kept secret."

The innkeeper brought the bag of coins to his ear, shaking it. His eyes lit up a bit at the sound of the coins, obviously surprised by the amount of cash that had been handed to him. That look didn't last long. He turned back towards Julian, frowning, "As you wish, your majesty, but I charge extra for housing creatures that are not aprimorads."

My heart pounded as his eyes rested on me once more, forcing another shiver to run through my limbs. Julian looked to me for only a split second before edging out in front of the innkeeper, trying to block me from his view, "We are all aprimorads, all citizens of Lorien."

"You cannot hide her scent from me, Prince Julian," the Innkeeper smirked, pointing a knobby finger in my direction. "Besides, I always thought that it was only dryads who allowed their women to take up arms."

Julian was silent for a moment, standing very still before the innkeeper. I could see the corners of his lips twitching in the light that flowed out from the inn behind him, making me wonder if it was a sly grin he was attempting to hold back. I had the sudden urge to run away, charge out of the village on my horse and onward to the Dia Mountains. Was it really necessary for us to stay here?

My ribs responded to that question almost instantly. A sudden ache began to shoot up my side, making me groan and hunch over my horse. The knight beside me reached out, placing a warm hand on my back as the pain continued to grow. It had been awhile since I had taken any Umbedium. The medicine worked miracles, but it fixed something such as broken bones a lot slower than the bruise I once had on my arm.

"You will house us immediately, sir, by the orders of King Jordan Wallace, ruler of the kingdom of Lorien of which you are a citizen," Julian demanded, yet again using his 'I-hold-all-power-over-you' tone. I lifted my head to see him take a step even closer to the innkeeper, whose pointed nose was almost brushing against the bridge of Julian's.

The innkeeper stood very still for some time, seeming reluctant to follow along with Julian's orders, but eventually doing so anyway. He dropped Julian's stare and bowed to his prince again, "Please accept my apology, Prince Julian. It has been a long time since the King and his royal family have ventured into this part of the country. In that time, it seems I have forgotten where I stand in comparison to you. It is not my place to refuse your wishes, especially those of your father."

A small voice at the back of my mind chuckled at his apology. Even with his head bowed in respect he didn't seem one hundred percent sincere about what he was saying. Something was off about him, something that even made my horse restless.

"You are forgiven," Julian responded, pulling five silver coins out of his pocket, but the Innkeeper shook his head, refusing the offer.

"Keep your treasure," he said, shaking his head. "I do not deserve your extra coin. You may still have your room and your stay shall be kept a secret."

He flashed all of us a reassuring grin, but it filled me with even more worry. I didn't trust this man nor did I believe the selfless act he was putting on for us. I was grateful though when he ordered two servants to take our horses to the stables for us, relieving me of the pain from riding on horseback for so long. I groaned as I followed Julian onto the porch, my ribs still aching and forcing me into a limp again.

The innkeeper led us into his inn, guiding us towards an empty table surrounded by men who were laughing and speaking louder than they probably imagined they were. Julian and I both dodged a man as he flung his head back, draining the last bit of booze from his cup.

"Here you are," the innkeeper said, gesturing to the table before us, "I shall fetch someone to prepare your room. In the meantime, why not enjoy a few drinks? Maybe a good meal?"

"We shall, thank you," Julian replied. The innkeeper flashed us a crooked smile before turning his back to us and making his way towards a small office at the front of the inn.

"I do not like him," Alexamian grumbled as we all took a seat at our table. I held my side, wincing as I bent to take my place. Julian quickly reached into his pocket and dug out a vial of Umbedium, sliding it across the table to me.

"I don't like this *place*," I added to Alexamian's comment after chugging back my medicine, choking on the strong taste I should have been used to by then, "Do we really have to stay here?"

"Yes, we do," Julian answered sharply. "If we are to have any energy to complete our journey, we must rest. This is the only village between Mitus and the Dia Mountains. The rest of our journey we will be making camp in the woods. This may very well be the best sleep you have in the next two days."

I sighed, knowing he was right. We all did and that was what kept us silent as a waitress delivered food and drinks to our table. Our knight's eyes instantly lit up at the tall cups of ale they were each handed and all took long swigs of it. I turned away, deciding to dig into the bread on my plate, taking little bites and picking at the crust. I didn't feel hungry, not with my whole body being so alert, so sensitive to every little sound around me. Suddenly, I was beginning to see everyone as a threat, especially three men who sat at the back of the inn, dressed in black cloaks with their hoods up. I was glad to have taken mine down, especially with the heat accumulating in the inn, radiating off the bodies of the men surrounding us.

I continued to stare at the group at the back, especially when the innkeeper slipped out of his office and approached them, pulling up a chair to join in their conversation.

"Do you not like this drink M'lady?" Alexamian asked me, gesturing towards my cup that was still filled up to the top. I stared at him a moment before answering with a shake of my head. Now that I was able to actually see his face, I began to recognize him as one of Abias' older brothers. The resemblance between the two was almost shocking. If Alexamian wasn't six foot two with shoulders as wide as two sets of mine, he and Abias would have seemed like twins. They had a similar chiseled jawline and brown curls, which was the one feature all the Wood boys seemed to possess.

My heart suddenly began to long for Abias' company. I regretted not telling him about my journey and about not saying goodbye before I set out. If it were Tyler, I would have gone to great lengths to do both those things, including asking him to come along. Tyler would have been at my side in a heartbeat, not even asking for my permission or waiting for an invite. I knew Abias would have done the same.

Suddenly, I found myself remembering snippets of my conversation with Julian, what he said about his sister's death, about Abias' "part" in it. I could almost hear Julian's voice in my head, knowing exactly what he would say if he could read my thoughts: *Abias would not have stayed at your side. He would have let you run off alone, to wander right into the hands of death, just as he did with Liana.*

I buried these thoughts, refusing to become like Julian and be quick to believe the worst about Abias. Instead I put on a smile – one I hoped would wipe the sudden look of worry off Alexamian's face – and responded to the question he had asked earlier, "No, I don't drink ale. Especially not here," I said, taking yet another look at the innkeeper and the shadowed men that were still seated at the back table, "I think I'd rather keep my brains."

Alexamian shrugged his shoulders and went to take another gulp of his drink when Julian suddenly swiped the cup out of his hands, placing it back on the table, "Olsen gives wise advice, Alexamian. I suggest – in fact, I *command* that you take it. You all need to be sharp and on alert, starting now and until the very end of our journey."

"Yes, My Lord," the knights all grumbled, giving their leader a disappointed expression, but following through with his command anyway and ordering water from a waitress who rushed by.

I looked to Julian as I took a sip from the cup of water that was placed in front of me, noticing that, unlike his knights, he had been ignoring his drink as well as his food. He seemed to be staring off past my shoulder, his jaw tight. I followed his gaze, wondering if there was another suspicious group like the one seated behind him, but instead I found it to be Mozko, standing beside his sister.

Talia stood with her arms crossed over her chest and looking quite flustered as Mozko spoke to her, not even a hint of the smile I had seen on her lips the last time I had seen her. Talia ran a hand through her hair and looked up, her eyes meeting with mine. I turned around immediately, focusing my attention on my food which I was still only taking little bites of.

"My brother speaks of you often, you know," Alexamian said to me. A playful grin lit up his face as he leaned into me, wagging his eyebrows, "In fact, I think he may be slightly in love."

I let out a laugh, giving Alexamian a slight shove, all the while knowing he was just teasing. It reminded me of Uncle Gabe, of how he used to tease Tyler and me about things such as this. I immediately forced all thoughts of my uncle out as my heart began to ache at the memory of him as well. *I can't wait until all of this is over, until I have my answers so I can climb back down that well and see them again.*

At first, I thought Alexamian's smile faded because he could feel my heart slowly growing heavier with worry, but I soon realized the tears that had begun to shine in his eyes were of admiration, not sadness.

"My brother has been through much in the past two years," Alexamian started. He spoke carefully, glancing at Julian every so often as if afraid the subject might make him snap. I gave Alexamian a nod, letting him know I knew about the manticore incident, and allowing him to continue, "Abias used to walk around with a flame of hope burning within him. Even as a child that flame spread like a wildfire onto all who were around him. Since two winters ago, that flame seemed to vanish, burn out. But just when I began to think all hope in my brother returning was lost, you came along. Now that flame seems to be burning within him more than ever. On behalf of my family – and of me – I want to thank you for that."

I flushed, answering with a nervous laugh, "I didn't do much. All I did was climb out of a well."

"And I have thanked you every day since," Alexamian beamed.

I returned his smile, feeling myself begin to blush even more.

"I will be back," Julian piped up, suddenly rising from the table. Alexamian and I both turned our attention towards him, neither of us bothering to ask where he was running off to. Julian's cheeks grew red in embarrassment, clearly recognizing that we had all noticed him staring at Talia from our table. Before he turned to go on his way, he gripped my shoulder, giving me a stern look, "No matter what happens, do not leave this group."

I opened my mouth to snap at him, to remind him that I wasn't a child, nor was I one of his knights, but saw better of it, especially when I noticed his eyes flicking over to the group I had been watching over his shoulder.

"I will only be half an hour. I expect to see you all in our room within that time," Julian said to the whole group, releasing his hold on me. We all nodded in agreement, none of us – except for Alexamian and one other knight – making any real promises.

Once Julian left the table to go see his fiancée and deal with her drunk brother, I was immediately looking back to the table the innkeeper once sat at, shocked to find he was no longer there. That none of them were there.

My heart hammered in my chest in sudden fear, but I soon let it pass. They probably went up to their rooms like several other people in the inn were beginning to do. Exhaustion immediately hit me like a wave at that thought. I felt my eyes beginning to grow heavy again and I started to nod off as the knights around the table struck up a conversation. Soon I found I couldn't stay awake any longer and excused myself from the table, ensuring them that I was just going up to our room, and made my way towards the stairs.

I weaved my way through the many tables, ducking my head as I passed Julian and Talia, and made my way up the steps. One of the employees guided me towards our room, handing me the key to unlock our door and bidding me a goodnight. Tiredly, I began to unlock it. As I fumbled with the keys in my weariness, I felt a cool breeze wash over me. Looking up, I discovered a set of double doors at the end of the hall flung wide open, allowing the cool air to fill the tavern.

There was a figure, a shadow that I could only just make out against the dark sky they were staring off into. Soon, I began to recognize the person, taking in his tall, slim figure and long arms that were stretched out across the railing. I continued to stare, finding that I was unable to pull away and also afraid to. Slowly, the innkeeper began to turn his head – as if he could sense me watching – and his glasslike eyes landed on me. I hoped that he hadn't seen me, that I was too far back for him to recognize my face, but I knew what a foolish hope that was. He was an aprimorad, one who seemed to see and hear better than the average.

I pulled the keys out of the lock immediately and turned with my head down in hopes I could make my way back to the group – all the while wishing I had forced myself to listen to Julian – but I hadn't even made it three strides. My head bounced off of what felt like a brick wall, but the odor that came off of it was strong, forcing horrible memories of that morbien cutting me open to flash before my eyes. I looked up at what I had bumped into, recognizing it as one of the suspicious men at the back table, but at the same time seeing him for what he really was. *A morbien.*

He was smiling down at me, flashing his rotten teeth, as he raised his chin towards the balcony. Slowly, I turned my head around, watching as the innkeeper turned to face me fully, leaning up against the wooden railing and folding his hands out in front of him. He wanted me to come to him. The look was written all over his face as if he had taken a permanent marker and drawn the words on his forehead.

"Move," the morbien hissed into my ear. I jumped slightly, startled by his words and the heat of his breath that blew across my neck as he spoke. I felt something tight wrap around my wrist and soon began to realize – as I dragged my feet towards the balcony – that it was the morbien's large hand clamped around me. He held my arms in place behind my back until I reached the doors at the end of the hall and the outdoor breeze was blowing against my face. He gave me a bit of a shove, forcing me to step out into the dark night. Then I heard the sickening sound of the balcony doors slamming shut and the click of the lock.

Panic surged through me, making my heart pound so hard that I could hear the quick *thump-thump* sound ringing in my ears. I looked back at the closed balcony doors worriedly, wanting more than anything to break them down, but found that all I could do was remain still. The innkeeper's stare had chilled me to the core, forcing me to remain frozen in fear.

He suddenly began to speak, breaking the eerie silence between us, and sending even more ice through my veins, "Good evening, Carter Olsen."

CHAPTER 11

THE FEARED ONE'S BANE

"Carter Leanne Olsen, the *human*." He didn't speak the word with disgust, instead he spoke as if it was foreign, marvelling at each syllable and sound. "Long has Elssador waited upon your arrival. Long, long have we waited indeed."

He shook his head, arms stretched wide as he looked me over, still smiling, flashing his yellow teeth. I shuddered, not just at the sight of his rotting teeth, but at the words he said before. *How does he know my name?*

"He has been expecting you, Carter Olsen, since the dawn of time, since the first age of this realm," the innkeeper said. "Legend says you bring hope with you, unity, which will chase off the Raging Storm, destroy the Ancient Evil who will one day rise."

I stared at him blankly, my mouth half open in bewilderment. Each word he spoke forced more and more questions to arise. My head pounded with confusion as he continued to speak, not bothering to question my silence. He probably thought I had become weak kneed in his presence, when really I just felt lost. The only thing I wished for at that moment was for someone who understood his words to be at my side, explaining everything to me.

"He understands the deep magic of this world, Carter Olsen. He can wield it. Yet here you stand, the Feared One's bane, with not even an ounce of fear within your bones," the innkeeper continued, now standing so close that I could smell him. The odor made me want to retch over the side of the balcony, especially when another memory of that morbien slicing my throat open leapt into my mind. Just like the morbiens, the scent of blood and sweat seemed to be soaked into his pores.

He works with them, I thought suddenly as Mortimer's words once again began to haunt my memory. His suspicion about traitors amongst his people seemed to be correct. This aprimorad was in allegiance with the morbiens. Did that mean it was his fault for the attacks? Was he the one who was hunting me?

"I know this all may seem so puzzling to you," the innkeeper said, his brows creasing in false sympathy, "but you will soon understand, my dear. Soon you will come face to face with Him and you will know of what I speak."

I had a feeling the *Him* he spoke of was not the Wanderer, the man I was heading out to see. Something about the way he said the word made me shudder and the wind seemed to pick up around me, blowing loose strands of my braid across my face. It also sounded as if the innkeeper was just a part of a bigger whole, like he was the rod and this other man he spoke of was the fisher. Either way, someone was after my blood and this man seemed to hold all the answers.

"What do you want from me?" I managed to say.

The innkeeper raised his brows, moving closer to me with a wicked smile still spread across his face. Suddenly, he reached for my hand and began to rub my knuckles with his bony thumb, "So the Lionheart speaks. The question is, what must I do to make her roar?"

I shivered, not wanting to know even a little bit about what that was supposed to mean. I tried to yank my hand out of his grasp, but his grip tightened, practically crushing all the bones in my hand. The palate of blood drowned my taste buds as I bit down on my tongue, forcing back a cry of pain. The innkeeper's sickening smile grew wider, the same enjoyment I had seen gleam in that morbien's eyes shining in his.

"Why are you after me? What do you want?" I repeated, using a tone that was much stronger than what I was beginning to feel.

"Why what runs through your veins of course," the Innkeeper beamed, pulling me even closer, allowing me to get a whiff of his rotten, hot breath, "your *blood.*"

That was when I struggled even more, stomping my foot down hard on his and attempting to make a run for it, but he grabbed me by the belt, pulling me back to where I stood a second before. He looped his claw-like fingers through the gap between the leather and my tunic, his hand hovering over my dagger.

I quickly grabbed his hand, twisting his finger back until he winced, loosening his hold on me, and drew my dagger. I slashed the blade in his direction, just nicking his jaw. He stumbled back, wiping the blood away with the back of his hand and drew his own weapon from inside his coat pocket. A whip, with sharp metal spikes running along it. He allowed it to uncoil and raised it with a sneer, about to strike when suddenly someone leapt out of the shadows. They grabbed onto the back of the innkeeper's coat, pulling him down onto the ground. His whip caught around my boot and – despite the pain of his fall – he pulled. I yelped as I slid down onto the ground, feeling my dagger fall out of my grasp, hearing it skitter away across the balcony. I immediately sat up on my elbows, watching as the person who saved me wrestled with the innkeeper, raising his weapon – a trident of sorts – and stabbing it down on the innkeeper's head.

The innkeeper was quick to move out of the way as the three pronged weapon crashed down beside his head. I continued to watch in shock as the innkeeper brought his fist to his opponent's jaw, knocking him backwards until his hood flipped off his head, revealing to me who my rescuer was.

"*Abias?*" I muttered as he fell to the ground, the innkeeper rising behind him. He looked to me for only a split second before jumping to his feet to kick the innkeeper back against the wooden railing, anger and focus gleaming in his grey eyes.

The innkeeper caught himself on the balcony and grabbed two knives from his coat, "*You,*" he growled before advancing toward Abias, slashing his knives in the direction of his neck. Abias quickly raised his pitchfork and blocked the Innkeeper's strike, once again shoving him against the railing. I expected the innkeeper to tumble off, but he again was able to balance, still managing to hold tightly onto his knives.

Before the innkeeper could even raise his hand to throw his blades, Abias had swung his pitchfork towards his head, striking him right across his face with the end of his weapon. The Innkeeper's eyes rolled back and he slid down to his knees, slumping over on the ground.

Silence fell upon us as we stared at the innkeeper, knocked out unconscious. Only a trickle of blood slid down his face from where Abias struck him. Something at the back of my mind hoped he was dead, but another part wished he wasn't, for Abias' sake. If the innkeeper was dead, then he would have to live the guilt of murder. But the way Abias let his weapon drop to the ground and turned to me, a look of worry plastered across his bruised face, indicated that he wasn't even a little bit phased by what he had just done. All he seemed to be able to think about was me and my safety, reminding me of my father and the deer. Abias was as calm as my dad had been when he drove his knife into the deer's flesh, digging out the arrow he had pierced it with.

"Carter," Abias said, rushing towards me. I could sense him kneeling down at my side, but all I seemed to be able to stare at was the innkeeper, torn between wanting him to be dead and hoping Abias hadn't murdered him. "Carter, are you hurt? Are you alright?"

I gave him a nod, afraid that if I spoke I would cry. The innkeeper had assumed wrong, I was afraid and only then did that fear begin to take hold of me. I absentmindedly allowed Abias to help me get up off the ground and stand steadily on my feet.

"You should not have come out here alone," Abias warned, sounding like Julian. I fought the urge to roll my eyes. "He was going to kill you."

"What are you doing here?" I exclaimed once I had broken out of my trance. I pushed away the hands he rested on my shoulders, wanting a full answer before I thanked him for saving my life. If Abias was here, if he followed us, that meant he knew about my journey. That meant someone told him and it sure wasn't me. "How did you know to follow us?"

"My brother told my family he was leaving us for a few days. When we tried to pry for more information he said he could not speak of it. So I followed him to the stables that night and when I heard your voice..." he trailed off for a moment, seeming to only be able to bite his lip and shake his head.

"I know you want to protect me, Abias, and I'm thankful for that," I replied, reaching out to him –but then at the sight of the innkeeper's limp body, thinking better of it. I was slightly afraid of Abias, still shocked by what he had just done. "But when Julian finds out you're here, he'll kill you. No one but he, Mortimer, King Wallace, and the six knights he brought with us are supposed to know about this journey, and traitors such as the innkeeper are the reason why," I pointed towards his body and Abias turned to look, but I couldn't. I glued my eyes to Abias, knowing that if I took one more look at the body I would fall back down to the ground.

"They are after you," Abias answered after a long pause, his eyes still transfixed on the innkeeper. "The morbiens and, most importantly, their masters."

My reason for staring at him became less out of fear and more out of curiosity. Last I checked, no one really knew if the morbiens had a master or not. The first attack made it seem as if they were just animals, beasts, who lived off murder and chaos. But the attack after, the one on Mitus... I suppose it brought suspicion to the people of Lorien, and this innkeeper proved that suspicion to be true. I wasn't being hunted by morbiens, I was being hunted by aprimorads.

Abias turned to me then, giving me a knowing look as if he too could sense what I was thinking, or perhaps he hoped I was thinking the same as he. After a short moment of staring, of a shared fear beginning to settle in our hearts, Abias opened his mouth to speak, but his words turned into a cry of pain as a knife came whizzing by, slashing across his arm. I ducked as the knife continued towards my head and heard the blade stick into the balcony rail behind me.

Abias spun around to find the innkeeper, alive and well, getting up from the ground. He sneered, another knife at the ready in his hand, and Abias' weapon at his feet. Suddenly, I felt something run through my veins, a foreign feeling that seemed to take over my whole body. I found myself reaching for my quiver, yanking my bow and drawing an arrow out of it. I quickly nocked the arrow just as the innkeeper raised his arm to throw the knife, and released the bowstring.

My arrow soared past Abias – just missing his ear by an inch – and sank into the innkeeper's wrist. He screamed into the night sky, his knife falling to the ground as the end of my arrow stuck into the railing behind him. I lowered my bow – with that odd feeling still pulsing through my veins – as Abias approached the innkeeper, grabbing his pitchfork and driving it into his stomach.

My body went numb – drained completely of that adrenaline I felt before – at the sound of Abias' pitchfork meeting the Innkeeper's flesh. His eyes went wide and blood began to drip out of his mouth, onto his clothing. Abias drew his weapon out of him, the blood staining the iron scarlet. The innkeeper looked at me, then up at Abias, and soon went limp, his head falling back against the rail.

CHAPTER 12

THE MARK

"Abias?" Alexamian exclaimed as he and two other knights raced down the hallway towards us. Abias had broken down the balcony door, practically knocking it off of its hinges after he tossed the Innkeeper's body off the side of the building. We were making our way down the hall, heading towards the stairs that would lead us down into the tavern when we pulled up, spotting Alexamian rushing down the hall, his sword drawn.

Abias didn't look at all happy to see his brother, nor did Alexamian seem pleased to find him. He looked furious as he approached his youngest brother, staring down at him, at the blood that stained his clothing and the bruise along his jaw.

"What happened?" Alexamian asked. His anger seemed to dissolve into worry as he continued to stare at the dark red stains on Abias' brown tunic. He waved off the two knights, ordering them to return to our table before cupping his brother's face with one hand to take a better look the bruise on his jawline.

"Let's just say all the bad feelings we had about the innkeeper were true," I informed Alexamian.

"He attacked Carter. I got to him before he could harm her," Abias added.

Alexamian looked from him to me a couple times before finding words to speak, "So it is true. We are being hunted. All Prince Julian did to ensure Carter's safety has failed,"

Alexamian sighed, slumping back against one of the doors along the hallway.

As we all stood still, silently agreeing with Alexamian's words, I remembered the morbien who had stopped me in this hallway, locked me on the balcony with the innkeeper. I began to wonder frantically where he had gone. *Where are the others that were with him?* I was about to warn Abias and Alexamian about them, when Abias began to speak instead. He stood with his hands at his hips, giving Alexamian a hard look, "Alex, he bore the Mark."

Alexamian whipped his head around towards his brother, eyes wide and fearful, "The Mark? Are you certain?"

Abias nodded, allowing for the two of them to fall into a state of silent communication, leaving me in the dark, "What mark?" I asked slowly, "I didn't see a –"

"It was on his left wrist. I saw it when I knocked him out," Abias said to his brother, cutting me off as if he hadn't even heard me speak. It was like they no longer recognized my presence at all.

Alexamian rubbed his lips together, running a hand through his light brown hair, and standing up straighter against the wall, "We should warn Prince Julian. It seems we cannot stay here this night."

I followed behind the two men down the stairs. They stayed a good few feet in front of me, whispering back and forth, every once and awhile looking back at me in hopes that I wasn't able to hear their conversation. I let out an audible sigh of frustration. Just because I was a human didn't mean I was deaf. I was easily able to catch some of the words they exchanged, but – just like their previous conversation – didn't understand what most of it meant.

"Alex, I'm staying," I heard Abias hiss. "I will not leave her, not like I did Liana."

"You are not safe here, Abias," Alexamian whispered back. "Did you know him? The innkeeper? Did he know you?"

"Yes, we knew each other. Not well, but well enough," Abias replied, his voice sounding hollow, drained of all its usual life.

My mind raced for an explanation for Abias' words. *How can he know the innkeeper? Why would he?* I suddenly found myself burying Mortimer's warning again, but no matter how hard I tried to extinguish the thought, it pressed at the back of my mind as Alexamian and Abias continued down the stairs in silence. *You must trust no one you meet on the road. Perhaps even those you think you may already know...*

We soon reached our table, where Julian was standing face to face with the knights Alexamian sent down earlier. He turned his attention to the three of us as we approached, his eyes growing wide with fury. He raised a hand, pointing an angry finger in Abias' direction, "No, absolutely not. He cannot come."

"He saved my life, Julian," I said sternly. "He – like all of you – has made a vow to protect me."

Julian shook his head, seeming only able to repeat his previous words, "He cannot come. Absolutely not. He cannot come..."

"Sire, please," Alexamian piped up, taking a couple steps towards his commander. "He's my brother."

"That means nothing," Julian snapped.

"My lord, it is far too late to refuse his company now. He knows too much of our journey," Alexamian responded calmly. "If he were to be captured, the morbiens would force all he knows out of him. If he returned to Mitus, King Wallace would want to question him. Then you – all of us – would be charged for treason."

Julian just stared at Alexamian with a blank expression, still not at all convinced. Although, I noticed his jaw tighten at the mention of his father, of the fate that would befall him if his father were to find out about our journey. Perhaps the only way to persuade a selfish prince was to turn the situation towards him, to make it personal. I instantly took a step closer to Julian, gripping his wrist and looking around at all the people in the tavern, still sitting and drinking as if their host was still alive, completely unaware that Abias and I had thrown his dead body off a balcony.

"No one is safe here, Julian. Not us, not your people, and not Talia." His eyes lit up at the mention of her name and his brow furrowed in confusion. I quickly explained to him what happened upstairs with the innkeeper and when I reached the part about his death, Julian's eyes widened, seeming as surprised as I was about Abias' ability to fend him off. I wondered if perhaps he felt angry too, maybe even jealous at the thought of Abias trying so hard to protect me, yet all he did was lay still in shock as Liana was killed. But in that moment none of those thoughts mattered to him. My persuasion tactic was working. Julian was about to give in to my demands.

"Prince Julian," Alexamian continued. I could feel him move closer as well, hovering behind me as I continued to stare at Julian, pleading with my eyes for him to agree to let Abias come along. I needed my reminder of Tyler, my small piece of home... "My lord, Abias tells me that the innkeeper bore the Mark," Alexamian said.

Julian paled, his eyes growing even wider than before, "The Mark? But that is impossible. No one has seen the mark for over an age!"

"He had it. I swear on my life," Abias spoke up.

Julian glowered, "I will hold you to that. For if it is a lie, I will personally drive my sword through your heart."

The tension between the two grew unbearably strong and I was thankful when Alexamian placed a gentle hand on Abias' shoulder, diffusing a bit of the rage burning within his brother, "We cannot linger," Alexamian said, looking at Julian.

Julian responded with a curt nod, then gestured towards our table, still glaring at Abias as we all sat around it. As I took my seat across from Julian, between Alexamian and Abias, I scanned the tavern, looking for any sign of the morbiens, but I couldn't find any. I couldn't even trace their scent. It was like they had just left, not bothering to assist the innkeeper if anything were to go wrong. Even as I thought it, I was weary to believe it. They may have been heartless, soulless creatures, but they weren't entirely stupid. They were somewhere, perhaps hiding in the dark shadows of the inn.

I only returned my attention to the group once Julian reached into his pocket, pulling out a map and smoothing it out across the table. Besides the stains and rips on its corners, it was quite beautiful. Thin black lines were drawn all across the parchment, marking the borders of different territories, squiggles outlining rivers, arrow heads indicating mountains, and small castles marking cities. At the bottom left corner of the map was the title, written in neat, cursive handwriting; *The Realm of Elssador*. Julian pointed to a line of mountains drawn down the centre of the map, the tip of his finger soon resting on the southern part of the Dia Mountains, only seeming to be a short distance away from Maycock.

"This is our destination, the Galdia Caves," Julian said. On the map it didn't seem that far, but I knew in reality it was going to be quite a trek.

"How long will it take?" I asked.

"It is about a two-day ride," Julian replied. "But if the Stable Boy is right about the innkeeper having the Mark, then we must try to make the journey in one."

"What's the Mark?" I said, not able to hold the question back any longer. "What does it mean?"

"We do not have time to explain," Julian responded. I stared at him, noticing the sudden change in his tone. It didn't sound nearly as strong as it had moments before, which made me wonder more about the topic. Julian held my gaze for a long moment, sending his feelings of urgency and slight fear into me. I gave him a slow nod of understanding and drew my arms back from the table, allowing them to fall onto my lap as I fiddled with my bracelet.

Soon we had all returned our attention to the map as Julian began to explain our route and the terrain we would be crossing. He then began to discuss provisions, taking stock of how much food we packed, where we could get water, all the necessities needed for the rest of the journey. I lifted my eyes at the sound of more guests entering the inn, but when I looked to see who they were, I froze. My eyes widened at the sight of them, at their gills flaring in and out as the exhaled, the familiar stench they brought in with them...

Discreetly, I turned to look at the back of the inn, finally able to see the three tall figures emerging from the shadows, joining their new morbien friends, whom they probably summoned. I looked back to the ones lingering in the entrance of the inn, staring until the one at the front – who seemed to be even more muscular than the average, with dark leather armour clinging to his arms and legs – met my gaze with his black eyes. I instantly dropped his stare, quickly ducking down under the table before he could register who I was, or rather *what* I was.

"Olsen," Julian hissed. "What in the name of –"

"Prince Julian," I heard Abias whisper, "we have company."

I looked up from my spot under the table, staring up at Abias' watchful eyes which I knew were glued on the morbiens that had just entered the inn. When Julian and the other knights began to reach down under the table to the hilts of their swords, I knew they could now sense who our company was.

Soon I was able to see the morbien's muddy boots from under the table, feeling their heavy strides as their heels met with the floorboards beneath them as they neared our table. The sticky sound of their gills opening and closing filled my ears, making me wonder if perhaps they were tracking me, picking up my human scent. I closed my eyes, held my breath, hoping that the odour all the alcohol being consumed around us and of all the aprimorads occupying the inn would cover up my scent.

But it seemed I was wrong. The three of them stopped right in front of our table and the others I could see were beginning to circle around the room, surrounding us and preparing to pounce at the right moment. To my surprise, the buffer morbien moved even closer to our table. I could hear the wood above me creak, allowing me to confirm that he was in fact leaning against our table. I swallowed hard and closed my eyes tightly. *He saw me. Now he's going to get me. He's going to get me...*

"Well, well, well," the morbien spoke suddenly. I slowly opened my eyes, surprised by how human his voice sounded. The other morbien that spoke to me sounded just like an animal, as did the others as they killed Julian's people. I quickly shoved these memories out of my mind. Now was the worst time for me to dwell on that past, to remember all the people that had been murdered because of me. I almost wanted to jump out from under the table, hand myself over to them so that no more people died, but some force deep within me held me back, practically gluing my hands and knees to the ground so that all I was able to move was my head and eyes.

"You are not welcome here," Julian said in response to his inconclusive greeting. "Your kind are not welcome anywhere."

"The innkeeper is a friend of mine. Or rather, he *was*," the morbien said. A short silence fell upon the group and I could only assume the morbien was staring right at Abias who shifted uncomfortably in his seat. "We found his body behind the inn. It seems you are still capable of your old ways, Abias Wood."

I continued to remain frozen under the table, slowly moving my eyes back towards Abias, wondering what this morbien meant. But the morbien answered my questions almost instantly, making my heart pound with rage.

"Yes, all across the kingdom know this tale well, Wood. The story of how you sat and watched as a beast ripped the flesh off your lover's back," the morbien said bitterly.

What happened next left me with no time to completely register what the morbien had said for Alexamian had jumped up from the table, sword drawn and slashing at the morbiens. I shifted under the table, watching as the morbiens around the room closed in, approaching the knights who met their blades with their own. I looked back at the others, watching as Julian's sword met with morbien flesh, splattering blood onto the floor before me.

The whole table was in a total uproar. The sound of swords clashing echoing throughout the whole tavern, making some of the drunk men cheer and the waitresses run off screaming in terror. I felt a hand on my arm and instantly turned, expecting it to be a morbien, but instead it was Abias, beckoning me forward.

"Come, we have to leave," Abias said. I gave him a nod and took hold of his hand, allowing him to guide me out from under the table and into the middle of a fight between the buff morbien and Alexamian. I yelped as the morbien's sword swung towards my head, but Abias had pulled me down just in time, gripping my hand even tighter and leading me towards the front door.

We dodged the blades of the knights and morbiens, navigated our way around the tables, until we had almost made our way to the entrance, almost out of the inn, and away from the battle raging behind us. But just as we reached the door, standing only at a four-foot distance, a morbien had leapt out in front of us. Abias and I both took a step back in surprise.

The morbien stood tall before the two of us, grinning as he looked me over, licking his pale lips, his black iris' suddenly gleaming red as he held his curved sword at his side. As I stared at the iron, single-edged blade, memories of that morbien pressing all his weight on me, of that blade cold against my neck, tearing my skin… I felt my throat go dry and in an instant I was frozen in my place, unable to move or even react to the morbien advancing towards me.

I felt Abias' body collide with mine, knocking me over onto the ground just as the morbien raised his sword to strike me. Abias met his blade with his pitchfork, holding it there until his strong arms began to shake. Before the morbien's blade could crash down upon him, he brought his foot to meet the morbien's leg, allowing for a sickening *pop* to echo throughout the tavern, followed by the morbien's loud cries. He dropped to the ground, gripping his knee, and Abias took that time to move towards him with his weapon aimed at his chest, but the morbien was up in an instant, parrying Abias' strike and sending him back a couple of steps.

I watched as their battle continued on, still on the ground, unable to move in my state of shock.

"Go!" I heard Abias shouting as he glanced at me between his movements against his opponent, gesturing towards the door and quickly spinning around to block the morbien's blade, which had nearly slit his face. "Run, Carter! Get out of here!"

All of a sudden, I began to feel my body coming back to life and before I knew it, I was moving again, rising from the ground and scrambling towards the door, only glancing over my shoulder once to see Abias run his pitchfork through the morbien's chest. I instantly turned away at the sight of his dark blood splattering across the floor, nearly charging right into the door. I pulled up in front of it and just as I reached out to grasp the handle, someone grabbed my cloak from behind, yanking on my hood and spinning me around to pin me up against the door.

It was the buff morbien, his face all bashed and bloodied from Alexamian's blows. His hold on my arms was strong as he continued to pin me up against the door, smirking as I tried to squirm out of his grasp, trying to break free of him. He began to chuckle coldly, the wound on his cheek opening up more as his lips spread, allowing more blood to trickle down his pale face. I supposed his laughter was to make me fear him, to drain all hope from my body, but all it did was make me angry and with that anger came that strange feeling that came over me when I fought the Innkeeper. It was some sort of adrenaline that made me aware of everything around me, allowing my eyes to capture just about every little detail as I looked around at the inn – Abias assisting another knight in defeating their opponent, the people rushing out of the inn through the back door, Julian jumping up onto the table in order to gain a better position against the morbien he was facing... But it was the buff morbien I had become the most aware of, finding that I was able to clearly see where it was best to strike him, where his weaknesses lay. It were almost as if I was playing a video game, watching as little targets lit up around him, guiding me to where I should attack.

The morbien's laughter seemed to die down, as if he were sensing this sudden awareness, as if he could see my plans for attack brewing within my mind, "You cannot escape me, human girl. You cannot escape your fate. No matter how much –"

Before he could finish his sentence, I brought my foot to his groin and smiled as he released me, stumbling backwards with a loud howl. I slid down the door the moment I was released, but balanced myself on my feet before I fell too far, nocking an arrow and aiming at the morbien's head. He snarled, glaring at me as he got up, recovering from his injuries quicker than I expected. Caught by surprise, I hadn't noticed that he had begun to advance towards me with his sword raised, but when I did, I was quick to re-aim my arrow, pulling back on the string and releasing the arrow so that it flew towards his leg, sinking into his flesh with a sickening sound. It was then that he truly cried out, falling to the ground and grasping the spot where my arrow stuck out of his leg.

The sudden nausea that rose within me as I watched the blood ooze out around his fingers snapped me out of that strange adrenaline, forcing my body back into its shocked, frozen state. *Did I really just do that?*

Suddenly, I became aware of another person stepping towards me. At first I flinched, afraid that it might've been another morbien, but looking to my left, I found it only to be Abias with just a trickle of blood dribbling down his chin from the corner of his mouth. He reached out to my shoulder, giving me that look Tyler always gave me when he was silently asking if I was alright. I felt tears rushing to my eyes and knew that I was far from okay. It wasn't just the memories of my home that forced these tears to sting my eyes, it was because of all the death I had witnessed, the killing. It had all finally begun to catch up with me, making my hands tremble, and my knees suddenly feel weak. In order to keep my tears at bay, I said nothing, only gave him a nod and a weak smile to assure him that I was okay.

I pulled my gaze away from Abias at the sound of a loud growl. Abias and I both instinctively reached for our weapons, expecting it to be another enemy, but we saw that all of them were slumped over on the ground, not a sound coming from their even paler lips. The growl had come from Alexamian as he rose from behind a table, gripping his sword tightly. I stared at his bruised and battered face and then back down to the morbien I wounded, the morbien Alexamian was charging towards. I noticed a vein pulsing in his neck as he stared furiously down at the morbien and brought up his sword to strike it, but before he could do so Julian had rushed to his side, grabbing his arm just as he had begun to lower his blade.

"Stand down," Julian said calmly, although I could see a flame of anger spark in his eyes.

"*Stand down?*" Alexamian bellowed, "Prince Julian, have you gone mad? He tried to kill us! He –"

"I know, Alexamian, but he may be of use to us," Julian responded.

It took Alexamian a few seconds to reluctantly sheath his blade and take a step back, allowing Julian to take his place before the morbien, who still hadn't noticed his arrival. All he seemed to be able to look at was me, even as Julian placed his foot on his shoulder, digging his heel into his side, "I know who you are. You are Trench, the Dark Hand, one of the commanders of the Third Morbien Legion."

The morbien didn't reply or give Julian even a little bit of his attention. All he seemed to be able to do was continue on with his wicked smile and stare at me, his eyes shifting between their dark, pit like-state and the red that brought back memories of the first morbien attack I had experienced.

"My father told me about you," Julian continued, "Seventeen years ago he and his armies drove your forces away, destroying your people's final legion and bringing peace to Elssador. In other words. Trench, you are supposed to be dead."

"And yet here I am," Trench said in reply, finally turning away from me to give Julian his full attention. "King Wallace was able to destroy many of our men, but not all of them. We are creatures born to endure. All your people were able to do that day was chase us into hiding."

"Then why have you come back? Even you would not be so daring," Julian said, his voice losing some of its anger and beginning to drip with the same curiosity that was rising within me.

Trench's eyes shifted back towards my direction and his gaze locked with mine, once more allowing me to shift uncomfortably under his stare, "She is the reason we have returned. She will destroy you all."

Julian suddenly moved forward in a quick motion, grabbing onto Trench's black collar and pulling his ugly face towards his. From where I stood I could only see the back of Julian's head, leaving me to assume that he was glaring down at the morbien, the angry shake in his voice confirming it, "Who sent you? Why are you hunting her?"

Trench grinned, allowing a chuckle to escape his lips as he slowly moved his arm towards the one Julian still had pinned to the ground. He slipped his fingers into his sleeve and pulled it back to reveal a symbol that seemed to be burnt into his skin. It was a thick circle with four lines drawn over it, unevenly placed around the ring. I stared at it for a long moment, not needing all the knights to gasp beside me or Julian to take a nervous step back from Trench to know that it was the Mark.

"An ancient darkness is rising, Prince Julian Wallace," Trench said through cold laughter. As he spoke, a strange sort of smoke began to cloud around him, forcing Julian and our knights to move further back. "A war is coming, one greater than you could even begin to imagine, and she – the human girl – will be the cause of it."

As he spoke his last words, the dark clouds around him grew thicker until we could no longer see him. Eventually even his wicked chuckle had been drowned out by the black smoke circling him. It wasn't long before the smoke began to clear, suddenly beginning to disappear into the air around us. As the smoke faded, I began to see the small pool of dark blood that had come from Trench's leg, but he himself wasn't in sight. It was like he had disappeared along with the smoke, vanishing into the murky substance that seemed to dissolve before our eyes.

We stood very still in silence for a long moment, each of us staring in surprise at the spot where Trench had once lay. I could sense that no one in our group was expecting such an escape as that, no one except Abias. He was the only one who didn't seem shocked by Trench's sudden disappearance. As we all remained still in our bewilderment, he took a step forward, moving towards Julian, who still stood with his back towards me. I felt a lump rise in my throat, knowing that Julian would take Trench's words personally. He would believe every word that morbien had said because he already believed it himself.

It seemed that everywhere I went trouble followed, that death travelled at my side.

As long as I was in Elssador I was dangerous.

"Prince Julian, you know we cannot stay here," Abias said, breaking me free from the dazed state my thoughts had put me in. "They will be back if we stay."

His voice oozed with strength, a strength that seemed to be missing from all the members of our group at that moment. Slowly, Julian turned towards the group as if Abias' words had begun to click inside his mind, snapping him back into action. He stared at the floor and nodded, silently agreeing with Abias.

"He is right," Julian said, sheathing his sword, "We must leave immediately. Zaldun and Abias, head to the stables and prepare the horses."

"Yes sir," Abias and the knight Julian was referring to said in unison before turning around and rushing out the door together.

I stood still, chewing on my lower lip as Julian gave orders to the other knights to stand guard while Alexamian collected everyone's things. Once they had left, Julian turned his attention to me, taking a couple steps forward with his hands on his hips. I could see that suspicion gleaming in his glowing eyes once more, the same mistrust that had filled them the day we met. But there was something else about his expression, something that made me wonder if my conclusion about his believing Trench were true.

"Do you have any knowledge of what Trench spoke of?" Julian asked quietly. When I didn't respond right away he took hold of my forearm, gripping it firmly. "Do you know anything about what he said, Olsen?"

"I have no idea." I shook my head and quickly began to blink back tears that had suddenly begun to sting my eyes. "I don't know anything about a war or an ancient…"

"Shush," Julian hissed, gripping my arm tighter. A strange noise escaped my throat as I swallowed back the rest of my sentence. I looked away from Julian, not able to meet his angry stare. *He believes Trench. He believes every word.* The thought repeated over and over again in my mind. Julian's hold on my wrist became less aggressive and when I turned to look back up at him, his eyes had softened, allowing me to assume that the fear of his believing Trench was true had taken hold of my expression. "Olsen, I do not know if I believe Trench or not. Morbiens are creatures of deceit, they have always had a way of twisting the truth. What I do know, is that our need to see the Wanderer has grown stronger."

I rubbed my lips together, nodding in agreement as Alexamian approached us, handing Julian one of the packs he carried. As I watched this exchange, only one thought seemed to take hold of my mind, pulling me away from the shock and relief that Julian's words brought me: *I should be leaving Elssador, not riding into the very centre of it.* The thought remained present in my mind even as we exited the inn, making our way off the porch and climbing onto our saddles. We began to gallop out of Maycock and towards the row of mountains I could just see in the distance under the moonlight.

CHAPTER 13

DUST & LIGHT

We rode for a whole day after leaving Maycock, only resting when the sun began to set. It was Julian who had forced us to keep moving and only when one of his knights had passed out upon his horse did Julian allow us to rest. I fell right to sleep the moment I lay down on the grass and only awoke when Abias shook me the next morning. The sun had just begun to rise when we all got up, preparing to leave for the Dia Mountains, which I could see even clearer in the distance. There were many of them, all seeming to be fairly tall and thick at the base with only a light bit of snow around their tips. I had never seen mountains before, only in pictures and movies, but they didn't even compare to what I was seeing, didn't even begin to capture their magnificence.

The sun rose higher as we left our camp, making the sky turn all shades of orange and red as we began our journey again. It was a beautiful sight, especially when the light began to shine upon the mountains, lighting up its many cliffs and edges. Staring at the mountains then made me realize how beautiful Elssador truly was, how much it seemed to resemble Earth. A quick thought of those morbiens and the story about the Manticore that devoured Julian's sister buried all those comparisons immediately. Elssador was far more dangerous than Earth, far more horrible than the cards dealt to me there.

The reminder of Earth made me think of Marlee again, and Tyler. At first this reminder filled me with hope, but as we continued to ride towards the mountains, that feeling seemed to slip away. I had been in Elssador for a long time. Even if there were a chance of my getting back to Earth, would there still be a home there for me? By now I could only assume that everyone thought I was dead. It was the thought of Marlee having to wake up to her nightmares alone that made me long for South River even more, that drove my desire to see the Wanderer more, to get my answers so that I could finally return home.

Julian was quiet as we continued towards the mountains, responding to everyone's questions with a nod or a short reply. Alexamian had asked him several times if he was alright and each time Julian assured him that he was fine, but I could see the dark rings around his eyes, the sudden red to them. He hadn't been sleeping. I could only assume that Trench's words were the cause of that, his prophecy about a war that was soon to come. A war that I would begin.

I shuddered at the memory, gripping my reins tighter as I rode beside Abias, behind our group of knights. *How could I be the cause of a war?* I wondered, fiddling with my bracelet once more. I didn't want to be caught in a battle, let alone start one. My mind suddenly raced to what Julian told me before we left Mitus, about how I was a mystery, one that needed solving. The more I got lost in the waves of my thoughts, the more I began to question myself, who I truly was. Was I beginning to see myself the way Julian was? As a puzzle? A dangerous menace?

"Are you alright?" Abias asked me, moving his horse a bit closer to mine.

"Yeah. I'm just tired," I assured him.

"You do not have to lie to me, you know," Abias answered with a small smile. I looked into his grey eyes that were pleading with me to trust him, to be truthful with him. I still trusted Abias, deep down I knew it, but there was also something inside me that resisted him. It was like a constant battle being fought within me, one only the absolute truth could solve. I wasn't the only one lying or keeping secrets. Abias seemed to have many and it was only then that I truly began to take that in.

"Neither do you," I replied. Abias drew back, but didn't seem offended by my words, or my sharp tone. He only looked surprised, as if he hadn't expected me to see right through him. "Julian told me about his sister, Liana."

Abias' eyes clouded over, his mouth forming a grim line, and he suddenly began to find an interest in the leather reins he had wrapped around his hands, "I was wondering how long it would take until someone told you. I suppose you will want nothing to do with me now, then?"

"I didn't say that," I said. I expected my words to force him to look at me, but he didn't move his eyes from his reins. Even so, I was able to see the tears shimmering within them, implying that he didn't believe me. "Julian told me everything, about how all you did was watch as she was being eaten."

Abias began to laugh then, a cold chuckle that cut off my words, making me shiver. The reaction was so unlike him, so different than the Abias I had gotten to know, "He has told the same tale to all, portraying me as a coward, but he does not know the true story, the *full* story. He was not there to see what really happened that night."

"I didn't believe him," I responded calmly, contrasting the angry tone he had suddenly begun to use. "I know you wouldn't have just stood back and watched as someone died, unless there was nothing you could do to help. You've proven yourself to me Abias Wood. You're not a coward. Julian's just saying that because he wants to blame someone for what happened."

"He chose the right person to blame," Abias said, finally looking up at me. I could see the tears in his eyes now, even the stains of previous ones on his cheeks. "I was supposed to watch her, Carter. I was her guard, her protector, and I failed."

"But not on purpose," I replied as Trench's voice slowly began to creep its way into my thoughts: *All across the kingdom know this tale well, Wood. The story of how you sat and watched as a beast ripped the flesh off your lover's back.* It was only then that those words began to sink in and I was allowed a deeper understanding to Julian's hatred towards Abias, why Abias was tearing himself apart. "You loved her, didn't you?"

Abias gave a slow nod of his head and once again turned his attention away from me, "Very much."

"So what happened, then? What *really* happened?"

Abias paused for a moment, seeming to be either swallowing back his tears or hesitant to lose himself to his memory, to allow that awful day to take hold of him. A reminder of how Julian reacted to my questions and the guilt that filled me afterwards almost made me want to tell Abias he didn't have to explain it to me. But he had already begun to speak, "King Wallace ordered me to watch over Liana that night, to stand guard outside her tent. He did not know how Liana and I felt about each other at the time, only that she always seemed to request me as her personal guard.

'That night we snuck off together, not far from the camp. We started a fire and lay down to watch the stars, something I knew she enjoyed doing, but I was aware of the real reason she had wanted to see me that night. There had been talk about the possibility of us running away together, about leaving Lorien and living in the Free Lands, with the others that dwell there. That night she had made up her mind, putting an end to our fantasy. She knew her responsibilities as princess and respected them, even if she did not enjoy attending to them. Liana had always wanted more, wanted to be free from the bonds of royalty. She desired to live simply and running away would have given her that. At the time I was frustrated, angry that she had made me wait so long for an answer, filling me with false hope... As you can imagine, what we intended to be a quiet conversation soon turned into a loud argument, one we knew the knights in the camp could probably hear, as well as anything else lurking within the woods.

'That was when we heard it, a distant roar echoing throughout the forest. Both of us had learned about the beasts of Elssador, created to protect the land from evil forces, but it was only when we raced back to the camp, where we heard screams and shouts – did we recognize the monster as a manticore. At first, the two of us stood still in shock, not just because of the dead knights scattered around the camp, but because we had always known the manticore breed to be dead. Legend states that the last one died out centuries ago, yet there it was, slowly turning towards Liana and me with her mother hanging out the side of its mouth.

'In her rage and fear, Liana took a sword from one of the dead knights before us, charging towards the beast. I called after her, grabbed her, did everything in my power to pull her back, but she would not listen. She lunged at the beast, stabbing it in the paw. The beast roared, dropping the Queen's mutilated body to the ground, and turning to Liana, snapping its teeth at her. I jumped at the beast then, leaping onto its back and avoiding its tail, but it smashed me up against a tree with its paw, forcing my sword into my shoulder.

'That was when I fell to the ground, laying helpless, dazed, and unable to move as King Wallace, Prince Julian, and their knights approached the beast, watching as it ran away into the forest with Liana in its mouth. No screams escaped her lips as the animal carried her away, allowing us to believe that she was dead."

We became quiet as Abias finished his story, his voice cracking at the end of his last sentence. I turned away from him, knowing that he was crying and not wanting the sight to force the tears in my own eyes to fall. Each of us fixed our gazes upon the road ahead, continuing on our way in silence.

* * *

"Faris, Zaldun, and Abias, you three will remain here and guard our horses. The rest of you," Julian ordered, pointing to Alexamian and two other knights, "will follow Olsen and me into the caves."

We were standing in a small patch of forest, beside a river that ran around the mountains we stood beneath. The sun was high in the sky, shining hotly on us and making me want to jump in the river to cool down, but I just stood still, marveling at the mountains, at their high peaks, until Julian made his command. His words snapped me back to reality, forcing me to grit my teeth and glare.

"Abias is coming with us," I said, placing a hand on my hip.

Julian had been standing beside Zaldun when I spoke, removing his saddle bag from his horse and passing it to Alexamian before turning to me, his familiar scowl ever present.

He stared me down as he approached, moving so close to me that I could see the little droplets of sweat glistening on his neck, "I am the one who makes the commands here, Olsen. I thought you were wise enough to know that."

"He's come this far with us, Julian, this far with *me*," I insisted, staring up into his tired eyes. "I don't have any intention of abandoning him now."

"For goodness sake, Olsen, must you be so dramatic?" Julian groaned, "His only job is to tend to the horses! You should be happy that I have not yet sent him home."

I could see Abias give a little roll of his eyes at that last comment before he turned towards the horses, following through with Julian's orders, not even bothering to say anything in his defense. It was almost as if he wished not to come, or knew better than to press his case with Julian, knowing that he would just repudiate all of his requests, just as he seemed to be denying mine. I was almost about to give up on trying to persuade him to allow Abias to tag along, but when Alexamian stepped forward, the same request rolling off his tongue, the need for having Abias at my side grew stronger.

"Prince Julian, please. Abias is not dressed to stand guard and we do not have extra armour to provide for him," Alexamian said, taking a couple of nervous steps towards Julian. "I am asking you as a friend, Prince Julian, that you allow him to come with us. I could not live with myself if something were to happen to him."

I could sense an argument about to escape Julian's lips, but instead he let out a sigh, shaking his head as if he was disappointed in himself for giving into Alexamian's plea, "He may come, but I will not attempt to protect him if something is to go wrong in those mountains."

I was about to snap at Julian, remind him that it was Abias who was able to kill that innkeeper, proving that he was more than capable of protecting himself. But Julian's choice of words forced down any remark I could send his way, "Why would something go wrong?" I asked.

"We are in the Free Lands now, Olsen," Julian replied, as he continued to adjust his armour, preparing to head towards the mountains. "We are no longer under the protection of the four kingdoms. The people of the wild roam free, live by their own laws. We are marching on their land now, on territory where aprimorads may be seen as the least welcome."

I suddenly began to realize why King Wallace had suggested we bring knights with us, as well as the true reason for his wanting Julian to take me on this quest. It was because of these lands, the Free Lands, and the creatures that dwell here. Memories of Marlee speaking about the dryads instantly began to fill my mind, forcing me to linger behind as Julian, Alexamian, and the other two knights moved on ahead. They appeared to be making their way towards the river and began to cross. It was Abias' warm hand on my shoulder that forced me back into action, guiding me towards the others.

"Julian meant the dryads, didn't he. When he spoke of the people in the Free Lands?" I asked Abias. We were catching up with the others, who were beginning to move across the river, carefully stepping onto the many stones spread out across it.

"The Free Folk are made up of more than just dryads," Abias replied after a pause. "They are people who are not placed under magwa rule, people who have been cast out because of their rebellion. Some of them are whole races, but others are individuals, people who have boldly stood against the laws, creating their own outside of the four magwa's protection."

"Why would they want to do that? Without the four magwas, aren't they vulnerable to more attacks?"

"To some extent," Abias replied. "The magwas may be the most powerful creatures in this land, but people who are strong in their beliefs are not afraid to stand up to them. There are some laws that used to cause discomfort amongst the people long ago. That law is the reason the dryads have been cast out, no longer under the laws of the four kingdoms, but free to continue to provide the kingdoms with items of trade if they should like."

"What was the law?" My question seemed to make Abias freeze up, forcing him to swallow down any form of response and continue on ahead towards the river. He stepped to the side, allowing me to take the first step on the stones unevenly placed across the river.

"The one against dryad and aprimorad marriage," Abias answered before I began to cross.

I pulled my foot back from the stone and stared at Abias, cocking my head to the side in confusion, "Don't you guys hate each other?"

A small smile began to form upon Abias' lips, "In this Age we do, but there have been times when our races were allies, strong in our unity. That tight bond is what corrupted that relationship today. There were aprimorads who could not resist the strength and beauty of the dryads, and dryads who could not ignore the same in aprimorads. That law against them marrying became shaky, which, of course, then sparked anger in the four magwas, making them more forceful and ruthless in enforcing it."

"I don't understand," I said, as I finally began to move across the stones after watching Julian gracefully leap down from the last one and land on the other side, the others following suit. "Why would that bother them? Wouldn't they want their people to be united?"

"When a dryad and an aprimorad mate, a magwa is born. The magwa rulers are the last of their kind and they are keen to keep it that way," Abias responded. I could sense him following close behind me as I reached the last stone, stepping off it and onto the grass where Julian and the others were waiting to regroup.

"But wouldn't they not want to be the last of their kind? Don't they want to have others like them? Or at least..."

"Our magwa rulers are pleased to be the last of their race," Julian said, clearly having overheard my whole conversation with Abias. I started up at him, noticing the tightness in his voice and somehow knowing that it wasn't just because I was asking an abundance of questions. "During my father's age, some of the other magwas became obsessed with their power and fell to the darkness. To protect the kingdom, the four magwas made that law against dryad and aprimorad marriage. The less there were who were blessed with such powers, the better. Now, there are several paths that we must take in order to reach the Galdia Caves. I suggest we stop lingering and get moving."

I gritted my teeth and reluctantly did as he ordered, the heat of the sun burning the back of my neck making me long for the shade of the mountains ahead. I followed the trail that our group had created, and making our way towards a narrow gap between two of the mountains, where I could just make out a graveled path. Staring up at the many stones and crumbling edges of the mountains, I nearly tripped into Alexamian who walked in front of me. I caught my balance immediately before Julian turned around to see what the noise was all about. He looked at me over his shoulder for only a second or two before returning his focus to the path ahead.

We moved along the winding road, following behind Julian, who seemed to have a good idea where we were headed. It took us about thirty minutes to arrive at our destination and when we did, I felt the sudden urge to turn around. It wasn't because I was doubting my decision to discover the reason for my arrival in Elssador, but because an eerie feeling had filled my bones when I stared at the massive, dark opening of the Galdia Cave at the end of our trail. I glanced at Abias wearily, wondering if he had the same instinct as well. The sight of his wide grey eyes confirmed my fears, forcing me to swallow the lump I felt rising in my throat.

"Prince Julian, you know the legend behind this place, do you not?" Alexamian whispered to his leader. I was surprised by the shake in his voice, making that unnerving feeling in my body increasingly stronger.

"Of course I know the tales. I have been learning about the history of Elssador my whole life," Julian snapped, arrogantly straightening up his shoulders. I held back a smirk, sensing that perhaps that arrogance was a way to cover up a similar fear rising within the rest of our group.

"Yeah, well some of us haven't," I piped up.

"There are spirits, ghosts of sorts, that dwell here," Julian began to explain with a loud sigh. "They were camping in these mountains, preparing to battle their enemy, the Great Galdia. But he arrived first, destroying all who remained here. The legend states that The Wanderer could not return those who perished to their original form, but he could preserve their spirits, save them as a reminder of a time when dryads and aprimorads fought side by side. Of course now, if the legend is true, it would just be a reminder of the reason why our races refuse to do so in this Age."

"Who's the Great Galdia?" I asked.

"Not *who*, but *what*," Julian responded. "It is a dragon, a creature formed at the beginning of our time. It had been missing for many years. Some believed that it had been captured, others thought it had died. But it returned, striking many villages, even cities. When it discovered that an army was coming to tame it, it crept upon those camping in these mountains, surprising them, and scorching them until none were left alive."

I found myself shivering as Julian spoke, visualizing his tale in my mind as clearly as I had when he told me about his sister and the Manticore. Around me, the other knights began to bow their heads, eyes closed, as if they too were trying to shove these images out of their minds. That, or it was a way of showing their respect for those who had died here, sacrificed themselves.

Abias had suddenly come up beside me, his eyes wide and mouth half open in shock. I followed his line of vision, standing on my tiptoes in attempt to see past Julian's head. Julian's whole body had suddenly straightened, his shoulders pulled back as he too faced the opening of the cave. That was when I noticed it. Dust. Beginning to swirl around in the small clearing before us, just outside of the dark mouth of the cave. I stared as the dust began to somehow collect itself, starting to form and shape itself into images of people. As the dust continued to swirl, rising above the ground, these figures began to appear in greater detail. There were men dressed in armour similar to that of Julian and his knights. Even some women began to appear, each of them with their dark hair either pulled back in a long braid or a pony tail, all of them seeming to carry some form of weapon, preparing to fight. Unlike many of the men, they wore brown leather armour instead of silver, resembling some of the other men beginning to form around them.

I suppose that legend is true then, I thought, still staring at the ghost-like figures appearing around the clearing.

Subconsciously, all of us seemed to reach for our weapons, unsure about what to make of the ghost-like figures. Only when voices began to escape their lips did we draw them, standing at the ready. I quickly nocked an arrow, but didn't raise my bow. We all stood still in surprise at a song these spirits began to sing, a chant which allowed goose bumps to form all along my arms, making me shiver even more.

> *"You have awoken us*
> *Awoken us you have.*
> *From the dust we have risen*
> *From the ashes we all shall rise*
> *We all will fight*
> *We all will fight*
> *We all will fight*
> *Until morning light."*

As more of them began to form – some around the clearing and others upon the ridges above us – the chant grew louder, forcing me to lower my bow even more in shock and curiosity as I began to take in the lyrics. Only when a faint light emerged from the darkness of the cave behind them did their singing die down. My eyes locked on the light that was drawing closer, beginning to fade as it met the light of day. Suddenly, a bare foot appeared from the darkness and a body followed out after it, emerging from the cave and stepping onto the gravel.

It was a woman, resembling the other ghosts assembled before the cave, but this woman's hair was loose, rolling down her shoulders in perfect waves. She wore no armour, but instead was fitted into a plain, green gown, making her forest-coloured eyes stand out even more against her tanned skin. The ghosts surrounding her parted as she moved, creating a clear path towards us.

She came to a stop only a few feet in front of our group, smiling as she slowly turned around to the ghosts behind her, beginning to speak to them in a language I did not understand and I couldn't tell if the others recognized it either, "*Lo! Ez da zure denbora da.*"

The ghosts seemed to glance at one another, some of them smirking, but all of them seeming to question what this woman said. Noticing this, the woman took another step towards them, her voice carrying an even greater strength and confidence than before. "The Wanderer commands it."

It was then that the spirit-like creatures gave her a nod before each of them raised their heads to look up at the clear sky above. A wind began to blow through the clearing, washing over the ghosts until they began to return to the particles of dust from which they had come. I shielded my eyes when some of the dirt lifted off the ground and began to blow against my face as the wind continued to gust. It was almost as if his name, The Wanderer, brought that wind. As if invoking that name was the only way to keep those ghosts down.

Once the wind had subsided, I removed my hand from my eyes and looked to the woman who stood before us with her hands folded in front of her and a smile brightening her dark features. It was hard to believe that she was a ghost. She seemed so solid, so alive, so present that it made me wonder if perhaps she really was dead like the others. There was that glitter of life in her eyes, the same sort of light I had seen in my father's eyes in the dream I had after I had jumped off the tower.

"I am Imogen Telmar, daughter of Lord Eli Telmar," the woman said and, to my surprise, bowed before us. As she lowered her head, I spotted a glittering object upon it, a tiara, marking her as royalty. Abias' short gasp beside me implied that perhaps that was true. There was certainly a look of recognition that had washed over his face at the mention of her name.

"You know her?" I whispered to him.

"All the people of Elssador know the Telmar name well," Abias replied, his voice even quieter than my own. "It is dryad lineage, the name of one of their five tribes, the one that dwells in the Forest of Growth."

I almost questioned the hush of his response, but then bit back my words as Julian began to speak, "We have brought someone who seeks The Wanderer's counsel. She has not come to speak with *dryads*." He spoke the word with such disgust and bitterness that it made me clench my jaw to keep myself from correcting his tone, or reminding him that I was capable of speaking for myself.

"I understand your hatred towards my people, Julian Uriah Wallace," the woman – Imogen – replied, her voice dripping with the kindness that was missing from Julian's response.

"How do you know who I am?" Julian asked, taking a nervous step back and cocking his head to the side as he loosened his hold on his sword in amazement.

"The Wanderer has revealed you to me, just as he has shown me the human girl, Carter Olsen, who has come to see him." Imogen's eyes finally moved away from Julian and rested on me, forcing the other members of our group to turn and stare as well. I began to chew on my bottom lip, uncomfortable with this sudden attention and the silence that followed the stares. Now that I was there, standing before the Wanderer's messenger, I realized that I hadn't rehearsed what I was going to say. The thought made me blush even more, forcing me to latch onto the first question I could think of.

"You – you were sent here by him?" I asked Imogen who responded with a slight nod of her head. More strands of her hair began to fall down her shoulder again, filling me with a sudden feeling of *déjà vu*. I knew deep down that I had seen someone else display a similar action, who had the same type of hair, a similar wide-set nose... But at that moment I couldn't quite figure out who it was she reminded me of.

"The Wanderer has saved me for this moment. He has sent me to lead you to him," Imogen said when I failed to react to her previous response. I immediately snapped out of my thoughts and slowly began to move towards her, pushing through the others until I was standing at Julian's side.

"I was told he's expecting me," I said. "Is that still true?"

Imogen's smile widened, forcing her eyes to grow even smaller. "Yes, he is. He is expecting you both."

It was then that I noticed her eyes darting between Julian and me. I knew for sure he had realized it too when through my peripheral vision noticed him turn to look at me. I looked to him as well, shrugging my shoulders at the puzzled expression he gave me. We both turned our attention back towards Imogen, questions beginning to pour from our mouths. Imogen raised her hand and I suddenly found myself biting my tongue, unable to speak at all, as if some power had forced me to stop.

"You will receive the answers to these questions soon, for only The Wanderer can give them to you. It is not my destiny to provide you with this knowledge. My purpose is just to lead you towards it," Imogen said, taking a step aside and gesturing towards the cave across the clearing, the one I had suddenly begun to feel drawn towards.

Uncertain of what that feeling could mean, I looked to Imogen, who gave me a reassuring smile, making me wonder – once again – who it was she resembled. I felt someone gently brush against my right arm, which made me jump slightly in surprise. Looking up, I spotted Abias, making his way through our group, and towards the cave, smiling at Imogen as he passed.

"Well come on then," Abias said, clearly noticing that we weren't following him. He grinned, turning as he walked backwards towards the cave. "You will not find the answers you seek just by standing around."

Alexamian and I shared a sidelong look as Abias continued to move towards the cave, practically skipping towards the entrance with Imogen following behind him. A look of thankfulness transformed Alexamian's face, allowing for his creased brow to soften and a handsome smile spread across his pinkish lips.

Thank you, I could almost hear him saying in my mind, as he too began to follow after Abias with me close behind.

CHAPTER 14

SINCE THE DAWN
OF TIME

The six of us followed behind Imogen, who led us into the dark cave, the only light guiding us coming from the torches that had suddenly lit the walls around us when we entered. I moved beside Abias as we continued to follow Imogen around another corner of the tunnel. It felt as though we had been walking forever, making me wonder more and more where on earth she was planning on taking us. *More like, 'where in Elssador?'* I thought to myself as we kept moving along the same path, heading for another tunnel straight ahead.

"Where are you leading us?" Julian questioned impatiently from the back of our line.

"To The Wanderer, Prince Julian," Imogen responded, continuing to flash him a kind grin. "Today he lives in the heart of this mountain."

"Today?" I said.

"He is The *Wandering* Spirit. One with such a title is not usually expected to dwell in one place for very long," Imogen answered, turning around to face the next path we were to enter. This time, I noticed a faint light at the end, shining into the tunnel we walked through. I let out a short sigh of relief at the sight of it, but then wondered why I had. The light that was shining through looked as though it was daylight, the bright rays of the sun outside of the walls of this mountain. Did Imogen not say she was bringing us into the heart of it?

"Where is he on other days?" Alexamian piped up.

"I know not. He is a man of mystery," Imogen replied with a shrug. Then she turned slightly, looking at me with a small smile. "Quite like the person who seeks him."

I felt my brows knit together after she spoke, turning back to face the light that was growing brighter in the distance. It wasn't that I was confused by what she said, but rather I was suddenly more curious, especially when I was reminded that King Wallace had said something similar before I started out on this journey.

Eventually, we reached the end of the tunnel, the light beginning to pierce my eyes as we drew closer to another opening at the end of our path. I squinted as I stepped out after Imogen and Abias into the new section of the mountain we were entering. Once my eyes had adjusted to the sudden bright sunshine streaming through the opening in the mountain, I began to see what lay beyond it, my lips parting in amazement at the sight.

I saw grass, lush green grass, acting as a shore for a deep pond of clear blue water that separated the land we were standing on and the one on the far side, where a small hut stood, surrounded by beautiful pine trees and flowerbeds. The sound of chirping birds made me jump in my skin and look to where they flew out of the trees beside us and across the pond towards the hut. The sight allowed me to fully take in the beauty of what I was seeing, forcing the corners of my lips to curve upward into a smile.

The beautiful and impossible sight allowed my past wonderings about this world being a dream slip into my mind, only this time I was hoping that it wasn't. I felt as though I had stepped into yet another world, this time one within a mountain. I gazed up at the cone-shaped ceiling above us, built from the rocky walls of the mountain. There was no sunlight, as I had thought there to be, no ball of fire lighting up the area like I had seen in an adaptation of *Journey to the Centre of the Earth*. It was like the light was just there. Like it just existed.

"This is not written on my map," I heard Julian mutter from the back of the line. I turned, watching as he slowly moved further into the area, glancing down at his map – which I assumed he had unfolded the moment we entered – and then back at the beautiful sight before him. "I do not recall this being written on *any* map."

"That is because no one has ever seen it, nor thought to find it," Imogen replied. "Very few know of its existence. Only those called by The Wanderer are lucky enough to lay eyes upon it, as well as those who stand in supporting them." She smiled towards the two knights, Alexamian, and Abias, giving them an assuring nod of her head.

"So where is The Wanderer, then?" I questioned, suddenly finding myself unable to wait any longer to receive my answers, to uncover the mystery that was myself.

"In there," Imogen said, pointing to the small hut across the waters. I was about to ask how we were to get across when I noticed a white boat docked on the edge of the shore to my right. We all then began to move with Imogen, starting towards the row boat, which seemed a lot smaller than it first appeared to be as we neared it.

"The boat only seats two, therefore only Julian Wallace and Carter Olsen may cross," Imogen said to the others. "You all may wait here for them to return."

I noticed the look of disappointment that crossed Abias' face at those words, but he nodded along with the others anyways. As if sensing his discouragement, Imogen moved towards him, placing a hand on his shoulder. I studied her curiously as her hand rested perfectly on his arm, once again making me wonder if she truly was a ghost.

"Your time to see the Master of the Portal will come, Abias Wood," Imogen said with a sweet smile. "When the time is right, all of you will see him."

"Do what must be done, My Lord," Alexamian said to Julian, who began to seem uneasy about going anywhere without his knights. "We are fine to remain here and await your return."

With a slight nod in reply, Julian began to step into the boat that shifted slightly under his weight. I began to step in after him, grabbing onto his arm for support as I began to lose my balance. I was not a very stable girl in general, but being around aprimorads – who I had realized had exceptional balance – made me seem even clumsier. I tried not to worry too much about the heat that I began to feel around my face and instead focused on the hut across the pond. My senses were tingling, my heart racing with excitement.

I am so close, I thought. *So close to knowing why I was brought here, to knowing my destiny.*

* * *

Julian and I were able to steer the white boat smoothly towards the shore on the other side of the pond. He was the first to get out, effortlessly tying the rope on a short wooden post hammered into the grass. I studied him as he continued to dock our boat, pressing his lips together in concentration. *What does The Wanderer want with him?* I thought, knowing that it was a question that was surly present in Julian's mind. That filled me with a sense of comfort, knowing that perhaps I wasn't exactly the only person who was beginning to view themselves as a puzzle.

Imogen stepped out of the boat next, which forced me to keep these thoughts locked away and focus on getting out of the boat without tipping it. Successfully, I made it out, stepping onto the grass and following behind Imogen, who had started towards the hut. As the three of us moved, the wooden handle on the door began to turn and the door slowly opened, allowing for a figure to step out onto the shore. I knew immediately who this figure was the moment my gaze locked with his silvery-blue cycs. His smooth pale skin, his long silver hair, it all seemed too familiar to me, although I was certain I had never met him before.

The door closed behind the man as he stationed himself just outside of his hut, folding his hands out in front of him. He was silent as we approached, even when Imogen came to a halt before him. All he seemed to be able to do was watch my every move, smiling kindly as he did so.

"My Lord," Imogen greeted, lowering her head into a bow.

"You have done your job well, Lady Imogen," the man spoke, his voice calming, mellifluous, powerful, and hypnotic all at the same time. The sound relaxed my muscles, relieving a bit of the nervousness that I had been feeling about meeting him, about receiving these answers. "Be at peace now, Princess. Be at peace."

Imogen gave the man one last bow before turning back around to face Julian and I, "Goodbye, young warriors. May you be strong, no matter what the future holds."

I found myself lowering my head in response to her kind, yet puzzling, farewell. Out of the corner of my eye, I could see Julian doing the same, bowing as she began to walk back down our path and towards the pond. She stepped onto the blue surface, beginning to walk towards the eastern side of the mountain. A light began to shine off her skin, consuming her as she continued to move across the waters. I watched until the light began to fade, until it was completely extinguished and Imogen was nowhere to be seen.

"Where did she go?" I asked, spinning around to face the tall man who still stood before the door, staring at the spot upon the waters where Imogen once stood.

"To a world far beyond this one," the man replied, his eyes suddenly seeming to fill with longing. "One far beyond your own, Carter Leanne Olsen."

"You are The Wanderer, the Master of the Portal," I said in proclamation, not surprised when he gave a slow nod of his head and confirming my statement with the words, "I am He."

"We have come for answers," Julian started boldly. "Answers to –"

"I know why you have come, just as I knew exactly *when* you would," the Wanderer replied. "I have been waiting for this day for over an age, since the dawn of time."

"But how is that possible?" I blurted out. "How could you have known who we were – who *I* am? I'm not from Elssador."

"I am the Master of the Portal, the Gatekeeper of Worlds," the Wanderer answered without even a bit of arrogance in his matter-of-fact like tone. "My knowledge exceeds the walls of this realm. I was there in the Beginning, when Earth and Elssador were one. I was there when they were divided into separate realms, just as I was there when their stories were written, recorded into the very soils of the lands themselves."

"Stories?" said Julian.

"Indeed, Julian Wallace, stories," the Wanderer replied, finally lowering his hands to his sides. Julian opened his mouth as if to point out that the Wanderer had not actually answered his question, but he seemed to hold it back, clearly noticing that the Wanderer was preparing to lead us into the hut behind him.

"We shall speak more in here," the Wanderer said as he pulled open the door, holding it for us so we could lead the way.

I was the first to step into the quaint hut, to see that it was not all that glorious compared to the one who occupied it. There was a small, perfectly made bed in the far left corner of the one-roomed home, just beside a table with a basket full of fresh fruits. In the centre of the hut was a round, wooden table with three chairs placed around it. Once the Wanderer had entered, he gestured toward the table, indicating that we should take a seat. Julian and I gladly obeyed his request, lowering ourselves into two chairs across from the one he had begun to seat himself on.

My nerves and excitement seemed to return again, making my leg bounce up and down, a gesture that seemed to annoy Julian. He shot me a quick glare before returning his attention to The Wanderer, "Why have you been so eager to see us?"

"It is as I said, Julian. I have been waiting a long, long time," The Wanderer said with a small smile. I almost smiled back, but his words reminded me about what the innkeeper had said, about how he too had been awaiting my arrival. *But why? Why is everyone waiting on me?* I almost asked aloud, but was forced to hold it back as Julian continued on.

"I do not doubt that you were there in the Beginning, sir, but what I do not understand is why you would possibly wait that long to meet a *human*? Did she do something wrong? Is she going to –"

"Everyone has done wrong in their life, Julian Wallace. If I called all who have made mistakes to greet me I would have the population of this world at my doorstep," The Wanderer answered with a laugh. "I wanted to speak to you because you – *both* of you – are a part of something greater than you can even imagine, of something that has been predicted many, many years ago. You two are the key to winning this war."

"A war?!" Julian exclaimed. He seemed as though he was going to jump out of his seat, draw his sword, and ride out to assemble his troops right then and there, but – thankfully – he didn't. I raised my brows, watching him as the memories we both had about Trench's warning all came back us. His body calmed, but when he looked to me to confirm I was remembering the same thing as he, his eyes were as wild as a lion's.

"We've heard a little something about that," I said to the Wanderer, slowly dragging my eyes back towards him. "We were attacked by morbiens on our way here and one of them warned us about some darkness that was rising, about a great war that – that I would begin."

The Wanderer paused, drawing his eyes away from me and rising from his seat. I noticed that his smile had faded, a grim expression forcing his lips into a firm frown, allowing me to fear the worst. He walked towards a small window carved into one of the walls of the hut, standing before it with his back to Julian and me, "This morbien speaks the truth."

My heart began to pound hard in my chest and I could feel my stomach beginning to twist and turn, "But – but, that doesn't make any sense. How could – how can – I can't begin a war when I can't even begin to understand what I would be fighting for!"

"You do not understand now, Carter Olsen, but in time you will discover what you will be called to stand for. But," the Wanderer started, turning back around to face me, "that is not the true meaning of the morbien's words. He is right about you being the cause of a war, but what essential piece of information he – I would assume – purposely left out is that you would not be the one to begin it. You are merely just the one to raise the evil that will."

"Is that supposed to make me feel better?" I said through my teeth, folding my hands together on my lap and digging my nails into my palms, holding myself back from slamming my hand down on the table in frustration. "I don't want any part of this, do you hear me? I'm not going to wake up some evil... thing to destroy thousands of people!"

"You have done nothing of the sort, Carter Olsen, at least not on purpose," The Wanderer responded, his eyes widening, pleading for me to understand what he was beginning to reveal to me. "This evil that is rising, the Ancient Darkness, is returning because *you* have arrived in this realm. He is returning because he knows of your destiny. He was there when the prophecy was made against him, when the coming of his end was predicted."

"*The* Ancient Darkness?" Julian asked quietly. I turned slightly to face him, noticing how pale his cheeks had become. "Do you mean to say that –"

"Yes, Julian. The Dark Diviner is returning." These words seemed to make Julian even more uneasy, they even sent an unsettling feeling though my own stomach, despite the fact I had no idea who or what they were talking about.

"The Dark Diviner?" I questioned, my eyes darting between Julian and The Wanderer's grim expressions.

"He is one of the first beings of Elssador, a powerful wizard who was tempted by the powers of the Portal he and his kin were instructed to protect," The Wanderer explained. "He allowed himself to fall into shadow, to give into that temptation. He used the Portal and travelled to a world beyond the realm of Elssador and of Earth, to a much darker world where he devoted himself completely to the evil in his heart. When he returned to Elssador, the other wizards turned on him when they saw what he had become, banished him to the Oscor Mountains. Legend states that they came together to cast a spell upon him, binding him to those mountains so he could never escape."

"Legend also states that he is dead, that he has been dead for over a thousand years," Julian argued, the colour finally returning to his cheeks.

"A powerful wizard such as he cannot be defeated so easily," The Wanderer replied. "He is immortal, therefore he can defeat age itself."

"You mean to say that he is still there? In those mountains?" Julian said, his voice uncharacteristically quiet.

The Wanderer nodded as he moved back towards his chair, taking a seat across from the two of us, but only seeming to be able to stare at me, "He is in hiding, gathering a mass army together from behind the walls of his prison, awaiting the proper moment to strike."

"But how can he possibly accomplish such a task without leaving the mountains?" Julian asked urgently.

"He is calling upon others; aprimorads, dryads, all the races of Elssador to join with him. Sadly, many have, and it is by their hand that his armies are growing larger and possibly even stronger," The Wanderer explained. "They all have the Mark that morbiens bear inked into their skin, showing that they have been claimed by the Dark Diviner. The Mark is how he binds his soldiers, shows that they no longer belong to themselves, but to him."

I nodded slowly, letting out a quiet sigh of relief as the weight of the question was lifted off my shoulders, but they still slumped forward, still heavy with unanswered inquiries.

"For years no one has seen such a mark except on the morbiens. The fact that it has been seen more than once these past days means all that has just been said is undoubtedly true," Julian mused, his eyes seeming distant as he spoke, his voice coloured with amazement. "The Dark Diviner is truly returning."

"He can be stopped though, right?" I said, looking back and forth between Julian and the Wanderer who leaned back in his chair, rubbing a finger over his upper lip. "Isn't there some other wizard or whatever that can defeat him?"

"The Diviner race became extinct ages ago, all of them destroyed by the Dark Diviner and his servant, Zeth, who died shortly after, destroyed by Elssador's current rulers," The Wanderer replied.

"Then can't *you* just do something about it?" I snapped, feeling my heart beat speed up again as King Wallace's words suddenly began to repeat at the back of my mind, *Maybe you are the one to call upon this evil, but perhaps you are also the one to break it.*

"I have, Carter Olsen," The Wanderer answered, staring at me intently, forcing my throat to go dry. *Perhaps you are also the one to break it.* Could that be what The Wanderer was meaning? Was I brought to Elssador for *this*? To finally put this wizard to rest? I pressed my lips together, trying hard not to laugh out loud at how impossible that was. I was just a human, a teenage girl; there was no way that I was able to destroy a powerful wizard. My internal laughter immediately began to subside as I looked back at The Wanderer, whose brows were raised, his small smile transforming into a frown. "I believe you have received a message, Carter. An object that bears your name."

I swallowed hard and nodded my head, suddenly finding it difficult to speak, especially with both Julian and The Wanderer's intense looks. I reached for my left hand and unclipped the silver bracelet, pulling it out from under the table and placing it on its surface, right before The Wanderer. His lips curved up into a slight smile. I almost thought he was going to reach for it, hold it, and examine it as King Wallace had, but the fact he didn't made me realize that perhaps he already knew what was written on it.

"Those are the Lost Runes," Julian mumbled, reaching out to the bracelet and running a finger over the back. The strange markings I had discovered just before I came to Elssador on the back of the bracelet were just visible from where I sat. "It is a language that has not been learned or used for centuries. It was only ever truly used to mark enchantments."

"That is correct, Prince Julian," The Wanderer responded. "This is the language you speak of. However, those runes are not all they seem to be. An enchantment was certainly used to place Carter's name upon that bracelet, but the runes serve as more than that. They are the message. It is the piece you have been missing to your mystery, Carter Olsen."

I could feel my heartbeat speeding up, but not from excitement. No, it was a different emotion entirely. It was anxiety, fear, "Well what does it say then?" I asked, sensing that perhaps The Wanderer was one of the very few people who could read this lost language.

"It spells the word *help*," The Wanderer revealed, without having to even look at the bracelet. Was it he that placed the enchantment upon it? Could he do that? The weight of The Wanderer's stare seemed to grow heavier as Julian passed the bracelet back to me, but a smile still pressed upon his lips. One that didn't make me want to do the same. Not now that I was beginning to truly see what all of this meant, that he was confirming my fears.

Julian had let a strange noise escape his throat, something between a mix of a laugh and a cough. Before, I would have found the courage to laugh along with him, but after discovering what all of this meant...I found that all I could do was stare back at The Wanderer, hoping that this wasn't true.

"*Her?*" Julian exclaimed, a look of complete surprise crossing his face. "You think that this human girl is the one to destroy the Dark Diviner, the Ancient Evil that has plagued these lands for centuries?"

When he said it like that, I realized even more how ridiculous the conclusion was, but The Wanderer remained firm in his answer, "It is her destiny to kill him, to destroy him, and finish him off once and for all."

"Why?" I asked, my tone coloured with demand, as well as the rising anger I was beginning to feel in my chest. "Why me?"

The Wanderer paused, rubbing his lips together and looking down at his hands. He knew the answer to that question, I was positive he did. But then why was he holding the answer back? Why not tell me? I continued to stare at him until he was finished with his pause, until he lifted his head again and his lips curved upwards into a mysterious grin, "That is something you must figure out for yourselves."

"Yourselves?" Julian and I chorused.

"Indeed. As I have said before, you *both* play a large part in the Dark Diviner's defeat. Carter Olsen may be the one to slay him, but when the Dark Diviner dies his armies will still remain. They will still fight for their master to which they are bound. *That*, Prince Julian, is where you come in," The Wanderer said. I heard Julian gulp beside me, making me wonder if perhaps he knew what The Wanderer was implying, just as I had when he revealed my destiny to me. "Elssador needs a king."

"Elssador already has a king," Julian snapped immediately. "The four magwas have ruled us well for years."

"Their time is ending," The Wanderer replied calmly. "Their duty was to unite the races of Elssador and they accomplished that, but over time their rule spurred more division. Elssador is in need of *one* king. One who will unite her people again and one who will lead them against the Dark Diviner's army."

Julian got up from his chair and began to pace, shaking his head back and forth, "You cannot be serious. You cannot," he muttered, clenching and unclenching his shaking hands.

"I am quite serious," The Wanderer said. "The Dark Diviner's army is greater than any Elssador has ever faced before and we cannot have victory unless you both accept your roles. This cannot be done with just one of you. You must work together in order for this darkness to end."

Julian and I shared a look, our brows raised. I felt like laughing again, knowing that the only thing that would come from Julian and me working together would be disunity and utter chaos.

"We cannot work together," Julian grumbled, voicing my exact thoughts. "I do not trust her and nor do I very much enjoy her company."

"That goes both ways," I piped up, shooting Julian a glare which he didn't seem to notice.

"If this is your way of attempting to change what has been written, then I must inform you that you cannot," The Wanderer answered with a smile. "This is the right path for you and it will come into play no matter how much you try to resist it. This will happen no matter what."

I was beginning to dislike The Wanderer, but more than anything it was the news he revealed to us that I disliked more than anything. Going up against a wizard, working with Julian… it was all mad, all completely ridiculous! But most importantly, it was wrong. I was a human, a being who had not even a lick of magic in her bones. I was an orphan, a broken child who couldn't even watch a deer fall dead to the ground. And yet *I* was the one to kill this dark wizard? My destiny was to become an executioner? *He's made a mistake*, I instantly thought. *He's wrong.* I felt some of my anger begin to dissolve as Julian turned to The Wanderer, the same rage bubbling inside me clear in his wide eyes and flushed cheeks.

"There must be another way, another path to victory," he said sharply. "And I will certainly go searching for it with every bit of strength I have left."

"Then you will be wasting your time, young prince, for there is no other way. Not one that will result in victory," The Wanderer insisted, contrasting the edge in Julian's tone, "Your destinies are entwined, connected. One cannot complete their task without the other. Therefore if one of you strays, it could be the cause of Elssador's destruction. Instead of saving this world you may put it in great peril."

His eyes flickered towards me then and I noticed something strange about them, something that made me wonder if he knew something about me that I did not. His words were obviously meant to be encouraging, but all they made me want to do was scream, they made me want to run as far away from Elssador as possible. I gritted my teeth and stared down at the wooden table as Julian strode towards the window, his jaw clenched as he leaned against the pane.

There is more to your destiny than you know, Carter, I heard The Wanderer say, but noticed that his lips hadn't moved. I shivered once I realized that he was speaking into my mind, fearing that he could read it also. *There is more that I cannot reveal, not yet, but what I can tell you is that together you and Julian will be stronger. He will help you fulfill your role just as much as you will assist him in fulfilling his. It will all happen in ways that you both will least expect.*

"I don't like this," I said aloud, shaking my head. "I don't like any of it."

I know, but it must be done, The Wanderer responded in my mind, reaching for the silver bracelet that was still on the table. He gently took my hand in his and slipping the silver bracelet into my grasp. I almost released it, no longer wanting anything to do with that wretched object, but The Wanderer's grip around my hand tightened, forcing my hold around the bracelet to do so as well. *It must be done, Carter. You will be saving more than you know, more than you can even imagine.*

CHAPTER 15

LET THEM GUIDE YOU

Julian and I had rowed the boat back across the waters in silence, docking it where it had been stationed previously, and meeting up with the others who rushed towards us. All of them were eager to know what The Wanderer was like, wondering aloud if we received the answers we sought, but both Julian and I remained silent, not daring to even look each other in the eye. I watched as he pushed past the others and stalked off towards the entrance we had come through to get here, his knights following silently behind him. I lingered at the shore for a moment, looking back out across the pond at The Wanderer, who I could see standing at the door, waving in my direction.

May the winds of destiny guide you, Carter. Let them guide you, I could hear him speak in my mind. The bracelet clipped around my left wrist seemed to vibrate against my skin when he spoke, forcing me to instantly turn around to the others and follow them back out of the cave.

I walked alongside Abias as we made our way back, the two of us trailing behind the others as we made our way out of the Galdia Cave and into the clearing where those spirits had once stood. I didn't remember if those ghosts had risen again as we passed, nor did I realize how long it took us to reach the river that would lead us back across to the small patch of woods where our knights were waiting for us. My mind was locked on other things, more important topics that continued to make my

189

head spin even more than it did before all my questions were answered.

I kept thinking about what The Wanderer told Julian and me, beginning to realize more and more how impossible that fate was. I knew that most people would kill for a destiny like mine, to be that hero that flies in to save the day, save the world, be praised by all. But I didn't want that. All I wanted to do was to return to that well, to South River so I could see Tyler and Marlee again.

He's mistaken. The Wanderer is wrong. I wasn't capable of killing a wizard, especially one who could defeat the curse of time itself. Even if what The Wanderer said was true and I *was* really the only one who could destroy him, deep down I knew I didn't have the heart to. I didn't *want* to kill the Dark Diviner, no matter how bad he was. Abias had told me once that I had a heart of courage, and my father made me promise that I would be brave, but they didn't know what stirred deep within my heart. What everyone was failing to realize was that I was still the little girl in the woods, trailing behind her protectors as they shot bullets and arrows at animals that ran by. I was still the little girl who ran away from her dad for shooting down a deer, still the girl who feared death.

If I hadn't been so upset then, so angry, I probably would have chuckled at the irony of the situation. Me, the human who is destined to be an executioner, who has the blood of Elssador's people covering her already dripping hands, is afraid of death?

The Wanderer is wrong, I assured myself, repeating the statement over and over again. They allowed encouragement to settle in my heart and began to calm my mind, but at the same time the words felt empty, useless. They felt like lies.

"You and Prince Julian are quiet," Abias said to me as we walked, only drawing half of my attention away from my deep thoughts, "and grim."

I looked up at him as we made our way towards the river, noticing that his storm-coloured eyes seemed pained, hurt. Perhaps it was because I refused to tell him all that went on within the walls of The Wanderer's hut. *Or maybe it's because he knows that you're seriously considering leaving all of his people alone to die because you're afraid.* I tried to gather enough saliva to swallow before responding and attempted to hold my hot tears of failure at the same time, "We just didn't get the answers we had hoped for. They weren't what we expected."

"Was it something bad?" Abias insisted, obviously understanding that if either Julian or I were to spill the beans about what happened back in the caves, it would be me. Julian was still silent up ahead, still swearing himself to secrecy and giving in to the anger that I was also feeling.

Your destinies are connected, entwined...

I shoved The Wanderer's words out of my mind instantly, then pulled my gaze away from Julian, forcing myself to focus on the ground beneath my feet, "It was in a way, I guess."

"Did it have something to do with The Mark?" Abias asked after a long pause. I jerked my head in his direction, feeling my brows crease together.

"Why would you think that?" I was aware of the sharpness in my tone. I hadn't planned for it to smother each of my words, but his question opened my chest, allowing for some of that internal anger to be revealed.

"I know what The Mark is, Carter," Abias responded, his soft voice contrasting with my hard one. "As do I also know whom such a symbol belongs to. You can trust me, Carter. You do not have to be afraid to tell me what happened in there." He reached out to me then, startling me by grabbing my hand and pulling me closer towards him. He dipped his head, drying to catch my eye as he continued to assure me that I could tell him anything when I knew that this was something I couldn't share with him. Not him, not anyone, "I will understand, Carter. I will understand."

I shifted uncomfortably under his gaze and then slid my hand out from his, "I can't. Not right now, at least. I just need – I need time."

"Oh, I see," Abias replied disappointedly, but he nodded anyway. He remained true to his words. I smiled weakly up at him before turning away and stepping on the first stone that would lead me across the river. We moved along the rocks in silence, one that didn't fill me with comfort, but curiosity. Even after all the times such a feeling deceived me, after knowing that it was because of that burning desire to know everything that got me into this mess, was I seriously still able to allow myself to feel such a thing?

I tried my best to push the feeling away as Abias' silence dragged on, assuring myself that the only reason he had closed his lips was because he was trying hard not to slip on the stones we placed out feet on. That, of course, was a ridiculous conclusion, one almost as unbelievable as my being destined to destroy a powerful wizard. No, Abias seemed silent for another reason, but for one I couldn't quite place my finger on. Was it because he knew something? Did he somehow know that my coming to Elssador had something to do with The Mark? The more his silence lasted, the more I wondered if *I see* was all he really had to say.

I stepped off the last rock and out onto the other side, sensing Abias coming up right behind me. I tried to focus on other things besides The Wanderer's words as we continued to follow the others back to the rest of our group, but they kept cropping up, no matter how much I tried to shove them away. *May the winds of destiny guide you, Carter. Let them guide you.*

"Abias," I said, with no real question to follow. I just needed another thought to latch onto, another topic that would soothe the headache that was pounding at the back of my head. But that plan failed. My life had suddenly become so complex, so dangerous, that I found nothing I could say that would take that headache away, could sooth the pain and fear I was dwelling inside me.

"Yes?" Abias replied, moving up beside me.

"Um...when... when we were back at Maycock," I started, clinging to the first question that slipped into my mind, "after the innkeeper – after we –"

"Yes," Abias said without even a shudder. How was it that he was so calm and content with what he did? How can he live with himself after murdering someone? I buried these thoughts, refusing to voice them.

"I heard what you and your brother said afterwards, about you and the innkeeper," I admitted. "You said that you knew him, but it didn't seem like Alexamian did. Yet you had?"

Abias fell back into his silent state as continued on our way, both of us aware that we had fallen behind. He hurried his pace and I did as well, trying to keep up with his long legs and to understand the strange emotions radiating from him. I had always been good at understanding how people felt, probably because I had felt every single emotion ever to exist within the first ten years of my life. But I couldn't predict this. I couldn't see his emotions clearly. All I was able to recognize was that his cheeks had gone pale and his gaze hard.

"Carter," he started, "before I explain, you have to understand that –"

But he never got the chance to continue with those words, for we had both bumped into the backs of Alexamain and one of the other knights who had accompanied us. I stumbled backward a few steps, but the others hadn't even budged. They were frozen, all four of them looking as if they had just been transformed into statues. The same state seemed to pass onto Abias as he stretched his neck, looking over his brother's broad shoulder, and letting out a quiet gasp at the sight he was seeing. Frustrated by my lack of height, I pushed through the frozen knight and Alexamian, making my way to the front of our group where Julian stood, his golden skin deathly white. I almost foolishly questioned what the holdup was, but the scene I had finally caught sight of glued me still, just as it did the others. All I could do was blink rapidly, hoping that what I was seeing wasn't true.

Blood. Dark pools of it stained the grass beneath our now fallen knights and smeared over the area between. I could just recognize Faris, his once tawny hair stained red by his own blood that oozed out of a wound on his forehead where a single arrow protruded. My gaze shifted towards Zaldun who was only now recognizable because of the broader-looking sword that lay in the palm of his hand. I swallowed back bile as I stared long and hard at the three claw-like slashes across his now pale face, unable to avoid noticing how different those revolting wounds made him look. The other knight lay several meters away from the first two, his body fallen onto the ground face first with an arrow sticking out of his back, the same kind of arrow as the one embedded in Faris' brow.

My knees felt weak as I continued to stare at the knights I had been riding alongside only an hour or two ago, whom I had laughed with at supper at that inn, knights who had protected me even though I had brought death upon their people. Their families, friends, people they had seen in the market might have been murdered in both the attacks the morbiens made on the people of Lorien. The attacks made on me.

"You do not have to look at this," I heard Abias' soft voice in my ear, but I didn't listen – I couldn't. My hand fell over my stomach and I found myself gripping Abias' arm tightly, afraid that if I let go I would fall right over.

"Who did this?" I croaked as I struggled to hold back my tears. The other knights had moved forward, stepping over the puddles of blood in order to move closer to their fallen partners, trying to get closer looks at the damage that had been done. I shivered at the sight of Zaldun's leg, at how torn and twisted it seemed. Thoughts of those morbiens began to leap into my mind, making me stumble over more in fear, but one look at the slashes across Zaldun's face and I knew that even they weren't capable of that. It looked almost as if he had wrestled with a lion. My whole body stilled as I thought back to the Manticore, hoping beyond hope that it wasn't that creature who had done this.

"The Free Folk," Julian announced, responding to my question. His voice was sharp, sharper than I believed it had ever been before, allowing me to come to a simple conclusion about who had done this.

"The dryads?" I exclaimed, suddenly finding the strength to release my hold on Abias and point to the deep wounds across Zaldun's face. "*They* are capable of doing *that*?"

"Yes, Olsen. The dryads are suddenly able to grow claws and attack highly trained knights with their teeth." His sarcasm made me clench my jaw, but I didn't say anything back in reply, didn't argue, because I knew why his cruelty was suddenly being unleashed. He was grieving for his friends, and when Julian grieved, he blamed and found ways to hide his pain, his brokenness. But he can't hide that from me, not while my heart still mirrors his.

"The dryads have allies," Abias began when no one else offered an explanation. "There were once creatures who lived with us in the four kingdoms, but, like the rest of the Free Folk, were driven away by the four magwas. It is the aldaket race, a people who at first glance could pass as aprimorads, but they have the ability to change."

"Change?"

"Yes. They can transform themselves into animals," Abias answered with a nod. "The most common of the race – and the only ones left in existence – are the lycanthropes, werewolves. To survive, they made allies with the dryads, sharing in their goods and serving them in their battle against us."

I looked back at our fallen knights, remembering how bitter Julian had been towards the dyrads, how he seemed to spit the name out as if it were the gross, metallic taste of blood in his mouth. Something told me that this was more than some silly rivalry, that something deeper had happened for these two races to despise each other. I once again found myself studying Julian as he moved over to Faris, closing his ghostly eyes and then reaching for the arrow. I swallowed back the sour taste of vomit in my mouth as he yanked the arrow out of his head, wiping the blood off in a dry patch of grass, and then studying the weapon.

The arrow was beautiful, the silver tip smoothly cut and sharp, the wooden shaft thin, yet quite firm as Julian grasped it in an angry fist. I noticed an engraving of a vine climbing up the shaft, how the design got more intense once it reached the lower sinew, and climbing up to the deep green fletches. I couldn't help but wonder how much work had gone into making such an arrow, how much time and care. Then, I found myself thinking about the dryads, wondering if they truly were as cruel as the act they and their allies had performed upon our knights.

I almost went on to ask why the dryads had attacked in the first place, hoping – and somehow knowing – that it wasn't just because they disliked aprimorads. It was becoming clearer to me that something bigger was happening, something that these five didn't seem to be willing to share. But my mind had quickly wandered onto another thought, one that made my body go cold as the familiar voice of a four-year-old girl found its way into my thoughts. She had told me once about this rivalry, about how this constant battle between them blinded them to the fact that an even greater war was brewing. *The bad man is coming back. A darkness is coming.*

She knew, I thought, my heart racing as the realization hit me. Marlee had known that whole time what was going to happen here, about this rivalry, about the return of the Dark Diviner. Did that mean she knew everything? Did she know more about this rivalry? About my destiny?

"We must move out," I heard Julian say, his command reeling me back to the matter at hand. I looked to him as he slowly rose from his crouch beside Faris. "If we linger, the dryads may return and then we will have to fight a battle none of us have the strength for. The horses had all of our supplies so we must begin tracking them immediately. They are our only chance of making it back to Mitus alive."

"Why did they attack? What was their reason for doing this?" I asked, looking from Julian to Alexamian, Abias, and then back to Julian who continued to refuse to meet my gaze.

"It is as I said, Olsen," he grumbled, tossing the arrow aside in disgust. "We are in the Free Lands, the kingdom of rebels and savages. Our races have despised each other for generations and this is the game we have been playing for years."

"This doesn't feel like a game," I said through my teeth, staring down at the three knights again, at the blood that was I was beginning to believe was shed for nothing. "This feels like war, a *pointless* one."

"They – the dyrads – began this rivalry," Julian spat, his angry stare locking on me. "They initiated it two winters ago when they failed to follow through with the vows our races had made with each other. When they failed to come to our aid when we most needed it. Now, we are enemies and we will always be so."

He ground out his last words and pushed past me, nearly nudging my shoulder in his fury. I slowly turned around to watch him leave, noticing how his shoulders seemed to slump over more as he stalked away from us. I sensed Alexamian come up beside me then and he placed a warm hand on my shoulder, giving me a weak smile.

"I would not go prying into that territory, M'lady," he said before I could even think to question what Julian had said. "We aprimorads despise the dryads, but Prince Julian has more a reason to hate them the most. Those savages might have betrayed the entire aprimorad race long ago, but their betrayal of Prince Julian went far deeper, something that will not be so easy for him to forgive."

And with that, he moved on, releasing his hold on my shoulder and following after Julian and the other two knights. I stayed back with Abias, watching as Alexamian made his way towards his leader, questions still stirring within me.

"What did they do to him?" I asked Abias, my eyes still fixed on Julian. "What did the dryads do to make Julian's hatred burn fiercer than yours?"

"The dyrads were there that night," Abias started with a sigh, his voice dropping to a whisper. "They came the night of the manticore attack. They came to an aprimorads aid, answered their call for help. The dryads were there and they saw what was happening, yet they did nothing. All they did was watch. They broke the oath made between our races, the vow that once united us long ago."

"But why didn't they help? What stopped them?"

"Pride, a desire for power, selfishness," Abias replied. "The curse of imperfection is upon us all. Whether human, dryad, aprimorad, or magwa, we all desire the power to make our own fate, to change and warp the story already written for us. Dryads and aprimorads were destined to be united, to fight for one another instead of against. But our desire to take destiny in our own hands was greater than our longing to accept the things the High Diviner had in store for us."

I listened to him carefully, considering all he had said. I was lost in my thoughts for only a short while before Abias placed a gentle hand on my back, guiding me towards the rest of our group.

CHAPTER 16

I AM WILLING

By nightfall we had convinced Julian to give up on his search for the horses. All of us were exhausted and our stomachs felt as though they were ripping themselves apart. More than once I could hear my stomach growling in the night and more than once Julian snapped at me to shut it up, even though he knew very well that my hunger was something I couldn't control, especially when there was no food in sight. The rest of our group were aware that Julian's snappy behaviour was a result of his weariness and hunger. We all were feeling quite grouchy by the time the sun began to set and were glad when Julian had finally agreed to let us rest for the night. I had let out an audible sigh of relief once I lay down on the grass beside the warm fire, staring up at the sky above, at the white stars that twinkled against the blackish-blue sky.

It had been almost an hour and I was still unable to allow myself to fall asleep. With my stomach continuing to moan in hunger, along with Alexamian's loud snores, and the thoughts of the past day still pressing hard at my mind, I found it impossible to even close my eyes. After a few more minutes of trying to force myself to get some sleep, I gave up and rolled over onto my side, staring past Abias' sleeping body at Julian who was still wide awake. He was seated some feet away from our fire upon a rock, his sword drawn and resting beside him as he stared out into the mass of flat land ahead. He had insisted he take first watch to make sure that Alexamian's monstrous snores didn't attract any unwanted guests. But I knew his reasoning was far deeper than that. He wasn't just staying awake to ensure our safety, he was doing it because – like me – he couldn't fall asleep, not after all we had just learned.

Slowly, I pushed myself up from the ground, quietly stepped over Abias and made my way to Julian. He didn't look up as I approached, nor did he speak. He kept his attention on a stick he held, on the hole in the mud he had created with it. I didn't say anything either, just stood there, hugging myself as a breeze blew over me, forcing even more strands of my blonde hair out of my already messy braid.

"I've been wanting to speak with you," Julian eventually said after his long pause. I probably would've jumped if I hadn't been expecting him to say something like this. We had both been dreading this moment, the moment where we would have to discuss what The Wanderer had said. I swallowed hard and looked down at my muddy boots, rubbing my lips together as the thought of what he wanted to discuss with me brought back the anger the solitude of our mini-campsite had buried.

"I don't think you want to know how I feel about everything he just said," I replied, feeling guilt mix in with my fury, and making my empty stomach suddenly feel a bit sick. "You'll hate me for it."

"I dislike you anyways, Olsen. Hatred towards you is just taking that distaste a couple steps further," he said with a surprisingly light tone. I felt the corners of my mouth curve upward into a smile, despite the horrible events that occurred so recently. The light of the campfire behind us lit up the side of Julian's face, revealing to me that he too found the strength to grin, even to chuckle a bit at his own tease. Even though I was sure we had both wanted this small, happy moment to remain, we couldn't fight the weight that The Wanderer's words had upon us. Our hearts were both too heavy to keep the moment rolling.

"You do not have to tell me how you feel towards The Wanderer's words," Julian said, finally turning to look at me with eyes that were slightly red, swollen, holding all the unspoken hurts that were burning inside him. "I understand that you do not believe what he has revealed to you about your destiny."

The moment he voiced my thoughts I let out a sigh and felt my body lowering to the ground beside him. I leaned up against the rock he sat upon, holding my knees against my chest as I stared out across the dark plain before us, wondering how the world had felt before I learned all that I had. I tried to think of a time when my world was just the small town of South River, but no matter how hard I tried to recall such a moment, I couldn't. Those memories seemed to be lost to me now, gone with the sliver of happiness that I had felt before this new weight was thrust onto my shoulders.

"He's mistaken," I said more to myself than Julian, but he was still all ears anyway, picking up every word that escaped my lips. "The Wanderer's wrong. He's chosen the wrong person for this job, Julian. You and I both know that."

"Perhaps a few hours ago I did," Julian responded, drawing his gaze away from me and staring down at the hole he had created in the mud. "When I was caught in my fury, my frustration. Now, however, that all seems to have changed."

"You can't be serious?" I said, feeling a sudden heat climb up my neck, despite the cool breeze that continued to blow against my skin. "You'd be a fool for believing something like that, that *I* am the one to destroy a powerful wizard."

"I have known about The Wanderer's existence my whole life, Olsen," Julian replied, his voice insistent and tight, matching my own. "My mother spoke of him often and made an effort to teach my sister and me about him since we were young children. If there is one thing I remember most about those tales is that The Wanderer is a man of truth. Each word he speaks is pure, good, and right."

"What are you saying, then? That you believe everything he said? That you're supposed to be a king and I..."

"I am saying that I wish all he said were lies and that I wish it more than you seem to understand. But I cannot find it in me to claim that what he has told us is anything but the truth," Julian answered, glancing up at me once more. I searched his eyes, his expression, trying to find some sort of joke or lie hidden within his gaze, but all I saw was truth. He believed every word The Wanderer said, meaning he also believed I was destined to save his people. *But I can't do it!* A voice at the back of my mind screamed. *I can't kill a wizard!*

"Then what are you suggesting we do?" I said, pressing my nails against my skin in attempt not to shout at him. "Throw some armour on me right now and send me off alone to his lair –"

"You are not alone," Julian cut in with a loud sigh. He dropped the stick he held and slid down off the surface of the rock, sitting down next to me and seeming to look even deeper into my eyes. I blinked, surprised by the strange care that filled his expression, the slight concern that decorated his tone. "If you believed The Wanderer's words just as I do then you would know that. We are in this together, Olsen, which means we either fight alongside one another on the road of our destiny, or try to dig our own paths away from it."

It took a while for his words to register within me, but when they had I felt understanding begin to calm my mind, "Let's just say The Wanderer is correct, just as you believe he is. Assuming everything he said is true, wouldn't that mean there is no other route to take?"

"Perhaps not," Julian replied with an exhausted shrug of his shoulders. "But maybe if we do walk down our own paths it will prolong the inevitable."

"So we run," I concluded with a slow nod of my head. "We run and keep running until we're forced to face our destiny?"

He returned my words with a small nod of his head and looked out at the dark land before us, his sea-green eyes glowing brightly in the darkness. I felt my heart begin to pound loudly as I began to understand more and more what Julian was suggesting, what all of it would mean. Running from our destiny would mean running for our whole lives. It would be a constant battle between the path we walk along and the one that chases us wherever we go. There was more, though, more that The Wanderer said that I was failing to realize was the reason for the tears in Julian's eyes. *There is no other way. Not one that will result in victory. Instead of saving this world you may put it in great peril.* Would Julian be willing to do this? To watch his whole world fall into itself just so he wouldn't have to take up his throne as king?

"Julian, why are you wanting to do this? Why are you refusing a throne you're destined for?" I asked carefully. A reminder of how he reacted to my asking questions about his sister warned me not to try to pry this information out of him. I waited patiently wondering when he would snap, wondering if he was going to ignore my questions, but he did neither. Instead he looked out at the land before us, swallowing hard as if he feared what he was about to admit.

"Because I am afraid," he eventually said. "I fear chasing after that throne because I know that if I do, more damage will be done. The world I know will fall even deeper into the darkness as all that's left of our unity slips away. I would not unite Elssador, instead I would be the cause of a rebellion, one that would lose greatly against the wrath of the four magwas."

I sighed and nodded, feeling the weight of his words as if they were pressing upon my own shoulders. Only when I recognized my own fear in my heart did I see that perhaps it was actually my own burden crushing me, dragging me down. Laughter seemed to want to rise within me as I continued to ponder on mine and Julian's fears. *Well here we are. Elssador's King and Lionheart, allowing their fear to control their next moves.* I shook the thought off as I felt a part of me want to get up and resist such words, to prove them wrong. Instead, I focused on home, on South River, allowing images of both Tyler and Marlee begin to cloud my vision, making me long even more for what my human heart truly desired.

"Would you really do it? Run away?" I said to Julian, breaking our silence. "I'm assuming you know the risk we'll be taking if we do, what will become of your world if we really do run from this."

"I know the consequences," Julian responded. I noticed his chest heaving then, felt his deep breaths brushing across my face even though I sat some distance away from him. "I know what I would lose, but it would be far less than what I would lose if we followed the path The Wanderer has set for us. It is a road

of suffering he's placed us on, Olsen. Th
is if we run in our own directions."

My own breaths began to grow hea
press hard against my chest. For a mom
hesitation, part of me knowing that wh
was wrong. My father always taught n
other's needs before my own. What wou
me now, suggesting something that wa
what he had always taught me to be? I
shaking his head in disappointment, pr
look his selfish daughter in the eye.

Is this really selfish, Carter? I asked
chance to change my mind. *Isn't Mar*
want to return to the Well? Isn't it so y

"I am willing, Olsen," Julian said,
to me. "Are you?"

I responded immediately, taking h
even a moment of hesitation, "I am wi

*   *   *

I woke the next morning with an ac
one that made me feel as though I was
as we began to move out, continuing
be – our endless search for our horses,
behind the others as they continued to
more than anything to snap at Julian
on this ridiculous search. But I didn't.
didn't have the strength to, but becaus
him now. We spent half of the previo
run away, suggesting how best to con
as I continued to follow our group o
of Elssador, that even though we had
plans together, we hadn't figured out
run from the path we were both dest
that we needed to stay as far from or
long as Julian and I were together, tl
our destiny would grow stronger.

The
leading
way w
closer
smoke
it mad
had be
at my
nostrils
the wo
over a I
of conc
"It's
all over
"Pri
Abias s
noticed
sting my
dark sm
I cou
Abias'
his body
pour up
"My
somethi
for me t
the figur
of five
which I
out for.
that the
They
all over
knights
lead hor
to have t
stop, as
hold on

trail that our missing horses left for us seemed to be
us further away from the Dia Mountains and back the
had come. As the minutes passed, we began to draw
nd closer to the village of Maycock. I could see the
rom the chimneys in the distance with such clarity that
me wonder if being in Elssador for as long as I had
un to give me aprimorad vision. I would have laughed
wn joke if an awful stench hadn't suddenly filled my
as we drew closer to the small village. The smell made
ziness in my stomach intensify, forcing me to stumble
t into Abias who caught me swiftly, flashing me a look
rn.

the – the smell," I stuttered, trying so hard not to vomit
him.

ace Julian, do you recognize that scent just as I do?"
id, his voice sounding hoarse. I glanced up at him and
iis eyes were watering. It wasn't until I felt something
own eyes did I realize that his tears were caused by the
ɔke that had drifted towards us from Maycock.

ld see Julian give a grim nod of his head in response to
iestion, but he never turned to face us. He stood still,
facing the small village where the smoke continued to
into the sky.

Lord, look!" Alexamian exclaimed, pointing towards
ig moving towards us in the distance. It took some time
 recognize what it was everyone was gaping at, but as
s began to move closer, I could just make out the shape
orses. My eyes naturally locked on the saddle bags
new contained the food my abdomen continued to cry
almost allowed myself to feel relieved, but the speed
iorses seemed to be galloping at buried those feelings.
were moving so fast that I feared they would run us
r try and pass us. But Alexamian and one of the other
vith us were quick. They grabbed the reigns of the two
es, digging their heels into the ground as if expecting
 wrangle them back, but the horses slowed to a steady
id the other three behind them. Puzzled, I released my
Abias and moved closer to our group, to the horses

who had strange scars along their hides that I knew were not there before. They also seemed restless and it wasn't until I moved past them to where Julian and his other knight stood did I understand why.

A man was being dragged behind them. A rope was tied around his left leg, the other end attached to a horse's saddle. Blood, grime, and grass covered every inch of the man's body, especially from his shoulder where something seemed to protrude. Julian knelt down at the man's side, his hands hovering above his body as if he weren't sure where to begin helping him.

"Cut the ropes, now!" he ordered. Alexamian was quick to follow instructions, immediately doing as his leader bid and cutting the man free from the rope with a swift motion of his blade. The man cried out as his leg flopped down to the ground and tears trickled out the corners of his eyes, creating trails around the dirt and blood that covered his face.

"Who did this to you?" Julian asked.

"They came in the night," the man started to respond, a strange gurgling noise coming from his throat as he spoke, "They came... with torches, pikes... and other weapons that common folk wouldn't recognize. They burned the village... killing everyone in their path. There were no survivors."

The man finished his sentence with a wet cough, allowing blood to shoot out of his mouth, missing Julian by only an inch. Julian and the knight beside him slowly rolled the man over onto his side as he began to choke on the thick, red liquid. I felt my stomach turn, especially when Julian reached towards the collar of the man's shirt, carefully lifting it to reveal the object that was protruding from his shoulder. It was a dagger, one that seemed to be deeply embedded in his body. There was a fresh, red line leading downward from the knife, but blood didn't seem to ooze out of it as much as his other wounds. Noticing the line as well, Julian began to pull off the man's shirt, drawing back a bit in shock once the man's whole upper body was revealed to us.

At first, I thought they were words that had been drawn onto his torso, but once I too took a step back, I recognized that it was a drawing, a drawing of The Mark.

"Morbiens did this," Julian murmured, looking deeply into the man's eyes which held the faint aprimorad glow. "Why? Why did they attack?"

"They were searching for someone... one... one of us. They asked me where he was... I refused to answer," the man explained, coughing again before continuing, "They tortured me until I spoke. When...when I did... they sent me out here... to you... with... with this message."

My initial reaction to this news was that the message was for me, from the morbiens who were reminding me that they still desired my blood. Then I realized he had said the morbiens asked for a *he* not a *she*. So then who was the message for? Was it for Julian? Did the morbiens know of his destiny too?

"Who is this message for, exactly?" Julian asked, voicing the question each member of our group had.

The man looked our group over for a moment, his eyes seeming to linger on me longer than the others, but he never raised an accusing finger towards me, never spoke my name. He just stared, as if taking in who I truly was, the scent of my blood, just as everyone in Elssador who met me had done. Then, his eyes shifted past me, his gaze landing on Abias who was standing very still, his fists clenched at his sides, and a look of recognition in his eyes. The man gave a slight nod and pointed towards Abias.

"H-him. The message –" before the man could continue, he began to gag, allowing more blood to stream out of his wounds. I felt the need to throw up again, but instead of bending over to do so. I turned my back to the man on the ground as he gagged, staring at Abias, who also lowered his head, not wanting to watch this man – who he somehow recognized – die. I found myself remembering the conversation I had overheard him having with Alexamian back at Maycock. Abias knew the innkeeper, he knew this wounded man, yet no one else in our group had. Why was that?

A heavy silence fell upon our group once the wounded man's gagging and wheezing breaths had come to an end. All of us stood still, taking in the wounded man's words and looking to Abias who seemed to be unable to turn away from the man.

His grey eyes were dry, wide, and unreadable. When I glanced down at Julian, I knew immediately that he was on the brink of explosion, but he found the strength to bite back his questions and contain his fury as he leaned over the man. I watched with creased brows as he rolled up the man's left sleeve and wiped off some of the blood and grime that covered the skin there, giving us a clue as to who this man was.

"He... he was one of them?" I said, my eyes darting between The Mark tattooed into his wrist and the one carved into his stomach. "He was part of His army."

"*His* army? Whose army?" one of the knights piped up. I closed my eyes immediately, biting down on my tongue hard. I noticed a strange look of suspicion in his eyes as they darted between Julian and me, making me wonder if he knew we were holding important information back from our group. And we were. Didn't they have the right to know what was coming? What my existence had awoken?

"Trench's," Julian lied lamely. Each one of our group members seemed to look at one another with raised brows, sensing the falseness of Julian's response. I pressed my lips together, holding myself back from saying anything. The last thing I needed was Julian to be upset with me for letting slip information we had promised to keep hidden. As if not being able to handle the tension of his knight's suspecting that he had been lying, Julian turned away to stare down at the man, then knelt down next to him and examined the tattoo of The Mark in more detail. "The true question is, why would the morbiens attack one of their own? If he bears the symbol of their maker, that means he fights with them, just as the innkeeper had. Why would they torture one of their own? Lessen the ranks of their army?"

"Because he is a traitor," Abias spoke up, his voice startlingly empty, drained of all the life his brother had claimed I had restored to it. I stared at him sadly, taking note of the fact that he had captured everyone's full attention, even Julian's. "Once you join the morbien ranks, there is no escape. Once The Mark is printed onto your skin, you are bound to one cause and one army. This is the price one pays for trying to sever that bond. It is what happens to those who betray the Dark Diviner."

I sucked in a breath, staring at Abias in surprise, wondering how he could possibly have known all of that. He returned my stare with a hard look, one that made me realize that he had known what we were hiding that whole time. He knew when I refused to tell him what happened behind the walls of The Wanderer's hut that this was the news we had received. But how? How could he have guessed such a thing when no one else had?

Julian suddenly swore loudly, nearly making me jump out of my skin. I whirled around to face him, noticing that he had shot up from the ground, his skin drained of all the colour it held before. We all immediately began to question what was wrong, wondering if he had realized something we had not. When he looked up at us, I knew what had made him suddenly so grim-faced. The feeling seemed to settle in my body as well when I too began to piece together what he had. I looked to Maycock, at the smoke that continued to billow up into the clear, blue sky above.

There were no survivors.

Everyone who was in Maycock was dead. Each person sent to stay there from Mitus had been murdered. All of them, including Talia Bennet.

CHAPTER 17

THE MAYCOCK EXECUTION

Julian darted towards the nearest horse without a word, quickly pulling his body onto the saddle and shooting off towards Maycock before even completely resting his body on his horse's back. Alexamian followed after him, scrambling onto his brown mare and galloping after his leader at a similar speed. Within moments, the rest of us had done the same, climbing into our saddles and riding out after Julian. I held onto Abias tightly as our steed jerked forward, starting off at a fast gallop with the other two knights trailing closely behind us.

Eventually we caught up with Alexamian and Julian, riding alongside them until we pulled up at the entrance to Maycock. As we moved into the village, our horses slowed, their hooves clicking loudly against the cobblestone road, breaking the eerie silence that loomed over the desolated town. I stared around at the damage in complete shock as Abias helped me down from my horse, looking to the inn we had stayed in to find it burnt down to rubble. Almost all the buildings had been cleared out and demolished. Some of their burnt furniture had even been tossed out into the street. The stench I smelt before was even stronger here, making me topple over, retching all over the road as I realized what that scent was.

It was flesh. Burnt flesh. Bodies of the village people, of the townsfolk from Titus, they were all burnt up to nothing inside that inn. Some bodies from the other demolished buildings were even scattered around the street, their faces unrecognizable even to those who probably knew them. My mind travelled to Mozko, to his cheery smile and then to his sister, whose image was surely the only image Julian was seeing as he lowered himself off his mare, approaching what had once been the inn. He was shaking his head, as if willing himself not to believe she had been buried under all that debris. Part of me wanted to approach him, to comfort him, but the other part of me wanted to continue to vomit all over the street. *What have I done?* I thought, feeling more bile rise up in my throat. *Why did I stay? This would never have happened if I hadn't stayed!*

"Someone is approaching," Alexamian said, breaking through my thoughts and snapping me back into motion. His words did the same for Julian. In an instant he had collected himself, drawing his sword. The others in our group slid off their horses and quickly came to join him, all of us moving together to form a line to watch the figure emerge from the smoke, our weapons at the ready. My grip on my bow tightened as the figure became clearer to me. I recognized him as the morbien I had shot back in the inn, the one I had been intent on killing. The feeling remained the same, especially when he approached us, smiling with two other morbiens coming up close behind him.

"Trench," Julian ground out as the morbien commander and his two minions pulled to a stop about four feet before us.

"Ah, Prince Julian Wallace. Welcome back," Trench responded, gesturing around the broken village surrounding us as if it were one of the most beautiful sights he had ever seen. He seemed to puff his chest out more in pride as he continued to grin at us, increasing the rage I felt towards him. "It is a shame, I suppose, that you and your human friend could cause such a mess."

"We did nothing," Julian growled. "You did this. You and your men took innocent lives! You murdered everyone!"

"Tell me, Prince Julian," Trench said as he took a few strides forward, almost crossing the invisible line that divided us. "Was it really your people that you came here to save? Is it *their* innocent lives that you care so much about? Or were you in search of a particular woman?"

Julian was wise not to answer, but the fearful look in his eyes betrayed the reasoning for his silence. Instead of making it seem as though he didn't know what Trench spoke of, it confirmed all that he said, allowing Trench's wicked smile to widen.

"I must say, Your Royal Highness, I thought it very unlike your kind to leave your woman here and run off with another." His black eyes shifted towards me and a flame of red seemed to pass over them as his gaze narrowed, his smile becoming tighter.

"How do you know her?" Julian demanded, drawing Trench's eye away from me and stealing his unwanted attention. Trench began to smirk as Julian too approached this invisible line, almost standing chest to chest with his enemy. "My fiancée, how do you know her?"

"I have to admit, it was quite an unfortunate meeting on her part," Trench started, purposely steering away from answering Julian's question, "I suppose I can relieve you of some of your pain and assure you that your fiancée was not burnt to the ground along with the inn where I found her."

None of us needed him to go any further in explaining what that meant. He had *found* her, meaning that he was the one to murder her. Tears immediately began to well up in Julian's eyes and his chest began to heave with pain, anger. This news set off a similar feeling inside me also, especially when Trench began to chuckle, a look of pleasure calming his features. My gaze turned even icier than before as his eyes swept over us, clearly enjoying our reactions to this news. He had obviously been expecting us to respond this way, to freeze in shock at what he'd done. The two morbiens at his side even laughed along with him, making my stare turn even colder.

It was only when I noticed that none of them were armed that all of those previous feelings began to slip away, replaced by suspicion… and confusion. All six of us were standing with our weapons drawn, preparing to attack them at any moment, yet they stood with their long arms at their sides. Not even a dagger seemed to be attached to their belts. I continued to look at each of them, trying to understand what was really happening, why they were weaponless, and why they seemed so pleased with themselves when they were clearly outnumbered. If the six of us moved to attack, we could've ended them in seconds. My heartbeat began to thunder in my ears as I realized what was happening, as I finally took in what Trench and his men truly were. A distraction.

"You see, Prince Julian," Trench continued, licking his thin, pale lips. He was savouring this moment, eating up the grief and terror that swept over Julian, which left him frozen in his place. He was unable to swing his sword at his enemy even though I was certain he wanted to. He was just in too much pain, too much shock to even blink back the tears that began to fall from his eyes. "I found her in the inn, sleeping in a room alone. You were foolish to leave such a beautiful creature lying around unguarded. Some men just cannot resist the temptation…"

Before he could speak another word, I released my arrow. It flew right towards his head, just nicking the top of his ear, allowing a small trickle of blood to drip down. He didn't jump back in fear, I hadn't expected him too. But his eyes were filled with astonishment as he looked me over, glancing at my arrow, my bow, and then back up at me, his eyes like flames. The other two behind him seemed less smug than they had before. Instead they looked worried. Did they not think that one of us would suspect something?

"You're lying," I hissed, glaring at Trench. My voice sounded strange in my own ears, strong, authoritative. It was a tone Julian would have used, the same one that allowed everyone below his rank to understand where they stood in comparison to him. Trench seemed slightly taken aback by my accusation, but my group looked proud, relieved that one of us was able to break free of their shock in time to understand what was really happening. "Talia's not dead, you're just using that lie to immobilize us, to shock us so that you can take us down in our fear. You want me, my blood. That's why you burnt this village to the ground, to lead me back here."

"That was part of the plan, yes, but there are other members of this group whose blood our master also desires," Trench responded, his eyes seeming to shift towards Abias who stood at my side. Before I could question it, his gaze had locked on me once more, making the hairs on the back of my neck stand at attention. "Blood that our captain will spill on our master's behalf."

"Your captain?" Julian asked, snapping out of his shocked state almost immediately. "You mean you did not lead this attack? Or the others before it?"

Trench silenced himself, staring down at Julian with a wicked smirk. Eventually he looked beyond our group, staring past us at someone else. Slowly, we turned around to see who it was he was staring at. I felt my heart stop the moment I laid eyes on the person, my jaw dropping open in shock as I looked him over. I would have recognized those reptile-green eyes anywhere, that slick, black hair that now seemed greasier than it had when I first met him. Then there was the woman at his feet, Talia, who wore only a torn nightgown, stained with blood that still trickled down from her nose, mixing with the tears that had washed her cheeks clean.

"Mortimer?" Julian asked incredulously, moving away from Trench and approaching the man who had Talia's hair wrapped around his hands. "What is this? What is going on?"

"Prince Julian, I do hope you are liking my wedding present," Mortimer replied, pulling harder on Talia's hair until the skin around her scalp pulled back. She whimpered and more tears spilled from her eyes, which were locked on Julian. But all he could see was Mortimer, his father's steward, the man who he had known his whole childhood, the man who promised to protect the Wallace family until his last breath.

"I don't understand," Julian said, shaking his head as if trying to snap himself out of a dream. "You did all of this?"

"Well, I had some help, of course, from my morbien legion. Even this wench's brother has shown himself to be quite useful," Mortimer said, gesturing to Talia. Julian paled even more at these words, his fists tightening at his sides as Mozko shyly emerged from one of the buildings that were still standing. A frown now replaced the charming grin that had once brightened his face. His eyes, which had once been glistening with drunkenness,

213

were now empty, darkened by who he had become. He stood beside Mortimer and lifted up his shirt, revealing the Mark, which was tattooed onto his hip.

"Moz..." Talia sobbed, shaking her head.

"Silence," Mortimer growled, once again yanking her hair. She yelped in pain, closing her eyes and allowing more tears to stream down her face. I looked to Julian, who finally began to take in the condition of his fiancée, at the injuries that had been inflicted on her. "You know, Prince Julian, I am quite surprised that neither you nor Lady Olsen picked up on this. I had, after all, given so many hints."

You must trust no one you meet on the road. Perhaps even those you think you may already know. Those were his exact words, the warning that I had been using throughout this whole journey to help me reach The Wanderer. The warning that even crept up on me when I had seen Abias fight off the innkeeper. I gritted my teeth, holding onto my bow even tighter until small splinters of wood began to burrow into my skin.

"You gave yourself away. Your warning. It wasn't about the people we were going to meet on the road. It was about you," I hissed, staring hatefully into his green, snake-like eyes.

"Smart girl," Mortimer noted with a sickening grin. He started to move forward then, dragging Talia across the rubble as he did so, creating more rips in her nightdress. Mozko steadily followed them, gripping the hilt of a morbien blade that was attached to his belt. How could he stand there and do nothing? This was his *sister*!

"Stop, Mortimer, please. This is unlike you," Julian said, his voice fearfully calm as Mortimer continued to drag Talia across the street. She whimpered even more, sobbed as her bare legs scraped against the stone road.

"No. For once, Prince Julian, you are seeing me as I truly am, who I always have been," Mortimer sneered. There was a strange amount of hatred swirling within his eyes, covering each word he spat out as he continued towards us. It was a deep hatred too, one that neither I, nor Julian, nor anyone else in our group seemed to understand. Eventually, he came to a stop, gesturing to Trench who immediately came to Mortimer's side, grabbing Talia gruffly as Mortimer passed her off to him. She yelped as strands of her hair began to rip out of her scalp at Trench's pull, but he didn't care. Neither did Mortimer. And neither did Mozko.

Mortimer began to roll up his sleeve then, revealing to us The Mark inked onto his wrist. "This symbol is revealing of who I really am. I am Mortimer Blackcrow, Captain of the Dark Army, follower of the Dark Master, and soon to be King of Lorien."

"Is that what you are truly after?" Julian asked sadly. "My father's throne? Is that why you decided to become so close to my family? So that one day you could use our weaknesses against us, murder us, and then steal my father's crown?"

Mortimer paused, his smile widening as he leaned forward dramatically, "Yes. Your father is my true target, Prince Julian. I am just using you as a way to break him, just as he had once broken me."

"Then do it," Julian snapped, tossing his sword onto the ground, despite Alexamian's protests. "Release Talia and take my life instead!"

"As much as I would like to, I am afraid that my master's cause must always come before my own," Mortimer replied tightly. "Unfortunately, I am not here to murder you today, Prince Julian. I am here to offer you a deal."

"A deal? What sort of deal?" Julian said.

Mortimer nodded to Trench, who instantly drew a dagger that had been hidden in his belt, pressing it against Talia's throat. "Hand over the traitor and her life will be spared. Give us Abias Wood and your dearest fiancée will be released."

I stilled, just as I had done when the wounded man pointed to Abias, silently letting us know that The Mark carved into his skin was a message for him. I found myself remembering how Abias stared down at the man in recognition, how he had claimed to know the innkeeper. Suddenly, Mortimer's motives became more confusing. I lowered my bow as I stared at Mortimer suspiciously, "Why do you want Abias?" I asked.

"He is a traitor, Miss Olsen," Mortimer said, beaming as the tension in our group began to rise. Abias stood next to me silently, his pitchfork held down at his side, his eyes almost like slits as he glared at Mortimer. "It is my duty to see justice on behalf of our master, to give his traitors what they deserve."

I shook my head, taking a step closer to Abias, standing in front of him as if my short body would protect him from such an accusation, "You're a liar, Mortimer. You and Mozko are the only traitors here."

Mozko lowered his head at my words, seeming to find a sudden interest in his boots. It was almost as if what I said hurt him, as if I smacked him across the face instead of speaking the truth. *Was he forced into Mortimer's schemes? Had he really chosen this path?* I found it difficult to wrap my head around it all. It found it so hard to even look at Mozko, the boy who had been making jokes with Julian only a couple days before this, the one who showed sympathy towards the mention of Liana's death. I couldn't even begin to imagine the thoughts that were shooting through Julian's mind, couldn't even begin to feel the same pain he was feeling.

"You may believe what you like about your *friend*, Miss Olsen, but that will not change the fact that my master seeks his blood just as much as yours," Mortimer said before returning his attention to Julian. "So what say you, little prince? Will you accept my offer?"

Julian was quiet for a moment as he stared at Mozko. I could see the anger in Julian's gaze, how it heightened as Mozko finally looked back at him, their eyes meeting. But there was also something else about the look he gave, something that made me wonder if perhaps Julian was sending a message to him, trying to get him to understand his thoughts. *Why would he do that?* I thought. *After all Mozko did to Talia, how could he?*

"You have a deal, Mortimer," Julian said, returning his attention to Mortimer.

"*What?*" Alexamian and I exclaimed in unison.

"My Lord, please," Alexamian started, but my shouts drowned out his arguments.

"Julian, you can't do this! Just because you hate Abias doesn't mean you can let them have him!" I yelled, stomping away from Abias and towards Julian just as a child might have done. "They're going to kill him!"

"Then he will be getting what he deserves," Julian snapped, whirling round to face me. To my surprise, he grabbed my wrist, holding it firmly. I stared up at him and noticed the intensity in his gaze, the urgency, desperation.

"Julian…please," Talia began to say. Slowly, Julian turned to her, but he didn't ease his grip on my arm. A look of confusion crossed his face as Talia continued to speak though her sobs. "Don't do this… please do not."

His bewildered expression deepened as he stared at his fiancée, probably wondering why Talia would say such a thing. Why would she give her life to save a stable boy? Eventually, I began to realize that she wasn't trying to rescue Abias. She was trying to save Julian. She was giving her life up so that he wouldn't fall into the dark pit of anger and grief within him. She was saving the last bit of compassion and kindness he had, the goodness that she so easily brought out in him.

"Tick tock, boy," Mortimer snarled impatiently, signalling for Trench to press his blade even harder against Talia's neck. She sobbed as a thick trail of blood began to trickle down her throat toward her chest. "What is your final answer?"

Julian sighed, slowly releasing my arm and running a hand though his unkempt hair, suddenly becoming indecisive, hesitant. Perhaps it was because he understood what Talia was trying to do by urging him not to give in to Mortimer's request, but perhaps part of it was a sign. I noticed how Julian looked upward as he moved, his eyes flickering towards the roof of one of the buildings that was still standing two doors down from the inn. Then, as he paced the other way, he gave Alexamian a hard look, his eyes shifting towards the mill behind us.

Very discreetly, I followed his line of vision, checking over my shoulder to find the other morbiens still standing there, grinning as their blackish-red eyes flickered upward in the same direction, towards two of the buildings that were still standing on either side of the street. That was when I noticed it, movement up on the roof of the mill and up on the other building near the inn. I couldn't quite make out what those shadows were, but I could guess.

My heart hammered even more in my chest as the realization hit me hard, like a gust of wind knocking me over. I felt winded, like I had fallen down from a tall building or tree. Trench told us that there was more blood to be spilt here, but what he meant by that went beyond me, beyond Abias, and even Julian. We were all brought here for the same purpose. We were all led to Maycock to be executed.

That time with my father and the deer suddenly popped into my head again, a memory of the tactic he used to hunt it down. We spent about an hour tracking it, then followed those prints all around the woods until they led us back to where we started. It was there we found the deer, eating the leaves off a nearby bush. Uncle Gabe, my grandfather, and my dad began to surround the helpless creature, box him in so that there was no escape. They cornered it so it had no place to run and then ambushed it.

Ambush, I thought, glancing up at the morbiens on the roofs and then to the weaponless morbiens surrounding us. *They are the hunters...we are the deer.*

This was a trap.

In an instant, I had lifted my bow, pulling back the string and aiming at Mortimer at the same time Mozko drew his blade, kicking Mortimer in the gut and knocking him out of my range. I blinked in surprise as Mozko leapt onto Mortimer, driving his sword down towards his head. But Mortimer was already beginning to vanish into that strange black smoke I had seen Trench disappear into. Mozko's blade stuck hard into the ground, spilling no blood. His attack however, set everyone else into motion. The morbiens above us began to shoot arrows from their positions on the roofs. Others began to emerge from the building that Mozko had come from, and Julian and Alexamian had gone straight for Trench, managing to break Talia free of his grasp. I watched as Talia fell into Julian's arms, as Alexamian began to slash his blade down upon Trench, who managed to dodge every one of his blows.

Our other two knights and Abias immediately spun around on Julian's command, advancing towards the weaponless morbiens behind us as arrows continued to rain down upon our group. Julian held Talia close to him as he shouted my name, gesturing for me to follow him. I could see his lips move, see the arrows flying so close to me, but my body couldn't seem to function. I couldn't move, not after what I had almost done, not after feeling what I had. I wanted to *kill* Mortimer. *I wanted to* kill him.

It was Mozko who sprang me back into action, practically lifting me off the ground as he rushed me towards Julian, to an alley where he and Talia were headed. I glanced over my shoulder as we moved, catching a glimpse of Abias, who had knocked down one of the morbiens, driving his pitchfork right through him. I turned away once Mozko, Talia, Julian, and I were behind the half-demolished wall of a building, safe from the arrows the morbiens continued to shoot. I shifted uncomfortably out of Mozko's hold, still unsure of what just happened, confused if he was to be trusted or not.

"Olsen, it's fine. He's with us. He has always been with us," Julian assured me, recognizing my discomfort and sensing my unease at being in the same vicinity as him.

I turned to Julian, feeling my brows knit together in bewilderment, "But the tattoo. He –"

"It is not real," Mozko responded, cutting me off. He lifted his shirt again to reveal what had once been The Mark, but was now just a black smear across his stomach. "Charcoal from a fire. I drew it on the moment I realized they had taken Talia. I would never betray my sister, nor my friend."

"Moz," Julian started, his focus returning to the matter at hand, in true military fashion. "You are going to guard Talia. Get her as far away from this village as possible. Do you understand?"

"Of course, Your Highness," Mozko replied, already moving towards his sister, gripping her hand tightly. "Where shall we meet once this battle is over?"

Julian hesitated for a moment, his eyes growing sad as he looked to his fiancée. Noticing the hopeless expression that took hold of his face, Talia moved closer to him, her pretty brown eyes filled with the same emotion that had been embedded in her brother's simple question. She reached out to Julian, placing her hand on his, on the one that gripped the hilt of his sword. "We will meet again, Julian. This battle will not be in vain," she assured him.

Julian paused for a moment, considering her before lowering his lips to hers, giving her a gentle, yet tender kiss before letting Mozko take her away, "We will meet in the woods, just south of here," Julian said. "Now go, quickly."

Talia held onto Mozko tightly as he put his arm around her like a shield before they darted out into the battle, dodging arrows and swords as they hurried towards the horses. I intended to watch them get to safety, to ensure that they hadn't been intercepted by any other morbiens, but Julian stepped in front of me, blocking my view.

"I am giving you a task, Olsen," he said, steadying his gaze, and ducking his head a bit in order to catch my eye.

"Mozko... did you..." I said, still caught in my confusion. "How did you know he wasn't..."

"Now would be the worst time for you to be asking such questions," Julian snapped, rolling his eyes. "Mozko would die before he saw her in the hands of a morbien. If he had not drawn The Mark on himself and acted as a traitor, they both would have been slain. He was lucky it was a morbien who first glimpsed The Mark and not Mortimer. Morbiens don't share our aprimorad vision. They would not have noticed that the tattoo was not real."

I nodded, showing him that I understood, and signalling for him to continue.

"You have to listen to me carefully, Olsen, okay?" he said. "I am giving you a task, just as I would with any of my knights. If we are to leave this battle alive, then you must allow me to treat you as such."

I sighed, reluctantly giving him another nod of my head, "What do you want me to do?"

"You must shoot at the morbiens stationed on the roofs," he said, pointing up at the archers who continued to release their arrows upon our group. I saw one shoot from the mill roof, catching one of our knights in the shoulder, piercing his armour. "And you must do it quickly," Julian added grimly.

"You want me to *kill* them?" I exclaimed, feeling afraid of myself, of unleashing the part of me that had wanted to kill.

"What else would I be asking?" Julian groaned, giving me another roll of his eyes. When he looked back at me, his features softened, making me wonder if he noticed the fear that began to take hold of me, if he finally began to understand the real reason for my stupidity in that moment. He moved closer to me then, speaking gently, "If you do not do this, more members of our group will die. More lives will be at risk if you do not impale those archers. It is either our lives or theirs, Carter."

I realized that this was the first time he had ever called me by my first time, the first time he looked at me as if I were more than just some human girl who wandered into his world, but rather someone he needed. As if I were someone he was choosing to rely on, despite all my shortcomings. I took a deep breath before drawing an arrow, loading my bow, and giving him a nod of my head.

"Think about what is at stake here," Julian said, coaxing my mind into the proper place, getting me to focus as I turned towards the battle before us. "Focus on *why* you must fight, *why* you must kill, not on the actual process of it."

"Will you stay with me?" I asked, my eyes darting between Mozko and Talia, who were continuing to make their way towards the horses, maneuvering around morbiens who stood in their path, and then to Abias and Alexamian who fought back to back against more of our enemies.

"I made a promise to my father that I would guard you with my life," Julian replied. I looked to him, unsure of whether his tone comforted me or made me even more nervous. "And I will be doing just that."

We shared a small smile, then a nod before racing out from our hiding spot and towards the battle ground. The moment I was out from behind the building, I took aim and fired up at the morbiens on the roofs, just as Julian asked me to. My first arrow soared straight towards one of the archers, shooting him right through his chest. I heard his distant cry as my arrow met its mark and watched as the impact knocked him over, sending him falling off the building.

Focus on why, not how, I reminded myself as I aimed at my next target. *Focus on why.*

My next few arrows brought down the rest of the archers on the one roof, but all my shooting seemed to draw the attention of some of the morbiens on the ground, especially Trench's. I could see him eyeing me from where he fought Alexamian, in between blocking his strikes. I glanced back at them, watching as Trench swung a fist at Alexamian, smacking him right across the temple and knocking him to the ground. Alexamian stumbled and blinked as blood began to trickle down the side of his forehead, shaking his head in attempt to steady his vision.

"Focus, Olsen!" Julian shouted at me from where he fought off two other morbiens. "Shoot them!"

I took a deep breath before repositioning myself, taking aim at the morbiens on the mill roof. Slowly, I drew my bowstring back, steadying my shaking arms as I aimed, and then fired. As I did so, someone's body collided with mine, making me lose my aim, and sending me onto the ground. I could feel the skin peeling off my hands, hear my sleeve rip as I rolled across the rubble. I groaned, the whole side of my body aching as I carefully rose, looking to my right to find Trench standing there with one of our knight's blades in his hand. His pale lips drew back into a smirk as he spun the sword around in his hand, staring me down like a predator would his prey, his black eyes transforming into that solid red colour as he ran towards me.

As I watched in fear as he came at me, something began to stir within me. That strange adrenaline I felt the last time I faced him suddenly began to pulse through my veins, triggering a sixth sense that made my body move faster than I believed it could. Just as Trench reached me, swinging his sword towards my head, I lifted my bow to meet his blade. The sound of the sharp metal crashing against my wooden bow made me nervous, afraid that if I continued to press as hard as I was against his sword, my bow would snap. Recognizing this anxiety, Trench pressed down on me with all his strength, making my arms shake and weakening my defense against him. That energy within me then urged me to move out from under him and quickly lift the lower limb of my bow to his temple before he could swing his sword at me.

Trench tripped over himself a bit as I moved to stand behind him, nocking an arrow and aiming for his back. I released the thick string and watched as my arrow headed straight for my target, but Trench turned just as I let my arrow fly, instantly deflected the arrow before it could get anywhere near him. I immediately reached for another arrow, but he was upon me just as I lifted my hand to my quiver, grabbing my wrist. I winced, feeling the pressure right down to my bones. I then swung my bow towards him again, the lower limb of my weapon just missing his cheek by an inch as he drew back, still holding my arm tightly. I attempted to hit him across the head with my bow once more, but he grabbed my other arm too, squeezing it so hard that I began to cry out, feeling my bow slip out of my hand. My heart sank into my stomach as I felt it fall from my grasp, landing on the road at my feet. Trench swiftly kicked it out of the way with his foot before shoving me to the ground.

I wheezed as the wind was knocked right out of my chest, struggling to rise and roll over to get my hands on another weapon. I could see a sword not far from where I was, attached to the belt of the knight I had seen get shot earlier. But each time I managed to roll over, Trench pulled me back, making my skin tear even more.

"This is what I came here for," Trench sneered as continued to try and drag me under him so he could pin me down. Memories of that other morbien doing the same thing to me days before popped into my head, making my heart pound even more with fear. "My master will praise me greatly when I return to him with you at my side."

I glared up at him, still struggling against his pull. The fury that I could feel rising in my chest making my adrenaline pulse even faster, draining every ounce of fear from my body. Before Trench could say another word, I kicked him square in the face, right where his nose should've been, and knocked him back a couple steps, giving me time to wiggle out of his hold and scramble towards the nearest sword. I could hear him growling like an animal behind me, could sense him moving closer as I grabbed the hilt, whirling around just in time to meet his blow.

Our swords met with a loud, screeching sound, but it was like music to my ears, fueling the foreign energy within me. Trench looked me over in surprise as I pushed against him and swung my sword towards his face. He quickly parried my strike before taking another swing at me, but I repeated his move, blocking the blade before it could draw blood from my arm. We went back and forth like this for a while until I was finally able to wound him, the tip of my sword scratching across his cheek. Blood spilt from the wound, but he continued to try and take me down, to push me back into a corner so he could have the advantage. But I seemed to be able to anticipate his moves before he made them and could, for some reason, guess where and when he would choose to strike. I tried my hardest not to think about it, not to worry about the strangeness of it all. Instead, I allowed my body to do what it wanted. I allowed that adrenaline to take control of me, surrendering my whole being to it.

Trench's confused look deepened as I suddenly began to gain the advantage, pushing him back further with my swings and strokes. He blocked my strikes, but only just. Eventually, I had him cornered, just as he had planned for me. His back was pressed against a crumbling wall, leaving him with nowhere to go. I smashed my sword into his blade, knocking it right out of his grasp, and then driving my sword into his stomach before he could retaliate.

His hot blood began to cover the hilt of my sword, spilling out on my hands. I stared into his eyes as he began to slide down the side of the wall and watched the life drain out of him. Suddenly, my body began to feel weak, exhausted, as if that vigour inside me had completely vanished from my system. A cold feeling replaced it, one I knew was caused by what I had just done. I stared down at my shaky hands, examining the dark blood that covered each one of my fingers. My gaze shifted from my hands and back to Trench who lay dead at my feet.

"What is happening to me?" I whispered through a sob. I could feel my stomach twisting again, could feel the vomit rising in my throat. *I killed him. I killed...*

Suddenly, a blood-curdling scream echoed in my ears, drawing me out of my shock and forcing me to turn towards the others, who were still fighting for their lives. I could see Abias not far from where I was, turning at the sound of the scream as well, looking to the spot where we had entered Maycock. Standing there was none other than Mortimer. Everyone froze in their places, staring at him as he held Talia upright against his body, placing the knife at her throat once again. I frantically searched for Mozko, eventually spotting him near Mortimer, lying motionless on the ground with blood trailing from the corner of his mouth.

"Drop your weapons!" Mortimer shouted, pressing his knife harder against Talia's neck. "Drop them now!"

Julian was the first to lay down his weapon, and he did it with the least amount of hesitation. Alexamian, Abias, and I, however, did it in full reluctance, the three of us sharing a quick look before returning our attention to Mortimer. My heart ached at the fact that we were all that was left. The two knights that had been with us were both dead, slain by this man who stood before us, this man who I hated more deeply than I ever thought I could. I glared at Mortimer, my chest heaving with anger, my fingers itching to draw an arrow and shoot him. But the sight of him still pressing that knife against Talia's neck, where a trail of blood trickled down her neck, forced me to remain still. All I could do was hate him and hope he felt it, even though I knew he wouldn't care that I despised him, that any one of us did. All he cared about was getting what he wanted, which is what was happening.

Julian's chest also heaved, but not with anger. It was with grief. His sea-green eyes were filled with tears as he gazed at Talia, as the knowledge of what was about to happen to her began to register. She was going to die and there was nothing any of us could do to stop it. It was for that reason that Talia seemed so calm, that not even a hint of fear glistened in her eyes. She knew that there was no escape, and she was choosing to accept it.

I noticed her lips moving as she looked back at Julian, who still continued to shake his head, silently urging her not to let this happen, to at least try and fight back. But it was out of her control. Mortimer was the one with the weapon, not her. It was only when she mouthed her words again as Mortimer steadied his knife, did I catch what she was saying. *We will meet again.*

Mortimer swiftly moved his knife, sliding it across her throat, and stepped back to watch as Julian cried out in horror and raced towards Talia to catch her. My heart throbbed at the sound of his sobs, at the sight of him rocking Talia's motionless body back and forth in his arms. What made my chest ache even more was the look on Mortimer's face, the satisfied smile that spread across his thin lips as signaled to the morbiens gathered that they should vanish into clouds of black smoke, leaving us in the empty streets of Maycock to watch Julian grieve.

CHAPTER 18

A TRAITORS TALE

It was nightfall by the time we reached the woods just south of Maycock, tied up the horses, and lit a warm fire. All four of us were tired, our stomachs still longing for food, our bodies desiring the escape that sleep would bring. But no one moved to do any of that. None of us could. Grief lay too heavy upon our group, especially on Julian, who seemed so distant in comparison to the rest of us, his eyes wide, watchful, as if he were seeing Talia being murdered once more.

We had buried her and the others before we left. We did it in the centre of Maycock, in the street where Mortimer had slain Talia. Julian stood back as we began the burial, closing Talia's eyes before Abias, Alexamian, and I started piling rocks and rubble on top of her, Mozko, and the two knights. Soon there were four perfect mounds of stone in the middle of the street, four piles which we stood around, silently saying our goodbyes. We took our time leaving the village, giving Julian more time to calm down, and trying to come up with a plan for our next steps. But no one had the strength to move on, even though we all knew we had to.

Our eyes were fixed on the fire as we sat in silence, each of us escaping into our own world of thoughts. I wrapped my cloak tighter around my shoulders as a cool breeze began to blow against my back, making me shiver, despite the heat of the campfire. My gaze shifted towards Abias as our silence dragged on, remembering how sick he looked as we were burying Talia. His cheeks had gone so pale, the corners of his lips drooping downward as he frowned, concentrating on assisting us in burying our fallen friends. But what I remembered most was how readable he had become. His eyes were filled with an emotion I recognized all too well, one that I knew I would possibly feel for the rest of my life. Guilt. He was feeling guilty for reasons beyond my understanding. Was it because he could have taken Talia's place, but he chose not to? Did it have to do with the message that was sent for him?

"I know what you are thinking," Abias spoke up, finally breaking our silence. At first, I thought he was speaking directly to me, but then I noticed that his grey eyes rested upon Julian, who still stared at the fire before us, his fists clenched on his lap. Anger blazed in his gaze as he continued to stare at the fire, looking as though he wished Abias would toss himself in it. I sighed, guiltily admitting to being annoyed with Julian. He couldn't possibly blame Abias for all of this too, could he?

"You think so, do you?" Julian responded tightly. He turned slightly, staring at Abias the way he had looked at Mortimer earlier that day. As if he had been betrayed. "If you truly know what I'm thinking, then answer me one question. Is it true?"

I looked from Abias to Julian, shifting to share a puzzled stare with Alexamian, but noticed I that his eyes were locked on the fire, his shoulders slouched further than ever.

"Is what true?" I asked.

"Were you really able to sense Mortimer's betrayal, but not this one?" Julian said, gesturing to Abias. "Even after everything that has happened, you do not suspect a thing?"

I knew exactly where Julian was going with this and I didn't like it, not one bit. I had suspected something about Abias, but it was just a suspicion placed there by Mortimer, by the warning he had given us before we left Mitus. "Julian don't," I said, shaking my head. "Mortimer is a liar. You should know that better than anyone right now."

Tears rose in Julian's eyes at the memory of that treachery, at what Mortimer had done to him. Yet he was persistent in his argument. "There is a reason he is being hunted, Olsen. There is a reason Mortimer would send such a message to him, a reason they all want him dead, and a reason that he knows so much about The Mark."

I laughed lightly, shaking my head and turning away from him. *It's not true*, I thought. *It's not true and I know it.*

"Mortimer may know the power of a lie, Carter, but he also knows the strength of the truth. He knows how to wield the hard truths and use them against others, a tactic I assume he adopted from his master," Abias responded quietly. I turned to him slowly, my brow furrowing in confusion. *Why is he agreeing with Julian's response? Why would he?*

I stared at him, both confused and afraid of what he meant. Abias sighed, noticing the bewilderment in my gaze, and reached up to the collar of his torn and blood-stained shirt. He began unbuttoning it, pulling it down over his broad chest, which bore strange scars, markings that made my head spin slightly with even more confusion. A black line became visible as he revealed more of his chest, making my heart stop. I drew back in shock at the sight of the four black lines and the thick circle inked into his chest, seeing this evil tattoo, but not believing someone so pure could bear it.

"You – you have the..." I stuttered, staring at his chest, at The Mark that was tattooed over his heart. I immediately blinked back tears, looking from The Mark to Abias in complete astonishment. "I – I don't get it. You're one of them?"

"No. I'm not. But I used to be," Abias answered, his voice hoarse. "Everything Mortimer said about me is true. The Dark Master does want me dead, for he demands that blood is spilt from all who betray him."

"You are lucky my father has not set similar laws," Julian hissed, his cold stare locked on Abias. "You aren't only a traitor to the Dark Diviner, but to aprimorads as well. Are you aware of what that makes you?"

Abias pressed his lips together, giving a slow nod of his head, "A rebel and an outlander, one of the Free Folk. If I had not chosen to return to Titus, I would have been all of those things, but I chose to come home. I chose to walk away from my path of darkness. I chose to swear my loyalty again to the four magwas, to your father –"

"Do you mean to say that he knows of this dark past? Did *you*?" Julian snapped, cutting Abias off and whirling around to Alexamian, who had remained silent throughout this conversation. Alexamian closed his eyes, giving Julian a small nod that made him look even more hurt, as if Alexamian had sliced a wound upon his heart similar to Mortimer's. "And no one decided to tell me?" Julian asked.

"Your father thought it would be wise to keep it a secret. As did I," Abias said. "He was aware of the dangers of my being in the city, and in order to protect his people – to protect you – we swore to tell no one else. For the past year only he and my family have known."

"I don't understand," I sighed, shaking my head, still finding all of this to be so utterly unbelievable. "Why did you chose to join him in the first place? Didn't you believe the Dark Diviner was dead?"

"Before I joined his ranks, before I swore an oath to follow him, I had no knowledge of who he truly was. I grew up listening to stories, tales of the Ancient Darkness, but, like most people in Elssador, I did not know he was still alive," Abias started. "At first, I did not join his army willingly. I had been in hiding on my own account. During the month after Liana's death, when I returned to Titus and saw the way everyone looked at me, I knew I could not stay there. They all saw me as a murderer, believing that I had let her die, just as you did, Prince Julian. Even though I knew it was not true, it still pained me. So I left, ran away to Gem, a village on the western coasts of Boron. I lived there for about a month, finding work as a blacksmith until the village was raided. Ships with dark sails docked on the coast and morbiens jumped out, running through the village, killing people and taking some captive. It was the first time I had seen a morbien. For years those in Lorien had believed the morbiens were either dead or in hiding.

'They took me as a prisoner after I attempted to fight them off, bringing me – beaten and blindfolded – to one of their ships. We sailed for days, weeks, perhaps even months before they reached their destination, the Oscor Mountains. The moment we arrived I knew what this all meant. I knew that those morbiens did not pillage Gem for their own entertainment. They had been sent by their creator, by the Dark Diviner."

"So he really does live then?" I asked, trying to mask the fear and worry I could hear rising in my voice. Julian and I had chosen not to tell anyone about the Dark Diviner's rising when all the while there were those in our company who already knew this. Abias and Alexamian had known all along what was coming, living in fear for the day he truly did make his appearance. But Talia had had no idea. Neither did Mozko and the rest of Elssador. They didn't understand the danger I had awakened, nor did I even fully understand it.

"Yes. He certainly does," Abias answered grimly, "He has been alive all these long years, building his armies, preparing to head to war, one that no world has ever faced before. I discovered all of this when I was first taken to him, when he persuaded me to join his ranks. That was when I swore my oath, when The Mark was placed upon me." Abias pointed to his chest, to the black tattoo over his heart, "This is more than just a symbol of the leader one serves, more than just a mark that strikes fear into all who lay eyes on it. It is an enchantment, one that binds someone to the Dark Master."

"Binds?" I asked.

"It means he can track those who bear it, speak to them, watch them as they perform his tasks," Abias explained. "When you swear to the Dark Master, you are swearing upon your own blood, therefore you must pay with it. I stood before him and drew my own blood, then allowed it to drip onto the orb upon his staff, where it was absorbed and will remain until the day I die. It is a bond that can never truly be broken, even if your heart desires to tread a separate path. In the eyes of the Dark Master, once you become his servant, you will always be one."

Silence came upon our group once Abias had finished his explanation, each of us taking in all he had said, and understanding. Everything began to make so much sense to me. That was why Abias could wield a weapon so easily, why he had known the innkeeper, why he was able to look past killing him. It was all because of this, because he was trained to fight the Dark Diviner's battles, because he had been one of his soldiers.

Even though everything made so much more sense to me, I was unsure about how I felt about all of this. Suddenly, Abias had changed. The joyful stable boy I once knew had transformed into a dark warrior. Any reminder of Tyler he had within him fading away because of one short conversation. I wrapped my cloak around me even more closely, my body feeling colder than it had before, but not because of the air around me. It was because of the shock of what Abias had just explained, of seeing Abias as he truly was, not as the boy Alexamian told me I had changed, who I had supposedly returned to his old self. Now Abias' eye looked even more like the storm they resembled. They were sad, guilty, and pained, especially as they locked on me.

"I wanted to tell you, Carter, truly, but I feared this. I was afraid of how you would react," Abias said. "I didn't want you to look at me any differently."

I swallowed back the lump that formed in my throat, trying to hold back the tears that stung my tired eyes. I didn't wanted to see Abias any differently either, but how could I not now? After all he told me, how could I not look at him as if this was our first meeting? A new, shattering thought entered my mind, one that made my empty stomach feel nauseous. Would Abias react the same way if I had told him the reason for my being in Elssador? If he discovered my destiny, which I planned to run from, wouldn't he look at me the way I was looking at him? Abias wasn't the only one keeping secrets, the only one to break the promise we made to tell the truth. My own secrets were still present and my mind screamed for me to reveal them, but Julian's hard look stopped the words in my mouth. He shook his head slightly, clearly recognizing my desire to speak the truth. It took everything in my being not to say anything, to keep my lips sealed as Abias continued.

"All that has happened is my fault," Abias admitted quietly.

"No, you can't take the blame for all of this, Abias," I snapped. "The Dark Diviner might be after your blood, but he's also after mine. And he probably has been for longer than I've been alive." Julian gave me a harder look once those words slipped out, but Alexamian's brow furrowed as confusion swept over him. I expected a similar expression to transform Abias' face too, but his gaze remained steady, his eyes filled with understanding.

"I know," Abias admitted. "I know why you were brought to Elssador, Carter. I have known this entire time, the moment I sensed your humanity."

I could feel my heart pounding harder against my ribs. This was the moment I feared, the moment where Abias would discover that I was going to let him down, that I was going to let this world fall apart all because I was scared to face my destiny. *I can't leave Marlee,* I assured myself. *I can't leave Tyler. I can't kill a wizard!*

"How?" I managed to ask.

"When I joined the Dark Diviner, when I chose to serve him, he gave me a task," Abias answered. "All of his non-morbien servants are given one, but mine was different. After six months of training, I was given a special mission, one connected to a prophecy made long ago that predicted the Dark Diviner's end. To aid me in competing this task, he gave me further understanding of the powers of the Portal, of the windows which it had opened. He told me how someone will one day come from the World Beyond to begin the war he has been waiting for, the war that he believes he will surely win."

My heart was beating even louder as Abias continued, my hands shaking as the fear pressed hard against my heart, threatening to overwhelm me. "It was you he was speaking about, Carter," Abias said. "Though he did not know your name or who you might be, he knew that it was a human who was destined to destroy him. In order to prevent that, he called upon me to hunt you. For almost two years I was in search of you, of the human who would be the cause of a great battle, but who would also be our saviour."

I didn't want to understand what he was saying, but it was as clear as day to all who sat around the fire with us. Even Julian's scowl faded into a look of surprise as this information sank in. Memories instantly rushed back to me. I remembered my first meeting with Abias, how he had known that I was a human the moment we had spoken. I hadn't remembered him explaining to me how he knew what I was when all the others like him could only sense that I was different. Now I understood. Now it all made sense. He knew I was human because he was sent to hunt me, to murder me.

"So you were an assassin then?" I said.

"Not exactly," Abias replied. "I was sent to stop you, yes, but not in the way you think. The Dark Master's lust for power is far stronger than it was during the first age of this realm. He is far too proud to send one lone aprimorad to kill you. He wants to destroy you himself, break the bonds of destiny which tie you to him. He wants to defy the powers of the High Diviner, show that he is stronger than the Wanderer and all the greater powers of this world and the next."

"So you were sent to capture me, to bring me to him so he can kill me?" I concluded, quite certain that this was the only reasonable answer. But Abias continued to shake his head, proving me wrong once more.

"It is not that simple. The Dark Diviner *fears* you, Carter. He fears the prophecy that you are bound to. People like us would want to eradicate that fear as soon as possible," Abias continued. Julian and I shared a nervous glance, one which I was sure Abias had seen, but had been too focused on his explanation to register. "But the Dark Master is different. He does not want to extinguish his fear. He wants to control it. He wants to use you, Carter. He wants to challenge and twist the powers of destiny."

"That will never happen," Alexamian piped up. I feared to look at him, knowing just by the strength in his voice that his chest was heaving with pride, his brown eyes alight with a hope. "Destiny has too great a pull, a force that no creature – human or wizard – can control."

I tried to muffle a sigh as I brought a hand to my temple, attempting to soothe a headache that I could feeling coming on. As I lowered my head, I caught Julian's eye again. This time I could see the words clearly in his expression, recognizing them as much as I would have if he'd spoken what was on his mind. I swallowed hard as I read the message he was trying to send me, allowing myself to accept the fact that it was time. The time to run was upon us. Abias and Alexamian knew too much about my destiny, about why I was brought to Elssador. If I waited longer to run, then I would hurt them even more.

I refused to make eye contact with Abias as I prepared to lay down next to the fire, claiming over-exhaustion. My body was weary, weak, and part of me truly did want to drift off into a deep slumber, but my brain was wired, more alert now that Julian and I were beginning to go through with our plans. I wrapped myself fully in my cloak, turning my back to the others, and closing my eyes, giving the illusion of sleep, just as Julian and I had arranged. It wasn't long before I heard shuffling in the grass behind me, the sounds of the others beginning to settle down as well. Julian asked to keep watch and we both expected Alexamian to protest, but he didn't. He knew why Julian would want to keep watch instead of resting, just as he knew that there was no use in arguing with a leader who already made up his mind.

I curled up under my cloak even more snugly, feeling a single tear begin to slide down the side of my face. *We are no better than Mortimer*, I thought painfully. *Playing with the hearts of those around us, those we consider friends. Does this not make us traitors as well? Is running really our best option? Will I truly be able to live with the outcome? With the guilt?*

The answer to these questions was simple, yet painful for me to dwell on. I might not have to carry the burden of my destiny with me wherever I went – running away from it would give relieve me of that – but I would have to lug this new weight along with me as well. The consequences of running, the deaths of those whom I leave behind, the hatred and disappointment Abias was going to have towards me… They were all results I was going to have to learn to live with.

*   *   *

I waited for Alexamian's loud snores to sound through the forest and for the feeling of Julian's warm hand on my shoulder before I opened my eyes. I rose slowly and quietly from the ground, navigating my way around our camp by the faint light from the last embers of our fire. I could just make out Julian's figure before me as he moved towards the horses, a saddle bag slung over his shoulder. He lowered it to the ground once he reached the mare furthest from our camp, lifting his glowing green-blue eyes to help guide me in the dark. He began to strap the bag to the horse's saddle once I reached him, glancing at me as he adjusted the thick, leather straps.

"Do you remember the way back?" Julian whispered.

"Yeah, I think so," I responded quietly.

Julian's glowing eyes returned to the saddle bag as he made his last adjustments. I looked over my shoulder at our camp, at the outline of Abias' strong back and could feel the guilt beginning to eat away at me again. I couldn't seem to shake off the feeling that something about this was wrong, but then an image of Marlee slipped into my mind, reminding me of why I was fleeing in the first place, why it was so vital that I escape the bonds of destiny and return home. I didn't want her to lose me the way I had lost my father. I didn't want anyone her age to have to go through what I had.

"Take this," Julian said, reeling me out of the depths of my thoughts. He held his map out to me, the tattered, folded paper that seemed to have a new stain added to the many that circled its crinkled edges. I stared at the map, at the dark red stain upon it that brought back the painful memory of Julian holding Talia's bloody body against his chest. It was Julian's touch that snapped me out of those dark thoughts, the feeling of his fingers brushing against my skin as he placed the map in my hand that calmed me. I studied his green-blue eyes, recognizing the strangeness in his gaze, the softness and care which I had only seen him lavish on Talia. But there was something else. There was another feeling embedded in the look he gave me that I didn't quite understand. It was fear, but fear for what? For me?

"Take it, just in case," Julian repeated, giving my fist a tight squeeze before allowing his hand to fall back down at his side.

I swallowed and peered over my shoulder, taking one last look at Abias and Alexamian. *This all feels so wrong, running away,* I thought. It seemed that no matter how many times I assured myself that I had good reasons for leaving, that uneasy feeling still found it's way into my mind. It still made my stomach churn, my throat tighten, and I could sense that a similar unsettling feeling had come over Julian too. I could see it in the way he looked at Alexamian, in the way he had aggressively attached the saddle bag to my horse. I could only imagine what he was thinking, could only guess that his thoughts were the same as my own. We were doing just as the Dark Diviner wanted. I was leaving, returning to the world where I belonged, to where I found more safety and comfort than I ever could here in Elssador. By doing this, weren't we allowing him to win? If both Julian and I fled, I would be seen as a villain to these people, as the human who raised a demon, not the heroine who I was destined to be.

Suddenly, I heard a voice ringing in my ears as Julian placed his hands on my waist, preparing to lift me up onto my saddle. The voice was a mixture of my father's and another's, a voice that I had learned to know well even though I had spent only an hour with him. It was the Wanderer's voice, his words, but I could see my father as they played through my mind. *Is that really the person you want to become, Carter? Do you really want to become the girl who began a war, one which no world has ever faced before?*

No. The answer was *no*. I didn't want to be that. But I also didn't want to leave Marlee, Tyler, Uncle Gabe, and especially the small town of South River. That small, rundown town was the last piece I had of my father. It held the last vestiges of his spirit which I could see in the greenish waters at Eagle Lake – the beach he always used to take me to – and even in the rustling of the leaves at Tom Thompson Park. Memories of my dad coloured every inch of that small town, and even though I feared to face them, was afraid to allow them to resurrect all the pain and anger that came with his death, I was always conscious of them being there. I was happy they were.

Maybe my reason for returning to the well is purely selfish after all, I wondered as the snippets of memories played at the back of my mind. Maybe it wasn't *just* Marlee I wanted to return to. Perhaps all I actually wanted to return to was my home, to the last pieces of my father I had to cling to. I realized that at the heart of all this, I wasn't just afraid of facing a wizard, of being destined to be a killer. There was another fear that I began to recognize, one far greater than all that. It was the fear of letting go. I was afraid to let go of my father.

"Be on the alert for morbiens and for Mortimer." Julian's voice broke through my deep thoughts, once again helping me focus on the task at hand. I held my bow across my lap, gripping it with one hand and wrapping the reins around my other as I glanced down at Julian, who stared up at me, wit that soft, caring look still in his eyes. "I do not know what he has planned next, but I am sure he and his men are still willing to do whatever it takes to take you to their master."

"I don't think they will," I replied, shaking my head. "I'm doing what the Dark Diviner wants, aren't I? Leaving his world, going home to get out of his way…"

"Olsen, did you listen to a word Abias said?" Julian hissed, stepping closer to my horse, gripping my saddle tightly. As he did, I willed myself not to dwell too long on the fact that he just used Abias' real name and instead to concentrate on the warning that laced his tone, "The Dark Diviner *wants* you to remain in Elssador. He wants to control you, to twist you, and wield you as one would a weapon. As long as you are not in Elssador he cannot do that. As long as the Portal is still destroyed and The Wanderer still controls its remaining powers, he cannot reach you."

I nodded slowly in understanding. This was another justification, something to help me bury the shame that came with running away from the path I was set on. It gave me even more of a reason to go home, to return to Earth where nothing from Elssador could touch me, not The Wanderer or the Dark Diviner. The only thing I couldn't wrap my head around was why Julian was so insistent on my getting out of the Dark Diviner's reach. On getting to safety. I wondered if it was destiny calling *him*, if this desire to keep me safe was something connected to the fact that our destinies were entwined, or if it was because he couldn't bear to lose someone else he knew.

"Just be careful, Carter" Julian whispered, his tone a little edgier than it had been previously, but that care was still present in his eyes. The look seemed to calm my mind, my body, making me less anxious than before. Julian then reached out to my bow, placing his hand just beside my own. "If you are attacked on the road, do not be afraid to use this, and make sure you don't miss."

I felt a small spark of joy ignite inside me and my lips curved upward into a smirk, "I never miss."

In the glow his eyes emitted, I could see him grin as he released me, taking a few steps back to give me space to ride ahead slowly towards the valley beyond the forest. Only when I reached the edge of the woods did I urge my horse into a gallop, gradually gaining speed as I burst through the trees, and out into open land, shooting off into the direction of the well.

CHAPTER 19

THE FIGHT FOR HOME

I could hear the sounds of war as I moved quietly through the familiar woods, recognizing it as the same forest we had stayed in just after the morbien attack en route to Mitus. Shouts, cries, the sound of metal screeching against metal, and of rock smashing against rock grew louder as I rode through the once-silent forest. I slid off my saddle as I neared the edge of the woods, pulling my horse behind me as I peered through a small break in the trees, looking out towards the city of Titus.

I sucked in a breath, caught only slightly off guard by the horrible sight before me, by the massive battle that was raging on the plains of Titus. My jaw fell open in shock as I stared at the land before the city, at the catapults that were set up a short distance from it. They were swinging massive rocks towards the turrets and destroying the walls of the city. Morbiens and knights fought on the field before Titus' gates as arrows rained down on them from the city's towers. I strained my eyes to get a better look at the archers atop the remaining walls.

They were morbiens, probably the same ones who had driven King Wallace and his people out of Titus in the first place. My attention shifted from the walls and to the warriors who fought on the ground. I scanned the area, recognizing the silver breastplates of Lorien knights and the purple tunics peeping out beneath their heavy armour as they fought the morbiens with their shining blades. My horse whinnied and drew back as one of the catapults fired, making a loud crash the moment it met one of the front turrets, taking it down completely. My grip tightened on the reins and I managed to persuade the horse forward so I could attempt to pull myself up onto its back. I led the horse closer to one of the trees, climbing up one of its lower branches so I could easily pull myself onto the saddle. Once I was seated with my feet secure in the stirrups, I looked again at the battle unfolding before me, trying to determine a safe path around the chaos towards the Forest of Growth, which lay beyond the battleground.

I noticed a familiar face as I stared, someone who I thought I was never going to see again. It was King Wallace, seated upon a white steed, dressed in full armour, which glittered faintly in the dim light from a grey sky growing darker with gathering storm clouds. He bore a similar frown to the one his son had given me only hours before I arrived here as he watched his knights defend his home. He shouted orders for more of his troops to close in. His men were in immediate motion, beginning to form a ring around the battle, moving in around the many morbiens who tried to make way their way towards the king. It was a smart plan, but the morbiens were too strong and too many. I could see more of them flooding out of the gates, already beginning to break down the aprimorad wall King Wallace had created.

When I returned my attention to him, I felt anger bubble and boil inside me as I caught a glimpse of someone who stood at the king's side. On his left was Lord Sebastian, but to his right was someone who I no longer believed deserved to stand by King Wallace and his armies. It was Mortimer Blackcrow, still acting as his steward, pretending to be the innocent advisor King Wallace believed him to be. But I knew better. I was there when he murdered Talia, when he declared his hatred for the Wallace family. I knew of his betrayal and who he truly was. I wished King Wallace would be able to see it, but he his mind was so preoccupied with the battle at hand that he couldn't see past the false fearful expression Mortimer so obviously forced upon his face. He was probably bursting with joy inside, suppressing a cry of glee as he watched his morbien army crush King Wallace's men.

My grip on my bow tightened as I continued to stare at him and as the desire to watch one of my arrows shoot through his skull sprang up inside me. I immediately forced myself out of this dark fantasy and willed myself to focus all my attention on getting to the well, on trying to find a safe way to the other side of the woods. I was drawn even further out of the dark corners of my mind as lightning suddenly split the sky. I glanced up at the grey clouds above me, then towards the battlefield as the lightning flashed through the plain once more. My eyes locked on King Wallace, who was still seated upon his horse. As he stretched out his hands in front of him, a bluish-white light shot out of his palms towards Titus, electrocuting some of the morbien archers on the walls. The sight of all that power shooting from him made me tremble. I never realized how powerful King Wallace was until I saw him in full action. Until I witnessed him shooting down enemies who had taken his city.

I suppose people will do anything to get home, I thought as I watched King Wallace continue to direct his lightning towards Titus. *Even if it means destroying it.*

My horse flinched beneath me as one of the catapults released another boulder on the city and I struggled to keep it from running off into the warzone before me. However, the noise had startled my horse, forcing it into a full-on sprint towards the forest. I swore under my breath the moment I was jerked forward and tried to muffle a yelp as my mare began galloping straight towards the battlefield. I tugged on the reins viciously, guiding the horse to the left, away from the battle and towards the edge of the forest. I galloped along the perimeter of the wood, ducking under low branches as I entered the Forest of Growth.

The sounds echoing from the battlefield began to muffle as my horse led me further and further into the deep woods. I yanked on the reins, pulling hard until my mare came to a sudden stop, nearly sending me flying. I breathed in heavy breaths, gently patting the horse's side, whispering soothing words into her ear to calm the creature down. I allowed myself and the horse to rest for a moment so I could regain my bearings, look at Julian's map, and make sure I was heading in the right direction. My lips curved upward into a smile as I compared the map to the clearing I idled in.

I'm close.

Suddenly, I became alert to the area around me, to a rustling in the trees to my right, which I sensed was not caused by the wind. I wrapped the reins around my hands more tightly, nervously glancing at the trees above me just in time to notice someone shifting in the branches. All of a sudden, an arrow shot down from the tree, heading straight for my horse, which had jumped up onto her hind legs in surprise, sending me flying off the saddle. I landed with a thud, watching as another arrow flew towards my mare, the black tip embedding itself in the horse's neck. I stared at the arrow that brought my horse down, recognizing the brownish-black fletches that only a morbien arrow seemed to possess.

I was on my feet in an instant, loading my bow and whirling around to face the morbiens who had concealed themselves in the trees. The five of them jumped down from their hiding places, their swords drawn, and the lone archer aiming his next arrow directly at my shoulder.

Standing in the face of danger seemed to trigger that adrenaline rush within me again. I could feel it shoot through my veins as I drew back my bow string and fired before the archer could even blink. The morbien fell backward the moment my arrow met his chest, which sent his companions into immediate motion. All four of them charged at me with their swords raised above their heads, leaving me with little time to figure out defensive a move. My heart pounded loudly, pumping more and more of that strange energy through my body as I loaded two arrows onto my bow, aiming for the morbien closest to me. The impact of both arrows sent him into the morbien beside him, forcing them both to fall to the ground, and giving me time to focus on the other two who had drawn closer to me than I anticipated. I ducked the moment I turned to face them as one of their blades swung over my head, just skimming my brow and releasing a trickle of blood.

I quickly got onto one knee and wiped the hot blood out of my eye before shooting an arrow in one morbien's direction, feeling relief flood through me as it pierced his chest. I could sense the other one beside me, could hear his heavy footsteps clearly as he advanced. I spun around, reaching for another arrow to load, but the morbien recognized the motion and immediately swung his blade downward before I could do as I wished. But I was quick to dodge his strike and spin out of his swing, yet still stood close enough to him to shove my arrow into his arm with my bare hands. The morbien growled, furious and confused about my ability to get past him so easily. I tried to supress my own bewilderment about how skillful I was as I drew another arrow, nocking it and firing in one swift motion. I didn't even wait to see whether my arrow had met its mark, knowing that more morbiens would probably follow if I lingered too long. Instead, I ran, scrambling up a small slope in the direction of the well.

What if there are more waiting for me? I wondered as I raced through the forest, jumping over various roots and rocks that were in my way. What if Mortimer stationed morbiens around the well in case I decided to escape? To ensure that I remained in this world? All of this became certain to me once I entered another break in the forest. I pulled up at the sight of a long line of morbiens that blocked the path I needed to get to my home, their swords drawn. I immediately turned around, planning to run back the way I came in hopes that I could find another path to get to the well, but more morbiens emerged from the bushes and the trees around me until I was completely surrounded. I swallowed, trying to moisten my dry throat. I helplessly loaded an arrow, aiming my bow at all of them as they began to move forward, circling me, and beaming as if they had already won. As if this was the end.

Is this it? I thought. *Is this the consequence for my leaving? For running away?*

Hot tears rose in my eyes, especially when the realization of what that could mean hit me. If this was my end, that meant I was never going to see Marlee or Tyler again and it would've been all my fault. I was going to lose them and it was all because I wanted to change my fate, because I wanted to create my own path. Anger instantly festered within me, along with my hatred towards the morbiens, to the Dark Diviner, Mortimer, The Wanderer, and even towards myself. It came upon me in one huge wave of emotion, making my eyes sting with even more tears.

I knew that my self-loathing couldn't save me, that hating myself wouldn't solve my predicament, but it brought an idea to mind, one that I knew would wipe those ugly smiles off the morbiens' faces. I stared into their redish-black eyes as I gradually lowered my bow, removing the arrow and slowly bringing it to my neck. I knew my plan was working the moment my arrow touched my neck, when I saw the fear sinking into their eyes. The cold, sharp tip of the arrow brushed against my skin, kissing it with little sharp pricks of pain as I held it against me as steadily as I could.

"Your master wants me alive, doesn't he?" I questioned loudly so all of them could hear. Many of the morbiens glued their feet to the ground, standing completely still as I pushed the tip of my arrow even harder against my skin. "If any of you take another step forward, your leader won't get what he wants! Then you'll all have to pay the price!"

Frowns replaced the arrogant smirks they all held moments before and they did exactly as I said, remaining frozen in their places and hesitantly lowering their weapons. I let out a quiet sigh of relief and was about to lower my arrow when a loud cry startled me, making me jump back and wince as my arrow scratched my neck slightly, drawing a thin trickle of blood. My eyes locked on the place where I heard the battle cry sound and a small smile tugged at the corners of my lips, despite the throbbing pain I now felt in my neck.

The shout had come from Lorien knights, several of them, as they leaped out from the path I had come from, swinging and slashing their blades at every morbien in sight. Questions immediately began to eat away at my mind as I watched the knights bring their swords down upon their enemies, spilling morbien blood just as their comrades were doing on the fields before Titus.

How are they all here? I thought frantically, slowly lowering the arrow I held at my neck in disbelief. *How did they know to come?* I knew King Wallace couldn't have sent these knights. He had no idea I'd even entered the boarders of his city, let alone that I was running back to the world I came from. The only person that knew for sure that I would be here was Julian.

Julian!

I blinked rapidly when my eyes caught sight of his figure advancing towards a morbien, driving his blade through his chest, and then turning swiftly to slash his opponent's arm. My mind raced for answers, frantically searched for an explanation that would justify when and why he had followed me here, but these thoughts all melted away the moment he rushed towards me. The sight of him pulled me out of my frozen state of relief and allowed me to fully release my hold on my arrow. I dropped it and instantly ran to Julian, pulling him into a tight hug, one that neither of us expected. I laughed lightly as he awkwardly placed his arm around me, then tightened his grip, holding me against him. My feelings of comfort and relief faded the moment we pulled out of our embrace and were replaced with anger, which I felt stir within me.

"What are you doing here?" I asked Julian furiously, shoving him slightly. We planned to run as far from each other as possible, to split up so we didn't need to tempt the powers of destiny. But there was another reason for my anger, another reason why I was both relieved and furious that he came to save my life. He could have died coming here. He was putting his own life at risk, but all for what? To make sure I was safe? To ensure I was out of his world for good?

"It's always a pleasure to see you too, Olsen," he smirked in response, brushing off my question with his sarcasm. I rolled my eyes, irritated by his this new sense of humour that he'd adopted. I yanked on his arm just as he turned to move further into the battle. I turned him around, forcing him to face me so I could search his eyes, so I could try to read what he was thinking, feeling...

"Why are you here?" I asked again.

"You cannot do this on your own, Olsen. No matter how much you would like to," Julian responded. "I knew there would most likely be morbiens waiting for you in this forest and

I knew the moment I sent you away what I mistake that was. Not long after you left, Alexamian and Abias awoke and we readied our horses immediately so we could follow you here."

It was easy for me not to focus too much on the fact that Julian had once again used Abias' real name, for my mind was locked on other things. It was locked on the fact that Abias and Alexamian were here too, that they were somewhere in this battle fighting for me, protecting me even though they certainly didn't have to. But didn't this also mean that they knew? That they knew I was running away to the well because I was afraid?

I was about to ask Julian what he'd told them, if he revealed to them all that had happened within the walls of The Wanderer's hut, if they knew about his destiny too, but he had suddenly tugged on my arm before I could speak a word. He pulled me out of the way and raised his sword to block a morbien who had snuck up behind me.

I stepped back as Julian moved forward, standing between me and our opponent, and swinging his blade around to strike him. The morbien brought his blade up to meet Julian's attack, blocking his blow. But before he could make another move against us, a three-pronged weapon drove in and out of the morbien's stomach. Julian and I watched in disgust as his blood splattered over us, his red eyes rolling back as he fell dead at our feet.

I looked up to find Abias standing where the morbien once did, his pitchfork dripping with blood as he lowered it to his side, staring back at me. I almost rushed forward to greet him with a hug just as I did Julian, but I didn't think he would have accepted it. I was expecting him to look me over as if this was our first meeting, as if we were strangers. I expected him to see right through me, to read me like an open book, a novel written in a language that he couldn't decipher. He could read the words, but he didn't know them. They were unfamiliar to him.

But none of that seemed to be embedded in Abias' gaze. All that filled his grey eyes was relief, joy, and exhaustion. I blinked, surprised as he rushed towards me, wrapping an arm around my shoulders and pulling me against him, hugging me as tightly as I had just embraced Julian. I hugged him back, but it felt wrong. I didn't deserve this. I didn't deserve this hug and I certainly didn't deserve to have him here, fighting for me.

"Did you think you could really sneak away so easily?" Abias jested as we pulled out of our hug. He was smiling, grinning the same way he had when I first met him. "We're aprimorads, Carter! There is nothing we cannot see!"

Just as he said those last words, a morbien came up behind him. Abias spun around quickly to face the enemy, but Julian hurled his sword at the morbien before Abias could even raise his pitchfork. Julian pushed past the two of us to retrieve his sword, his lips set in his usual frown as he moved back to us, shooting an irritated look in Abias' direction.

"Go to Alexamian," Julian ordered Abias as he pointed to another figure I recognized. Alexamian was in the crowd of knights that had stormed through the clearing, fighting off three morbiens some distance away from where the three of us stood. "The two of you follow close behind Olsen and me with as many knights as you can bring along with you. I do not believe that these are the only morbiens we shall encounter."

"Yes, My Lord," Abias answered with a slight bow of his head. His expression transformed into one of focus and determination as he turned away from Julian and me to get to his brother.

As I watched Abias take down two morbiens and then disappear behind the crowd of our knights and enemies, my heart warmed with gratitude towards Julian. *He didn't tell them,* I thought as he grabbed my arm and began to pull me away from the battle and in the direction of the well. *Abias still doesn't know why I'm here.* Part of me was relieved that he didn't know, that my last memories of him weren't going to be about his disappointment in me, his shame at having once called me friend. But the other part of me was sick with guilt. Didn't he deserve to know? Didn't he have the right?

These thoughts quickly faded from my mind as Julian started off into an even faster jog, pulling me along with him. I glanced over my shoulder as we moved, spotting Abias and Alexamian sprinting up the path behind us, along with several knights who followed them. Eventually, they all caught up with us just as Julian and I turned down a slight bend in the road. As we did, I noticed movement upon a boulder to our left. I spotted a massive figure whose blue, human-like eyes were locked on our group. However, it wasn't the size of the creature's eyes that worried me, but rather the amount of rage that filled them. My lips parted in surprise as the beast began to lumber out of the shadows and into the grey light that streamed through a break in the trees, revealing even more of its large body.

"Julian," I gasped, pulling up slightly to gape at the creature, hoping beyond hope that it wasn't what I thought it was. The others came to a stop beside us, all of them staring at the creature I pointed at with wide eyes. Julian stared at it too, fear and terror settling in his sea-green eyes as he shared a look with Abias, whose face had turned deathly pale.

This creature was exactly what I thought it to be.

Julian hesitated for a moment, caught in a daze as he stared back at the creature, which lowered itself onto the boulder, preparing to pounce. Julian released my hand and drew a second blade from his belt, his eyes still locked on the beast as it shook its large, knotted mane. My heart hammered in my chest as I was suddenly brought back to my conversation with Julian in the armoury at Mitus, when he had given me a vivid description of this beast, of the manticore, the monster that destroyed his family.

"We must hurry," Julian urged our group. His words pulled me away from the animal, drew me out of my thoughts so I could focus on fleeing from it, from the beast who had tilted its head and roared into the sky. The ground rumbled beneath us as we raced towards the well at an even faster pace, the leaves blowing off their branches above us from the wind that escaped the monster's mouth.

I swallowed hard, attempting to quell the sudden fear that was rising within me.

This journey home was going to be more difficult than I thought.

CHAPTER 20

MANTICORE

The roars of the beast were now above us as we reached a familiar clearing. I could see the well from where I stood at the end of the path that led to this break in the forest. I could practically feel the cold stone under my hands at this distance. I was so close, so close to going home. These thoughts filled me with excitement, with that foreign energy I felt before. It surged through my veins as I ran alongside Julian, Abias, and Alexamian, charging towards the morbiens that stood in my way, just as we expected they would.

Another roar sounded above us as I shot down a morbien whom I had seen sneaking up behind Alexamian. I nervously glanced up at the grey sky, at the shadow that was circling the clearing, gradually lowering itself closer to the ground. I forced my eyes away from the creature as another morbien charged at me, aiming his sword at my chest. I quickly met his strike with my bow, just as I did with Trench, and swiftly slipped out from under him, drawing another arrow, and bringing it to his neck. I ignored the feeling of his hot blood splattering onto my hands, my clothing, and drew the arrow out to meet another morbien, who I sensed was creeping up on me. The moment the arrow slit open his throat, I loaded the bloody arrow, shooting down a morbien who was heading straight for Abias.

My arrow struck the morbien before Abias could raise his weapon to block his opponent's strike. He looked up, staring at me as if I were someone he had seen before, as if all that was happening around us was giving him a sense of *déjà vu*. I noticed his eyes clouding over with memory, with horror as the manticore above us continued to lower itself into the clearing, its massive wings and spiked tail crushing several trees that stood in its landing space.

Gradually, I began to understand why Abias was looking around at the battle before him as if it were nothing but a dream. I could see the same look in Julian's eyes as he continued to fight our morbien enemies, glancing over at the beast every so often with terror gleaming in his eyes. This had already happened for the two of them. They had faced this monster before and lost greatly. This was the creature that took Julian's mother and sister from him, that ate them, murdered them. Every time Julian and Abias laid eyes on the Manticore, every time they heard it roar, they also heard the screams of Liana Wallace, the cries of the young girl whom they both had loved.

After a moment's pause, Abias leapt over the morbien I saved him from and raced towards me. I waited for him with a loaded bow, preparing myself to charge out deeper into the battle with him, to continue fighting my way towards the well with a friend at my side. *At least I hope he's still my friend,* I thought painfully. I was about to abandon him to a greater battle than the one we were fighting now. I was about to leave him and all the people of this world to clean up after me, to deal with the consequences of my refusal to face the Dark Diviner.

Once Abias reached me, he grabbed my arm tightly and pulled me towards the well. "You must leave, *now*," he said. The urgency in his tone puzzled me, made my brows knit together in confusion as we continued on towards the well. *Why does he want me to leave?* I thought. *Didn't he come here to change my mind about leaving?* I searched the unreadable look in his eyes as best I could while we ran, not understanding any of this. It wasn't until we came to a stop a short distance away from the well that I could recognize his expression. I didn't need him to explain once I saw the fear in his eyes, but he explained anyway, and the words made his eyes water. "I cannot have you die by that beast as Liana had. I cannot see it murder someone else I care about."

I swallowed back my own tears. I knew Abias cared for me, that I was probably the closest thing he had to a friend, but that love in his eyes, that care...it was different from the way Tyler loved me. Abias didn't see me as a sister as Tyler always did, he saw someone else, someone King Wallace had seen in me too. He was seeing Liana, the part of me that was like her although neither I nor her brother could see it.

Suddenly, Abias pulled me into a tight hug as he had before, and held me against him longer than I wished. Yet, I allowed him to do it, knowing that this was the last time I would ever see him, the last time I would ever see anyone who lived in the realm of Elssador. But Abias held me even closer, embraced me longer than I expected. He hugged me as if this was the last hug he would ever have, as if this would be the last time someone showed affection towards him. When we pulled away from the hug, I stared up at him nervously, my hands gripping his strong arms with a strength matching his own.

"What are you doing?" I asked through a shaky breath. "What are you planning to do?"

He dropped my gaze for a moment and I watched as his eyes shifted over to the manticore as it landed in the clearing, beginning to make this battle far worse than it needed to be. I watched in shock as the beast brought a large paw down on a group morbiens and knights, how its tail took out a whole line of people when it turned to roar at someone who struck it. But my attention was quickly captured by Abias once more, especially when he brought a gentle hand to my face, forcing me to stare into his eyes.

"Will you promise me something, Carter? Will you make me a promise and swear to keep it?" he said, shaking me slightly. I was startled by the sudden intensity of his gaze, by the tears that slid down his cheeks when he stared down at me. I nodded my head slowly, afraid that if I spoke, my own tears would begin to fall. "I know you are afraid of your destiny, Carter. I knew the moment you stepped out of the Galdia Caves, after you had spoken to The Wanderer and all you could do was frown.

I know you came back to the well for that very reason. But you are our only hope, Carter. You are Elssador's only hope."

"What do you want me to do?" I replied, trying my best to bury my surprise and hide the blush I felt spreading upon my cheeks. *Now I really don't deserve this,* I thought. So Abias did know, but it wasn't Julian who had told him. He figured it out on his own. I bit my tongue, trying so hard to keep myself from falling apart, to hold myself together. That task become easier as a small smile tugged on the corners of Abias' lips, sending warmth through my being despite the guilt I felt pressing heavily against my chest.

Suddenly, it became clear to me what Abias was about to do. I understood why he wanted me to make a promise, why he held me as if it were the last piece of affection he was going to receive. He was going to face the manticore. He was going to defeat the monster who haunted his dreams at night, the beast who had stripped him from his future, from who he was, and had led him down a path from which he could never truly break himself free.

He was going to die.

"Promise me, Carter, that if you ever do return to Elssador it will be to save it. That you will do everything in your power to do so," Abias said, his voice cracking slightly as he leaned in closer to me, nearly closing the narrow gap between us. "Promise me, Carter, please."

I rubbed my lips together, sniffling as I took one last look at him, "I promise."

With that, Abias turned away, giving my arm one last squeeze before charging towards the manticore, hurling his pitchfork at the beast to catch its attention. I forced myself to move, to turn and hurry on towards the well as Abias instructed me. I imagined myself jumping up onto the stones, lowering myself into the dark abyss the moment I laid hands on the cold stone, but something held me back. Realization hit me hard, freezing me in place so all I could hear were the muffled shouts and cries of wounded knights, the loud growl of the manticore that made the ground rumble. This was it. I was returning to South River, to Earth, the place where I belonged. Once I climbed down this well, once I left, I would never come back, and hopefully would never want to. But the promise I made to Abias would weigh on me. I would have to carry it for the rest of my life, along with the guilt, the shame of running from my destiny.

A deep, blood-curdling scream sounded through the clearing and I knew exactly whose scream it must've been. It had to have been Alexamian, which meant that Abias was gone, that the manticore had slain him before he could do even a little bit of damage. Instead of turning, instead of looking to see where my friend had died, I slung my bow over my shoulder and lifted myself onto the rim of the well. I carefully twisted my body around, keeping my eyes fixed on the darkness below me, on the small cracks between the stones where I placed my feet. Then I began to climb down, to disappear down into the well, where I could still hear the sounds of the battle that raged above me. Eventually though, that all began to slip away, to fade as if a heavy door had been shut above me, blocking out all the sounds from above. Soon, I was climbing down the well in complete silence.

*   *   *

I stared at the stone wall of the well for several minutes, pressing my hand against the cold rock, taking in the silence that consumed me. *I should be happy with the quiet that had come over the well*, I thought, *rejoice in the fact that I can't hear the sounds of war anymore.* This was what I wanted after all, wasn't it? To leave Elssador, to be gone from it forever. As I continued to press my palms against the cool stone, I began to realize that everything that happened in Elssador was already beginning to feel like a distant memory, one that felt far off, yet always leapt back into your mind when you least expected it, no matter how hard much you wished to forget it. This feeling made me slam my fist against the wall of the well and grit my teeth in fury. It seemed that no matter how much I wanted to forget Elssador, I couldn't. The things I had seen, the things that I had done, the people that I had met and hurt, they would stick with me forever. They would cling to me just like the promise I made to Abias before he walked to his death, like the guilt that came with refusing to fulfill my destiny.

I was then struck with a sudden thought, *Can I really go back to living the way I did before?* That whole time I was in Elssador, I longed for my life back. I longed to wake up to Marlee's bright blue eyes, to meet with Tyler at Tom Thompson Park, to hear the low rumble of Uncle Gabe's laughter, to argue with Sophie and her mother... That was my life. That had almost always been my life. But now it felt like something else entirely. Something was missing from this life, something that only Elssador could fill...

I immediately forced these thoughts out of my mind, for I already knew where I belonged. South River was my home, Earth, the world where humans roamed was my place of true belonging. I supposed I was just going to have to forget in order to move on, to leave that world behind me completely and treat it as if it were only a dream.

Eventually, I found the strength to pull away from the wall, especially when cold air and light flakes of snow began to fall through the opening above me. I smiled slightly as I began to recall what life had been like before I had discovered Elssador. For once, I was excited to see a land covered in snow, to see the trees being weighed down by it. But more than anything I was excited to see Marlee, to race home from Tom Thompson and let her know that I was alive, that I was okay. To tell both her and Tyler that I had been gone for almost fifteen days, away to the place Marlee always dreamed of. They would ask questions, I knew they would, and I would explain, but they wouldn't believe me. And I'd be alright with that. If they didn't believe, then it would be easier to forget.

My heart suddenly began to beat louder in my ears as I thought about Marlee, about the questions she would ask me. She was the only one who would believe my story and I knew she would want everyone around her to believe as well. But I couldn't let that happen. Marlee wasn't stepping foot in this well. She wasn't going anywhere near it. The Wanderer had control over who travels through these two realms, he chose who to allow in, and I was certain I was one of those people. He wanted me back in Elssador to fulfill my destiny, to become Elssador's Lionheart, and I knew he might use Marlee to accomplish that goal, to get me to return. But it was more than that. If the Dark Diviner discovered who Marlee was, what she meant to me, he would use her to reel me back to that world as well. Marlee was now a target, someone who could be used as a pawn in a game she had no reason to be part of. I needed to protect her, to ensure that she – or anyone else –would never come near this well again.

This was my last trip to Tom Thompson Park, the last time I would ever step foot in that clearing. It was a sacrifice, a great sacrifice, but I was willing to give it all up for Marlee. For her, Tyler, and myself. This was the way it had to be, the way I wanted it to be. And this was how it was going to remain.

ACKNOWLEDGEMENTS

First and foremost, I would like to thank God for giving me the ability to write and for placing the idea for this novel in my mind. I can confidently acknowledge that could not have written this book without Him and without the help of the many people He placed in my life, the people who continuously keep pushing me to continue with this story. These people include my family who have shown me their love and support since two-thousand and eleven when I told them that I started writing a book. Thank you parents and my dear brother for putting up with my many, angry moments of writers block and for listening to me ramble on about characters that don't exist. I would especially like to thank my dad for always being there to help me through this whole process and being the best manager a daughter could ask for! You have sacrificed so much of your time working with me through this publishing experience, time that you could have used to do better things, but I want you to know how touched and grateful I am for that sacrifice.

In addition, I would like to thank my close friends who have also stood by me through this whole process. I thank Samantha Tai who painfully read the very first draft of this book and still told me that she loved it. I also want to thank Ciara Dempsey, my Inkling, who has been my writing buddy for almost two years! Thank you to Shelia Brewster who is my favourite critic and one of best writing instructors that God has placed on his Earth. Thank you for all of your suggestions and for all you've taught me over the years. I would also like to thank my editors, Lydia Mountney and Donna Nabel, who read through and

Charlotte E. Craig

critiqued the two most important drafts of this novel. I thank you so, so much for your honesty and for taking time out of your busy lives to edit this book.

I also must thank those who supported me financially. Words cannot describe how thankful I am. I would specifically like to thank Jason and Gillian Keon, David Meslin, Paul Gray, Dick and Bev Craig, Marijke Dyke, Liz and Jim Craig, Pauline Craig, Lily Magnus, Lisa Tam, and everyone else who donated towards the publication of this novel. Without your generous hearts, publishing this novel would not have been possible. Thank you so, so much! Without everyone's love, assistance, and support, the doors of Elssador would not have been opened. Thank you so much for allowing me to have this incredible opportunity!

- Charlotte E. Craig

of suffering he's placed us on, Olsen. The only way to escape it is if we run in our own directions."

My own breaths began to grow heavier and guilt began to press hard against my chest. For a moment, I caught myself in hesitation, part of me knowing that what we were about to do was wrong. My father always taught me to be selfless, to put other's needs before my own. What would he do if he could hear me now, suggesting something that was the polar opposite of what he had always taught me to be? I imagined he would be shaking his head in disappointment, probably not even able to look his selfish daughter in the eye.

Is this really selfish, Carter? I asked myself before I got the chance to change my mind. *Isn't Marlee the true reason you want to return to the Well? Isn't it so you can be there for her?*

"I am willing, Olsen," Julian said, stretching his hand out to me. "Are you?"

I responded immediately, taking hold of his hand without even a moment of hesitation, "I am willing."

*   *   *

I woke the next morning with an aching pain in my stomach, one that made me feel as though I was going to throw up. Even as we began to move out, continuing out on – what seemed to be – our endless search for our horses, I still felt woozy. I trailed behind the others as they continued to track the horses, wanting more than anything to snap at Julian and force him to give up on this ridiculous search. But I didn't. Not only was it because I didn't have the strength to, but because I knew I needed to trust him now. We spent half of the previous night making plans to run away, suggesting how best to conceal our escape. I realized as I continued to follow our group out across the open plains of Elssador, that even though we had spent hours placing our plans together, we hadn't figured out how Julian was going to run from the path we were both destined for. All we said was that we needed to stay as far from one another as possible. As long as Julian and I were together, the chances of us fulfilling our destiny would grow stronger.

The trail that our missing horses left for us seemed to be leading us further away from the Dia Mountains and back the way we had come. As the minutes passed, we began to draw closer and closer to the village of Maycock. I could see the smoke from the chimneys in the distance with such clarity that it made me wonder if being in Elssador for as long as I had had begun to give me aprimorad vision. I would have laughed at my own joke if an awful stench hadn't suddenly filled my nostrils as we drew closer to the small village. The smell made the wooziness in my stomach intensify, forcing me to stumble over a bit into Abias who caught me swiftly, flashing me a look of concern.

"It's the – the smell," I stuttered, trying so hard not to vomit all over him.

"Prince Julian, do you recognize that scent just as I do?" Abias said, his voice sounding hoarse. I glanced up at him and noticed his eyes were watering. It wasn't until I felt something sting my own eyes did I realize that his tears were caused by the dark smoke that had drifted towards us from Maycock.

I could see Julian give a grim nod of his head in response to Abias' question, but he never turned to face us. He stood still, his body facing the small village where the smoke continued to pour up into the sky.

"My Lord, look!" Alexamian exclaimed, pointing towards something moving towards us in the distance. It took some time for me to recognize what it was everyone was gaping at, but as the figures began to move closer, I could just make out the shape of five horses. My eyes naturally locked on the saddle bags which I knew contained the food my abdomen continued to cry out for. I almost allowed myself to feel relieved, but the speed that the horses seemed to be galloping at buried those feelings.

They were moving so fast that I feared they would run us all over or try and pass us. But Alexamian and one of the other knights with us were quick. They grabbed the reigns of the two lead horses, digging their heels into the ground as if expecting to have to wrangle them back, but the horses slowed to a steady stop, as did the other three behind them. Puzzled, I released my hold on Abias and moved closer to our group, to the horses